Secrets to

STEVE FRECH

ONE PLACE. MANY STORIES

HQ
An imprint of HarperCollins*Publishers* Ltd
1 London Bridge Street
London SE1 9GF

www.harpercollins.co.uk

HarperCollins*Publishers*
1st Floor, Watermarque Building, Ringsend Road
Dublin 4, Ireland

This paperback edition 2021

1

First published in Great Britain by
HQ, an imprint of HarperCollins*Publishers* Ltd 2021

ISBN: 9780008471033

MIX
Paper from
responsible sources
FSC
www.fsc.org FSC™ C007454

This book is produced from independently certified FSC™ paper
to ensure responsible forest management.

For more information visit: www.harpercollins.co.uk/green

Printed and Bound in the UK using 100% Renewable Electricity at
CPI Group (UK) Ltd

For Mom and Dad.
Thank you for everything.

Chapter 1

Patricia Crawford pumped her arms as she rounded the corner onto Willow Lane. The motion caused her nylon windbreaker to send a steady *thwick-thwick* out into the morning fog.

Ten pounds. That was the goal. Ten pounds gone by the time summer rolled around.

It was tough going at first, dragging herself out of bed before Stan and the boys were up, but she did it, and now that she had established a routine, she loved it. This was her time. She listened to audiobooks, music, or her new obsession: true-crime podcasts. That particular morning, it was music. Through her earbuds, a now-defunct pop group of women was seductively trying to convince their man not to go to work. Patricia began to quietly sing along, unaware that she was doing it. It wasn't the first time. At the gym, she only realized she was doing it when she got an odd, amused smile from someone on the machine or treadmill next to hers. She would stop and apologize with an embarrassed grin, but with no one around, her volume grew.

She alternated her workouts. Some mornings she went to the gym. Other mornings, like this one, she would take long power-walks, which were her favorite. Once she had explored her own neighborhood, she began branching out to explore others. That's how she found Meadowgate. Over the past two decades, Atlanta had become blanketed in subdivisions that offered only four different models of homes, creating streets that repeated themselves over and over.

Not Meadowgate.

There was variation to the upscale homes. The lawns were bigger, unlike other subdivisions where the houses sat on small lots with only patches of grass masquerading as front and back yards. The wide lawns of Meadowgate and the varying houses reminded her of the neighborhoods in Indiana where she grew up.

That morning, the thick fog hid the houses on Willow Lane from view, which was a bummer, but Patricia reminded herself that it wasn't about the houses; it was about the ten pounds.

… But they were such nice houses.

Willow Lane sat in a secluded corner of Meadowgate, like a mini-subdivision unto itself.

Out of curiosity, she had looked into the asking price of the house under construction at the end of the Willow Lane. The previous home had burned down earlier in the year. She didn't know how it had happened, and no, she and Stan weren't thinking about moving. It was just for fun but turned into a bucket of cold water. They would never be able to afford a house on Willow Lane.

If only we didn't have two bright sons who had to go to college, she thought and laughed. She would take Ricky and Mason over a house on Willow Lane any day.

Still, it was nice to dream.

The combination of her wandering thoughts, the music blaring through her earbuds, her absent-minded singing, and the dense fog, caused her to almost pass right by the object in the street.

At first, it looked as though someone had dropped some clothes in the middle of Willow Lane. It was the hair that caught Patricia's attention.

These weren't some discarded articles of clothing.

It was a young woman.

Patricia stopped singing and pulled the earbuds from her ears. It was unnaturally quiet. Even the birds were silent.

"Hello?" Patricia said.

The young woman didn't move.

She was lying face-down, wearing a blue sweatshirt, gray sweats, and socks, the soles of which were covered in fresh grass stains. Her wavy, chestnut hair fanned out across the pavement.

Patricia took a cautious step closer. "Excuse me?"

There was still no movement from the young woman.

"Ma'am? Are you okay?"

Patricia closed the few remaining feet between them and crouched. The discovery had been so sudden, her senses hadn't caught up, but now her pulse began to spike and her breathing quickened.

"Are you all right?"

She nudged the young woman's shoulder, which brought no reaction.

Maybe she passed out, Patricia thought.

"Hey," she softly said. "You need to wake up. We need to get you out of the road."

As gently as she could, Patricia rolled the young woman onto her back. She then gasped and recoiled.

The young woman was in her teens. Deep bruises encircled her neck but the most unsettling feature was the eyes, which stared lifelessly upwards.

That's when Patricia Crawford began screaming.

Chapter 2

Detective Meredith Somerset sat at her desk, filling out paperwork and signing off on requests for lab work. She glanced up at the clock on the wall for the fourth or fifth time, confirming that it was well past eight. She picked up the old, red sponge ball from her desk and rolled it between her hands for a few moments before turning to the open office door behind her, through which she could see Sergeant Wheaton sitting at his desk, peering at the computer screen over the rims of his glasses, and pecking away on the keyboard.

"You want me to call him?" she asked. "See where he's at?"

"I do not," he calmly replied. "He gets here when he gets here. Then, he can tell me what was more important than being on time his first day."

"That's a little harsh."

"Yes," Sergeant Wheaton replied, pushing his glasses back up the bridge of his nose and continuing to type.

Meredith didn't envy her new partner, Tyler Foles, but Sergeant Wheaton was right. It was a bad look to be late on your first day. And why hadn't he called? It happened, morning traffic in Atlanta was obscene, but there hadn't been any word from him. Tyler Foles was late, hadn't checked in, and wasn't doing himself any favors.

The phone on Meredith's desk rang. She quickly grabbed it.

"This is Somerset."

"Hey, Meredith. It's Jackson."

"Hey, Jackson. What's up?"

"Got one for you. Female. Mid-to-late teens. No ID. Found in the middle of the street in a nice neighborhood."

Meredith grabbed a pen from the coffee mug on the corner of the desk and pulled a notepad in front of her.

"Go ahead."

"She was found this morning by a jogger. The street is Willow Lane. Nearest address is 147. It's in a subdivision called Meadowgate."

"You said no ID?" she asked, jotting down the information.

"Nothing."

"Any idea when it happened?"

"No, but Lewis is on his way there. Eddie, too, to take some photos."

Lewis Moore was one of the crime scene techs. Eddie Sheldon was a photographer. Meredith knew them both.

"Great. Anything else you can tell me?" she asked.

"That's all I got."

"Okay. Thanks, Jackson."

"My pleasure, detective. Until next time."

Meredith hung up the phone and ripped the paper containing her scribbled notes from the pad. Her chair squeaked and groaned as she stood and walked to Sergeant Wheaton's door.

"What have you got?" he asked, not looking away from the screen.

"Young girl. No ID. Found on a street in a nice neighborhood."

He stopped typing. "Please tell me it's not a sex thing."

"Won't know until I get out there but I don't think so. Jackson would have said something."

Sergeant Wheaton went back to tapping on the keyboard. "Okay. See ya."

"You want to text Foles? Tell him to meet me there?"

"Nope. I want to welcome him to his first day of homicide and let him know that he is off to a spectacular start. Then, I'll send him to you."

"Gotcha," Meredith said, knocking on the doorframe before turning and walking out.

She did not envy the ass-chewing Sergeant Wheaton had in store for Tyler Foles when he arrived.

Chapter 3

Meredith pulled up to the end of Willow Lane, the entrance to which was blocked by two patrol cars. She showed her badge to the officers standing next to the cars as she walked past, and then tucked the badge onto her belt.

The morning fog had burned away and Willow Lane stretched out before her. Meredith would have guessed that it was about a hundred and fifty yards to the opposite dead end. There were two houses on each side of the street, with a fifth under construction at the far end. Halfway down, in the middle of the street, there was a knot of uniforms and techs. Through the spaces between their legs and crouched forms, she could see the girl lying in the road. Eddie was circling the body, snapping photos. There was nothing frenzied or dramatic about his actions. Just a guy doing his job. Sitting on the curb, about twenty yards away from the body in Meredith's direction, was a woman in a nylon windbreaker who was giving a statement to an officer. Meredith pegged her as the jogger who found the body.

Meredith took in the picturesque street as she began walking. The houses were large but not opulent. They were constructed of that famous Georgia red brick and cedar-planked siding. The yards were well kept. Everything about it proclaimed "upper middle class".

As she drew nearer, the team standing around the body came into focus. Eddie continued taking photos. Lewis, their forensic tech, was kneeling next to the dead girl, closely inspecting her hands. Three more officers formed a loose circle around the scene. Just outside the circle was a mountain of a man standing with his back to her. His arms were folded across his chest, causing his shirt to strain against his muscular frame. He noticed the heads of the men around him pop up at Meredith's approach and turned.

"Sheriff Howell?" Meredith asked.

"That's me. You Somerset?"

"Yep."

"Nice to meet you."

Meredith's hand disappeared into his rock-crushing grip as they shook.

"Eddie. Lewis," Meredith said, nodding to each one in turn.

"Hey, detective," Eddie said.

"Hey."

They barely acknowledged her, but not out of indifference. They were absorbed in their work.

"What've we got?" she asked Sheriff Howell.

Sheriff Howell consulted his notes. "Female. Mid, maybe late, teens. Looks like manual strangulation. She was found a little after 7 a.m., by Patricia Crawford on her morning jog," he said with a nod to the woman sitting on the curb. "She says she didn't see or hear anyone, but it was pretty foggy, and she was wearing headphones."

"Talk to any of the residents?" Meredith asked.

"Not yet. It's been quiet. Figured I'd leave that for you."

"Thanks." Meredith looked around. "Wait. No one's come out to talk to you?"

"I've seen some faces in windows, but no one's come outside."

"Huh … Okay," Meredith said.

That was odd. Most times, especially in residential areas, people wanted to know what was going on right outside their doors.

"No one's driven off from these houses, right?" she asked.

"Nope. We locked it down as soon as we arrived."

"Thank you, Sheriff."

Sheriff Howell motioned to the crime scene. "She's all yours."

Meredith stepped forward and crouched down to join Lewis next to the body of the girl.

"So, Lewis. What are we thinki—?"

As her eyes rested on the face of the dead girl, Meredith's chest constricted. The hair. The high cheekbones. Strong jawline. It was the spitting image of someone she hadn't seen in twenty-five years. Meredith suddenly lost her balance and had to place her hand on the pavement to steady herself.

"—tective?"

Meredith blinked.

"You okay, detective?" Lewis repeated.

"Yeah. Fine. Just tried to squat too fast."

Lewis went right back to his work.

Meredith shook it off.

"What are we thinking?" she asked, once she had centered herself.

"I'm willing to bet it happened right here." Lewis pointed to her feet. "Grass stains on the soles of her socks. She was probably running from her attacker."

Meredith glanced around. "No way to know which direction she was going. Let's hope someone saw something," she said, putting her attention back on the body and ignoring the face for the time being.

"The knees on the sweatpants are pretty scuffed up …" she observed and moved to the arms. "As are the elbows. You're right. Whoever was chasing her caught up and tackled her right here." Her gaze drifted up to the bruises on her neck.

Lewis saw where she was looking. "Manual."

"Yeah." Meredith pointed to the darker bruises. "These deep ones here are fingermarks."

"She fought like hell," Lewis said. "Check out the hands."

Meredith got closer to the dead girl's right hand. The fingers were slightly curled. There were scratches, and the fingernails on the middle, ring, and index finger were cracked. Meredith moved around and examined the left hand, which had similar scratches and two more broken nails.

"Let's hope she got some of the guy's skin under those nails. Can you bag the hands, please?"

"You got it," Lewis said, pulling two plastic bags from his kit, which was sitting on the pavement next to him.

"And can I get a pair of gloves?" she asked. "Left mine in the car."

Lewis pulled a pair of latex gloves from the kit and handed them to her.

She snapped them on as Lewis carefully placed the bags over the corpse's hands.

Finally, she moved up to the victim's face. The momentary shock of seeing something akin to a ghost had passed and her training and instincts were in control.

"There are some small cuts around the mouth," she said.

"I saw those. You think he hit her?"

Meredith peered closer, trying to play the scene in her mind. "No. They're small and individual. If he had hit her, it would be one big bruise." She turned to look over her shoulder at Sheriff Howell. "Did Mrs … umm …?"

"Crawford."

"Right. Crawford. Did Mrs. Crawford move or touch her in any way?"

Sheriff Howell once again checked his notes. "Yes. She found her lying face-down and wanted to help her. Didn't know that she was dead until she turned her over."

"Okay," Meredith replied calmly, but mentally cursed. She couldn't blame Mrs. Crawford for trying to help someone she thought might be in trouble, but the body's original position may have given them a better idea of what happened and in which direction she was coming or going.

Meredith moved past the lifeless eyes. There was a broad scrape on the right side of the forehead that disappeared under the girl's auburn hair.

"You're right, Lewis. Either this guy tackled her or she fell and hit her head on the pavement. There are bits of asphalt in the wound. Eddie?" Meredith asked over her shoulder in the direction of the sound of the digital camera shutter behind her.

"Right here."

"You get close-ups?"

"Only about a hundred."

"Thank you. Lewis, have you taken the temperature, yet?"

"Only external. I haven't taken a rectal temperature. I was waiting until you got here to give the all-clear to move her, but do you want to hear another one of my best guesses?"

"Fire away."

"She was alive three, maybe even two and a half hours ago. Rigor is just starting to set in. Bruises look fresh. Again, this is only my best guess, but I don't think she was dead very long before the jogger found her."

"Agreed," Meredith said, and moved back down to the feet.

She carefully inspected the socks; the soles had fresh grass stains and dirt, but the tops were clean. A slight bulge in the sock near the ankle caught her eye. Meredith took out a pen and gently pressed the tip against it. The small bulge moved but fell back against the fabric when she pulled the pen away.

There was something in there.

"All clear to move her?" Lewis asked.

Meredith stood. "Not yet. I'm gonna let the new guy take a look first."

"That's today? Where is he?"

"Good question," she said. "Give me a few more minutes. If he's not here in ten, then we'll load her when the ambulance arrives."

"Got it."

Meredith walked past Sheriff Howell in the direction of Mrs. Crawford, who was still sitting on the curb, talking to the officer.

Mrs. Crawford got to her feet as Meredith approached and the officer moved to meet her.

"Detective Somerset?" he asked.

"Yep."

"I'm Officer Hawthorne."

"Nice to meet you, Officer."

"Same. I've got her statement but didn't want to send her on her way until the two of you spoke."

"Thank you."

Meredith stepped over to Mrs. Crawford.

"Mrs. Crawford, hi. My name is Detective Somerset. Thank you for calling us. I'm really sorry about all of this."

Patricia Crawford nodded. She seemed mostly calm, even though her eyes were bloodshot.

"I know you've already told Officer Hawthorne what happened, but could you please tell me?"

"Uh, okay. Um. I was doing my morning walk and I came across her lying in the road, and I thought maybe she was hurt or passed out, so I tried to help her. I, uh, I rolled her over and saw … saw … that she …"

"Take your time," Meredith said reassuringly.

"I, uh, saw that she was dead and I started screaming and then I called 911."

"Did you happen to see or hear anybody nearby when you found her? Maybe a car driving away?"

Patricia Crawford shook her head. "No. It was really foggy and, uh, I was singing—I mean, I had my earphones in. I took

12

them out when I found her, but I didn't hear anything."

"Okay. You're doing great. Now, did anyone come out of these houses when you started to scream?"

"I don't know. I wasn't really paying attention. I only saw … her." Her voice trembled. "And, I'm sorry that I touched her. I know I shouldn't have. It was just that—"

"It's okay. It's okay. You did absolutely nothing wrong."

Meredith's words had some success in calming her down and she waited a few moments for Patricia to regain her composure before continuing.

"Before the police arrived, did anyone drive by or did you see anyone drive off from any of these houses?"

"Uh, no. No. I didn't see anyone leave."

"You're sure?" Meredith asked gently. "It's important."

Patricia Crawford nodded. "Yes. I'm sure."

"Great. Thank you. Do you live nearby?"

"No. I live over in Kennesaw. I like to take my morning walks in different neighborhoods."

"Have you walked in this neighborhood before?"

"Yes. A few times … I like the houses."

Meredith smiled. "Okay. Is there anything else you can remember?"

Patricia's eyes darted around as she tried to recall. "No. No, I don't think so."

"Patricia—may I call you Patricia?"

"Yes."

"You've been great, Patricia. And thank you for sticking around to talk to me. I want you to take my card," Meredith said, pulling one from her pocket. "And if there is anything else you remember or if you have any questions, please don't hesitate to call me. All right?"

"Okay," Patricia said, taking the card.

"Do you need a ride back to your car or your home?"

"No. I'm parked a few blocks over. I can walk."

Meredith turned to Officer Hawthorne. "Got everything you need?"

Officer Hawthorne tapped his notepad. "Yep."

"Great. Officer Hawthorne is going to walk you back to your car, okay?"

Patricia nodded.

"Thank you again, and like I said, if you have any questions or you remember anything, please call me."

Patricia nodded.

"Drive safe, Patricia."

Patricia and Officer Hawthorne began to walk away in the direction of the patrol cars parked at the end of the street.

As he was walking away, the radio piece on Officer Hawthorne's shoulder squawked to life.

"Sheriff Howell?" a voice said.

"Go ahead," came Sheriff Howell's reply.

"Let Detective Somerset know that the ambulance is here, and that she's getting a teammate."

"Copy that."

Meredith looked toward the end of the street, where the patrol cars were being moved to allow the ambulance to pass. There was also a tall guy in a rumpled blue button-down shirt showing his badge to the patrolmen who waved him through. He hurriedly walked up the street, tailing the ambulance.

Meredith met him halfway so they could talk in private.

He was in his late thirties, tall, thin, short-haired, with a face that was somehow simultaneously care-worn and boyish. Without a jacket, his firearm was on display in his shoulder holster and even though he was late, he walked with a self-assured swagger.

"You Foles?" Meredith asked as he drew near and stopped in front of her.

"Yep. You Somerset?"

"Yeah," she replied dryly.

"Nice to meet you. I'm Tyler." He had a languid drawl that sounded more surfer than southern.

"Where were you?" she asked, skipping the pleasantries.

"I went to the station and Sergeant Wheaton said you were already here. He should have just called and told me to come straight—"

"Yeah. Sergeant Wheaton doesn't like that."

"Doesn't like what?"

"People being late. Especially on their first day."

"Don't worry," he said. "I got the message."

"Where were you?"

"Taking care of some stuff."

"What stuff?"

Meredith assumed he would simply tell her. Even though they were technically partners, she was the superior officer.

His posture stiffened. "Won't happen again."

It wasn't a bad answer. He was acknowledging that he was in the wrong, but also saying that it was his business.

"It had better not."

"Like I said, I got the message."

"All right," she said, and began leading him back toward the body. "Here's what we've got so far; Victim is female. Mid to late teens. Appears to have been manually strangled. The body was found around 7 a.m. by a jogger; Mrs. Patricia Crawford."

Tyler looked around. "And where is Mrs. Crawford?"

"She's already given her statement to me and another officer. We sent her home."

"I would have liked to talk to her."

"Then you should have been on time."

They continued walking in silence. Tyler waited for more info, but by the time they were nearing the body, he realized he wasn't getting any.

"Wait. That's it?" he asked.

"No. There's more."

15

"You're not gonna tell me?"

"I want to see how you work a scene," Meredith said.

Tyler stopped.

It took a few steps before Meredith realized he wasn't following her. She turned back to him.

"Problem?" she asked.

He glanced over to make sure that they were still out of earshot from the rest of the officers and techs. "Listen, Detective Somerset—"

"You can call me 'Meredith.'"

"Great. Hi. You can still call me Tyler, and you know this ain't my first rodeo, right? I did five years in narco and vice. Pretty good at it, too."

"Yeah. I know."

"So, I don't need someone holding my hand to see if I know how to work a scene. I got no problem following your lead, but I don't want us to start out by measuring our dicks—" He threw it out with the casualness of something he had said dozens of times, but caught himself. "Apologies for the phrasing."

"Listen, Detective Foles—"

"Tyler."

"Tyler. This is your first homicide. I want to know how you work a scene. That's it. No one's measuring dicks, okay? This is for me."

He inhaled through his nose and looked toward the body. The crew had noticed the new guy in their midst.

All right, Meredith thought. *He can take responsibility for himself, has a spine, but also a big chip on his shoulder.*

She understood.

She had the same mix of bravado and nerves the first time she stepped onto the scene of a homicide and was mentored by then Detective Wheaton. He handled her exactly the same way: by telling her to put the emotions away.

Tyler exhaled. "Okay, Somerset. I got you."

She nodded and resumed walking. "And it's a good thing we're not measuring dicks because mine's bigger."

Tyler was at a loss for words, but only for a moment.

"That's cold, Somerset."

Chapter 4

Tyler had regained a little bit of his swagger by the time he rejoined Meredith at the loose ring of people surrounding the body.

"Gentlemen," he said. "Nice to meet you. I'm Detective Tyler Foles. It's a pleasure to be on the team for this, my first homicide." He stepped over and crouched next to the body before anyone had a chance to respond.

Sheriff Howell gave a questioning glance to Meredith, who shook her head to let him know she had it under control.

"You mind if I bum a pair of rubbers off you?" Tyler asked Lewis.

Lewis blinked. "Rubbers?"

"Yeah, man. Rubbers."

"I think Detective Foles is asking for some gloves, Lewis," Meredith said.

"Yeah. Gloves," Tyler confirmed.

An annoyed Lewis reached into his kit and pulled out a pair. "Then just say 'gloves.'"

Tyler smiled, pulled the gloves on, and inspected the body. He started at the head and worked his way down. Every minute or so, he would look up at the surrounding houses, mumble to himself, and then continue with his examination of the corpse.

"Okay to touch her?" he asked.

"Be gentle," Meredith replied.

Tyler inspected the bagged hands, working the fingers, checking for rigor mortis.

So far, so good, Meredith thought.

Tyler looked up again and studied the surroundings.

"No one's come out of one of these houses, screaming that this is their daughter or niece or something?"

"Nope."

Tyler furrowed his brow and went back to the body. Finally, he arrived at the feet.

Meredith found herself holding her breath.

Tyler finished and stood.

"Done," he announced.

"You want to step over here?" Meredith asked, giving him the opportunity to give his findings away from everyone else, lest he make a fool of himself at his first homicide.

"Nah," Tyler replied. "We don't need to go over there."

"Okay, then. Let's hear it."

"One question."

"Shoot."

"This is it?" he said, motioning to the body. "This is everything? No one picked up any shoes or a coat or nothin'?"

"Nope. This is it. Mrs. Crawford did touch the body to turn her over because she didn't know the girl was dead. Other than that, the body was found as is."

Tyler nodded. "Okay. This newbie to homicide," he said, indicating himself, "thinks she was killed right here. The scrape on her forehead has got some road in it. She was running from the guy. He caught up with her right here on the street."

"'He'? What makes you think the killer was a guy?" Meredith asked. She thought the same, but wanted him to show his work.

19

"Playin' the odds," Tyler said. "Fast enough to catch her. Strong enough to overpower her. Strangled her bare-handed, but first, he tried to keep her from screaming."

"What makes you say that?" Again, it was a question Meredith already had the answer to.

"Bruising around the mouth. Dude didn't slug her. He was trying to keep her from waking the neighbors. Whole thing might have been an accident."

"An accident? Strangulation requires time, effort. How could it be an accident?"

"It might have started with him tryin' to shut her up and things got out of hand. I'm just sayin'; we don't know."

Meredith marked it as another positive. He was thinking but not locking anything in.

"She also didn't run very far," Tyler continued. "No shoes. No coat. We should probably search the yards, but I doubt we're gonna find 'em. Grass stains on the bottom of the feet but the rest is clean. This was a sprint. Doubt both shoes fell off. She probably wasn't wearing them, which means she started from somewhere nearby. Street's kind of by itself back here. Only five houses. I'm guessing she may have run from one of them." He turned to Meredith. "How am I doing?"

"Good," Meredith said.

"What, like an A minus? Solid B?"

"Eh. C plus."

Tyler looked down at the body. Meredith's remark was enough to let him know that he was missing something. He could resume his inspection, but that would mean everyone standing around waiting for him to find something Meredith already knew.

"Okay. What did I miss?" Tyler asked.

"Here," Meredith said, breaking from the perimeter of people. She crouched next to the feet. Tyler followed her lead. She pointed with her gloved finger toward the small protrusion in the sock. "Right there."

Tyler gently pressed his finger against it, recreating the experiment Meredith had done earlier.

"Something's in there," Tyler said.

Meredith turned to Lewis. "Can I get a bag?"

Lewis came forward and reached into his kit, pulled out a plastic bag, and handed it to her.

"Grab the sock for me," she said to Tyler.

Tyler gently lifted the foot with one hand and slowly pulled on the toe with the other. The sock slid off and he lowered the dead girl's foot back to the pavement. Tyler held the sock up by the toe and gently shook it while Meredith held her hand under the opening.

Something slid out and flashed in the morning sunlight as it dropped into her palm.

At first glance, it looked like a coin, but as she brought it closer, they could see that it was a heart-shaped medallion, roughly the size of a fifty-cent piece. It was worn and scuffed. On one side was some sort of symbol made of one circle with two lines coming down and wrapping around a smaller circle.

On the other side was a single word: SOSH.

Meredith deposited the medallion into the bag Lewis had provided. She and Tyler studied it.

"What do you make of that?" he asked.

"I don't know," she said, handing the bag to him. "Hold it up for me."

Meredith took out her phone and snapped a few photos of the medallion, then aimed her phone at the face of the dead girl.

As she focused the lens, she had that feeling again, the sensation of the past rushing up from the depths to meet her.

Through the image on the screen, the dead girl's eyes opened and looked directly at her.

The dead girl's lips parted. "I miss you, Meredith."

Meredith almost dropped her phone but was snapped out of it by Tyler handing the bag to Lewis.

21

"Can you log that, please?" he asked.

"Sure."

"Thank you ... uh ..."

"It's Lewis."

"Thank you, Lewis," Tyler added.

"You got it."

Meredith took a breath and looked back at the body. The eyes were closed, as was the mouth. Everything was as it should be, as far as finding a dead girl in the street went.

She glanced at Tyler, who was once again studying the houses.

"What's on your mind?" she quietly asked.

"I know this is my first homicide but why does this feel so weird? It's weird, right?"

"It is weird," Meredith concurred. "She's young. She didn't run far and your gut was right; why isn't anyone coming out of their house to see what's going on or claiming that this is their daughter or someone they know?"

"You thinkin' what I'm thinkin'?"

"What's that?"

"Someone on this street knows something."

Meredith nodded. "Yep."

Tyler grinned. "Time to knock on some doors, Somerset."

Good, Meredith thought. *He likes the chase.*

Chapter 5

They started back toward the end of the street where Meredith and Tyler had parked, with the house with slate-blue siding.

Meredith stepped onto the porch and rapped on the door while Tyler stayed a few steps behind. Her knock was answered almost immediately by a striking figure of a man. He had salt and pepper hair and a strong jawline that was sprouting the perfect amount of stubble. His tailor-fitted clothes accentuated his lean body.

"Mr …?" Meredith asked.

"Bowers. Scott Bowers."

"Mr. Bowers, I'm Detective Meredith Somerset with the Cobb County Police Department. This is Detective Tyler Foles," she added with a nod over her shoulder. "Sorry to bother you, but do you mind if we talk to you for a minute?"

"Of course not. Please, come in."

Scott led them down the hall to the kitchen, where he offered them a seat at the gleaming glass-topped kitchen table.

"Can I get you something to drink? I hate to play into stereotypes, but some coffee? I promise you it's really good coffee."

"That'd be great. Thank you," Meredith said. She had already had coffee but if it would make him feel more at ease, she wasn't going to refuse.

Tyler hadn't heard Scott's offer. He was too impressed by his surroundings.

Meredith couldn't blame him.

The outside of the house was perfectly fine, nothing spectacular, but the inside was like the showroom of a stylish furniture store.

The kitchen was black and white marble with top-of-the-line appliances. It opened to the living room, which held a sleek, sectional leather couch in front of a wide fireplace with a large flat-screen television mounted above.

"For you, sir?" Scott asked Tyler. "Anything?"

Tyler emerged from his reverie with an expression as though being addressed as "sir" was foreign to him.

"Nah, man. I'm good. Thanks."

"Your loss." Scott smiled, working his coffee brewer, which would be more at home in an upscale coffeeshop in Paris rather than his kitchen. "Cream? Sugar?" he asked Meredith.

"Black is fine."

"I wasn't going to say anything, but this coffee is better without it." Scott pulled a mug from one of the cabinets overhead. "It's called 'Ospina', from Colombia. The beans are only grown at altitudes of over seventy-five hundred feet in soil with a high volume of volcanic ash."

Tyler whistled. "Sounds expensive."

"It is. Over a hundred dollars per pound and it's worth every penny." He finished pouring the coffee into the delicate mug.

"Oh, you didn't have to do that," Meredith said as he placed the mug in front of her on the table.

"I insist. I love sharing it every chance I get."

"Why is that?" Tyler asked.

"Just watch," he said and nodded to Meredith.

Meredith held the steaming mug under her nose and inhaled.

It was heaven in her nostrils—rich, nutty. She took a sip. The hot liquid opened on her tongue with hints of vanilla and spice. It was unlike any coffee she had ever tasted and she was sure that she had tried almost all of them.

"Oh my god," she breathed.

Scott smiled. "There it is."

"This is the best coffee I've ever tasted."

"I'm glad you like it."

As he turned back to the coffee machine, Meredith and Tyler exchanged a glance, each asking the other, "Who is this guy?"

Meredith savored another sip and set the mug down.

"We're sorry if we're keeping you here," she began. "I'm sure you have places to go. We just want to ask you some questions and we'll be on our way."

"No, please," Bowers said, turning off the coffee maker. "You're not keeping me from anything. I'm working from home today. I simply can't believe something like this happened here, on this street."

"What kind of work are you in, Mr. Bowers?"

"Architecture. I design buildings."

"Anything we would know?" Meredith asked, more out of personal curiosity than an official capacity.

"Possibly. I designed The Mandioc in Peachtree Plaza."

"Really?" Meredith asked, impressed.

"Is that the all-black glass one that kinda looks like a crystal?" Tyler followed up.

"That's the one."

Tyler snorted. "My auntie always called it the 'high-falutin' lump of coal.'"

If that was going to be Tyler's contribution to the interview, Meredith thought it might be better if he stayed outside, but Scott laughed.

"Not the first time I've heard something like that."

"Do you live alone, Mr. Bowers?" Meredith asked.

"Yep. Bachelor for life, I suppose."

"Damn straight," Tyler muttered appreciatively under his breath.

Meredith pulled out her phone and brought up the pictures of the girl she had taken outside. She zoomed to crop out the bruises around the neck while leaving the face visible. "I hope you don't mind looking at some photos?"

"Not at all."

"Do you recognize her?"

Scott reached for the phone. "May I?"

Meredith handed it to him. He studied the image carefully, but eventually shook his head.

"I'm sorry. Can't say that I do," he said, handing the phone back.

Meredith believed he was sincere but that didn't mean much at this stage in the investigation. She had seen a guy pretend not to recognize his fiancée an hour after stabbing her to death.

"This all happened right outside?" Scott asked.

"There's a lot that we don't know, but it looks that way," Meredith answered.

"That's crazy."

"Do you mind telling us where you were this morning?" Tyler asked.

Even though it was going to be her next question, Meredith would have preferred if Tyler would let her do the questioning.

"Not at all. I was here, exercising in my basement," Scott confidently said with a nod toward the basement door.

"Let me guess." Tyler smirked. "You got one of those exercise machines where you link up with virtual classes and shit."

"Detective?" Meredith said, quietly.

To her surprise, Scott laughed again. "Guilty as char—Oh god. Sorry. That was almost a very poor choice of words."

It was Tyler's turn to chuckle. "Don't sweat it."

"Yes," Scott said, after recovering. "You are correct. Have you ever used one?"

"You kidding? The gym back at my old station was a couple of cinderblocks and a jump rope."

"I really enjoy it. As I said, I live alone and it's always a good motivator to work out with other people. It pushes you, even if you're not in the same room."

"And the people you work out with; can they see you?" Meredith asked.

Scott cocked his head. "Well, yes and no. The instructor can see me, but if you're asking if they could vouch for me? Probably not. There were about a hundred people in the class this morning. The instructors can swipe through their monitor to see everyone, but I don't think they look too hard. If I had to put money on it, the instructor isn't going to remember my face."

"Do you remember the type of class or the instructor's name?" Meredith asked.

"Body pump," Scott answered without hesitation. "It's usually taught by a guy named Lance on Thursdays but there was a sub this morning; a woman named Tracey." He suddenly lit up. "And I did log in. My workout was recorded and the results uploaded to my personal workout account. It keeps track of calories burned and heart rate and everything. It's probably not the same as an ironclad alibi, but it might count for something."

"It does," Meredith acknowledged while writing in her notes. "Thank you."

"I still can't believe it," Scott said with a shake of his head. "Right outside."

"You didn't happen to hear anything this morning, did you?" Meredith asked.

"No. I was up at six. Class started at six-thirty. It lasted for an hour and I cranked the music pretty loud. If I'm being honest, I couldn't hear my own thoughts."

"Have you noticed anything unusual on your street recently? Strangers? Any neighbors behaving oddly?" Meredith asked.

Scott hesitated and then quietly laughed.

"Something funny?" Tyler asked.

"No, detective. It's just an odd question. I don't want to speak ill of my neighbors, and I can't believe they would have anything to do with this, but who doesn't think their neighbors are a little weird? You've got the Whitakers across the street. I have no problem telling you that Thomas Whitaker is a piece of work. Then there are the Morgans. They're a little—how can I put this? They're a little 'fanatical' about their kids. Next door, you've got the Ansleys. I guess they're the closest to normal ... You're going to ask everyone the opinion of everyone else on Willow Lane?"

"Probably." Meredith nodded.

Scott quietly laughed, again. "If you do, I would love to know what they say about the bachelor living at the end of the street."

"Is there anything else you can tell us?" Meredith asked.

Scott searched his memory. "No. I don't think so."

Meredith took a card from her pocket and stood. "Well, if you think of anything we may have missed or if you plan on going anywhere, please give us a call."

"Of course." Scott accepted the card and took one of his own from his wallet. "And here. If you need to get in touch with me."

"Thank you."

He handed a card to Tyler as well.

Meredith turned the card over in her hand. It was black and sturdy with his name and contact info, and was embossed with his personalized logo.

"And one last thing," Scott said, retreating to the pantry, which was hidden in the wall of the kitchen. He opened the door and took out a small stack of thermal paper cups and pulled one from the top. He brought the cup over to Meredith, and poured her coffee into it.

"It'd be a shame for it to go to waste."

"Thank you, and thank you for your time."

"I wish I could have been more help," he replied. Scott led them back down the hall and opened the door. "Have a good day."

28

"You too," Tyler replied as they stepped back into the morning sunlight.

The door closed behind them.

"What do you think?" Meredith asked, stepping off the porch.

"Seemed pretty chill for a rich guy. It is a little odd, though."

"What's odd?"

"The dude said he was working from home."

"And?"

"Is that how you'd dress if you were working from home?" Tyler asked.

"I have a feeling that's about as 'casual' he gets."

Meredith suddenly stopped and turned back to the house.

"Somerset?" Tyler asked.

She stayed rooted to the spot.

"Somerset? What's up?"

Meredith stared at the door a moment longer.

"I thought I heard something," she said.

She slowly turned and they resumed walking toward the street.

"Hey, let me get a hit of that coffee," Tyler said, reaching.

Meredith held the cup away from him.

"You had your chance."

*

Back inside the house, Scott Bowers pulled his hand from the crater he had punched in the drywall, next to the door.

The calm, helpful veneer his face had worn while in the presence of the detectives was gone, replaced by one of seething rage.

It was only a matter of time now.

They were going to find out. It was going to come to light and everything that he had worked for, everything he had built, was going to come down.

He stared at the depression he had created. Had he hit a stud behind the drywall, the bones in his hand would have been pulverized.

As he stared, the calm veneer slowly returned. His expression of rage morphed almost imperceptibly into one of civility and cooperation. He would have to control himself. His survival depended upon it. It was how he had gotten this far.

But now, the clock was ticking.

Chapter 6

Meredith and Tyler made their way up the driveway and along the concrete path to the front door of the Cape Cod-styled house neighboring Scott Bowers'. In the street, the body of the girl was being placed into a body bag.

"Listen," Meredith said as they approached the porch. "Your questions back there were fine, but from now on, unless I give you the go-ahead, let me do the interviews."

"If the questions were fine, what's the problem?"

"No problem, but until we get to know each other's methods a little better, I'll do the interviews."

"I know what I'm doing, Somerset. I've been doing interviews for years."

"Not with me."

"I told you, I don't have a problem with following your lead, but I don't know how many ways I have to tell you that I—"

As they were about to step onto the porch, the front door opened and out stepped a woman in her forties. Her hair was slightly frazzled, and she had an intense stare that turned Meredith and Tyler into stone.

There was a brief standoff where neither Meredith nor Tyler knew what to say.

"Mrs …?"

"Meghan Ansley," the woman said.

"Mrs. Ansley. Hi. I'm Detective Meredith Somerset and this is Detective Tyler Foles. We're sorry to bother you, but is it okay to ask you a few questions?"

Meghan cast a glance toward the street and folded her arms. "Okay."

"Can we come inside?" Meredith asked, not wanting to conduct the interview with the backdrop of a murder scene.

Meghan reluctantly nodded.

*

The house of the Ansleys was a much more modest affair than that of Scott Bowers. The furnishings were provided by the likes of JC Penny rather than Neiman Marcus. Meredith and Tyler were sitting on the couch in the living room while Meghan Ansley stood, looking out the window into the spacious backyard, which lacked a fence but had a large work shed in the far corner.

"Again, thank you for taking the time to talk to us, Mrs. Ansley. I know this is all very upsetting."

"It is," she said, turning toward them. "And I don't allow guns in my house."

Meredith glanced down to see the grip of her Sig Sauer P226 9mm protruding from the shoulder holster under her jacket.

"I understand," Meredith said, buttoning her jacket to conceal it.

Meghan looked at Tyler, who seemed oblivious to the fact that his firearm was on full display due to his lack of a jacket.

"It's just that we have a son and I don't want a gun anywhere near him," Meghan added.

"I have a daughter," Meredith said. "When I get home, my gun goes right into a safe that only I have the combination to."

She was trying to reassure her and while it was true that

Meredith did have a daughter, she had conveniently omitted the fact that her daughter lived across town with her ex-husband and his girlfriend.

"Do you have any children?" Meghan asked Tyler.

"Not that I know of," he snorted.

Meghan's expression twisted as though something unpleasant had passed under her nose.

Meredith shot Tyler a side glance.

Tyler's chuckle died a slow, embarrassing death and he sat back on the couch. "No, I don't have any kids."

"What's your son's name?" Meredith asked.

"Anthony. He's seven."

"Is he here?"

"He's upstairs. You're not going to need to speak to him, are you?"

"Did he see anything?"

"No," Meghan answered, sternly. "As soon as I heard that woman scream, I looked out the window. When I saw what had happened, I sent him to his room and told him not to come out."

Meredith was writing in her notes. "Does anyone else live here?"

"Yes. My husband."

"Is he here?"

"No. He left for work early this morning."

"Have you spoken to him since he left?"

"I called him to tell him what was happening."

"Did he see anything out of the ordinary as he was leaving?" Meredith asked.

"No," she answered sharply. "I'm pretty sure he would have told me."

Meredith couldn't tell if Mrs. Ansley was on edge from the events of that morning, or if she was always this way.

"What type of work does your husband do?"

33

"What does that have to do with what happened?" Meghan asked, her frustration growing.

"We're simply trying to find out everything we can about what happened. I know it might seem unimportant, but getting a complete picture, like what time your husband left this morning, really helps."

"And we're very grateful," Tyler added.

"He's an engineering consultant."

"Can you give us his name and contact info?" Meredith continued. "He may have seen something important this morning and not have realized it."

Meghan turned back to the window. "His name is Greg. He works at Hopewell and Associates downtown." She rattled off his cell number, which Meredith wrote down.

"Do you remember what time he left this morning? It might help us clarify the exact time the murder happened."

"He left a little before six. He wanted to beat the traffic."

Meredith made a note of it.

"And you, yourself, Mrs. Ansley; did you happen to see or hear anything out of the ordinary this morning?"

"No," she answered, rubbing her eyes. "Greg got up and left. I slept for a little longer and then got up around six-thirty to make Anthony some breakfast. I heard the woman scream. I looked out the living-room window and I saw … what was going on. Anthony kept asking what was happening and wanted to go see, so I sent him up to his room … Do you know who the girl was?"

"Not at this time." Meredith pulled out her phone. "But would you mind looking at some photos to see if you recognize her?"

"How did she die?"

"It appears to have been strangulation."

Meghan seemed to search for a reason to decline, but relented.

"Fine." She exhaled and took the phone from Meredith.

She peered at the photo, her face contorted in painful disgust. "No. I don't know her." She handed the phone back.

"Have you or your husband seen anything or anyone strange on Willow Lane, recently?" Meredith asked, sliding the phone back into her pocket.

"I can't speak for Greg, but no, I haven't. Honestly, we don't see that much of our neighbors. Scott next door seems nice enough, but we don't really talk. The Whitakers are … they're a mess, and the Morgans across the street are just odd."

Meredith was unsure of how to respond. "Well, uh, I believe that's all, for now. Detective Foles? Anything?"

Tyler shook his head. "Nah. I'm good."

Meredith stood and took out a card. "Thank you, Mrs. Ansley. If you happen to think of anything or have any questions, please call me."

"Thanks," Meghan said, grudgingly accepting the card. "Let me show you out."

They walked back down the hall. Meghan opened the door.

"Have a good morning," Meredith said as they stepped outside.

"You, too," Meghan replied, barely getting it out before closing the door.

Meredith and Tyler walked back down the concrete path to the driveway and toward the street, where a stretcher, upon which rested the body bag, was being loaded into the ambulance.

Tyler glanced back toward the house. "She didn't sit right."

"Nope," Meredith agreed.

*

Meghan Ansley still had her hand on the door. She could feel the blood pounding against her temples.

"Mommy?" a quiet voice behind her asked.

She turned and looked up the stairs to see Anthony peering around the corner.

"It's okay, sweetheart. Go back to your room for a few more minutes, okay?"

The boy slunk back around the corner and moments later, there was the sound of his bedroom door closing.

Meghan Ansley slowly walked back down the hall to the kitchen and sat at the table, staring out the window to the backyard, and waited …

Chapter 7

Once the stretcher containing the body bag was loaded into the ambulance, the officer closed the door and gave it two hard slaps. The driver acknowledged with two quick hits on the siren and pulled away, driving off down Willow Lane.

Meredith and Tyler watched it go as they crossed the street to the next interview.

"Since you're running the questions, Somerset, why aren't you asking about the thing we found in her sock?" Tyler asked.

"I want us to find out more about it, first. That way, we don't tip our hand too much."

"Got it. And how are we gonna do that?"

"Same way everyone finds stuff: Google."

They stopped next to Lewis and Eddie, who were talking to each other in the middle of the street, watching the ambulance drive away.

"How's the hunting?" Eddie asked.

"Vague," Meredith answered. "You find anything else?"

"I took a rectal temperature and it confirmed what we were thinking; she hasn't been dead very long," Lewis said. "I'll send you everything this afternoon after I do the write-up."

"Thanks, Lewis. That'd be great," Tyler said.

"No problem. I also called Mike in the Morgue. He'll do the tox screen tonight and the autopsy in the morning."

Eddie was fiddling with his camera. "I'll upload the photos to the CCPD folder when I get back to the office so you can take a look."

"Thanks, guys," Meredith said. "Great work. You need anything else from us?"

"Yeah," Lewis said. "I need you to restock the 'rubbers' in my kit."

Tyler shrugged and smiled. "Gonna have to talk to budgeting on that."

"Well," Eddie said, "we'll leave you to your hunting. See you back at the precinct."

"Later," Meredith said.

Lewis and Eddie turned and walked down the street toward their cars.

"Look at you, Tyler," Meredith said. "Making friends and everything."

"They're just a couple of nerds," he replied. "But I have been told that I need to work on my people skills."

*

They finished crossing the street to the house with the deep-red siding and hunter-green accents.

Out of the four completed houses on Willow Lane, Meredith would have said this one was the nicest, not only because of its aesthetically pleasing design, but also the yard, which was a rich green that matched the accents of the house. The bushes lining the walkway were meticulously shaped.

Meredith's knock on the front door was answered by a man in his late forties with short hair and glasses.

She lifted her badge from her belt for him to see.

"Hi. Mr …?"

"Uh. Doctor. Dr. Richard Morgan." There was nothing rude in his correction, only a clarification.

"Dr. Morgan. I'm Detective Meredith Somerset. This is Detective Tyler Foles. We're sorry to bother you, but is it okay to come in and ask you a few questions?"

He opened the door wider and stepped aside. "Of course. Of course. Please, come in." The hardwood floor of the foyer gleamed under the light from the small chandelier overhead. To the right was a family room that landed somewhere between the stylish furnishings of Scott Bowers and the lived-in feel of the Ansleys. To the left was the living room. The blinds had been drawn over the windows looking out to the front yard and there were two identical twin girls, somewhere around eight years old, sitting at desks. In front of the girls was a whiteboard with math problems written in red marker. It was a classroom for two. Standing next to the whiteboard was an attractive woman in her late thirties. Her hair and features matched that of the girls. It was as though one of the girls had traveled back from the future and stood before them. The two girls stared at the detectives, as did the woman.

"Kathy," Richard said. "This is Detective Somerset and Detective Foles."

Kathy Morgan stepped over to shake their hands, doing her best to mask her concern from the twins.

"It's nice to meet you," she said.

"We're sorry to interrupt," Meredith replied.

"No, no, no. Not at all. These are our daughters, Cassidy and Fable."

"Hello, girls," Meredith said.

Tyler suppressed a laugh.

The girls continued to stare, impassively.

"We just had a few questions, if that's okay," Meredith said to Kathy and Richard.

"Anything we can do to help," Richard replied, placing a hand on his wife's shoulder.

"Let's go into my office," Kathy offered and turned back to the twins. "Keep working, girls. I'll be back in a few minutes."

Without a word, the twins went back to the papers on their desks.

*

"Your house really is lovely," Meredith said as they stepped into the office that opened from the kitchen.

"Inside and out," Tyler added. "That front yard looks like a putting green or something."

"Thank you," Richard said, closing the door once they were all in the room. "Do you golf?"

Tyler's face dropped a little as he sat in one of the chairs. "No."

"Richard and I love this house," Kathy said, taking her seat behind the desk, upon which sat photos of her and the children. On the wall were photos of a younger Kathy with a group of people in front of different buildings.

"We moved here, what has it been, honey?" Richard asked.

"Fourteen years next month."

"And it's you and the girls?" Meredith asked.

"Yes," Kathy said. "And our son, Trevor. He's up in his room."

Meredith was taking notes on her notepad. "Again, thank you for taking the time to talk to us. I'm sure you have places to be."

"Well, just Richard. His practice is over in Alpharetta," Kathy said, nodding to her husband sitting in the chair next to her.

"What field of medicine are you in, Dr. Morgan?"

"Pediatrics, and Kathy's right. I've had to push some appointments this morning, but I'm more than happy to help in any way I can. I mean, that poor girl." He was quickly struck by an idea. "I should say that I could see the body from the front window when the police arrived. I didn't want you to wonder how I knew it was a girl."

Kathy forced a light laugh. "Richard enjoys too many detective shows."

40

"It's true. I've always been interested in how accurate they are."

"Not very," Tyler mumbled.

"He really likes those medical mystery shows, like *House* and *The Good Doctor*." Kathy gave Richard a playfully scolding look. "He's a little insufferable. I can't be around when he's watching them."

"I can't help myself." Richard smiled. "And I know what you mean about those detective shows not being accurate. The medical shows aren't much better. I did my residency as part of a pilot program where for a year and a half, I traveled around the country, working in different hospitals. We were pulling fourteen-hour shifts. None of us looked as glamorous as the doctors on television."

This is good, Meredith thought. She wanted them to be as relaxed as possible and gently tried to guide the conversation.

"And you, Mrs. Morgan?"

Kathy Morgan snapped out of her loving gaze toward Richard. "Hmm?"

"What do you do?"

"The children are my occupation," she said with intense pride. "I used to work in construction contracts, but that was a while ago." She motioned to the photos on the wall. "It was a lot of traveling." The photos were of a younger Kathy with a group of people. The faces in most of the photos around her stayed the same while the buildings behind them changed. There was one that had the Seattle skyline in the background. In one of the photos, Kathy was smiling with the group as they stood next to a sign that read "McCormick Place Convention Center". There was another with a blue and green glass-paneled building behind the smiling faces. "I was traveling, while Richard was on the road for his residency. Once he finished, we decided to start our family. I quit the job, and we moved here to raise and homeschool our children."

"There's simply too much filth in the public school system," Richard said.

Kathy nodded in agreement. "We know what's best for our

children. We've been handling their education for years. I keep this room as my little teacher's office."

Meredith wasn't sure whether to include it in her notes, but she remembered Scott Bowers' and Meghan Ansley's opinion of the Morgans.

"We're trying to get a better understanding of what happened this morning and we're asking everyone on the street if they saw or heard anything," Meredith said.

"Well," Richard began, "I was still getting ready to go to work when Kathy came in and told me that something was going on outside."

"I was prepping today's lessons for the children," Kathy added, "and I heard someone scream, but ..."

"What did you do?" Meredith asked.

"Nothing," Kathy replied, embarrassed. "But you have to understand; the girls were watching television. I—I thought the scream had come from the show they were watching. I asked them to change it to something less violent."

Meredith didn't think it was too much of a stretch to assume that the scream had come from the television rather than the discovery of a dead body in the street outside your door.

"We're very mindful of what our children watch," Richard chimed in. "There's a lot of violence and ... other objectionable things we'd rather they not see. We allow Trevor, our son, to play video games, but only for an hour a day in the basement, and only games that we've approved."

"And what happened then?"

"It was Trevor who came down from his room and told us that there was a body in the road," Kathy said. "We thought he was playing video games in the basement before school, but I guess he had gone back upstairs."

"That's when I looked out the window and saw what was happening," Richard said. "I had everyone stay inside and pulled the blinds so the children wouldn't see."

"And how is Trevor handling it, since he saw the body?" Meredith asked.

"He seems okay," Richard said.

"Would it be okay if we talked to him?"

"I think so," Richard replied, looking to Kathy.

"We can ask," Kathy said.

*

Upon entering the upstairs hallway, Kathy tapped on the first door they encountered on the left.

"Trevor?"

"Yes?" a voice on the other side of the door answered.

"Sweetheart, there are some people here who would like to ask you some questions about what you saw this morning. Can we come in?"

"Okay."

Kathy smiled at the detectives as she pushed open the door.

Trevor was awkwardly standing in the middle of the room. Meredith guessed he was in the neighborhood of fourteen. He wore a blue T-shirt and jeans, which, like his posture, were stiff and formal. The walls were adorned with posters of sports figures.

"Trevor," Richard began after everyone had entered. "This is Detective Somerset and Detective Foles."

"It's nice to meet you, Trevor," Meredith said.

Trevor was mute, his face a mix of anxiety and uncertainty.

The moment was so uncomfortable, with everyone in such close proximity, that Meredith wasn't sure how to proceed.

Tyler stepped in and casually held out his hand. "How you doin', Trev?"

Trevor didn't move. Meredith worried that Trevor was about to shut down, completely. Even the Morgans looked concerned.

Then Trevor loosened slightly and tentatively shook Tyler's hand. "Hi."

"I like the room, man," Tyler said, glancing around. He motioned with a knowing smile to a poster for the Carolina Panthers. "All except for this. You not a fan of my Atlanta Falcons?"

"I like Cam Newton," Trevor said, relaxing further.

"Yeah, but he's flopping in New England, now. Don't tell me you're hopping on the Patriots bandwagon."

Trevor shook his head. "No way."

"Good. Tell you what, your Panthers can have Matt Ryan for your quarterback. I'll be glad when the Falcons get rid of him."

"He's past his prime," Trevor said. "If he couldn't get the Falcons a Super Bowl ring, he can't do it for the Panthers. The Falcons aren't going to be good for a long time."

Tyler fake-groaned and placed a hand over his heart. "Now, you're just hurting my feelings."

Tyler had managed to get an honest-to-God smile from the boy. They were two guys talking football and Meredith recognized that Tyler was using the same tactics she had been using with Trevor's parents.

Tyler saw the open book on the desk by the window. "Getting your studies in?"

"Yeah."

"Cool. Listen, Trev, you ain't in any kind of trouble. Everything's chill. We just want to know what you saw this morning and then we'll get out of here. Trust me, I'd like to get away from that as soon as possible," he said with a thumb toward the Panthers poster.

Trevor's back stiffened but Tyler had put him at ease enough that he began to speak.

"I was reading in my bed and I heard someone scream outside."

Tyler and Meredith stepped over to the window and looked down onto Willow Lane.

"What was going on?" Tyler asked.

"There was a girl lying in the road and a woman standing next to her."

"What was the woman doing?"

"She was on her phone."

"Did you tell your parents what you saw?" Meredith asked.

He fidgeted. "Not right away. I just kind of watched."

"Did you see anyone else other than the girl in the road and the woman on the phone?"

"No."

"Then you told your parents?" Meredith asked.

"Yeah," Trevor said, tensing.

"It's okay if you were scared, Trevor," Meredith said, trying to calm him.

Tyler scoffed. "You don't scare so easy, do you Trev?"

Again, Tyler had worked some sort of magic and Trevor regained control. "I was a little scared, but then I went downstairs and told my parents."

Tyler gave Trevor a nod to let him know it was all good.

"Thank you for your help, Trevor," Meredith said.

"Thanks, Trev," Tyler said. "We'll let you get back to your studies and misplaced love of the Panthers, but if you remember anything else, you tell your mom and pops, okay?"

"Okay," Trevor said.

*

They walked back downstairs, leaving Trevor alone in his room.

At the bottom of the stairs, Richard opened the front door to show them out.

"It was nice to meet you," Meredith said to the girls who were still seated at their desks.

Cassidy and Fable glanced up.

"Girls? What do we say?" Kathy asked.

45

"Bye," one said.

"Goodbye," said the other.

The detectives and the Morgans stepped through the door and onto the porch.

*

Meredith, Tyler, and the Morgans walked away from the door and into the yard to ensure that they wouldn't be heard by the children inside.

"We only have a few more questions," Meredith said. "Have you noticed anything strange on your street recently? Have your neighbors mentioned anything unusual recently?"

"We don't really talk to our neighbors," Richard said.

"We also don't allow our children to play with any of the neighborhood kids," Kathy added.

"Why is that?" Meredith asked.

"They are horrible influences," Richard said with a hint of disgust.

"Okay," Meredith said and quickly moved on. "There is one last thing and I'm sorry to end with this, but would you be okay with looking at a photo to see if you recognize the victim?"

"I'm okay with it," Richard said. "Kathy?"

She was less certain but agreed.

Meredith took out her phone, pulled up the picture, and handed it to Richard.

They studied it. Kathy groaned and gazed out to the road.

"I'm sorry," Richard said. "I don't recognize her. Sorry."

"I don't either," Kathy said.

Richard handed the phone back to Meredith.

"You've been very helpful and thank you again for taking the time to speak to us," Meredith said, handing them a card. "If you, or the children, remember anything, please give me a call."

"We will," Richard said.

"That really was amazing what you did with Trevor," Kathy said to Tyler. "He's nervous and shy around people but you got him to open up. Do you have kids?"

Tyler looked like he was about to crack a joke, but reconsidered. "Nah. I just know how that kind of stuff works."

The Morgans smiled.

"Well," Meredith said, "We'll let you get back to your day. Thank you for your time."

They all shook hands one last time.

"Have a good day," Meredith said as they walked away.

"You, too," Richard said, draping a comforting arm over his wife's shoulder. They walked back onto the porch, through the front door, and closed it behind them.

Meredith waited until she and Tyler were in the street before speaking.

"So, how do you like homicide interviews so far?"

"Beats the hell out of trying to get answers out of meth-heads and dealers."

"You prefer talking to the Stepford family back there?"

"Shit. That wasn't no Stepford family. That back there? That was *The Shining.*"

Meredith laughed. "That was really good work with Trevor."

"Little man's got it rough."

"What do you mean?"

"You see his room? That ain't no fifteen-year-old's room who's trying to express himself. That's a kid's room. They're putting him in a box."

"Still, thanks for the save."

Tyler shrugged. "Got one more interview to go. Plenty of time for me to screw this up."

They continued walking to the last house on Willow Lane.

Had they looked back over their shoulders; they would have seen Trevor Morgan anxiously watching them from his window as they walked away.

Chapter 8

"She was killed right outside our house?" the girl asked, a little too enthusiastically.

"Kendall," her mother chided from the other side of the kitchen table.

"Well, was she?"

Meredith shifted uncomfortably in her chair. "We're trying to figure out what happened."

She wanted some backup from Tyler, but he was too busy watching the guy who was pacing on the other side of the kitchen, adamantly talking on his cellphone.

"No. Listen to me; keep your mouth shut and I'll be there as soon as I can …" Thomas Whitaker was saying. "That's my point! Don't talk to the cops. Don't talk to the guy in your cell! Tell them that they're going to have to talk to me … No … No, I'm stuck here until they clean up this shit outside my house."

"We'd clean this 'shit' up a lot faster if you'd put down the phone and talk to us," Tyler said quietly, pinning Thomas Whitaker with a glare.

Thomas stopped and looked back at the table where his wife, Natalie, his thirteen-year-old daughter, Kendall, his fifteen-year-old son, Ashton, and the detectives waited.

"Just a couple of questions and we'll be on our way," Meredith said.

Thomas huffed and went back to his phone. "Listen, stay quiet until I get there, got it? Great." He hung up too quickly for a response and put the phone in his pocket. He impatiently made his way over to the table and stood behind Ashton, who was slumped in his chair, hair in his eyes, tapping away on his phone.

"Okay, okay, okay. Come on. Let's go," Thomas growled. "I know how this works."

Meredith stole a glance at Natalie, who continued to stare at the table.

From the few minutes they had spent inside the Whitakers' home, Meredith had quickly come to the conclusion that this was a family on the rocks.

"What kind of law do you practice, Mr. Whitaker?" Meredith asked.

"Criminal law."

"Any particular specialty?"

"Dad defends drunks, dealers, and prosti—" Ashton was cut short when Thomas smacked him in the back of the head.

Meredith tensed, as did Tyler.

"You like that phone?" Thomas asked his son. "You like living in this house?"

The boy didn't respond, nor did he look back at his father.

"Then don't get smart," Thomas finished and turned to the detectives. "And, yes, I represent a wide variety of clients."

An uncomfortable silence fell on the table.

It hadn't been a forceful hit, but if this man was fine doing that in front of detectives, Meredith wondered what happened when no one else was around. She could tell that Tyler was itching to call him out. Meredith sympathized but it wasn't the time.

"We're asking everyone on the street if they happened to see or hear anything this morning that might help us figure out what happened," Meredith said.

"Then someone did kill her," Kendall said, still too enthusiastically.

"Of course someone killed her," Thomas said, already getting his phone out, again.

"Could you please tell us where you were this morning?"

"We were here, in the house," Thomas said, punching in a text.

"All morning?" Meredith asked.

Thomas continued texting as he spoke. "No. I went for a run around five-thirty. I got home around six-thirty and since I know what you're going to ask next; no, I didn't see or hear anything."

"What about when you got back? Did you see or hear anything out of the ordinary?"

"You mean like a woman screaming hysterically? Yeah, we heard that."

"What did you do?" Meredith asked.

"I took one peek outside, saw the body, and I tried to get out of here."

"And why would you do that?" Tyler stepped in, slightly awed at the man's unabashed tone.

"So that I wouldn't be here, talking to you right now. I have an arraignment in thirty minutes."

"You didn't go outside to check on what was happening?" Meredith asked.

"No. One look and I knew that I didn't want any part of it. I told everyone to stay inside while I got ready to leave."

Meredith turned to the others at the table. "Everyone heard the scream?"

Thomas looked up from his phone. "Yes. I just told you—"

"And we're very grateful for your perspective, Mr. Whitaker," Tyler said, cutting him off. "But we're gonna hear it from them."

Even Meredith was a little thrown by Tyler's tone. His languid drawl was surprisingly menacing when he put some intensity behind it.

Thomas reluctantly got the message, shook his head, and went back to texting.

"Mrs. Whitaker?" Meredith asked.

"He's right. We were here. I was making breakfast. Kendall was over there, watching television, and we heard the scream. I think Ashton was in his room. Thomas came downstairs and told us not to go outside."

"You were upstairs?" Meredith asked Thomas.

"Yes. I told you," he responded, irritably. "I went for a run and then came back to get ready for work. I was just about to jump in the shower when she started screaming. I tried to hustle it up, but you guys arrived before I could get out of the garage."

"Very sorry about that," Tyler said dryly.

"What time did you wake up?" Meredith asked.

"Thomas got up around … five?" Natalie asked in Thomas's direction.

"Five o'clock," he muttered in agreement.

"The kids got up around six-thirty," Natalie said.

"And you were all home?"

"For the second time, yes," Thomas muttered.

"I was down here with Kendall," Natalie quickly added. "We didn't see or hear anything until the scream."

"Have any of you heard or seen anything strange on Willow Lane, recently?" Meredith asked.

"Whole place is full of weirdos," Thomas said. "That Bowers guy across the street. The 'sad-sack' Ansleys. The 'better-than-everybody' Morgans."

"Have you got anything specific?" Tyler asked. "Or just opinions."

Thomas matched Tyler's stare. "Opinions."

"Thank you," Meredith said, attempting to break the tension between the two.

51

"Great," Thomas said, returning his phone to his pocket. "Now, if there's anything else, it's gonna have to wait because—"

"One last thing," Meredith said, reaching for her phone.

"No. I told you, detective, I don't have time for your—"

"One more minute, man. Then you can go," Tyler said.

Meredith pulled up the picture of the dead girl. "I want to know if you recognize the victim."

Thomas took Meredith's phone and stared at it for a fraction of a second before attempting to hand it back.

"Nope."

Meredith made no motion to receive it. "Can you be sure for us, please?"

He reluctantly took another look. "No. I've never seen her before."

Meredith took the phone back and offered it to Natalie.

"Do you recognize her, ma'am?"

Natalie took the phone in her hand. Meredith caught the quick subtle movement of her eyes as she glanced at her husband, who was watching her. Tyler spotted it, too.

"I'm sorry," Natalie said. "I don't recognize her."

"Let me see," Kendall said and made an attempt to snatch the phone from her mother's hands.

Natalie pulled it back out of her reach just in time.

"Kendall!"

The girl was only slightly chastened, but still tried to see the screen while Natalie passed the phone back to Meredith.

"Thank you," Meredith said.

"That's it? Can I go, now?" Thomas asked.

Meredith got out her card. "Yes. Thank you and if you remember anything else—"

"Leave it with my wife," he said, already dialing his phone while bolting for the door to the garage.

Ashton remained slumped in his chair. Kendall was still staring at them.

"Thank you for your time," Meredith said.

Natalie Whitaker smiled sadly and took the card.

*

"Fuck that guy," Tyler said, once they reached the street. Thomas Whitaker's BMW had just disappeared from view in the distance. "I hope it was him. I want it to be him."

"I was worried you were going to get us into trouble," Meredith said.

"What do you mean?"

"The man's a lawyer."

"Nah. He ain't a lawyer. He's a con artist. You know how many of his kind I had to deal with working in narco and vice? Shit. Most times, I would have rather we locked up the lawyers instead of their clients."

"I get it, but leave out the commentary."

Tyler motioned to the empty street as they walked back to their cars. "Ain't nobody here but us chickens, Somerset." Tyler took a breath and changed gears. "You got any ideas?"

"Nothing, yet."

"Come on, Somerset. We usually had a pretty good idea of who our perp was within the first few minutes of showing up."

"This one's different."

Tyler smiled. "How did I get so lucky for my first homicide?"

They finally reached their cars, which were parked one in front of the other at the end of Willow Lane.

"Seriously, though," Tyler persisted. "You gotta be thinking something."

"We'll talk about it back at the office. There's too much we don't know."

"You're killing me, Somerset. Catch you back at the precinct."

"See you in a few."

Tyler slid into his driver's seat, closed the door, started the engine, and waved to Meredith as he pulled away.

She waited a second longer and got out her phone. She had wanted to make the call the moment she had seen the dead girl's eyes open, but wouldn't do it around Tyler.

She flipped through her contacts until she found the number.

Her call was answered on the second ring.

"Dr. Kaplan's office."

"Hey, Joanna. It's Meredith Somerset. Does Dr. Kaplan have a few minutes this afternoon?"

Chapter 9

Back at the station, Meredith and Tyler spent the rest of the afternoon writing their reports. Since Tyler was still waiting on a desk of his own, he worked off one side of Meredith's.

Despite being in such close proximity, they barely said a word to each other as they wrote down their own version of the events and observations so that they would be able to compare them later. Thankfully, it was a pretty standard practice across all departments and Meredith didn't have to walk Tyler through it. Occasionally, one might ask the other about a minor detail, such as a name or a time. Tyler had been so hung up on the charming Thomas Whitaker, that he had forgotten the names of the rest of the family. Meredith worked off her notes and didn't ask much of him.

Tyler finished first and waited for her to catch up while he read, then reread his own report. Satisfied, he picked up the red sponge ball from Meredith's desk, leaned back in his chair, and casually flipped the ball in the air to himself over and over while he waited.

"All right." Meredith exhaled, looking up from her notes. She paused when she saw Tyler tossing the ball up into the air. Her knee-jerk reaction was to tell him to put it down, but she shook it off.

"You ready to tell me who you think our primary is?" Tyler asked.

"No."

"Really? No one tickles your fancy?"

"We don't know anything. We've got to find out who she is, then we can start connecting dots."

Tyler leaned forward. "Okay. First question; why didn't she have ID?"

Meredith held up her hand.

Tyler grinned and tossed her the ball, which she confidently snagged.

"There's a chance she didn't have any on her. She might not even be old enough for a driver's license. There's also the chance that the killer took anything that could have identified her but didn't know about the thing in the sock."

"If she had ID, you think the killer might still have it?"

"It's possible," Meredith said. "Let's hope they're not smart enough to get rid of it." She threw the ball back to Tyler.

"But we're in agreement that this wasn't some rando. This guy knew her, right?" Tyler asked, throwing the ball back to her.

Meredith caught it. "Absolutely. He knew her and we both agree that she didn't run very far. Willow Lane is pretty isolated. So, the most likely answer is someone on that street."

"But you're not ready to start playing 'Guess Who'?"

"Not yet and I don't want us starting down any roads that we're gonna have to walk back. First thing we need to do is find out who she is." She tossed the ball back to him.

"Fingerprints?"

"Mike's downstairs with the body, doing the tox screen and the rape kit. He'll take the fingerprints, too." Meredith thought and shook her head. "We can run them through IAFIS, but they'll only have a record of her prints if she's committed a crime." The Integrated Automated Fingerprint Identification System was a database of convicts maintained by the FBI.

"We could get lucky. Maybe she was naughty," Tyler suggested.

"Not going to hold my breath. Also, she was a minor. Our best bet is NamUS."

Tyler groaned and tossed the ball in the air to himself. "What are the odds on that? We wait seven, maybe eight weeks, just to be told that she's not in that system, either?"

Meredith couldn't argue. The National Missing and Unidentified Persons System was another database run by the DOJ and the National Institute for Justice. Every year, 600,000 people went missing in the United States. Most were found, but tens of thousands weren't. There were also over one thousand bodies recovered every year that no one could identify. NamUS tried to match missing persons to unidentified bodies.

"It's all we can do, for now," Meredith said. "But someone, somewhere, is wondering where that girl is."

"And what about the medallion thing we found in her sock?"

Meredith pulled up the pictures of it on her phone.

"I'm guessing it's the closest thing we've got to an ID."

"What do you make of the symbol?" Tyler asked.

Meredith examined it, but couldn't decrypt the two circles or the lines emanating from them.

"I don't know." She swiped to the next picture, which showed the other side of the medallion with the word "SOSH" engraved upon it. "We've got a better chance trying to find out what 'sosh' means."

Tyler sat up. "I'm actually ahead of you on that. I was looking it up on the drive back."

"You were Googling and driving at the same time," Meredith said with the mock rebuke of a parent.

"I will not apologize for my hustle," he said, taking out his phone. "I even bookmarked it."

"And?"

Tyler cleared his throat. "There's a couple of things. There's an old, defunct art show that was called 'Sosh' in Seattle. There is also 'Sons of Sam Horn', which is a message board for Red Sox fans. Pretty safe to rule those out. The only like, real possibility I found was 'sosh' as in 'social media'. At least, that's what Wikipedia and Urban Dictionary are giving me."

"What's 'Urban Dictionary'?" Meredith asked.

Tyler was about to answer but stopped. "You know what, don't worry about that one. The only other thing that I can find is that it's Scottish slang for 'association store'." Tyler stared at his phone for a moment longer, then looked up at Meredith's underwhelmed expression.

"Though I commend your hustle, Tyler, it has brought us nothing."

"No, it has not."

"And don't Google and drive. It's dangerous."

"You and Dad gonna take away my car keys?" Tyler asked, lofting the ball into the air toward Meredith.

"Speaking of which," Sergeant Wheaton said, stepping through the door, and heading toward his office.

Meredith took her eye off the ball to glance at him.

The ball fell past her hand. As she grasped for it, her hand hit the pen-filled coffee mug on the corner of her desk, scattering the pens to the floor.

She quickly attempted to gather them up.

Tyler was instantly out of his chair and on the floor to assist her.

Sergeant Wheaton watched them with a bored expression.

Once Meredith had assembled the pens back in the cup and returned it to her desk, she and Tyler stood.

"Why don't you two follow me?" Sergeant Wheaton said and walked into his office.

Sergeant Wheaton motioned to the chairs in front of his desk. "Have a seat."

"Am I in some sort of trouble already?" Tyler asked, as he awkwardly settled into his seat.

"Not unless you still haven't figured out how to tell time," Sergeant Wheaton replied.

Tyler was a deer in headlights. Meredith turned her head so he couldn't see the grin she was struggling against.

Sergeant Wheaton was the King of Quick Wit. It could be intimidating at first, but once you got to know him, as Meredith had, you appreciated it, and knew he never made jokes if he was serious. No matter how deep his cuts were, if he was making them, whatever you were talking about wasn't a big deal. Tyler being late on his first day was a bad foot to start out on, but as long as he showed up on time from here on in, no harm done. If he kept doing it, Sergeant Wheaton would stop joking about it. Then, Tyler would be in trouble, but he didn't know that, yet, and Meredith would let him learn for her amusement.

"Now," Sergeant Wheaton said, bringing his hands together on his desk. "Tell me how the first day went. What did you find?"

"Unidentified female," Meredith began. "Mid-teens. Manually strangled. Left lying in the middle of the street. No ID."

"You said the neighborhood was 'nice'?"

"It is."

"And no one, none of the neighbors, could identify her?" Sergeant Wheaton asked.

"No one would identify her."

Sergeant Wheaton stopped. "There's a difference between 'no one *could*' and 'no one *would*'. You think someone is lying?"

"It's possible."

"Any chance the body was dumped there?"

Meredith was about to speak but Sergeant Wheaton held up his hand and pointed at Tyler.

"I'd like to hear from the new guy."

Tyler looked to Meredith for guidance. She nodded.

"Don't think so," Tyler said. "The victim wasn't wearing any shoes and the grass stains on the soles of her socks were pretty fresh, indicating that she hadn't run very far. There are also signs of a struggle in the road."

"Maybe she got the wounds when the body was dumped from a car," Sergeant Wheaton offered.

Meredith knew what Sergeant Wheaton was doing. It was the same method she had used at the crime scene. He didn't believe for one second that the body had been dumped from a car. This was a test to see if Tyler would stick to his guns.

"I suppose it's possible," Tyler said, unsteadily. "There's a lot we don't know, but it wouldn't make a whole lot of sense."

"Really? And why not?"

"Why dump a body there? It only makes sense if you're trying to send a message to someone, but there are way less risky ways to do it without the possibility of someone seeing you or catching your plates, right?" As he spoke, Tyler gained confidence and his drawl thickened. "And if you're looking to get rid of a body, why stop on a residential street in a nice neighborhood and take the time to push it out of the car where it can be found ten minutes later? It's the single worst place to dump a body if you want to keep a secret. Nah. No one planned this. She was killed right there."

When he stopped, Tyler glanced at the two of them as though he had forgotten they were there.

"That's just what I'm thinkin'," he concluded.

Meredith agreed with everything he had said.

Sergeant Wheaton glanced back and forth between them before his eyes settled back on Tyler.

"You know something, Detective Foles, it just occurred to me that because you were late this morning, you haven't sampled the lovely coffee we make here. Why don't you go try some?"

"Thanks, sarge, but I'm good. I don't drink coffee this late in the day. It always keeps me up—"

"Detective Foles, I need you to step outside so that I can openly discuss your performance on your first day with Detective Somerset."

Tyler's mouth hung slightly open.

Sergeant Wheaton smiled and nodded.

Tyler hesitantly stood. "That's … That's all you had to say."

He turned and walked out of the office.

"Close the door, please," Sergeant Wheaton called after him.

Tyler reached back through and pulled the door shut.

Once he was gone, Sergeant Wheaton turned to Meredith. "How is he?"

"Little unpolished around the edges but he's solid," Meredith replied.

"I took him on as a favor to Doc McElwee. You know that, right?"

"Yeah, but his instincts are good and he can handle himself."

"What about this case?"

"What about it?"

Sergeant Wheaton measured his words. "This case sounds like it could get complicated."

"It feels that way," Meredith said.

I miss you, Meredith.

The flash across her mind of the dead girl speaking caused Meredith to inadvertently flinch.

"Listen," Sergeant Wheaton said, misinterpreting her reaction. "If you think that this might not be the best case for his introduction to homicide, you need to tell me, right now. I'll explain to him that it's nothing personal and he's on the next case, but if this gets weirder, if it gets out of hand, and the press starts sniffing around, I don't want a rookie homicide detective mucking it up. You need to be 100 percent positive, because if you're only 95 percent, I'm bringing in someone else. So, I'm going ask you, again; Do you think Detective Foles is up for this?"

There it was. No jokes. No sarcasm. No quips. Sergeant Wheaton was dead serious and he was right. It would have been better if this was more of a straightforward murder but it wasn't.

It wasn't just her ass on the line. It was also his and he was asking for her opinion because Meredith had earned his trust.

"He'll be fine," she said.

Sergeant Wheaton nodded, accepting her verdict.

"Make sure he buys a watch," he said, ending their conversation.

*

Meredith and Tyler spent another hour going over the interviews until it was time to call it a day. They wouldn't have anything new until tomorrow, after the autopsy was performed.

"What now, Somerset?" Tyler asked as they walked out the door to the parking lot. "Want to grab a bite to eat?"

"Some other night."

"You got somewhere to be?"

"Maybe."

"So," Tyler said, stepping closer and lowering his voice. "Tell me what happened in there with Dad?"

"Don't worry about it."

"He asked you if you thought I could handle this, didn't he?"

"Tyler, I'm not gonna tell you."

"Come on, Somerset. I can take it."

Meredith grew quiet and looked down at the pavement.

"Okay," Tyler said. "Well, since he didn't call me back into the office to break some bad news, I assume you told him I'm good, yeah?"

She met his eyes. "Just don't prove me wrong, okay?"

Tyler broke into a wide grin. "I got you, Somerset. Go do your thing." He turned and walked away.

"Try being on time tomorrow," she called out.

"Shit. I've just been told I have some job security," Tyler said over his shoulder. He held up his arm and tapped his wrist. "About to go buy me a Rolex!"

Chapter 10

The door to the office opened and out stepped a woman in her fifties with glasses and dark hair that was pulled into a ponytail.

"Meredith," she said, her face lighting up.

"Hello, Dr. Kaplan."

They embraced.

Since they had known each other for years, Dr. Kaplan had told Meredith to call her Susan many times, but Meredith refused. Meredith insisted on titles, formalities, and structure. Ironically, it was Dr. Kaplan, herself, who had told her to use and rely on them for her own well-being.

"Thank you for seeing me on such short notice," Meredith said.

"It's always good to hear from you. Please, come on in."

Dr. Kaplan's office was as stereotypical as you could imagine for a psychologist. There was the couch and a wall of books which Meredith wondered if Dr. Kaplan had actually read. Another wall was dotted with framed degrees and photos of Dr. Kaplan with her family, at different symposiums, and some of the charity work she had done.

Meredith knew the drill without being told and sat on the couch. Dr. Kaplan closed the door and then relaxed into a leather chair across from her.

"How are Peter and Allison?" Dr. Kaplan asked.

"Good. Really good," Meredith replied.

This was also part of the routine. You didn't just come in and unload. It was best to ease into things, something Meredith had incorporated into her interview techniques.

"And Heather?" Dr. Kaplan asked, a little more reserved.

"She's great," Meredith answered with a smile that was sincere. Meredith truly liked her ex-husband's girlfriend. Pete and Heather had been together for years. For the sake of Allison, their daughter, Pete and Meredith wanted to be on the best of terms with each other to make Allison's life as smooth as possible. They were good friends and always would be, and Heather had been very understanding of the complexity of the relationship. She, too, wanted what was best for Allison, and was completely supportive of Meredith playing a large role in their lives. Meredith would even go so far as to call Heather a close friend.

"Good," Dr. Kaplan said. "That's really good ... Any word from your mother?"

"No, and I'm not expecting any."

Dr. Kaplan nodded.

There was a slight pause. Even though Meredith had worked through some of her deepest, darkest issues, and had come to the hardest decisions of her life in that very room, it had been a while since she had been on the couch.

"So," Dr. Kaplan said, recognizing that Meredith had struck a roadblock. "What's up?"

Meredith bit her lip before answering. "Got called to the scene of a homicide this morning."

"Okay."

"The victim was a young woman. A teenager ... She looked a lot like Alice."

"Not Allison?"

"No. Alice ... and it really got to me ... It's been a long time since something like that happened, but it got to me ..."

"How long has it been since you've thought about Alice?" Dr. Kaplan gently asked.

"I still think about her a lot, but nothing like before. I'm doing better … It just threw me, that's all."

Dr. Kaplan gave her a disapproving look.

"Meredith, you didn't call to see me at a moment's notice simply because you saw someone who looked like your sister."

Meredith sat back in resignation. "No. I didn't."

"Okay. Tell me what happened."

"I was a taking a photo of the victim on my phone to show the neighbors and ask if they recognized her and I had one of those things that … that hasn't happened in a long time."

"Meredith, I'm not going to guess. You have to tell me what you saw."

"Through the screen on my phone, I saw the girl open her eyes, look at me, and say, 'I miss you, Meredith.'"

Dr. Kaplan waited and then asked the most basic of psychological questions. "And how did that make you feel?"

When Dr. Kaplan had asked that question in their first session, Meredith lit up and railed against the bullshit of it all. Dr. Kaplan had listened with stoic acceptance and explained that she had seen Meredith's reaction to that question many times from many people and the sooner Meredith recognized the importance of that question, the sooner she would understand that her honest answer was the first step in addressing her problems. Not solve them. Dr. Kaplan had made it very clear in that first session that it was not her job to solve Meredith's problems. It was her job to help Meredith see her problems clearly and make a decision for herself. It had worked. Since then, she had always been honest with Dr. Kaplan. In fact, it was Dr. Kaplan's most important rule: do not lie. Meredith had to be honest with Dr. Kaplan and herself, or their sessions were a waste of both their time.

"I was confused," Meredith said. "I was irritated. I thought that this was all behind me."

"You know it's never going to be entirely behind you. It's perfectly normal that upon seeing someone who looked like Alice, who may have suffered a similar trauma, it would trigger something like this."

Years ago, Dr. Kaplan mentioned that Meredith's sister may have suffered a terrible fate and Meredith lost it. Dr. Kaplan explained that it was something that Meredith needed to confront, acknowledge, and accept but not dwell on. Bringing it up used to unleash a wave of anguish. Now, the suggestion of what may have happened to her sister merely felt like a kick to her gut. In other words, it was progress.

Meredith knew she was right but shook her head, as if she were somehow disappointed in herself.

"When you saw her speak, did you at any time, even for a moment, believe that what you were seeing was real?" Dr. Kaplan asked.

"No," Meredith answered assuredly. "No. I knew what it was."

"Good."

Meredith had never once suffered a psychotic break. Never had she questioned her sanity, which is to say that she knew these types of flashes were the result of the emotional and mental anguish she had suffered. They were intense, shocking moments, to be sure, but she recognized them for what they were. To keep her job, which meant everything to her, she made sure those moments didn't interfere with her work.

"Did anything else happen with this girl? Any other 'incidents'?"

"No. Just the one, but I wanted to talk to you, in case things start to get worse."

"Then you did exactly the right thing by getting in touch. If it keeps happening, you need to call me."

Meredith contemplated her shoes. "I'm worried about the nightmares starting, again."

"You remember what I told you about nightmares?"

66

Meredith smiled. "Yeah. I remember."

"Have you told James?"

While Dr. Kaplan called him James, he was always "Sergeant Wheaton" to Meredith. He and Dr. Kaplan also had a past.

"No," Meredith answered, suddenly worried. "Do you think I should?"

Dr. Kaplan considered it for a moment.

"No. We'll treat it as a blip, for now. I'm sure even he has had past trauma intrude on his mind from time to time at a crime scene. You're doing exactly what you should. If it really starts coming back, then you and I can talk some more about what to do. Sound good?"

"Perfect."

After everything they had been through, Meredith trusted Dr. Kaplan with her life. She had come to the same conclusion about a course of action before setting foot in Dr. Kaplan's office, and it was the world off her shoulders to hear Dr. Kaplan agree to it, unprompted.

"Anything else troubling you?"

"Nope," Meredith said, lightly slapping her knees as she stood from the couch. "Thanks for fitting me in."

"Of course." Dr. Kaplan smiled. She rose from her chair and walked Meredith to the door. "And call me anytime, Meredith."

"Thank you, Dr. Kaplan."

They hugged and Meredith headed out the door to face Atlanta's fearsome rush-hour traffic home.

Chapter 11

Upon stepping into her apartment, Meredith went straight to the bedroom and placed her sidearm in the small safe inside the closet. She closed the metal door, which emitted a small beep, followed by a click. Now, the safe could only be opened by entering a four-digit combination on the keypad. While she was the only occupant in her apartment, this was a routine she had established when she, Pete, and Allison were all living under the same roof, and Meredith had never lapsed in it. Ever. No taking a few minutes to unwind upon walking in the door and then putting the gun away. It went right into the safe as soon as she came home. No exceptions.

As she slid the closet door closed, her phone pinged with a text from Eddie.

Photos uploaded. Not my most artistic work but I'm still proud of it.

Thanks, Eddie. Will check them out tonight, she replied.

Copy that. Thanks, Eddie, Tyler added and Meredith saw that he had been included in the original text.

Get some beauty rest, especially you, Foles, Eddie replied.

Meredith stripped down and jumped in the shower, taking her time.

It was already starting. The obsession that accompanied the beginning of a new case, especially an intriguing case like this. In the majority of cases she had handled in her decade of working homicide, the killer was pretty clear from the start, just as Tyler had intimated about narco and vice. It was only a matter of collecting the evidence to give the district attorney the strongest case. The girl this morning left so many open questions that Meredith's thoughts were already starting to spin.

Once out of the shower, she changed into a T-shirt and pajama pants. She poured herself a healthy glass of cabernet, sat on the couch, and opened her laptop on the coffee table in front of her. She logged on to the CCPD server with her username and password and found the casefile in the directory. She had to input her information again, since only detectives assigned to the case could access the specific casefiles.

Recently, the Cobb County Police Department had upgraded to a new system that allowed detectives to access their cases from anywhere. For some old-school detectives, the new system was a bit of a headache. There was a certain comfort in separating work and home. Of course, a lot of detectives still worked cases when they got home, but it was more in the abstract. They didn't have access to the materials of their cases at all times. The new system changed that, and while they could simply choose not to use it, it didn't change the fact that it was always there.

For Meredith, it was a godsend. She never drew that line between work and home. She fixated on her cases. She was relentless. Her life may have been different if she had been able to draw that line, but the new system hadn't been the cause of that particular problem. That problem had been set in motion almost twenty-five years earlier.

As Meredith pulled up the first photo of the girl's face, she couldn't help but think of Alice. The Jane Doe in the road wasn't the spitting image of Meredith's sister, but the high cheekbones and auburn hair were more than enough. Meredith began flipping through the photos and as much as she told herself to focus on the crime in front of her, her mind was already being pulled back to a place she had spent way too much time revisiting. She spread her notes out on the table around her laptop, along with her written report, in an attempt to corral her thoughts to the task at hand, but she could smell the chlorine. She could taste it.

And then, she was there.

*

Mom had dropped them off at the community swimming pool in the small town of Dalton, Georgia on that scorching, humid summer afternoon, just as she did on most of the days of their summer vacation.

Meredith and Alice loved it. They insisted on it, even when they were little kids. Now that Meredith was turning sixteen and Alice was eleven, their swimming activities had begun to diverge. Alice still liked splashing and playing games. Meredith's attention had begun to focus less and less on swimming and more and more on friends and boys. She was finding Alice's insistence on playing together to be annoying, but it was an unspoken agreement with their parents that Meredith was to keep an eye on her. It didn't require much. The grounds of the pool were fenced in with the main entrance being the only way in or out, except for a large swing gate that remained padlocked. Outside the fence, the grounds of the pool were surrounded by trees on three sides and a field across the road.

Meredith and Alice got along well enough most of the time. They were still sisters who shared a fierce, loving family bond. The times they fought were no different than any other siblings who were separated by a few years.

That day, though, had been bad, and while the pool grounds weren't huge, the place was packed. Meredith wanted to hang out with her friend Kelly Brocklan, while Alice wanted her to play.

One of the lifeguards, sitting in a chair above the water, let loose a long blast on her whistle, signaling that the fifteen-minute adult swim at the end of each hour was over, and everyone could get back in the pool.

All the kids who had been perched on the edge of the pool, eagerly anticipating the lifeguard's whistle, jumped in, causing one huge, collective splash.

"Come on, Meredith!" Alice pleaded. She was wearing her new, light-purple swimsuit she had been so proud of; she had written her initial on the tag. In her hand was a red sponge ball. "I wanna play gutterball!"

"I'm going to stay here, okay," Meredith declared more than asked. She and Kelly were doing that most grown-up of pool activities: sunbathing. They were being adults. They had been gossiping about their friends and taking note whenever a boy glanced in their direction. Meredith had no interest in playing a childish game like "gutterball".

"Please?" Alice whined.

Meredith rolled her eyes. "Go find someone else to play with. Leave me alone."

Alice stared at her, hurt, and said, "I miss you, Meredith."

Meredith assumed that she meant to say, "I miss playing with you, Meredith" and while she found it annoying at the time, she had no idea how much those words would come to haunt her.

Alice turned, walked to the side of the pool, and jumped in without her usual flare.

Meredith and Kelly went back to talking, checking out everyone else, or not talking at all, and soaking in the sun. Every couple of minutes, Meredith would prop herself up on her elbows and check on Alice. It would normally take a minute or so to find her, but eventually she would see Alice splashing around or emerge from under the water after seeing how long she could hold her breath. One time, it took a little longer to find her and Meredith had begun to feel the first tiny stabs of panic until she heard the familiar shout and turned her head just in time to see Alice hit the water after jumping from the high dive. Meredith berated herself for worrying, lowered herself back down onto her towel, and closed her eyes.

Alice was fine.

Her attempts to check on her sister grew further and further apart. Finally, she looked around and didn't see her, but Meredith wasn't going to let it bother her. Alice could be in the bathroom or maybe Meredith just missed her in the crowd. It was almost time for adult swim again, anyway. Alice would be back to annoy her in a few minutes when she was forced out of the pool.

A short while later, there were two long whistle blasts from the same lifeguard as before, signaling the start of "adult swim".

Kids reluctantly pulled themselves out of the water, taking their sweet time. Instead of exiting at the nearest ladder, some of the more rebellious kids swam to the exact opposite end of the pool to prolong their time in the water, or to simply defy the lifeguard's authority.

Meredith waited, but after a few minutes, Alice hadn't returned.

She looked up, half-expecting to see Alice as one of the last kids exiting the pool, but the pool was empty.

"Alice?" Meredith called out, but not too loudly.

"What's wrong?" Kelly asked.

"I don't see my stupid sister," Meredith said, standing up.

Kelly also made a move to rise. "You want me to help?"

"No. She's here. I'll find her, but keep an eye out for her."

Meredith fully believed what she had said to Kelly as she walked away.

Why would she doubt it?

Alice was here, just not by her and Kelly, or in the pool, which left plenty of other places on the crowded grounds.

First, Meredith walked around the perimeter of the pool, scanning the chairs and bodies lying on the towels spread out on the grass, but no Alice. She checked the women's locker room and knocked on the bathroom stall doors. She had to apologize a few times, as some of the stalls were in use, but no Alice.

Meredith went back outside and looked over at Kelly who helplessly shrugged. Meredith searched over by the concession stand, kiddie-pool, and even began looking at the parking lot on the other side of the fence and the woods beyond. There was no sign of Alice.

Annoyed, Meredith went back to the concession stand and butted in front of the line. The high school boy on the other side of the counter blinked at her while Meredith ignored the protests of the people behind her.

"Will you please call Alice Somerset over the PA and tell her to come to the concession stand?" she asked.

Without a word, the boy lazily reached for the microphone they used to announce someone's soft pretzel or slice of pepperoni was ready.

"Alice Somerset to the concession stand, please. Alice Somerset," he mumbled, his voice carrying over the speakers around the pool.

Meredith turned and exited the line to wait for her sister to appear, fully prepared to wring her little neck.

But the opportunity never came, because there was no Alice.

Minutes passed.

Meredith was feeling anxious again. She took another long scan of the grounds. She didn't see Alice.

What she did see was the red sponge ball, floating in the empty pool.

A terrified, fifteen-year-old Meredith began crying.

*

It was as if Alice had simply vanished; raptured out of the pool without a trace.

Meredith's crying and calling her sister's name brought

everyone at the pool to a halt. They began searching, eager to help, but there was no sign of her.

Meredith's parents were called and arrived at the pool in less than half an hour. The police came shortly after. Statements were taken but no one could recall seeing her leave. People searched the parking lot, the surrounding woods, and even the field across the street.

At first, Meredith's parents were comforting, but as time passed with no trace of their daughter, they grew frantic. Meredith had already burned past being frantic and had slid into shock.

The police grabbed the footage from the two security cameras that were mounted to the light poles above the pool. However, it was a time before security cameras had reached their digital clarity. The footage from the cameras was recorded on VHS tapes that were used over and over again until they broke and had to be replaced. The tapes that were in use that day were toward the end of their life, so the images were grainy. In short, the cameras were more to instill a sense of security, rather than actually provide it. To make matters worse, the cameras were focused on the grounds inside the fence and not much else.

Meredith's father hovered over the shoulders of the two police officers as they scanned the footage in the office behind the concession stand.

"There!" he said, nearly pushing the cops aside as he pointed. "That's her!"

Thankfully, the footage had a timestamp, so they were able to find the time in question quickly. Meredith and her mother, who had been sitting on the other side of the office, stood and ran to join them.

Everyone strained their eyes at the image. It was from the camera that was pointed at the area by the diving boards. The image was blurry, but Alice's light-purple bathing suit was unmistakable.

She was standing at the back of the line to the high dive, a few feet from the fence behind her. She suddenly turned as if someone had called her name from the other side of the fence. The camera angle prevented them from seeing what or who she was looking at. She appeared to say something. She continued to look through the fence, paused for a moment, then started walking out of frame.

Everyone in the office turned their attention to the footage from the second camera, which was playing in synch with the other camera on a second television, and was pointing at the kiddie-pool and main entrance.

Alice walked into frame, her back to the camera.

"No," Meredith's mother whispered. "No, no, no, no …"

But Alice continued, walking past the kiddie-pool and out the main entrance, unnoticed by the girl working there, who had her back turned to talk to a friend.

Alice made a right and disappeared.

Meredith's mother began sobbing.

And just like that, Meredith's life changed forever. A few hours earlier, she had been the average teen in a happy family.

Never again.

*

The days immediately following Alice's disappearance were a hazy whirlwind. The police tried to interview everyone who had been at the pool, but again, no one could remember seeing Alice talking to anyone outside the fence. No one remembered seeing her get in a car. It had been too busy for anyone to notice.

The police did their best to reassure them that they would do everything they could to find her, but Alice could have gotten into a car and who knows where she could have been taken?

A hotline was set up. Hundreds of calls came in. Most of the calls were people trying to be helpful. A handful of others were people volunteering their psychic abilities to find Alice. And the rest were people giving their sick "confessions" of what they had done to her.

It was a horrible dream from which Meredith could not wake.

Then came the worst, and the worst was absolutely nothing. The search stretched from days, into weeks, and then months. There were no messages from whoever took her. There was no small clue or scrap of evidence to move the investigation forward. There had been a brief flurry of excitement when Wallace Hogan, a mentally unsound loner who lived in the woods near the pool, said he saw a girl with a man, but it came to nothing when he his story included talking birds and monsters.

Alice was gone. It was as though she had never existed.

The police search wound down. The calls to the hotline tailed off. The brief influx of news vans that had descended on the small, northern Georgia town departed.

Everyone was moving on.

Everyone, except the Somersets.

The marriage of Meredith's parents never stood a chance.

Meredith began to wish that they would find Alice's body, just to have it over with. Even a horrible, painful closure would be preferable to the unending anxiety, brought on by a status that never changed. Some days, there was the cruelest hope—a new tip, or someone possibly remembering something from that day— but it always came to nothing, resulting in a whole new cycle of misery.

And Meredith blamed herself for all of it.

She was supposed to be watching Alice. Her sister was her responsibility and if she had taken it more seriously, Alice would never have wandered off, which meant she would still be there, which meant that her parents would have never divorced, and her father would have never started the drinking that would eventually take his life, and her mother might still talk to her from time to time. Her mother, Bethany, never said out loud that she blamed Meredith for Alice's disappearance, but she didn't need to. The coldness with which she treated her remaining daughter from that moment on said everything.

Before Alice's disappearance, Meredith had begun contemplating her future and what she would like to do. She dreamed of working somewhere like the UN. She wanted to do something big, something important, something that required her to travel around the world.

As the search for Alice fizzled out and her family fell apart, the lead detective, Detective Reed, a man with jet-black hair who wore a constant sneer, took her aside and told her that they would probably never find Alice. Meredith hated him. She never believed that, not entirely, anyway. She always believed they could find Alice and after her talk with Detective Reed, Meredith decided that she was going to be a detective. She made this decision not with any bright-eyed, youthful enthusiasm about making a difference for good in the world. She had chosen it as though she could somehow make up for something she believed was her fault or could stop this from happening to another family. It became a singular obsession, enflamed in the mind of a young woman whose life had irreparably changed.

Her obsession served her well at the academy. She was focused, driven, and made no secret that she was going to work homicide, but no matter how hard she worked, Alice haunted her. While she had been able to channel her intensity into productive energy, there was still plenty left over to screw with her head. When she graduated, she followed her mother to Atlanta in the hopes that she would one day mend their relationship and possibly earn her mother's forgiveness. Meredith began working her way up to detective. She thought that her progress would make it easier to cope. It didn't. She was exceptional in her posts, but the closer she got to homicide detective, the more frustrated and anxious she became.

She suddenly decided that maybe being a homicide detective and getting back her mother's approval wasn't the way she was going to get over her sister's disappearance. Maybe the best way to feel normal again, was to indulge in more "normal things" and that would lead to a "normal life", like the one that had been taken from her.

She began dating, something that she had largely avoided since the nightmares made it difficult to trust anyone. It was awkward at first, but eventually she believed she was opening up, when she was actually deceiving herself. She knew what people in relationships were supposed to say and compromised with herself in the hopes that she was getting closer to a normal, healthy life, but it wasn't healthy. It was a toxic time bomb.

She met Pete and they hit it off. He was a teacher, kind and understanding. She shared more with him than she had anyone else in her life at the time. Meredith believed that she was finally processing her grief, but it was only coming to the surface. They both felt like they were in love, and she thought there was no doubt that they were.

They married after only a year of dating. They had their disagreements, like any other couple, but Meredith wanted that "normal life". Then, they became pregnant. It was difficult for Meredith as the delivery date drew nearer. Pete was as supportive as possible, but after the birth of their daughter, Allison, named after Meredith's sister, the toxic time bomb went off.

The stress of a newborn child combined with Meredith's unaddressed trauma was a devastating combination. She and Pete fought all the time. It was a year and a half of hell. They kept telling themselves it would get better when Allison began sleeping through the night.

It didn't.

Three years in, Meredith was angry and depressed. Her anxiety and frustration skyrocketed. She couldn't focus and Pete didn't know how to handle it.

By that time, she was working homicide with Detective Wheaton, who had recruited her after she grilled him when he came to speak to her class at the academy. He was the one who recognized the horrible pain Meredith was in. He had been there himself when he lost his wife and daughter in a horrible car crash caused by a drunk driver years before. He recommended a doctor who worked with family members of the victims of violent crime: Dr. Kaplan. He had worked with her after the death of his wife and daughter and told Meredith if she didn't confront it, it was going to tear her life apart, like his tragedy almost had.

Meredith agreed.

Those conversations were the hardest Meredith had ever held. Dr. Kaplan was able to pinpoint that Meredith's trauma couldn't be overcome in a few months.

It was going to be years and Meredith had to focus on herself.

She and Pete separated and Allison went with him. Meredith was devastated but she knew it was for the best. It was what was best for everyone, and Pete agreed. Once they had made the decision, all the barriers between her and Pete came down. They both knew that they had married too quickly. They still loved each other, and they were going to make what they had work for Allison's sake, and Pete wanted to help Meredith in any way he could. It was odd, but it led to Meredith and Pete becoming closer than ever before. As Allison grew, they made sure that she spent as much time with both her parents as possible. While Pete had custody, Meredith was always welcome at their house and Meredith spoke to Allison every night.

When Pete started dating Heather, he made it clear to her what the deal was and Heather was on board. The four of them had dinner together from time to time. Meredith liked Heather and Heather cared for Allison.

Was it messy? Sometimes, but so was any personal life. Meredith grew to accept that there was no such thing as the "normal life" she thought she craved, and she was happy with the way they had solidified their relationships.

That didn't mean that sometimes she didn't feel alone in her apartment or maybe wished that things had turned out different, but they were what they were and she and Pete and Heather made the best of it.

She worked for years with Dr. Kaplan and had gotten to the point where every victim in a case wasn't her sister. Meredith accepted that Alice was gone. She still occasionally felt pangs of guilt, but had largely been successful in silencing the demons that had continually whispered in her ear, "It's all your fault."

Which was why that morning's little episode had been unsettling. That had been the "Old Meredith".

She shook it off and checked the time. It was getting late.

"Damnit."

She had meant to study the photos from that morning, but had gone down the memory rabbit hole, instead.

She grabbed her phone and dialed.

"Hey, Mom," Allison answered.

"Hey, baby. What are you up to?"

"Heather and I are finishing up my homework."

"Hey to Heather."

"Mom says 'hi'," Allison said, away from the phone.

"Hey, Meredith!" a voice in the background said. "You're going to have to help Allison with math because I'm terrible at it."

Meredith laughed. "Can't help you with that. I'm terrible at it, too. I just called to say goodnight."

"Are we still hanging out this weekend?" Allison asked.

"Of course. We can do our usual visit to the farmers' market or we can do something different if you want."

"No. I want to go to the farmers' market."

"You sure?" Meredith asked.

"Yep."

"Okay. The farmers' market it is. Goodnight, baby."

"Goodnight, Mom."

"Goodnight, Meredith!" Heather said.

"Goodnight, Meredith!" Pete called from somewhere further in the background.

"Goodnight, everyone!" Meredith said.

"Love you, Mom."

"Love you, too, baby."

The line went dead.

Meredith took a breath. Allison was happy, loved, and supported. That was the important thing.

Her phone pinged with a text from Mike in the Morgue.

Got a head start on your Jane Doe for tomorrow. Tox negative. Rape kit showed no signs of sexual assault. See you tomorrow.

Thanks, Mike. Goodnight, she replied.

She looked back at the picture of the dead girl on the screen. Nothing was going to be solved tonight. She turned off the laptop, downed the rest of her wine, and got off the couch.

*

Meredith rested her head on the pillow and turned to look toward the bedside lamp, which was the only thing separating her from the darkness. She wasn't thinking about Allison or Peter or the dead girl in the street any longer. She was worried about something more primitive and basic.

She was worried about the nightmares.

They had plagued her for years and with the help of Dr. Kaplan, she had vanquished them, but Meredith wondered if that morning really had been just a blip or the return of something that had almost consumed her years ago.

'*You remember what I told you about nightmares?*' Dr. Kaplan had asked that afternoon.

Meredith remembered.

*

At that same moment, over on Willow Lane, Richard and Kathy Morgan were tucking Trevor into bed. He wanted to stay up, but he never argued with his parents.

"Goodnight, Trevor," his father said.

"Goodnight, Dad."

"Goodnight," Kathy said. She bent down and kissed his forehead. "Sweet dreams."

"Goodnight, Mom."

Kathy and Richard walked back to the door. The light from the hallway spilled over them and into the darkened room, casting them in silhouette.

"We love you very much," Richard said.

"So much," Kathy reiterated.

"I love you, too," Trevor replied.

His parents smiled and shut the door.

Richard and Kathy crossed the hall to the pink and white room that belonged to the twins, Cassidy and Fable, and repeated the ritual of tucking them into bed. The girls were wearing matching nightgowns but they could still tell them apart, even if no one else could. Cassidy had a small scar on her chin from where she had nicked herself with her own fingernail when she was an infant. Kathy would never forgive herself for taking off their tiny mittens for that brief moment allowing them one moment where she didn't put the tiny mittens on their hands. The irony was that that was the moment they finally became distinguishable. Up until then, there had been plenty of moments where Kathy had mixed them up, unsure which was which. She never told anyone and Richard had always taken her word, even though she had lied plenty of times when he had asked which girl he was holding.

"That's Fable," Kathy would say or "Cassidy" even though she wasn't sure, which she felt made her a terrible mother but would never admit that.

Kathy had played along because she believed that, as their mother, she should be closer to the girls than Richard. That's the way it was supposed to be. She wanted to be the perfect mother in a perfect family, and now, she had that.

"Goodnight, girls," Richard said, kissing them on the forehead.

"Goodnight," they said, not in perfect unison but close enough.

Kathy came over and did the same.

"Goodnight, my little munchkins," she said.

"Goodnight, Mom," they replied.

Kathy and Richard stepped back into the hall and closed the door behind them.

Richard slid his hand around her waist. She leaned into him and he kissed the top of her head.

Together, they walked down the hall to their room and closed the door.

Back in the darkness of the bedroom, Trevor waited until he heard the sound of his parents' door closing before he threw off the blanket and quietly jumped out of bed. He went to his desk and opened the bottom drawer. He took out the cheap cellphone he had buried under the notebooks and papers.

The little blue dot was glowing. He had received a text. The phone was on silent. It was always on silent because his parents would be livid if they knew he had a cellphone.

He unlocked the screen. The alert showed that the message had arrived only fifteen minutes ago. He opened it.

Did the police talk to you? it read.

He hesitated before answering. The shaking of his fingers made typing almost impossible.

Yes.

There was a painful minute or two of nothing. Trevor worried that he'd have to wait until tomorrow for a response but then a message appeared.

Did you tell them anything?

No! I didn't tell them anything! I swear! Trevor typed. He hit send and waited … and waited …

After a minute, the phone went into sleep mode and Trevor

was surrounded by darkness. He started to replace the phone in the drawer when the screen lit up with a response.

Trevor read it and his pulse raced. Beads of sweat popped on his brow.

You can never tell anyone. Ever.

*

Across the street, Meghan Ansley was lying on the bed, her back to the bathroom door as Greg stepped out.

She heard him pause and waited for him to speak.

He must have reconsidered because he stayed silent. They hadn't said much since that morning.

Greg climbed into bed and turned out the light.

Meghan's eyes remained open.

There would be no sleep that night.

Her fears would not allow it.

*

As Greg Ansley was turning out the light, Thomas Whitaker stood in a corner of his backyard, smoking a cigarette.

Yes, he had given up smoking years ago, or so he had told Natalie, but she had to have known. He practically chain-smoked at work. He blamed it on the clients, but she had to know. Even his "morning runs" were a joke.

They were both resigned to the lies, the lies about his smoking, his affairs, his business.

He took an angry drag and cursed every aspect of his life: the house, the kids, his wife, his job. He was making money and what was it all for? He was still in over his head in debt and his family brought him no satisfaction.

Nor did his job.

He was so tired of representing the ones who had no hope;

84

the ones who had screwed up, and he would take their last dime to provide the lamest defense to the prosecutor in order to get their client the most major of misdemeanors, rather than the lightest of felonies.

He needed more. That's why he was doing his side-hustle.

In his line of work, he saw the gains that could be made. Not from the desperate idiots who made a dumbass decision upon leaving the bar to drive home. Yes, that was part of his practice, and it was profitable, but he also represented those in other areas of "harmless crime", and he saw where he could expand his fortunes, or at least pay off his debts.

But he had never believed it might come to this. If the police started poking around …

He had to keep them away.

He took another long drag and savored the tingling in his nerves as the nicotine rolled through his body. He happened to look up at Scott Bowers' house across the street just as a car was pulling into the drive.

The driver's door opened and a figure stepped out.

Thomas angrily exhaled plumes of smoke through his nose.

"Are you goddamn kidding me?"

*

The girl's heels clicked on the concrete walkway as she approached the door.

She straightened her dress before pressing the illuminated button next to the doorframe.

It was answered by the handsome figure of Scott Bowers.

"Hi," he said.

"Hi," she replied.

He opened the door further. "Come on in."

She stepped across the threshold and he closed the door behind her.

She was struck by the modern, expensive décor, which was in sharp contrast to the outside of the house.

"This way," Scott said, walking down the hall toward the kitchen.

She was about to follow when she saw the hole in the drywall. She paused for a second too long, catching the man's attention.

"I was hanging a picture and thought there was a stud back there," he said.

"Oh." She smiled, not really believing him.

He politely motioned for her to follow and she continued walking.

He sized her up as she approached. Early twenties. Beautiful, in a girl-next-door kind of way. Perfect.

She entered the kitchen and spotted the expensive coffee maker and the designer furniture in the dimly lit living room.

The man stepped over to a door and held it open. She did her best to portray confidence but hesitated as she looked down into the darkness.

"It's right down here," he said.

She smiled, uneasily, and began descending the stairs.

*

A few miles away, against the flickering glow of a television, a razor blade dipped into the small white mound that rested on the small mirror and began tapping it into a nice, neat row. The blade continued to sculpt, making sure every fine granule was added to the row.

Waste not, want not.

The razor blade was set aside and a rolled-up dollar bill descended and hovered over the edge of the mirror. In a quick, carefully practiced flurry, the line of powder disappeared up the rolled bill.

As soon as the powder was gone, the bill was tossed unceremoniously onto the table next to a waiting cigarette.

Tyler Foles sat back, pinching his nose, not wanting any to run back out onto his lips.

Waste not, want not.

The effect was instant.

There was the burning at the back of his throat as the cocaine crossed the mucus membrane and entered his bloodstream. His eyes watered, but only for a second, and after that, he didn't care. His pupils dilated. His pulse was sent aloft. His brain released a flood of endorphins, filling him to the brim with a wave of euphoria.

Tyler let it wash over him, the sensation that everything was fine. Everything was great. That was where Tyler was going to live for the next few hours. Some addicts would have run around the room, convinced that they suddenly had all the answers to life's problems, only to crash when it was over.

Not Tyler.

He was a pro. A veteran. He knew that this was the best it was going to get and he was okay with that. There would be a crash, but it was manageable. That's what the cigarette was for.

Just enjoy it for a bit, was the motto he lived by when the lightning in his skin began to crackle.

It was his first hit in a while; the last had been weeks before he left narco and vice. He'd thought he might have kicked it, but the pressures in his life had been mounting. He simply needed something to take the edge off; just a little boost, then he'd put it away, again. He had to be careful. Back in narco and vice, he had a guy in internal affairs who would let him know when the tests were coming and Tyler was careful. He knew just how much he needed to achieve his desired effect.

It was a little riskier doing it the first day on the new job he had worked so hard for, but the odds were he wasn't even in the system yet to get popped for a test. Also, who knew how long it would be before he could cozy up to someone in internal affairs who could warn him when drug tests were coming? This might have to be his last chill session for a while before he figured things out.

Endorphins still pumping through his veins, Tyler licked his finger and wiped it across the small mirror to get any stray powder and ran his finger across his gums.

Waste not, want not.

*

Meredith contemplated the soft glow of the lamp.

"Nightmares are our minds letting the monsters run around at night, so they won't hurt us during the day," she said and then reached over and turned off the light.

Chapter 12

The smell of antiseptic, cold metal, and a hint of decaying flesh filled Meredith's nostrils as she watched the minute hand of the clock on the wall dip below the '3'.

It was 8:16 a.m., and there was no sign of Tyler.

"Detective?"

An oblivious Meredith continued staring at the clock.

No way, she thought. *No way he's late for his first two days.*

"Detective?"

Meredith finally tore her attention away from the clock to look at Mike Redding, or as he was colloquially known, "Mike in the Morgue". It was easier and so much more fun to say. Mike in the Morgue.

He was standing next to one of the metal tables with the raised edges that he fondly called "cookie sheets". Upon the cookie sheet rested the nude body of Jane Doe. While it sounded macabre, he wasn't wrong. They looked like cookie sheets.

That was the thing about Mike. You would think someone whose job it was to cut open and dissect the victims of heinous crimes would be awkward and employ a dark sense of humor but not Mike. He was one of the most affable guys Meredith had ever met.

The room resembled a large, high school science lab. The walls were tiled. The top half was tan. The bottom half a dark green. The floor was smooth concrete and almost imperceptibly sloped toward the drain in the middle of the room. The tiled walls and concrete floor made it easier to clean the room of the aroma of human decay. There were two "cookie sheets" on either side of the floor drain. The back wall was the "meat locker". It held rows and columns of metal doors. Behind some of the doors were bodies lying on stainless-steel slabs.

"Detective?" Mike asked, a little louder.

"Yeah. Sorry, Mike."

"Can I start? I've got four of these before lunch."

"Yeah. Please. Walk me through it."

"You want me to record?" he asked, working his way around the cookie sheet.

"That'd be great."

Mike stepped directly behind Jane Doe's head. He used his foot to press down on the pedal on the floor underneath the table, which activated the microphone that hung down from the ceiling above the cookie sheet.

Meredith had been trying to avoid looking at the girl's face but was forced to as she watched Mike place his gloved hands on either side of her head.

"This is Mike Redding, Cobb County forensic pathologist. It is …" He checked the clock that Meredith had been watching. "Eight-eighteen on the morning of March seventeenth. I am joined by Detective Meredith Somerset. I am presenting her with my preliminary findings for case number …" He consulted his notes, which were resting on a small tray hooked to the ledge of the cookie sheet. "Four-four-seven-one-nine. We have a Jane Doe. Mid-teens, height five-foot-five …"

As he continued talking, Meredith couldn't look away from that face.

It was Alice.

This was the closure she and her family never got. The autopsy that would have been horrible, devastating, but would also have been the end of it. There would have always been a scar, but at least there would have been some healing.

On the table, her head cradled by Mike's hands, Alice opened her eyes and stared at her sister.

Mike's talking faded. The air blowing through the vents overhead slowed. The motors powering the fans in the meat locker came to a stop.

The sisters stared at one another in the silence.

Alice opened her mouth.

"I want to come home, Meredith."

Meredith could feel the hot tears starting to well in her eyes.

The door to the morgue suddenly burst open.

Tyler jogged in, carrying two cups of coffee.

"Sorry! Sorry! My bad," he said, out of breath. "I thought we were meeting upstairs."

The spell of Meredith's vision was broken. The air conditioning was still blowing from the vents. The fans in the meat locker were whirring away. The girl's eyes and mouth were closed.

And Tyler's excuse was total bullshit.

"You were upstairs?" she asked.

"Yeah," he replied, but wilted under her stare. "Coffee?"

"I've already had some."

Appeasing her was out of the question, so Tyler turned to Mike.

"How about you? You want some coffee?"

"I'm fine, thanks," Mike said, eager to get through his findings.

"Okay," Tyler said, setting the coffee down on the other cookie sheet and eagerly extending his hand to Mike. "I'm the new guy, by the way—Detective Tyler Foles."

Mike looked down at his gloved hands, which were still on the sides of Jane Doe's head, and then back at Tyler. "I'm Mike."

"Got it," Tyler said and stepped back to Meredith's side.

"Okay," Mike said. "We all present and accounted for? Ready to do this?"

Tyler motioned for Mike to proceed.

"As everyone just heard, Detective Somerset and I have been joined by Detective Foles, who may or may not understand how everyone else's time works."

Meredith had seen Mike's foot come off the pedal as he spoke. That last bit hadn't been recorded but she was enjoying the ribbing Tyler had coming to him.

"I apologize for my tardiness," Tyler said in the direction of the microphone. "Seriously, I am sorry. Please, continue."

Mike turned back to Jane Doe.

"You're oh for two," Meredith whispered.

"Sorry. It was just—"

"*The victim*," Mike said loudly to shut them up, "is female, mid-teens. Height: five-foot-five. Weight: one hundred and seven pounds. Hair: brown. Eyes: brown. Cause of death is manual strangulation, judging by the pattern of bruises around the neck. There are distinct finger marks."

Meredith and Tyler stepped closer to the table for a better look.

"Strangulation is also suggested by the presence of petechiae around the eyes."

Meredith leaned toward Tyler and whispered. "Petechiae is when the capillaries burst under the skin. It can be caused by trauma, like strangulation."

"Thanks, Sherlock, but I knew that one," Tyler whispered back.

"A rectal temperature was taken at the scene," Mike continued. "Eighty-eight point three. The ambient temperature combined with the absence of rigor led the crime scene specialist to conclude that the victim had been killed no more than an hour before the discovery of the body. Combine that with the bruising, I concur with his assessment. There are small contusions and cuts around the mouth, consistent with someone possibly trying to smother or silence her. I found no adhesive residue or fibers around or inside the mouth to suggest that tape or a gag had been used, which reinforces the theory that it was done manually. There is a scrape on the right-hand side of the victim's scalp near the hairline. In the scrape, I found small pieces of stone and asphalt, which I'm fairly confident will match the road upon which she was found." Mike worked his way down to the arms. "There are other indications that the victim struggled. There is bruising at the elbow. Like the scalp, it is mostly likely from where she fell, and there is distinct bruising around the wrists consistent with finger marks. It suggests that her killer tried to restrain her."

Meredith raised a finger. "You said that the killer was trying to smother her with his hand. Any chance she bit him as he was trying to shut her up?"

"It's possible," Mike said. "But based on my preliminary findings, I'd say no. There would be bruising inside the mouth as the killer tried to pull free. I didn't find any bruising in the mouth other than where her lips were pressed forcefully against her teeth."

Meredith nodded.

Mike returned to the body. "As stated a moment ago, there is bruising on the wrists that points to her attacker trying to restrain her. However, while she struggled, it appears that she was able to scratch her assailant."

"You think she got some of this guy under her nails?" Tyler asked.

"Can't be sure but there was matter under the nails. I was able to collect it and sent it off to the lab this morning. We should have the results in two or three weeks."

Tyler silently pointed at the pedal, indicating that he'd like Mike to stop recording, which he did.

"Any chance we can get moved up to the front of the line at the lab? Maybe you put in a good word for us?" Tyler asked.

Meredith grimaced.

Mike stared at him in disbelief. "You really are the new guy, aren't you? Listen, everyone asks that. I should make cards and just give them to new detectives when they walk in the door that say, 'Your case is not special.' It's gonna be two or three weeks."

"Come on, man—"

"If you're lucky."

"Look at her," Tyler said, gesturing to Jane Doe. "She ain't special?"

"Tyler," Meredith said, but it was too late.

"Listen, Detective Foles," Mike said, his frustration boiling over. "I'm sure you're gonna do fine and all, but allow me to bust your balls for a moment." He went over to the meat locker. "Pick a door. Any door."

Tyler stared at the gleaming latches and faltered. "Umm …"

"No. You were late and I don't have time for you to pick." Mike turned, opened a door, and pulled out the slab, upon which lay the body of a young man with the side of his head caved in. "This is Gavin Whitacomb. Found last night by his parents. There was lots of blood on his clothes but there was some on his arm that was inconsistent with his injuries and might belong to his killer. I guarantee you his parents are going to ask the detectives, who are then going to ask me, to put a rush on it." He slid the slab containing Gavin Whitacomb back into the meat locker and closed the door. He then proceeded to another door, pulled open the latch, and rolled out the slab, which held an elderly woman. "Agnes Fuller. Raped and murdered. Found about the same time as your Jane Doe. Which means that there's a family that wants to know who raped and killed their grandmother and yes, the detectives have already asked me to expedite the lab tests." Mike returned the slab, closed the door, and reached for another latch but Tyler held up his hand.

"Okay, okay, okay. I get it."

Mike sighed. "It's not that I don't want to move you up, detective. I just can't."

"My bad," Tyler said.

"Speaking of tests results," Meredith said, eager to get back to the matter at hand. "Any signs of sexual assault?"

Mike walked back to the cookie sheet containing Jane Doe. "I guess if anything here can be called 'good news', it's that I didn't find any. There's no bruising around the genitals. No tearing of the labia. Still, as standard procedure, I ran the rape kit last night and sent it off, but my guess is, it'll come back negative."

"Small favors, I guess," Tyler said.

"Yeah," Mike agreed.

"Anything else you can tell us?" Meredith asked.

Mike pressed his foot onto the pedal.

"As I was just explaining to the detectives, there were no signs of sexual assault."

"Any idea how she spent the night before her death?" Tyler asked.

"What do you mean?"

"I mean, anything to indicate if she had slept outside? Was she homeless?"

"There are no signs of long-term exposure. If I had to guess, I don't think she was homeless. Her teeth are healthy, so she's been taking care of them. No signs of malnourishment. However, her stomach was empty. If she was homeless, she wasn't homeless long. She was pretty clean, other than the scrapes and bruises from falling on the pavement and struggling with her killer."

Mike took his foot off the pedal.

"I won't say it on the record, but if I were to put money on it, I'd say she spent the night somewhere inside."

Meredith and Tyler exchanged a glance.

"She was on that street," Tyler said.

Chapter 13

Meredith and Tyler stood side by side, watching the floor numbers climb on the display above the door and listening to the steady hum of the motors as they ascended in the elevator.

"Just like yesterday, I'll take the lead," Meredith said.

"You are *killing* me, Somerset."

"I'll do the talking. He might already be pissed that we're late, which is your fault."

Tyler continued watching the display. "One question. Let me ask one question."

"Fine," Meredith sighed. "But only if it's a good one."

"Oh, it's gonna be so good," Tyler said with a smirk.

Meredith felt her stomach rise as the elevator came to a stop with a final ping. The doors slid open to reveal an office floor comprised almost entirely of glass, offering a sweeping view of the city. On the wall in front of them was a directory of the offices located on the floor.

Hopewell & Associates was down the hall and around the corner.

They walked past frosted-glass doors with stenciled letters announcing the occupants. There were a lot of law firms, a few investment groups, and businesses that had a single, impactful word like Cynergistics or Leviathan, Inc. that were accompanied by indecipherable logos.

They finally arrived at the door to Hopewell & Associates. Tyler held it open for Meredith and they stepped into the small lobby.

Like the rest of the floor, it was almost all glass. There was a desk with a receptionist. Behind the receptionist were three conference rooms that looked out upon downtown. There were also two offices to the left and right. The interiors were obstructed by the opaque glass.

The receptionist greeted them with a practiced, cheerful tone.

"Good morning. Welcome to Hopewell & Associates. How can I help you?"

Tyler went to reach for his badge, but Meredith gently placed her hand on his arm to stop him.

"Hi," she said, stepping forward. "We're here to see Greg Ansley."

"Do you have an appointment?"

"We do. It was at nine-thirty. Sorry. We're running a little late."

The receptionist smiled with forced politeness, picked up the phone on her desk, and tapped a button.

"Mr. Ansley? Your nine-thirty is here."

The receptionist listened.

To their left, Meredith and Tyler heard muffled speech through one of the glass walls.

"Of course, Mr. Ansley," the receptionist said. She hung up the phone and stood. "Right this way, please."

She led them to one of the conference rooms and opened the door for them to enter.

"Mr. Ansley is on a call. Please, make yourselves comfortable."

"Thank you," Meredith replied.

"Can I bring you anything to drink? Sparkling water? Coke?"

Meredith sat in one of the plush, leather chairs at the conference table. "I'm fine, thanks."

"Anything for you, sir?" the receptionist asked Tyler, who had strolled over to the window to take in the view.

"I'm good. Thanks," he answered.

"Mr. Ansley will be with you shortly."

The smiling receptionist turned and left, allowing the glass door to swing silently shut behind her.

"I think I can see my shitty apartment from here," Tyler said, once they were alone.

Meredith quietly laughed.

"Why'd you stop me from flashing my badge, Somerset? Aren't we supposed to identify ourselves?"

"There's no need for it, here. It's his place of work. Either the receptionist knew we were cops and it wouldn't have mattered or she didn't know, and it would have made things awkward for him. Right now, we need him to be relaxed and trust us."

Tyler scoffed. "That ain't how we ran things in narco and vice."

"You catch more flies with honey than you do with shit."

"You and your polite ways would not last one day in narco, Somerset."

A form passed by the glass wall and a moment later, Greg Ansley opened the door. He was early fifties and starting to fill out around the waist, but still attractive.

Meredith noticed the bags under his eyes as she stood to greet him.

"Mr. Ansley, thank you for meeting with us. I'm Detective Meredith Somerset. This is Detective Tyler Foles."

"Hi," Greg said, shaking their hands.

"Sorry we're a little late. I hope we haven't inconvenienced you."

"No, it's fine," he said, stepping back toward the door. He pressed a button on what looked like a light switch mounted on the glass wall, and the clear, surrounding walls became opaque.

"That's a neat trick," Tyler said.

"Sometimes we like to show off our clients, and other times, we need some privacy, but it is a busy day for us and as you said, we're running a little behind. So, please," he said, motioning to the chairs as he himself sat at the head of the table.

Meredith resumed her seat while Tyler stayed over by the window.

"We understand," Meredith said. "And again, we apologize."

"It's fine. What can I do for you?"

"Just to get the preliminaries out of the way, Mr. Ansley," Meredith began, taking out her notepad and setting it on the table. "What kind of work do you do here at Hopewell?"

Greg hesitated. "I'm not in any sort of trouble, am I? I don't need a lawyer or anything, right?"

"No, no, no. Not at all," Meredith said. "I mean, you can certainly have a lawyer present, if you'd like. This is for our records. We're asking these questions of everyone on Willow Lane to see if anyone saw anything. They may not have known it at the time, but little details can be important."

"And what does my work have to do with anything?"

"It doesn't, necessarily. It's more out of curiosity and to ascertain everyone's whereabouts."

Greg's shoulders slumped. "I'm sorry, detective. I was being rude. This whole thing has me and my family on edge. It was a shock for my wife and son, and as you can probably tell," he said, pointing to the dark circles under his eyes, "it was a rough night. My apologies for being short with your questions."

"It's all right. It took a toll on your neighbors, as well."

Greg nodded. "We're having a little neighborhood meeting tonight for everyone on Willow Lane. It's been surreal. Anyway, please, allow me to start over. I'm a consultant. Here at Hopewell & Associates, we work with companies to help streamline their productivity. We use a concept called 'LEAN'. Ever heard of it?"

"No," Meredith answered.

"Well, a very simple way to put it, is if a worker has to take ten steps to move a product from one stage of manufacture to another, we try to find a way to make it seven steps. It may not sound like much, but little changes like that can save a company millions of dollars over time."

"Cool," Tyler said, impressed.

"And how long have you been with the company?" Meredith asked.

"About twelve years. Since we moved here to Atlanta."

"And before that?"

"We lived in Charleston, South Carolina. I was still in the consulting field, but I did a lot more traveling back then. It was rough on my wife, Meghan, and I. So, I took the job here and, after a couple of years, we had our son. That enough for the background info?"

"Thank you," Meredith said as she jotted in her notepad. "It's very helpful. Can you give me a rundown of your morning yesterday?"

"Sure. I woke up pretty early—"

"How early?"

His eyes meandered up to the ceiling. "I think around four-thirty."

"Do you normally get up that early?"

"No. I usually get up closer to five-thirty. I tried to go back to sleep, but couldn't and decided to beat the traffic."

"Anything in particular keeping you up?" Meredith casually asked. She thought it was a harmless question, but a shadow crossed Greg's face.

"Things are a little stressful," he said. "Work has been slowing down and … and, well, I don't know if this is what you are looking for but the slowdown at work has made things difficult at home."

Meredith nodded. It was more than she had been looking for, but it was another piece of the puzzle. Whether or not it was relevant remained to be seen.

"I appreciate your openness, and I promise you, unless it

becomes important to our investigation, nothing goes beyond myself or Detective Foles," Meredith said, nodding to Tyler.

"Our lips are sealed," Tyler agreed.

"Thanks," Greg said, less than certain of their guarantees.

Meredith went back to her notepad. "What time did you leave for work yesterday morning?"

"I think I got in the Honda around five-forty-five. Got here around six-thirty."

"That is early," Meredith said.

"I didn't come straight up to the office. I got a bagel from the walk-up window at Selnan's down the street and sat in Centennial Park for a while. Like I said, things at home are not optimal and I took a little time for myself."

"When you left home, did you happen to see or hear anything out of the ordinary?"

"It was still dark and the fog was pretty thick. I didn't see anything but, honestly, she could have been lying there and I still might not have seen her."

"How did you find out about it?"

"Meghan called and told me. I couldn't believe it. I'm sorry that I missed you. We could have done this sooner."

"We appreciate your time," Meredith said. "You said the name of the bagel place was 'Selnan's'?"

"Yes."

"There is one last thing and it might be a little traumatic."

"Okay …"

"I was wondering if you could look at a photo of the victim to see if you recognize her."

"Um sure. If it'll help."

Meredith dug into her pocket and brought out her phone. She pulled up the same photo she had shown the residents of Willow Lane and handed the phone to Greg.

He stared at the screen and his face dropped. "No. I'm sorry. I don't recognize her," he said, handing it back.

"That's okay. You've been very helpful. I think that's all I have."
Meredith looked over at Tyler. "Detective Foles?"

"That sucks about the home and work-life, man," Tyler said.
"I've been there. I found it worked best if I could distract myself.
You got any hobbies, something to take your mind elsewhere?"

Greg regarded him with skepticism. "I do woodworking. I have
a shed in the backyard where I build things."

Tyler nodded. "I get that. You being an engineer and all."

"Yeah," Greg said. "Been doing it since I was a kid."

"What do you make?"

"Little things. Pens, custom wine stoppers, a small table here
and there."

Tyler smiled. "You get me in that shed, I'd probably lose a
thumb in under five minutes."

"You do any woodworking?" Greg asked with what may or
may not have been sarcasm.

"Nah. I tried doing models as a kid. I kept gluing my fingers
together, but it did take my mind off of stuff."

"What do you do now to, you know, take your mind 'off of
stuff'?" Greg asked.

Tyler paused. "I read."

Chapter 14

"What'll ya have?!" the cashier in the yellow hat and red shirt called out to the couple stepping up to the counter from the endless line that stretched out the door. It was the signature cry from the cashiers at The Varsity in Midtown, one of Atlanta's more famous burger joints.

Meredith and Tyler had already braved the line, answered the call, found a booth, and were seated with their burgers, fries, and fountain drinks, and going over the interview.

They had paid a visit to Selnan's but it was a dead end. Neither of the cameras had a view of the walk-up window.

"So, tell me," Meredith said, running a perfectly spiced curly fry through a blob of barbecue sauce. "What was the point of that last question about his hobbies?"

Tyler took a sip from his soda. "I don't know. Curiosity, I guess."

"Bullshit. Come on. You're good with questions, like with Trevor Morgan. Tell me, what were you hoping to find out?"

Tyler took a bite of his double-decker burger to give himself some time.

"Tyler?"

"You know the game, Somerset. You asked all the right questions.

103

You didn't leave me anything. I figured, 'Hey, let's find out something about this guy'. I decided to ask him a question that had nothing to do with the investigation because it might tell us a little more about who he is."

"Him telling us that work was bad and his marriage kinda sucks wasn't enough?"

"Okay. So, how does a guy like that deal? Is he drinking? Is he creepin' on his wife?"

"Is he strangling women outside his house?" Meredith asked.

"Or that."

"And?"

Tyler shrugged. "And what?"

"What did his answer tell you?"

He waved a fry at her. "No, no, no. I was the one who asked the question. You tell me what his answer told you."

"Fair enough." Meredith considered her response. "He likes structure. He likes to build. He likes order. It seems that his job and his hobby overlap."

"I agree, 100 percent. I also think that this guy likes his 'alone time'."

Meredith nodded. "His wife was way on edge when we questioned her. I would have chalked it up to the discovery of a murdered girl outside her door, but after hearing him talk, maybe she was already on edge before the murder."

"Great minds think alike."

"You think you have a great mind?"

"I was going to say 'average minds' but I didn't want to insult you," Tyler said and washed down his fry with another sip of Coke.

"You think Greg Ansley is our guy?" she asked.

"I don't know. I don't like anyone on that street. Bowers strikes me as too nice. So nice that something has to be up. Don't know what Thomas Whitaker's deal is. He might just be your average, run-of-the-mill asshole. Might be more. The Morgans are a little out there. And the Ansleys are keeping secrets."

"Just because their marriage is on the rocks doesn't mean that someone is capable of murder. Marriage is tough."

"I wouldn't know about that," Tyler said.

"Oh yeah? No 'Mrs. Foles' at home?"

"I have my fun, but I'm steering clear of the whole marriage thing."

"Why's that?"

"Because you women are messed up."

Meredith gave him a look. "You men aren't much of a prize, either."

Tyler shook his head. "No, we are not."

They smiled and toasted their fountain drinks.

Tyler snatched up a napkin and wiped the grease from his hands. "All right. We've talked to everyone on that street. Mark in the Morgue—"

"Mike in the Morgue," Meredith corrected him.

"Mike. Thank you. He thinks she stayed the night somewhere nearby. I'm not seeing the kink in anyone's story just yet. You?"

"No."

"What's the next move?"

"I still want to give NamUS a little more time to see if they get an ID."

"That could take weeks, and in the meantime?"

"We run background checks on everyone we've interviewed," Meredith offered. "See if there's anything interesting."

"Same playbook we ran in narco and vice, but normally, we'd get back a bunch of fake IDs."

"Won't happen here. These people have families, homes, mortgages, kids. They'll have paper trails."

"What about Jane Doe?" Tyler asked. "I know you want to give it more time but there's no way we sit around for weeks, waiting for the FBI or for the lab tests, which might not tell us anything, anyway."

"What would you suggest?"

"There's the obvious, and I'm wondering why you haven't brought it up."

"And what's that?" Meredith asked in mock innocence as she took another bite from her burger.

"Why aren't we getting a Picasso to sketch her for all to see? I had tons of junkies turn up on a slab without an ID. Getting the face out there was the only way we could get someone to come forward, tell us who our victim was, and shake the investigation loose."

Despite the playfulness they had been enjoying, Meredith grew somber. "This is different. I don't mean to sound callous, but the public doesn't care about a junkie in an alley. I'm not saying that's a good thing. I'm just saying—"

"You ain't hurtin' my feelings, Somerset. I want to know how my homicide brethren operate. Lay it on me."

"The press would devour this. A young, attractive girl with no ID, strangled in the middle of the street in an upscale neighborhood? It'd be a circus. I'm not saying that we never go down that route. I'm saying it's too early."

"But you know the longer we wait, the worse it'll be if gets out, right?"

Meredith reluctantly agreed.

"So, what do we do?" Tyler asked. "How can we get some help from the public without them knowing what they're helping us with?"

Meredith popped another curly fry into her mouth and began to chew but stopped, her eyes lighting up.

"Somerset?"

"Thassit!" she said through a mouthful of French fry. She stood up, still chewing, and grabbed her tray. "C'mon. Let's go."

Chapter 15

Robbie Slonhaus was one of the department's IT guys. Fresh out of Georgia Tech, and as the fight song claimed, "A hell of an engineer". He and a group of four other young programmers handled the department's webpage, email, and file system. Sadly, they were the product of too many episodes of *CSI*, who thought they were stepping into a world of cyber-Sherlock Holmes, only to have their illusions crushed by underfunding.

"What we need," Meredith was saying, sitting at her desk with Tyler sitting on the corner, and Robbie in a chair off to the side, "is a photo at the top of the page, front and back of the medallion. At the bottom, we need a link to a mailbox where people can send their responses if they think they know what this is."

Robbie studied the engraved symbol on the medallion, then flipped it over.

"*Sosh*?" he asked.

"That's where we need the assistance of John Q Public," Tyler said.

"Is that doable?" Meredith asked.

Robbie shrugged. "You want a dedicated page with pictures and a link to a separate inbox. That it?"

"Can you do it?"

"I can have it up in ten minutes," Robbie said, standing from his chair. "Gotta warn you, though—I'll set it up and send out some feelers to some of the message boards we normally deal with, but after that, you're on your own. I've got to update the script for the evidence logs and archive bodycam footage. I don't have time to sort through the crazies who are going to try to give you tips as to what this thing means. You get to comb through the responses."

"That's perfect," Meredith replied.

She knew exactly what Robbie was talking about.

From her experience working with tip-lines while on the force, as well as her sister's disappearance, Meredith knew the minute that they asked for the public's help, there was going to be flood of lunatics offering advice. It was bad enough when it was a simple sketch of a face and a plea for help in identifying a victim, but something as vague as the medallion was sure to bring out the whackos who would claim it was the Illuminati or aliens.

"Okay," Robbie said. "I'll send it back down to evidence when I'm done."

"Thank you, Robbie," Meredith said.

"Thanks, man," Tyler added.

"Good luck," Robbie tepidly offered.

*

The sunlight outside the window had long since surrendered to darkness when Tyler stood and slipped on his jacket.

"All right, Somerset. You need me for anything else?"

"Thanks, but I think I got it," she said, typing away on her keyboard. "Just going to send off the background checks and call it a night."

"Cool. If you need me, you know where not to call me."

"Lovely."

"Have a good night, Somerset," Tyler called out as he walked out the door.

"Goodnight, Tyler."

Meredith was about to hit send on the background checks, the fields of which held the social security numbers, birthdates, driver's license numbers, etc., of everyone on Willow Lane, when her phone lit up with a call.

She picked it up off the desk, checked the ID, and quickly hit the answer button.

"Allison?"

"Hey, Mom."

"Is everything all right?"

"Yeah … Everything is fine."

She might not have been living with her daughter, but Meredith knew enough about her daughter's speech and mannerisms to recognize when something was wrong.

"Allison?"

"Everything is fine, Mom" Allison lied. "Are we still going to the farmers' market tomorrow?"

"Of course we are. I'll pick you up at noon, just like we always do."

"Okay …"

"Baby?"

"Yeah, Mom?"

"I need you to tell me, right now; are you in trouble? If you are, tell me where you're at and I'll come and get you."

Years ago, Meredith had made it clear to her daughter that if she were ever in trouble, no matter what it was, she would come and get her, no questions asked. That wasn't to say there wouldn't be a litany of questions and repercussions later, but Meredith would walk through fire, lava, or a nuclear blast for her daughter.

"Allison?"

"I'm okay, Mom. I promise. I just wanted to be sure that we were hanging out tomorrow."

Meredith could tell that wasn't the reason, but was comforted by the knowledge that Allison wasn't lying about not being in danger.

"Is there something you want to talk about?"

"Yes," Allison regretfully admitted. "There's something I want to talk to you about tomorrow, but I'm fine."

The tension flowed out of Meredith.

"Okay, baby. I'll be there to pick you up at noon."

"Okay," Allison said. "I love you, Mom."

"I love you too, baby. Goodnight."

"Goodnight."

The line went dead.

Meredith exhaled.

If Allison wanted to share whatever was wrong with her in person, that was fine. If it was pertinent, and with Allison's permission, she would share it with Pete and Heather.

Meredith rubbed her eyes and was suddenly filled with the urge to be home, on her couch, with a glass of wine.

One tap of the key, she thought, *and you're done.*

She leaned toward the computer screen, double-checked the info to make sure she had entered it correctly, scrolled the cursor over the send button, and clicked.

Meredith stood, grabbed her jacket off the back of her chair, and waited for confirmation that the information had been sent. She then powered down the computer, and walked out …

*

Seconds later, the phone in Scott Bowers' pocket vibrated.

As he crossed Willow Lane, heading toward the Morgans' home for the neighborhood meeting, he held up the phone to see that he had a text message from his monitoring service. Someone had just run a credit check on him. He knew exactly who it was and that it wasn't merely a credit check. It had to be part of a wider background check. He was also certain that everyone attending this little neighborhood get-together had also just been submitted to that same background check.

Had it been a simple credit check, Scott would have been fine, but this was the first time he had been submitted for an extensive background check in a while and he knew what they would find. At first, it would appear to be a simple mistake, as though someone had made a clerical error years ago, but if they grabbed that thread and started pulling, "Scott Bowers" would unravel. He couldn't treat that as something that *might* happen. He had to treat it as something that *would* happen. It was why he had been so careful for so long. He was trying to avoid something like this at all costs.

"I have to talk to you."

Scott looked up from his phone to see Thomas Whitaker striding purposefully across his lawn toward him.

"Not now," Scott replied.

"Yeah, now," Thomas said, saddling up next to him and matching his stride. "What the hell were you thinking?"

"I don't know what you're talking about."

"Bullshit. I saw the car at your house last night. Are you out of your damn mind?"

"You have got to calm down."

"Listen, pal. Let me remind you that if this shit gets out of hand, we're all screwed."

"I'm aware of that," Scott said, keeping his voice as steady as possible.

"Are you? Then what the hell was that last night?" Thomas sneered.

"I said, I don't know what you're talking about."

"Oh, I think you do," Thomas spat. "Which is why I'm telling him to cut you off."

Scott had been scanning the street to see if anyone was watching them. Satisfied that the coast was clear, he grabbed Thomas's elbow and pulled, hard, spinning him so that they were face to face.

The calm, charming face that Scott Bowers wore for the rest of the world was gone. What remained was the Scott Bowers who punched holes in walls. It was the Scott Bowers that hid in the shadows. In fact, it wasn't Scott Bowers, because Scott Bowers wasn't real.

Thomas knew the man who lived across the street was some sort of freak, but he had never seen this person before. His stare was one that somehow blended icy indifference, as if Thomas was nothing, with a fire that hinted at unspeakable things this stranger could do to him.

"You're not going to tell anyone about anything," Scott said. "Understand?"

Thomas futilely tried to wrench his arm out of Scott's grip. "Let go of me."

"Say you understand me," Scott hissed.

Thomas didn't think it possible, but Scott's grip tightened, clamping down on the ulnar nerve at the elbow, causing Thomas's knees to nearly buckle.

"Yeah. I understand. Let go of me!"

Scott gave another squeeze to drive his point home before finally relinquishing his hold.

Thomas massaged his elbow. "Fine. I won't say anything, but no more. You're going to get us both arrested. If I see another car at your house, I'm telling him you're cut off. Got it?"

Scott glowered at him.

"Say you understand me," Thomas said, attempting to mock him.

Scott continued to glare, demonstrating that Thomas's threat was a waste of breath. He wasn't one of Thomas's clients who he could bully. Scott Bowers was something different.

"Fucking freak," Thomas said, turned, and continued walking toward the Morgans'.

Scott watched Thomas walk away.

The beast that Thomas had just encountered slunk back into the shadows. The countenance of the Scott Bowers everyone on Willow Lane knew slowly returned.

He didn't care about Thomas's threat. It was stupid, hollow, and ultimately unnecessary, but he wasn't wrong. The woman last night had been a risk but one Scott needed to take. It had been planned a week before and after the events of the previous morning, it would be his last "play-time" until things settled down. He could have told Thomas that, but he had no interest in giving him the satisfaction. No one told him how to conduct his life or his urges. Besides, he had a lot more to worry about.

*

Natalie Whitaker had stayed home to watch Kendall and Ashton, which is to say that she was in the master bedroom, sitting up in bed, and staring blankly at the television.

Years ago, a doctor had prescribed one sedative an hour before bed, but she preferred two whenever she wanted. It put the world on ice. It didn't necessarily make her feel better. She simply didn't feel. She didn't feel the misery of her marriage or the stinging words from Thomas. She knew he had secrets, so many secrets, but any time she attempted to help, he'd either ignore or berate her. She'd learned long ago that there was nothing she could do except numb herself. The only thing better than not paying a price was not caring. So, there she sat, eyes glassed, staring at an episode of *The Donna Reed Show* she had seen dozens of times before. She used to watch the reruns while growing up as a kid. She longed for the innocence, for the simplicity. She didn't take the same enjoyment now, with her brain swimming in sedative. She just didn't care about anything.

Nor did she particularly care when she heard the sound of footsteps in the hall outside her bedroom descend the stairs.

She thought she might have heard the back door close, but she didn't move. She may have blinked, but it was difficult and pointless to do anything if you didn't care.

*

"We were thinking of starting a neighborhood watch," Richard Morgan said, standing next to the fireplace with Kathy sitting on the ottoman at his side, lovingly gazing up at him.

Greg Ansley, Thomas Whitaker, and Scott Bowers sat on the couch and loveseat in a loose circle in front of them in the Morgans' living room.

Scott did his best to avoid looking at Thomas and kept his focus on Richard, although occasionally he would steal a glance at Greg, who looked exhausted.

"That way," Richard continued, "we can really keep an eye out for each other and our families."

"What are you suggesting?" Greg asked. "We arm ourselves and start patrolling the neighborhood?"

"We do own two firearms if you'd like to borrow one for protection," Richard offered, as though it was a perfectly natural suggestion.

Greg was stunned. "My wife doesn't allow them in the house but … thanks?"

"You really think it's safe to pass out guns?" Scott asked. "I'm pretty sure the police think it's one of us."

Thomas shot Scott a poisonous scowl before speaking.

"Look. I know this is all really messed up, but I've had experience with this and I'm telling you, it's a one-time thing. This isn't the start of some string of brutal murders on Willow Lane."

You're a DUI lawyer, not Perry Mason, Greg wanted to snap, but he had made up his mind to say as little as possible at this get-together. He wanted to get back home. He and Meghan still hadn't said more than ten words to each other since the previous morning. Then, there was that interview with the detectives. He had panicked and started oversharing about his work and marriage. He had spent all afternoon calculating the ways in which he may have made everything worse.

"Still …" Scott shrugged. "It's not a bad idea to start a neighborhood watch. Couldn't hurt to keep an eye out."

Thomas almost laughed at the irony of this crazy man making that suggestion. Scott was the one they should be watching. Or the Morgans, who were bizarre. Thomas would have come up with a reason to suspect the Ansleys. Anything to keep the cops away from him.

Kathy rose and put her hand on her husband's arm. "We just think it's best to help protect all of our families, which is the most important thing. I mean, that's why most of us moved to Willow Lane; because it was a safe place to raise our children."

*

As Kathy Morgan was giving her opinion on protecting everyone's family, her son, Trevor, who had been downstairs in the basement, getting in his daily allotment of video games, slipped out the backdoor and into the yard.

He approached the figure standing at the fence. The figure wore his hood up, obscuring his face.

"What do you want?"

"I wanted to talk to you," Trevor replied, his voice laced with anxious uncertainty.

"We don't have anything to talk about."

"But the police and the girl—"

The figure pulled the hood back to show Trevor the anger in his face.

"So, what?" Ashton Whitaker asked.

"Don't you think we should tell someone what we—?"

Ashton took a step toward the fence. "I told you. You can never tell anyone."

Trevor cast his eyes down to the grass.

"Are we ever going to hang out again?" he asked.

Ashton rolled his eyes and began walking back toward his house.

Trevor bit his lip to keep it from trembling. He jammed his

hands in his pockets and walked back toward the basement door. He had to get back inside. It was getting close to his daily limit of video game time and his parents might come down into the basement to tell him to turn off the Xbox, but before he stepped inside, he made sure to wipe the one or two fearful tears from his cheek.

Chapter 16

"Dad's going to ask Heather to marry him," Allison blurted out.

Meredith blinked at her daughter as they stood in one of the stalls that sold jars and straws filled with flavored honey at the Marietta Farmer's Market, which was held just off the town square the second Saturday of every month.

It was tradition that they'd buy straws of different flavored honeys and enjoy them while cruising the stalls for knick-knacks, old books, or fresh strawberries. Once they had worked their way from one end of the market to the other, they would sit on a bench in the town square and talk. Meredith had been prepared to wait it out over the course of the day until Allison was ready to tell her what was on her mind, but they had been at the market for all of five minutes.

"Mom, did you hear what I—?"

"Yeah, baby. I heard you."

"Aren't you going to say anything?"

"Baby, is that what's been bothering you?"

Allison glanced around at the nearby shoppers. Meredith could see that she was becoming upset and put her arm around her.

"Hey, hey, hey. It's okay. Come on. Let's go talk."

*

They didn't say much on the walk through the market to the town square. The shock of the news had worn off and Meredith had questions. Nothing in the way of questioning Pete's decision to ask Heather to marry him. She had known for some time that it had to be coming sooner rather than later. Nor did Meredith expect Pete to discuss it with her, but she was surprised that he hadn't given her a heads-up.

"When did he tell you?" Meredith asked once they had found a bench on the edge of the square.

"He didn't. I was using his laptop to do some English home-work and he left a website open. It was a website for engagement rings."

"Oh. Okay."

Pete hadn't really told Allison, so Meredith could put that to rest.

"Baby, why is this upsetting you so much?" Meredith asked, gently stroking her daughter's hair. "You like Heather, right?"

"I do," she replied. She was calmer than she was at the honey stall, but still unsettled. "I don't know why I'm upset … I'm just worried that things will change."

"Like what?"

"Like, what if they decide that we should move?"

"Your dad has a really great job that he likes and Heather has family in Atlanta. And you're in school. If they do move, I don't think it'll be anytime soon."

"But what if they do?" Allison insisted.

"Well, if it comes up, we'll all sit down and talk about it. It'll be fine."

Allison grew quiet.

"What else is bothering you, baby?"

"What if … What if, after they're married, Heather wants me to call her 'Mom'?"

Quite unexpectedly, a fire erupted in Meredith's stomach. She had never contemplated her daughter addressing anyone else as "Mom" and she didn't like it. Not at all.

"Did she ask you to call her that?"

"No."

"Would you like to call her 'Mom'?"

"I don't know ..."

Meredith suddenly understood what this was. Allison wasn't worried about specifics. She was worried about the uncertainty of what would happen. Allison was smart and knew her family was "different". It was complex and Allison was afraid that it was fragile. Meredith knew that it was strong, but there was a growing sense of unease building in her gut. However, for the moment, she needed to reassure her daughter.

"Baby, look at me."

Her daughter's eyes, which had been firmly planted on the ground, found her through the strands of hair that fell about her face.

"Heather loves you and she loves your father. You love her, too, right?"

Allison nodded.

"And she's been helping to raise you and if she wants you to call her 'Mom', we'll talk about it."

"But you're my mom."

"Yep. And I will always be your mom and you will forever have to call me that."

Allison's gaze returned to the ground.

"Listen," Meredith said. "It's not something you have to worry about, right now. It's not something you'll have to worry about, ever, because no matter what you choose, me, your dad, and Heather, are going to support it, okay?"

Allison silently nodded.

"Okay," Meredith said, lightly slapping Allison's thigh in an attempt to cheerfully change the subject. "We've got the rest of the market to check out and I want you to help me find something for my kitchen. Let's go!"

Meredith hopped off the bench. Allison's face brightened a little, happy to have spoken her mind, but also relieved to move on.

Meredith was happy to move on too, because while she was being honest in her praise of Heather, there was also that knee-jerk, territorial reaction.

Of course, Allison shouldn't call Heather "Mom". Meredith was Allison's one and only mom. The "mama bear" instinct had stood on its hind legs and roared. Meredith had been able to check it, but only just.

*

A few hours, some frozen lemonade, two roasted corn-on-the-cobs, a small wooden, hand-painted sign for her kitchen that read, *To reduce stress, I do yoga! Just kidding. I drink wine in my yoga pants!*, and Meredith and Allison were pulling into the driveway of Pete's home.

Pete casually stepped out onto the porch and down the walkway to greet them.

Like wine itself, Pete was getting better with age. He was that professor that all the female students had a crush on.

"Hey, you two," he said as they exited the car.

"Hey, Dad," Allison said, hugging him.

"Hey, Pete," Meredith smiled and also gave him a hug, once Allison had cleared the way.

Pete kissed Meredith on the cheek, as was his custom.

"How was the farmers' market?" he asked.

"I loaded our daughter up with sugar. She should be good to go."

"Great," Pete theatrically moaned. "Because we were just setting up for dinner."

"Then my work here is done," Meredith replied.

"We're making tacos," Pete said. "You want to stick around? We've got plenty."

"I'd love to but I can't. Working on a case."

Normally, she would have joined them, but that uneasiness that had started back at the market was growing and while she was sure she could hide it from Allison, there was no way she would be able to hide it from Pete and Heather.

She wasn't even doing a good job of it at the moment because Pete could see in her face that something was up.

"Allison, sweetheart, why don't you go inside and see if you can help Heather set up, okay?" he asked.

"Okay," Allison replied, eager to get taco night underway. She turned and embraced Meredith. "Bye, Mom. Thanks for today!"

Meredith kissed the top of her head. "Bye, baby. I'll call later to say goodnight."

Allison broke away and went inside.

Pete took a step away from the door.

"What's going on?" he asked.

Meredith paused, uncertain if she should bring up the proposal or Allison's concerns about what to call Heather.

"Meredith?"

She decided to go with the one that was a certainty.

"I don't know what to say because I'm not sure I'm supposed to know."

"Know what?" Pete asked.

"That you're going to propose to Heather."

Pete's eyes widened.

"How did …?"

"Allison told me, but it's not her fault, Pete."

Pete glanced back at the door and tried to keep his voice low. "How did she know?"

"She was using your laptop and you left open a page where you were shopping for engagement rings."

"Shit."

"Don't be mad at her."

"No. I'm not mad. I was waiting to tell you guys until I was all set to go."

"When are you pulling the trigger?" Meredith asked.

"Maybe a month or so. How is Allison taking it?"

"She's concerned. I think she's worried that it will bring a lot of changes."

"Meredith, you know that I would always talk to you and her before—"

"Pete, don't worry about it. It's fine. I just wanted you to know that she knows. You probably want to have that conversation with her sooner rather than later."

"Thanks." Pete nodded. "How are you taking it?"

"You proposing to Heather? I think it's great. You know how I feel about her."

"So, you approve?"

"Pete. Come on. It's your life. You don't need to ask my opinion."

"No, but I want it. It's officially making her a part of our family. I know that much isn't changing, but it's a step and it's important to me and to Heather that we have your ... I don't know what to call it."

"My 'blessing'?"

"Would we have that?"

"Of course." Meredith smiled, but all the while the knot in her stomach was tightening.

Chapter 17

Meredith's hands slashed through the cool night air. Her legs fired like pistons on the pavement and her quick breaths left a smoky trail in her wake as she sprinted down the street in the direction of her apartment.

This was how she would normally spend her mornings, not her Saturday nights at ten-thirty. She should have been ready for bed or on her couch, going over a case, which she had tried to do. She had showered, changed into comfy clothes, booted up the computer, and had even poured herself a glass of wine. She had sat on the couch, but her brain would not stop going back to Pete and Heather.

She couldn't focus on the case and she didn't want to sit around the apartment, thinking about it. Instead, she pulled on the leggings, threw on a sweatshirt, laced up the shoes, and headed out the door.

She pushed herself on her morning runs, but that night, she practically sprinted the entire route. She wanted to be tired. She wanted to exhaust herself. Her legs were melting and her lungs were begging for mercy, but she had been unable to outrun her troubled thoughts and frustrations.

She completed the circuit and reached the pathway leading to her building. She leaned forward, rested her hands on her knees, and pulled gulps of air into her chest. The chill caused her to cough a few times but the cold air felt good on her sweat-covered cheeks.

She gritted her teeth and grunted, not out of exertion, but irritation.

Pete and Heather had been together for years. They were a great couple. Hadn't Meredith known that this was in the cards? Shouldn't she be happy?

"I am," Meredith said to herself, but it was a lie.

What was it that was eating away at her?

Somewhere, from the back of her mind, the answer stepped forward. It was as if her subconscious wanted her to be physically exhausted before presenting it.

It was bothering Meredith because Pete and Allison, and yes, even Heather, who Meredith viewed as a friend, were moving on. They were starting a new chapter in their lives and there was Meredith, alone, still in the same job as when she and Pete had split, and in some ways moving backwards. At least, that's what it felt like, now that she was seeing her sister's face on a dead girl. It was just as before when the search for Alice dried up. The rest of the world moved on, except for Meredith and her parents. Now, Meredith was on her own, and while she had been telling the truth to Allison that much wouldn't change in the short term, she felt it was only a matter of time before they would drift away from her.

Don't be ridiculous, Meredith thought. *They're not going anywhere. They're just getting married.*

But the more she tried to reassure herself, the more the seeds of doubt began to grow.

What if Allison was right? What if they did decide to move? What if this new chapter also called for a change of scenery? After all, Meredith didn't know what Pete and Heather were discussing for their future. They could be on the couch or in bed right now, talking about where they'd like to go. Pete had always talked about moving back to the town in Vermont where he grew up.

"Stop it," Meredith said. "You're driving yourself crazy."

But she couldn't help taking out her phone, thumbing through her contacts, and stopping at her mother's number. The closest Meredith came to contacting her was when things were trying with Pete, Allison, and Heather. Her mother was the only other person who understood the situation, but Meredith had never actually called her. Once every couple of months, Meredith would bring up her mother's number and stand there with her thumb hovering over the call button, wondering if it was worth taking the chance to vent her frustrations.

Thankfully, at that moment, her phone vibrated with an incoming call.

She hit the answer button. "This is Somerset."

"Oh. Hey, detective," Robbie Slonhaus said from the other end. "Sorry to call you this late on a Saturday. I hope I didn't wake you up or anything."

"No," she said in between breaths. "I was taking a run."

"On a Saturday night?"

"Yeah."

"And people think IT guys are the ones with no social lives."

"Yeah, yeah, yeah," Meredith said, walking to the door of her apartment. "What's going on?"

"I set up the webpage for your medallion thing. It went live last night."

"Okay ..." Meredith said, unlocking her door and stepping inside.

"I figured there probably wouldn't be too much activity over the weekend, but I wanted to make sure everything was functioning properly and the confessions from the crackpots were being displayed where only we could see it."

"Has anyone posted, yet?"

"Are you near your computer?"

"Yeah. Give me one second." Meredith set the phone down on the kitchen table. She quickly pulled off her damp sweatshirt. She picked up the phone and carried it to the couch. Her laptop was still open and her glass of wine waited next to it. She brought the laptop out of "sleep" mode and brought up the CCPD website.

"Logging in now," she said.

"The page is set up in the bulletin boards section. I made it so that the email responses are displayed like a comment thread. That way, you don't have to open each individual email," Robbie replied.

"Thanks."

Meredith found the page and clicked.

The top of the page showed two pictures; one was the front of the medallion and the other was the back. Underneath was a short description and a plea for help from the public in identifying the medallion. There was no mention of its connection to an anonymous dead girl.

"Okay, got it," Meredith said.

"Scroll down."

Meredith brushed her finger over the pad on the laptop and the screen moved.

True to Robbie's word, the bottom of the page looked like a comment thread and already, there were weirdos claiming they had done "it", even though they didn't say what "it" was. One of the posts claimed that the medallion was part of a satanic cult. Three posts down, and someone had already brought up the Illuminati.

Meredith scrolled past a few more ridiculous posts until she came to one that made her stop.

SOSH – Sisters of Sacred Heart.

"You seeing it?" Robbie asked.

"Sisters of Sacred Heart," Meredith said.

"Keep going."

Meredith continued down the page. There were more replies with the answer to the acronym.

Sosh = Sisters of Sacred Heart

s.o.s.h. is Sisters of Sacred Heart

(S)isters (O)f (S)acred (H)eart

Then came the first picture.

It was a guy in his twenties with short dark hair and a smile. He was holding something up to the camera.

A medallion. Identical to the one they found in the sock of their Jane Doe.

Meredith kept scrolling.

There were more text-only responses but as she continued, there were more and more photos.

They were of people of all ages, holding up the same medallion. There were couples with young children, where the child was holding the medallion. There were a few of smiling couples holding babies, while displaying the medallion.

It was like an online community had suddenly sprung up around the medallion.

"Whoa …" Meredith breathed.

"Right?!"

"Robbie, this is great."

"Thought you might want to see it. Now, if you'll excuse me, I'm going out on the town, because unlike some detectives, this IT guy has a social life."

Meredith kept scrolling. "Have fun. Do a shot for me."

"What did you say? Do five shots for you?" Robbie dramatically asked. "Okay. If you say so. Goodnight, detective."

"Goodnight, Robbie. Good work."

Meredith quickly hung up the phone and brought up another browser on the laptop. She entered "Sisters of Sacred Heart" into the search bar. The results took her to the homepage of a Catholic church and children's home in the northern most part of the Bronx in New York. At the top of the page was a symbol. It was the same as the one on the medallion but more detailed to show that it was actually an adult cradling a baby.

Meredith quickly picked her phone back up and dialed.

The ringtone purred once ... then twice ...

"Come on, come on, come on."

Just when Meredith thought that it was going to go to voicemail, Tyler answered.

"Somerset?" Tyler's voice was scratchy. He coughed, sniffed, then cleared his throat. "You okay?"

"Yeah. I'm fine. What are you doing, right now?"

Tyler cleared his throat, again. "Just hanging out at home. What's going on?"

"Do you have a computer?"

"Of course, I have a computer. You think I'm some caveman who—"

"Have you gotten your CCPD login, yet?"

"This morning. Why?"

"Check out the tip page Robbie set up for the medallion."

"All right. Hold on."

Meredith heard him moving around.

"Booting it up ... Okay. Got it."

"You're on the page?"

"Yeah," he said.

Meredith could tell by his tone that he was seeing what she was seeing.

"What is this?" he asked, his excitement rising. "Wait a sec. I'm looking up 'Sisters of Sacred Heart.'"

There was the clicking of keys from Tyler's end and then silence.

"You got it?" Meredith asked.

"Holy shit, Somerset. Our girl was an orphan."

Chapter 18

The dawn had barely broken the next morning when Trevor Morgan quietly crept down the stairs and into the kitchen.

The refrigerator hummed as he passed by on his way to the pantry.

He once again asked himself why he was doing this. He had been asking himself all night. The answer was that he knew it was wrong to lie to the police.

Does that mean it's okay to lie to Mom and Dad to make it right? the voice in his head countered.

Trevor didn't have an answer for that.

He cautiously opened the pantry door and grimaced as the hinges softly squealed.

He waited, eyes glued to the ceiling overhead.

There were no footsteps, no shouts from his father from the top of the stairs, warning any intruders that he had a gun.

The house remained silent.

Trevor stepped on the pedal to the stainless-steel garbage can, causing the lid to slowly rise. He looked down into the contents of the three-quarters full bag. An overturned coffee filter lay on the top. Its spent grounds coated nearly everything. Trevor kneeled down and carefully rummaged through greasy napkins, opened wrappers, and discarded food scraps.

He pushed aside a stained, wadded-up paper towel and found the first piece of what he was looking for: a scrap of stiff paper with some printed letters and numbers. He plucked it out and set in on the floor. He sifted through more trash; a small, Styrofoam tray that had held the chicken breasts his mother cooked for dinner two nights ago, an empty packet of oatmeal, the remnants of a salad, a snot-filled tissue.

There. Two more scraps. He lifted them out and set them on the floor, next to the other scrap.

He dug around some more and found three more bits of paper. He plucked them out, brushed off the coffee grounds, and added them to the small pile.

Trevor began to worry that he wouldn't know when he had all the scraps he needed, but he was past the point of no return.

He found a few more scraps at the very bottom of the trashcan. To fish them out, he had to sink his arms into the garbage up to his shoulder. He used one hand to hold the garbage to one side and snatched up the pieces with the other.

Once he had retrieved them, he looked at the tiny mound of torn, stiff bits of paper lying on the floor.

That was it.

He couldn't risk taking any longer.

He scooped up the scraps into his grime-covered hands and carefully placed them in the pocket of his pajama pants.

He crossed the kitchen to the sink, slowly lifted the faucet handle, and quickly rinsed his hands. There was no time for soap.

After drying his hands on the dishtowel next to the sink, he quietly pulled open the junk drawer and removed a roll of Scotch tape which he added to his pocket.

Now came the part that he had been dreading. It was going to be way more unpleasant than rooting through the garbage. He went back to the pantry and removed two granola bars from the box on the shelf. He tore open the wrappers, quickly scarfed down the bars, and then tossed the wrappers into the trash. He walked back over to the sink, grabbed a cup from the cabinet, filled it with water, and chugged it down. He refilled the glass and downed it, again. And then another. And another. And another.

His stomach uncomfortably full, he dried off the glass and the sink with the dishtowel and returned the glass to the cabinet.

Trevor took a quick survey of the kitchen. Satisfied that it looked exactly as it had upon his arrival, he made his way back to the stairs.

He reached his bedroom door and heard muffled voices and footsteps coming from his parents' bedroom at the end of the hall.

Trevor ducked into his room and quietly closed the door. He went to his desk, deposited the roll of tape and scraps of paper in the bottom drawer and climbed back into bed.

Over the next fifteen minutes or so, he listened as the house came to life. The door to his sisters' room opened and he heard them head to the bathroom. Minutes later, footsteps from his parents' room traveled down the hall and stopped outside his door.

There was a knock.

"Trevor?" his father asked. "Time to get ready for church."

"I'm awake," he replied, attempting to sound weak and miserable.

"You okay?"

"Yeah," Trevor responded, but did his best to come across otherwise.

"All right. We're leaving in half an hour."

"Okay."

His father's footsteps receded down the hall.

Trevor waited until he heard the sound of his sisters vacating the bathroom and returning to their room. He got out of bed and went to the door. He ruffled his hair and plastered a weary expression on his face before stepping into the hall.

The door to his parents' bedroom was partially open. Trevor walked slower than usual. As he reached the bathroom in the hallway, his mother passed by the open bedroom door and caught sight of him.

"Trevor, honey, what's wrong?"

"I don't feel good," he said.

She looked him up and down. "Well, after church, we'll get you some soup and you can lay on the couch."

Trevor nodded.

She smiled and resumed getting ready.

Trevor went into the bathroom and closed the door.

That was why he knew he couldn't try to fake it. His parents insisted on attending church, and normally, Trevor loved it. Not for the sermons, but for the social interactions he got to have with the outside world. He had friends at church. It was a chance to talk to people, but today he had to convince his mother and father that he couldn't go.

Trevor kneeled in front of the toilet and steadied himself. He held two fingers near his mouth and then shoved his fingers past his lips. They connected with the soft, slick flesh at the back of his throat.

The effect was instant.

His stomach lurched and sent its contents up into his esophagus. Trevor leaned forward and loudly retched as the water and granola mixture flew from his mouth and into the toilet. His eyes watered as another convulsion racked his body, bringing up more of his hastily consumed breakfast. He took deep breaths, tasting the foul, acidic bile in his mouth.

"Trevor?" his mother called from the other side of the door. "Are you okay?"

"Yeah," he moaned.

"Can we come in?" his father asked.

"Okay," he answered.

Trevor could have flushed before they opened the door, but he wanted them to see. It was the only evidence that would definitively convince the two-person jury.

The door swung inward to reveal his parents standing side by side with worried expressions.

"Oh, sweetheart," his mother said upon seeing the mess in the toilet.

"I'm sorry," he replied, flushing the handle.

"Really not feeling well, are you, sport?" his father asked.

Trevor shook his head.

"Okay," his father said. "Back to bed."

Trevor nodded and pulled himself to his feet.

He trudged down the hall, back to his room, and slid under the covers.

His parents followed him into the room. His mother sat on the edge of the bed and pressed her hand to his forehead.

"You don't feel warm."

"Probably just a stomach bug," his father said. "You'll feel better after you rest."

Behind his parents, Cassidy and Fable watched from the doorway with those unreadable expressions they always seemed to wear.

"We'll be back in a few hours," his father said comfortingly, but then grew severe. "You're to stay in bed. No television. No video games. Understand?"

"I understand."

"Get some rest," he said and walked out of the room. "Come on, girls."

The twins followed their father down the stairs.

His mother remained sitting on the bed, stroking his hair.

"Are you sure you can't come to church?" she asked. "I don't like how it looks if we're not all there."

"I want to, Mom, but I don't want to barf during the service."

She sighed in disappointment. "I suppose you're right." She kissed his forehead, got up, and walked to the door. "Feel better. I love you, honey."

"Love you, too, Mom."

She gave him one last glance and closed the door.

Trevor lay motionless and listened.

A few moments later, he heard the sound of the garage door opening and the car driving away.

He leaped out of bed and hurried to the desk. He pulled open the drawer and scooped out the scraps of paper and the roll of Scotch tape. He placed them on the desk and began frantically piecing the torn bits of paper together like a puzzle. Once finished, he laid strips of tape across the completed puzzle to hold it together.

Done.

He had reconstructed the card he had seen Detective Somerset give to his parents.

He'd known it was in the trash.

After the girl had been found in the street that afternoon, Trevor had been lying on the couch, reading a book. His mother didn't know he was there. He had peeked over the top of the couch and watched as his mother ripped the detective's card to pieces and then threw it in the trash.

Chapter 19

"Sisters of Sacred Heart. This is Sister Mariah. How can I help you?"

"Hi. This is Detective Meredith Somerset with the Cobb County Police Department in Georgia. I'm sorry to be calling you so early ... and on a Sunday."

Sister Mariah lightly laughed. "It's quite all right. What can I do for you?" Her voice was soft and gentle without the slightest hint of a Bronx accent.

"Well, I wish I was calling under better circumstances, but something's happened, and I can't stress enough that the information I'm about to share with you hasn't been made public yet, and we'd like to keep it that way."

"All right," Sister Mariah replied after a slight hesitation.

"A few days ago, a young woman was murdered and we found one of your medallions in her sock."

"Oh no ..."

"The medallion was the only identification on her person, and I was hoping you could help us identify the girl."

"Whatever I can do to help," she said, her voice unsteady.

Meredith leaned closer to her laptop.

"I got this number from your organization's home page. There's an email address under the number. Is that the best place to send a photo?"

"Yes. You can send it there."

Meredith had the distinct feeling from Sister Mariah's tone that she had an inkling of who she was about to see.

"I have to warn you, Sister Mariah, the photo I'm sending you isn't pleasant."

"I understand."

"Okay. Sending it, now."

Meredith had already composed the email with the photo of Jane Doe in a separate browser. She hit the send button and waited a moment.

"There. You should have it," Meredith said.

She thought she could hear the faint click of a mouse. Then Sister Mariah emitted a pained sigh and swallowed hard.

"Sister Mariah?"

There was a wet sniff. Sister Mariah was fighting back sobs.

"You've found Alice," she said.

Meredith's vision swam. She felt the couch fall away beneath her.

"What did you say?" Meredith asked.

"I said, you've found Alex," Sister Mariah said. "Her name is Alexa, but everyone called her Alex."

Meredith leaned back and stared at the ceiling, the phone still pressed to her ear. She tensed every muscle in her body, fighting back a panic attack, gritting her teeth, and willing herself back to calm.

"Her name was Alexa?" she finally asked.

"Yes," Sister Mariah confirmed.

"Can you tell me anything more about her? Her surname? The last time you saw her? Anything you can tell me that will help us find who did this to her."

There wasn't a sound from the other end of the line.

"Sister Mariah?"

"I'm sorry, detective. I'm afraid I'm going to have to call you back."

"Why? What's wrong?"

"I assume that you'll want information about Alexa, such as information about her birth parents, correct?"

"We'd like to know everything we can."

"We really do want to help but for these types of questions, you'll have to speak with our Reverend Mother, Sister Anna. We're very careful with sharing information about our children here at Sisters of Sacred Heart."

Frustration coursed through Meredith to the point that she held the phone away from her face.

"Fuck," she whispered before bringing the phone back to her ear. "I understand."

"I … I realize that this is frustrating, detective, and we'll do everything we can, but it's necessary for our organization."

Meredith wondered why she said that until she was struck by a shameful thought.

"You heard me swear just now, didn't you?" Meredith asked.

"Yes."

Meredith grimaced. "I apologize."

"It's all right. I might, too, if I was in your position, but please know that we both want the same thing."

"I appreciate that."

"I'll speak with Sister Anna. We'll set up a time for all of us to talk and answer any questions you might have."

"That would be great. Thank you, Sister Mariah."

"Is this the best number to contact you?"

"Yes."

"We'll be in touch as soon as possible," Sister Mariah said.

"Thank you."

"Have a blessed Sunday, detective."

"You, too," Meredith replied, not sure if that was the correct response, and then added. "And thank you."

"Goodbye."

Meredith hung up the phone, pressed the heels of her palms to her eyes, and cursed again, louder this time.

She understood. She did. Sisters of Sacred Heart had to protect itself, but it was obvious that Sister Mariah had answers to share. The case could have taken a massive leap forward in a matter of minutes but now could become mired in a legal swamp and if Sisters of Sacred Heart refused to answer questions, what then? Were they going to subpoena them? Would Sisters of Sacred Heart go to court to fight it? The word would get out and the press would go nuts. Also, since they were in New York, that made it a national story, and whatever circus they were hoping to avoid with the local press would become a national spectacle.

And she had heard Sister Mariah say "Alice".

It was an innocent mistake and not totally outside the realm of understanding. Still, should she call Dr. Kaplan? She probably should have called her after the episode in the morgue.

No, Meredith told herself. *Not yet.*

Her phone began to buzz.

"That was fast," she said, but when she checked the screen, she saw that the area code was local.

Most people, if they didn't recognize a number, would have simply allowed it to go to voicemail. If it was important, the caller could leave a message. If it was a telemarketer, they could get bent, but detectives didn't have that luxury.

"This is Somerset," she answered.

There was no response, only the sound of short, nervous breathing.

"Hello?" she asked.

Still no reply.

"Listen, whoever this is, if you're not going to talk to me, then you can—"

"It's Trevor Morgan."

It took a second for Meredith to process, but she quickly

remembered the nervous, awkward boy standing in the middle of his room at the Morgan house.

"Trevor? Is everything all right?"

"I need to talk to you."

"Oh. Okay. Are your parents there?"

"No. They don't know that I'm calling you. They don't know that I have a phone."

"I see …"

Meredith was hopping from one legal minefield to another. Trevor was fifteen. If he was sixteen, he could ask to speak to her without his parents present, but not fifteen.

If Trevor had said that he only *wanted* to talk to her, Meredith would have suggested they wait for his parents, but Trevor said that he *needed* to talk to her.

She made a decision to roll the dice.

"Okay, Trevor. What's up?"

"I can't tell you over the phone. Can you come to the park at the entrance of my neighborhood right away?"

"Um. Sure. I can be there in fifteen minutes."

"And the other detective has to be there, too."

"Well, Trevor, I can be there but I don't know if Detective Foles is available."

"He has to be there," he insisted, his voice about to break.

"Okay, Trevor," she coaxed. "We'll be there."

"Okay. Bye."

"Trevor?"

He had already hung up.

Meredith quickly dialed Tyler's number.

He answered on the second ring.

"Somerset?"

"Tyler, I need you to meet me at the park at the entrance to Meadowgate as soon as you can."

"Somerset, I'm kind of in the middle of something."

"I just got off the phone with Trevor Morgan. He wants to

meet. He said he needed to talk to us, but he'll only do it if you're there."

"Now?"

"Right now."

Tyler took a breath. "Okay. I'll be there as soon as I can."

"Hurry," Meredith said, reaching for her keys.

Chapter 20

Meredith and Tyler arrived at the park at the entrance to Meadowgate within moments of each other. It wasn't much of a park; more of a patch of woodchips with a swing set, slide, see-saw, and a small fort to climb on.

Trevor Morgan was sitting in one of the swings, watching as Meredith and Tyler stepped out of their cars. The sky was an expanse of gray, wooly clouds.

"What's going on, Somerset?" Tyler mumbled as they walked toward Trevor.

"No idea," Meredith muttered back.

As they drew nearer to Trevor, Meredith could see that he was nervous, anxious, and maybe even a little ashamed.

"Hey, Trevor," Meredith said, trying to sound as casual as possible.

"Sup, Trev?" Tyler added.

Trevor kept his eyes level, staring past them toward the trees.

"Are you okay?" Meredith asked.

"Can I … can I talk to Detective Foles, alone?" Trevor asked.

Meredith turned to Tyler, who appeared just as confused as she was.

Tyler shrugged. "Yeah, man. Absolutely."

"I'll just, uh, I'll just wait by the car," Meredith said. She turned and took two steps toward the street, which brought her even with Tyler.

"You good?" she asked quietly.

"Yeah. I got this."

"If you need help, I can tap in."

"Copy that."

Meredith continued walking, leaving Tyler and Trevor alone.

There was a long, awkward pause, where neither spoke. Trevor still had that thousand-yard stare toward the trees.

Tyler gestured to the empty swing next to him. "Mind if I join you?"

Trevor didn't answer.

Tyler stepped over and eased himself into the swing. He looked down at his feet and casually ran the toe of his shoe through the soft layer of woodchips that covered the ground.

"You know, when I was a kid, this all would have been concrete. We used to see who could jump off the swing at the highest point. Can't tell you how many times we sprained our ankles." He glanced at Trevor and smiled. "We weren't the smartest kids on the play-ground."

While it didn't make Trevor laugh or even smile, it did break his stare and he glanced down at the woodchips.

"What's going on, Trev?" Tyler asked.

He waited for a response, but Trevor continued to stare at the ground.

"Listen, Trev, you can talk to me. You've obviously got something on your mind that—"

"I lied to you." Trevor suddenly uttered.

"About what?"

"Seeing the girl." Trevor's tone wavered as he spoke. "I mean, I did see her, but I wasn't in my room."

"That's okay," Tyler said. "You're telling me now. It's all good. So, where were you?"

Trevor kicked at the woodchips, still unable to look Tyler in the eye.

"I was in the house that's being built next to ours."

"What were you doing there?" Tyler gently asked.

Trevor's lips tightened and his eyes suddenly glistened with tears.

"Listen, Trev, it's just you and me. You're not in any trouble. No one's gonna be mad. Just tell me what happened."

Trevor inhaled but didn't speak.

"Were you alone?" Tyler asked.

Trevor shook his head.

"Who was with you?"

Trevor hesitated, then answered, "Ashton."

"Ashton? Your next-door neighbor?"

Trevor nodded.

"What were you guys doing?"

Trevor was barely holding it together as he spoke. "We kinda grew up together. We used to always hang out and play and stuff. My parents didn't know. He got to do all the things I wanted to do. He went to school. He got to watch movies and play video games. I really thought he was cool. We were, um … friends. A while ago, he gave me a cellphone so we could text at night when everyone thought we were asleep but he started getting new friends because he goes to school … but we still hang out, some-times, and I started to …" Trevor stopped to wipe the snot that had begun seeping from his nose.

"Started to what, Trevor?"

Trevor looked back at the trees.

"I'm different, detective. I don't want to be, but I am," he said. "I started to like Ashton … but like, in a way that I'm not supposed to."

The dam broke. Tears poured freely from Trevor's eyes.

Tyler finally caught up.

"Trev, buddy … you telling me you like guys?"

143

"I don't know," Trevor said in a miserable way that let Tyler know that was exactly what he was telling him.

Tyler was walking a tightrope. His experience with situations like this was virtually nil but his heart went out to the kid, who was clearly hurting.

"Trev, my man, if that's who you are, there ain't nothing wrong with it."

Trevor continued to stare at the trees.

"Do your parents know?" Tyler asked.

Trevor fearfully shook his head. "I don't think so. I mean, I don't know, but I asked Ashton if I could kiss him and Ashton said okay, and we kissed." He turned to Tyler with wide, panicked eyes. "I had wanted to kiss him for a long time. But that's all we did because I told Ashton that I liked him and he got really mad. He said that I could never tell anyone what we did! I know that it's wrong to feel that way about boys and I try not to. I really try because I know my parents—"

"Hey. It's okay, Trev," Tyler said, reassuringly. "Listen, I'm gonna do everything I can to keep this between you and me, all right?"

Trevor nodded and looked back at the ground.

"I just need to know what you saw," Tyler said after giving him a moment.

Trevor calmed to a degree and began to speak.

"I told my parents that I was going to play video games in the basement before school, but I had texted Ashton and asked if he wanted to meet at the house. We'd done it before. My parents would kill me if they found out, but he said 'yes', so I snuck out."

"Do you remember what time this was?"

Trevor took out his cheap cellphone and brought up the text messages. He showed it to Tyler. The timestamp on the texts read 06:34.

"So, you two met up at the house that was under construction?"

"Yeah. I met up with him in the house and I asked him if I could kiss him. He said 'yes', so we did and, I swear, that was all

144

that we did. I told him that I liked him and that I had liked him for a long time. He got really mad and said that …"

"Trev, it's okay. You don't have to tell me what happened. There's nothing wrong with what you did. I just want you to tell me what happened with the girl in the street."

Trevor collected himself.

"We heard a sound, like a girl trying to yell, but she couldn't."

"Like someone stopped her from yelling?"

Trevor nodded.

"And you and Ashton were in the house?"

"We were in the—I don't know what it's called, but it was the front room. When we heard her, we looked out the window but it was too foggy. We waited and a little while later, we heard another woman scream really loud."

"How long do you think it was between screams?" Tyler asked.

"I checked my phone because I was worried that I had been away from the house for too long and my parents might check the basement. It was, like, maybe five minutes or something."

Tyler's head was spinning. The second scream Trevor had heard had to be that of Patricia Crawford when she found the body, but the first attempted scream had to have been the murder, itself. Trevor's account had dramatically closed the gap between when Alexa had been killed and when her body had been discovered.

"What did you guys do?" Tyler asked.

"We ran. I ran home. I went in through the basement and snuck up to my room."

"Anyone see you?"

"No."

Tyler nodded. "Okay."

"Please! Please, don't say anything to my parents. They don't know that I'm talking to you. They don't know about me."

"Trevor, listen to me; I'm not going to say anything to your parents. I'm not going to say anything to anyone about what was going on in the house between you and Ashton."

145

Trevor raised his eyes and looked at Detective Somerset, who was standing by their cars.

"Not even Detective Somerset," Tyler said. "It's just between you and me, okay?"

"Okay," Trevor replied and directed his eyes to the trees as fresh tears began to fall. "If my parents ever found out … They said that people like me are bad. That people like me end up in hell."

Tyler nodded and took a breath.

"Well, Trevor, that's what they think and, believe me, they love you, but I'll tell you this, parents can be wrong. My old man was wrong about a lot of things. So was my mom. Parents don't have all the answers, but sometimes, they feel like it's their job to pretend that they do."

It had some effect on Trevor and he wiped his nose with the sleeve of his jacket.

"Can I ask you something, Trevor?"

"Uh okay."

"Why'd you want to only tell this to me?"

"You were nice to me. I don't meet a lot of people and when I do, they treat me like I'm weird. I mean, I know I am weird, but you were nice. I didn't feel weird."

Tyler took it in.

Trevor stepped out of the swing. "I have to get back before my parents come home from church."

"Got it," Tyler said. "Get home safe."

Trevor began to walk toward the entrance to Meadowgate.

"Hey, Trev?"

He stopped and turned back to Tyler.

"You did the right thing in helping us catch the person who killed that girl, even if it meant telling me what you told me. Thank you … You're not weird. You're brave, and exactly who you're supposed to be. And if you ever want to tell your parents about who you are and you want someone to back you up, you let me know. I'll be there."

It wasn't much, but Tyler thought he saw a weight come off Trevor as he turned and walked away.

Tyler pulled himself out of the swing and made his way across the park to Meredith, who was still standing by their cars.

"What was that about?" she asked.

"Trevor Morgan and Ashton Whitaker were in the unfinished house next to the Morgans' when the murder happened. They heard our girl try to scream only a few minutes before she was discovered by Patricia Crawford, which means our killer was close by."

Meredith's mouth hung open. "What were they doing?"

Tyler shook his head.

"You're not going to tell me?" Meredith asked.

"Nope."

"Why not?"

"Not relevant."

Meredith looked at him, pressing for an answer.

"Not relevant, Somerset," Tyler repeated, "and I made a promise."

Chapter 21

"How was 'Taco Night'?" Meredith asked, her legs curled under her on the couch, phone pressed to her ear.

"Messy," Allison said.

"All of your homework done?"

"I still have some math."

"'Some math'? How much is 'some math'?"

"A few geometry problems."

Meredith checked the time on her phone. "You need to get on those. It's getting late."

"I will … Mom?"

"Yeah, baby?"

"I'm sorry I was upset at the farmers' market, yesterday."

"That's okay. It's okay to be upset."

Even a little pissed, Meredith thought.

"I think Dad's going to ask Heather soon."

"Yeah. I may have told him to speed it up."

"Does that mean you want him to ask Heather to marry him?"

"Doesn't matter what I want, baby. It's their decision. Your dad loves Heather, she loves him, and they both love you."

"But do you want him to ask Heather?"

"Baby—"

"Do you?" Allison insisted.

Meredith winced.

Why was she having such a hard time answering Allison's question? She had made peace with the fact a while ago that it was an inevitability.

Okay, Meredith thought, *then say yes.*

"I want what's best for you, and your dad, and Heather, and if they want to get married, then yes, I'm all for it," Meredith answered instead, and couldn't help noticing all the qualifiers. "Yes, baby, I think it's great if they want to get married," Meredith added, hoping to clarify.

"And if Heather wants me to call her 'Mom'?"

"Allison, we went over this, if she asks you—"

"She asked me."

Meredith's mouth hung open. "When?"

"Tonight. We were going over my homework and I guess I was thinking about it because I accidentally called her 'Mom'. I told her that I was sorry, but she smiled and said it was okay if I called her 'Mom'. I thought she was going to cry."

"Oh."

There it was—that white-hot ball of rage in her stomach. It was one thing when it was theoretical, but now it was real, and the calm, rational demeanor that Meredith had always employed when talking about such things was barely holding the line.

"And what did you say?" Meredith asked, a tad too earnestly.

She regretted the question as soon as it left her lips. It wasn't fair to do this to Allison. Heather was the one she needed to talk to.

"Baby, I'm sorry. I shouldn't have asked you that. We can talk about it later, okay?"

"Okay."

"All right. Finish up those geometry problems and get to bed. You hear me?"

"Yeah."

"Goodnight," Meredith said.

"Goodnight."

"I love you, baby."

"I love you, too, Mom."

Allison hung up, as did Meredith.

I love you, too, Mom.

Damn right, Meredith thought.

Chapter 22

Early the next morning, Meredith stepped into the office to find Tyler sitting at her desk, going over photos from the crime scene on her computer.

"Who are you?" she asked.

"What?"

"Who are you? What are you doing here?"

Tyler looked around the office. "Somerset, I have no idea what is happening, right now."

"What have you done with Detective Foles?"

"I am … he?"

"No, no, no. I know Detective Foles. He doesn't show up for another thirty minutes or so."

"Oh. Ha, ha, ha," Tyler laughed sarcastically. "Now I know why you went into policework."

"Yeah? Why is that?"

"Because you're shit at comedy," he said, giving her finger guns.

Meredith laughed. "Get out of my chair."

Tyler pushed himself away from her desk and stood. "See? Even when I try to show initiative, you're going to give me flak."

"Showing up on time isn't 'initiative'. It's 'competence',"

Meredith said, dropping into her chair. "You been going through my stuff?"

"Relax. I was using my account. Your porn is safe."

Sergeant Wheaton walked through the door and stopped when he saw the two of them.

"Detective Foles, is there something wrong?" he asked.

"Sir?"

"You normally wouldn't grace us with your presence for another hour or so."

Tyler bit his lip.

Sergeant Wheaton was thoroughly pleased with himself.

"Tyler?" Meredith asked. "Do you want to tell Sergeant Wheaton why *he* went into policework?"

"I don't know what you're talking about," Tyler muttered.

"How's our Jane Doe going?" Sergeant Wheaton asked.

"It's going," Meredith replied.

"Can you give me a rundown before lunch?"

"Sure."

"Good," Sergeant Wheaton said, walking past them to his office. "Get back to work."

Meredith logged in to her account to discover that she had two new emails; one was from Sister Mariah at Sisters of Sacred Heart, asking if that morning would be a good time to talk with Sister Anna.

"That was fast," Tyler said, hopefully.

Meredith had explained her phone call with Sister Mariah after their meeting with Trevor the day before, but she didn't share in Tyler's optimism.

"Alexa, our Jane Doe, was a minor. I don't know if they can be held responsible for losing her or if they can legally tell us anything about her past, like her parents or if they even know anything about them."

"Then it'll be a short conversation."

Meredith pulled up the other email, which were the results of the extensive background check she had ordered for the residents of Willow Lane.

Greg Ansley had a DUI in Boston from sixteen years ago.

"Boston?" Tyler asked, looking over her shoulder. "What the hell was he doing in Boston? Wasn't he living in Charleston?"

"Might have been for work. He said that he did a lot of traveling for his job at the time."

"How wet was he?" Tyler asked, pulling up a chair.

Meredith checked the report. "He blew a .12 in a rental car. He paid the ticket and did his alcohol awareness classes in Charleston."

"Any other ghosts in the Ansleys' closet?"

"You mean skeletons?"

"Whatever."

Meredith scrolled through the rest of the info on the Ansleys. "No. They moved to Willow Lane twelve years ago."

"I don't think a drunk joyride from sixteen years ago jumps him up the list of suspects. What about my boy, Thomas Whitaker, Esquire?" Tyler asked, elongating "esquire".

Meredith found the info about the Whitakers.

"Sorry to disappoint you, but clean as a whistle." She continued scrolling and grimaced. "Oof."

"What is it?"

"Terrible credit score."

"Doesn't surprise me," Tyler remarked.

"Want to know what it is?"

"Nah."

"Why not?"

"Glass houses and shit," Tyler muttered.

Meredith continued reading.

"The Whitakers have been on Willow Lane for eight years. The Morgans are clean, too," she said, studying the screen.

"I could have called that one."

No priors, no reports, not even a parking ticket.

"The Morgans have lived on Willow Lane for fourteen years. Before that, they lived in Providence, Rhode Island."

"Why are you telling me where everyone used to live and how long they've lived on Willow Lane? What are you going for, Somerset?"

"If it was someone on Willow Lane, Alexa has to be tied to their past."

"Point taken."

Meredith's eyebrows creased as she came to another section.

"What's up?" Tyler asked.

"Scott Bowers."

"He dirty?"

"No, but the date on his birth certificate and his social security don't match and it looks like his employment history only goes back to when he moved to Atlanta."

Tyler leaned in, his face close to Meredith's, as they both peered at the screen.

It was as if Scott Bowers' life had started seven years ago, when he moved to Willow Lane.

"What do you make of that?" Tyler asked.

"Probably an admin error. A software glitch somewhere."

Tyler continued to stare at the screen, his forehead creased in concentration.

"You're probably right …"

"But?" Meredith asked.

"I'm most likely seeing things from working in vice so long, but we would have flagged this. It looks like someone trying to hide something."

"We can ask him if he knows anything about it," Meredith said. "Give him the chance to verify his info and then run the check again."

Tyler straightened up. "Or, I've got a guy who can run a deeper check than we can. He knows how this shit works."

Meredith leaned back in her chair.

"Would this guy be from your days in vice?"

"Maybe."

"Would this guy also happen to be a criminal who helps people set up fake identities to escape criminal pasts?"

"Maybe …" Tyler answered again, but more coyly.

"And if we were to find something that could help us, we would never be able to use that info in court, correct?"

"I'm not saying we make it official, Somerset. I'm just saying someone owes me a favor. He can run it down, and if it is an admin error, fine. No harm, no foul, but if there is something, he'll point us in the right direction. That way, we don't tip off Mr. Scott Bowers that we know he's dirty."

"*If* he's dirty."

"Yeah. That's what I meant."

Meredith took a contemplative breath.

Her first thought was *What could it hurt?* But those were always the things that came back to bite you in the ass. If Scott Bowers was their guy and Tyler's fishing expedition got out after he was arrested for Alexa's murder, his attorney would have a field day.

"Let's sit on it, for now," she said.

"Fair enough," Tyler replied, but he was already making plans.

Chapter 23

"Sister Mariah?"

"Yes?"

"Hi. It's Detective Meredith Somerset. I'm here with my partner, Detective Tyler Foles."

They were situated around Meredith's desk. She and Tyler had phones pressed to their ears on a conference call to Sisters of Sacred Heart.

"Good morning, Sister," Tyler said.

"Nice to meet you, Detective Foles."

"Likewise."

"I'm here with our Reverend Mother, Sister Anna," Sister Mariah said.

"Good morning, detectives," a voice chimed in. "How are you?"

Meredith had expected an authoritative tone belonging to a commanding, heavyset woman in a habit with rosary beads bouncing off her hip as she walked, ruler in hand.

Instead, Sister Anna's voice was sweet, almost grandmotherly.

"We're good, Sister Anna," Meredith said. "Thank you for taking the time to talk to us."

"Of course. Sister Mariah told me of your phone call yesterday and I want to make clear that we'll do whatever we can to help you find who did this to Alexa."

Tyler and Meredith glanced at one another. The words Sister Anna had spoken were right but the tone was off. It sounded full of caveats and fine print.

"We're happy to hear that," Meredith replied. "We'd like to start—"

"But I also want to make clear that we need to protect the staff and practices of our organization. Sisters of Sacred Heart have done wonders for our children and placed them with kind, loving families all over the country and will continue to do so. With that in mind, I've advised Sister Mariah and the rest of my staff that all questions regarding Alexa should be handled by me."

Tyler placed his hand over the mouthpiece of the phone he was holding. "This nun go to law school or something?"

Meredith shook him off. "We appreciate any help you can give us."

"Wonderful. Let me begin by telling you what I can; the young woman's name was Alexa. She grew up here at Sisters of Sacred Heart. Last week she ran away. No one had seen or heard from her until you sent Sister Mariah the photos. We don't know how she got to Atlanta, but she may have hitchhiked."

Meredith and Tyler waited for more but Sister Anna remained silent.

"That's it?" Meredith asked. "That's all you can tell us?"

"You may now ask any questions you'd like, Detective Somerset," the honey-toned voice replied. "I will do my best to answer while protecting our organization."

"Can you tell us Alexa's last name?" Meredith asked.

"I'm sorry, but no. It might reveal the identity of her parents, who have a right to privacy. We at Sisters of Sacred Heart jealously protect the identities of the parents who give us their children. Their anonymity is guaranteed and if we were to break

157

that promise, distressed parents may be hesitant to trust us with their child."

"Sister Anna, it's important that we know Alexa's last name. It could help us—"

"If you want, you could file a subpoena but I have to warn you, we have excellent legal representation who will advocate for us very vocally."

There it was. Sister Anna was laying it on the table, letting them know that if they tried to subpoena Sisters of Sacred Heart, the case would go public. It was the most pleasant-sounding threat Meredith had ever heard.

"Got it," Meredith said. "Can you tell us why Alexa may have kept the medallion in her sock?"

There was a pause and they heard Sister Anna say, "Go ahead."

"The medallions are given to the children as soon as they arrive at Sisters of Sacred Heart," Sister Mariah spoke up. "For some, it's the first possession they ever have, and it holds a special place for them. It's not uncommon for some of our children to hide them in their socks for safe keeping. Alexa treasured hers. She might have been worried about someone stealing it, especially if she hitchhiked from here to—"

"Thank you, Sister Mariah," Sister Anna said, cutting her off.

Meredith bit her lip in frustration. "Are they given any other form of identification?"

"Yes," Sister Anna answered. "When they're older, they're given an ID card from the orphanage. Alexa had one of these ID cards."

"Can you tell me more about Alexa and her time at Sisters of Sacred Heart?" Meredith asked.

There was a slight delay as the nuns conferred.

"She was a troubled child," Sister Mariah said, her voice wavering. "But she was also very intelligent and was helping me with our computers. That's where she found the name—"

Sister Anna stepped in, again. "I'm afraid that's all we can say."

"Do you know the identity of Alexa's parents?" Meredith asked.

"That's another one we can't answer on privacy grounds," Sister Anna replied. "While some parents do leave information, others do not. Sisters of Sacred Heart is a 'safe haven'. Babies can be brought here and left, no questions asked. Any more details might jeopardize the parents' privacy, who most likely, have nothing to do with this."

"Sister Anna," Meredith sighed. "Can you tell me if you know the identity of her parents without telling me their names?"

"Sadly, I cannot," Sister Anna said.

"Is there *anything* you can tell us?" Meredith asked, exasperated. "Because for such a wonderful organization who has done so much for the community and professes that they want to help us, this isn't a lot of help."

"Detective," Sister Anna said, her gentle tone unchanged. "I understand how—"

She was suddenly drowned out by Sister Mariah's pleading voice.

"I loved Alexa. I wanted nothing more than to keep her safe. I did everything I could to stop her, but she wouldn't listen. She said she was going t—"

"Sister Mariah!" Sister Anna snapped, suddenly sounding a lot more like the woman Meredith had envisioned. "Step outside."

There was another pause, longer this time.

"Step outside, now," Sister Anna demanded.

Meredith and Tyler stared at one another in the silence that followed.

"I apologize for Sister Mariah's outburst," Sister Anna finally said.

"Yeah," Tyler said. "How terrible of her to try to help us catch the guy who killed the young woman she cared for so much."

"Detective, I don't enjoy this either, but I'm doing the best to protect my children here at Sisters of Sacred Heart and the loving families we've helped create in the past and will create in the future. Everyone wants this solved as quickly, and as quietly, as possible, as I'm sure you do. Right now, it's taking all I've got to keep the press at bay."

Meredith and Tyler were suddenly alert.

"What do you mean by that?" Meredith asked. "Have the press been asking about Alexa?"

"No, not yet, but they were asking about the medallion. We received a phone call from the *Atlanta Journal-Constitution*."

Meredith rubbed her eyes.

There was only one place that a reporter could have gotten it.

She thought they had been so clever in putting up that tip-line about the medallion without any mention of Alexa's murder. They knew that reporters watched the pages where the police asked for help from the public, and even though they hadn't mentioned the murder, a reporter might be interested in finding out what the medallion was. It wouldn't take a super sleuth to start connecting the dots.

Suddenly, the lack of cooperation from Sister Anna wasn't the worst part of the phone call.

"What did you tell them?" Meredith asked.

"I told them we didn't know why one of our medallions was posted on a police website. I confirmed that it was from the orphanage, but apart from that, we knew nothing."

"If that could remain your official position for a little while longer, we'd really appreciate it."

"I can do that, but if you subpoena Sisters of Sacred Heart for the name of Alexa's parents—"

"Yes," Meredith said. "We understood the threat the first time."

"It's not a threat, detective," Sister Anna said in her kind, grandmotherly tone. "Is there anything else?"

Meredith looked to Tyler, who shook his head.

"No," she said. "But if you think of anything, you'll be sure to tell us, right?"

"Of course. Have a good day, detectives."

"You, too."

Sister Anna hung up.

"Damnit," Meredith said, returning the headset to the cradle.

Tyler hung up his phone and ran his fingers through his hair. "If the *AJC* is starting to put shit together, it's only a matter of time before someone talks. We gotta speed this up."

Sergeant Wheaton popped his head out of his office.

"All right. Let's go, you two. I want to hear what's up with our Jane Doe."

Chapter 24

"Where are we?" Sergeant Wheaton asked from his chair behind the desk. "What do you know?"

"Not much," Meredith began as she and Tyler sat in the chairs on the opposite side. "We know her name was Alexa and that she was strangled. She fought her attacker and possibly got some of her killer's skin under her fingernails. Mike in the Morgue is waiting on the lab results. There were no signs of sexual assault."

"I guess that's something. Did Mike give you a timeframe for the lab results?"

"The tests themselves only take a few hours, but the lab is backed up, as always."

"How long did Mike say?"

"Possibly a couple of weeks."

Sergeant Wheaton frowned and moved on. "If it wasn't sexual assault, any idea on motive?"

"We're looking into that," Meredith said. "We've also been able to narrow down the timeframe between when she was killed and when her body was discovered. It looks as though she was strangled around six-fifty and the body was found shortly after seven."

"That's pretty damn specific. How were you able to pin that down?" Sergeant Wheaton asked, impressed.

Meredith hesitated. "I'm sorry, Sergeant. I didn't quite catch that last question."

Tyler was about to answer but Sergeant Wheaton spoke up.

"I asked, 'What else have you found?'"

Tyler was baffled but it was a code that Sergeant Wheaton and Meredith had worked out long ago. If it was better to not answer a question, Meredith or Sergeant Wheaton would respond that they "didn't quite catch that last question" and pretend they hadn't heard. Since the information had come from a minor without their parents present, Meredith thought it was best to leave it out for now.

"We're running extensive background checks on everyone on Willow Lane."

"Anything juicy?"

"We're following up on some stuff."

"What about that thing you found in her sock?" Sergeant Wheaton asked.

"We were able to track it down. It's from a children's home in the Bronx called Sisters of Sacred Heart."

"She was an orphan?"

Meredith nodded. "We spoke to the head of Sisters of Sacred Heart, Sister Anna. She said that Alexa ran away from the home a week ago."

Sergeant Wheaton looked between Meredith and Tyler. "Why wouldn't you lead with that when I asked you what you've found?"

Meredith shifted uncomfortably in her chair. "Because things have gotten a little complicated."

Sergeant Wheaton stopped.

"How complicated?"

"Sisters of Sacred Heart know a lot more than they're willing to tell us."

"Like what?"

"Her last name, the identity of one or both of her parents, and why she ran away."

"You're sure they know?"

"Yes."

For the first time since they had entered his office, Sergeant Wheaton directed his attention at Tyler. "You agree with that assessment?"

"Absolutely. I was on the line, too," Tyler answered.

Sergeant Wheaton turned back to Meredith. "And why won't they tell us anything?"

"Sister Anna claims it's a privacy issue. She's worried that other parents might not trust them if she gives up the name of Alexa's parents."

"Even though she was murdered?"

"Yeah … and it gets worse."

Sergeant Wheaton locked eyes with Meredith. "How much 'worse'?"

"We created that tip-line to help us figure out the meaning of the medallion. It's how we found the children's home."

"Okay …"

"The press watches those message boards, looking for stories."

"Yes …"

"Sister Anna said that she had been contacted by the *Atlanta Journal-Constitution*, asking them why the medallion showed up on a police tip-line website."

Sergeant Wheaton leaned back in his chair and looked up at the ceiling. "Goddamnit."

"Sir, there was no way we could have known—"

Sergeant Wheaton waved her off. "No, no, no. You two are fine. It was the right call. It just means that the shit is a lot closer to the fan than I would like." He scratched his chin. "Did this Sisters of Sacred whatever give you anything else?"

"No. All they would tell us is her first name and that she was intelligent but troubled. It sounds like Alexa may have found one or both of her parents' names in their computer records."

Tyler sat up. "One of the nuns, Sister Mariah, she wanted to tell us more, but Sister Anna shut her down."

Sergeant Wheaton thought it over. "Okay. If they're not going to cooperate with us, I could talk to Kelly Yamara over in the DA's office. Get a subpoena."

Meredith shook her head. "Sister Anna made it clear; the moment we file, they go public."

"Of course they do," Sergeant Wheaton exhaled. "And there was no mention of a murder on the page about the medallion, right?"

"None."

"And am I correct in assuming that Sisters of Sacred Heart aren't in a rush to admit one of their kids ran away and was murdered?"

"They said they would stay quiet for the time being and only confirm that it is one of their medallions."

"Is this going to go public? Who knows about it?"

Meredith calculated in her head. "There's us, the crime scene unit, and while I'm fairly certain none of them would say anything, I can't guarantee it. I'm more worried about the residents of Willow Lane or one of the other residents of Meadowgate. If it breaks, it'll be from there."

"In other words, this is going to break?"

After a pause, Meredith nodded.

Sergeant Wheaton again looked at Tyler. "You agree with her?"

"Yep."

"Good. You're learning." Sergeant Wheaton leaned forward in his chair. "You said you had leads you were chasing down?"

"A couple."

"Okay. First and foremost, Detective Somerset, I'm going to ask you again, and because time is of the essence, I can't be diplomatic." He pointed at Tyler. "You still good with him?"

"Yes. Detective Foles has proven himself more than capable."

Meredith's answer had been so quick, there wasn't time for Tyler to be offended by Sergeant Wheaton's question.

"All right," Sergeant Wheaton said. "I want this wrapped up as quickly and quietly as possible before it gets out. What do you need? Where can we hit the gas?"

"Well, there is one thing," Meredith said.

"Name it."

"Someone's not gonna like it."

Sergeant Wheaton shrugged. "*Someone* will get over it."

*

Mike looked up from the corpse on the cookie sheet at the sound of the doors opening, to see Sergeant Wheaton walking into the room, followed by Meredith and Tyler.

"Mike!" Sergeant Wheaton jovially announced. "How we doing?"

"Um, good."

"What are you working on?"

"Uh, stabbing victim. Early thirties. Most likely killed by a short, serrated—"

"Boy, that's great," Sergeant Wheaton said. "Listen; I understand that Detective Somerset and Foles have a young, strangled Jane Doe."

"Yes," Mike replied, casting his eyes to the detectives standing behind Sergeant Wheaton.

"They also told me that Jane Doe put up a fight. Clawed at her attacker. Maybe got some of his skin under her fingernails?"

Mike deflated, fully aware of where this was going. "Yes, she did. I sent the samples off to the lab."

"Perfect," Sergeant Wheaton exclaimed, all smiles. "And how long is that gonna take?"

"At least a week, probably more. Just like every other—"

"A week, probably more?" Sergeant Wheaton said in mock

surprise and then made a *tsk-tsk* sound with his tongue. "That seems like an awful long time, Mike. From my understanding, these tests only take a couple of hours."

"They do, but the lab is really backed up."

"I get that, Mike. I really do," Sergeant Wheaton said sympathetically. "But the press is starting to crawl all over this. They're going to make a stink. I need you to tell the lab techs to move it up."

Mike's shoulders slumped. "You want me to tell them you want the results expedited?"

"That'd be great. Thanks, Mike."

Meredith tried to make herself as small as possible. She believed that Sergeant Wheaton wanted to speed up the results because of the press, but there was also a perception around the precinct that Sergeant Wheaton had a favorite, someone he gave preferential treatment, and that someone was her. While she didn't want it, she knew it wasn't entirely untrue.

"Can I tell them to contact you when they start chewing me out?" Mike asked.

"That'd be fine. I'll just hang up on them," Sergeant Wheaton said. He turned back to the door and began walking.

Meredith and Tyler tried to keep up.

Mike called after them. "You know, you're ruining a really great lesson I taught Detective Foles about lab work."

"I can live with that," Sergeant Wheaton said as they passed out the door and into the hall.

Chapter 25

"Now that we have the big man's blessing, how long you think we gotta wait for those lab results?" Tyler asked as they walked out of the station to their cars at the end of the day. They had spent the rest of the shift going over the interviews, again, and asking Kelly Yamara in the DA's office if there was any way around Sisters of Sacred Heart's policies and were told that no, there wasn't.

"Depends," Meredith said. "Could be a few days, a week, but hopefully not much more than that. You know how it is."

Tyler nodded. "Rush don't mean *rush*."

"They'll get it to us as quickly as they can, but like Mike said, they get 'expedited' requests all the time."

"Yeah, but we're special now."

"You're always special, Tyler."

"Damn straight." He glanced around the parking lot. "Thanks again for having my back in there."

"Didn't have your back. I gave him my opinion."

"Still, *gracias*. What are you gonna do with your evening?"

"Keep digging. I feel like we're missing something."

"No parties to attend?"

"No," Meredith scoffed. "Going to comb through those photos

over dinner, have a glass of wine, call my daughter, tell her good-night, and turn in."

"Don't party too hard," Tyler said, breaking from Meredith to go to his car.

"You too."

"Don't worry. I ain't got no kids to call," he said, opening the door. "Goodnight, Somerset."

"Goodnight, Tyler."

*

Tyler climbed into the driver's seat and put the key in the ignition, but didn't start the engine.

Instead, he watched as Meredith got in her car and drove away.

Once she was out of sight, he took out his phone.

He scrolled down to a rarely used number in his contact list. Meredith had said it wasn't necessary to call him yet, but Tyler saw no harm in it. After all, it probably was an admin error that caused the weird results on Bowers' background check, but after the ribbing he had received that morning, why not show a little initiative?

Tyler dialed and the call went immediately to voicemail.

"The number you have dialed is not available," the automated woman announced. "Please leave a message after the tone."

Beeeeeeeep.

"I'm sorry," Tyler said. "I was trying to get in touch with Simon Templar. I guess I got the wrong number."

He hung up and started counting backwards from thirty.

At fourteen, his phone rang with a call from a blocked number.

Tyler answered. "Yo."

"As I live and breathe, Detective Foles," the voice on the other end said. "To what do I owe the honor of this inconvenience?"

"'Sup, Granger?"

Tyler had only met "Granger" face-to-face once when his unit raided an apartment that was a hub for churning out high-quality fake IDs.

As agents swarmed the apartment, which was filled with computers, boxes of PVC cards, magnetic strip encoders, bottles of UV ink, and holographic decals to match the licenses of every state, Tyler found an exit cut into the wall of the back bedroom. Tyler went through and began chasing a guy in his mid-twenties with an elongated nose, bird's nest of hair, and thick glasses into the stairwell. The guy was trying to use his cellphone and run down the stairs at the same time. His feet tangled, sending him tumbling and causing him to drop his cellphone. Tyler quickly grabbed the phone and drew his weapon, which lead to a standoff on the landing.

Tyler asked him his name. He said it was Granger. Tyler knew that he couldn't bust him, since he wasn't in the apartment, but they both knew he had been, so Tyler made him a deal. He told Granger he would never go after any of the contacts in the guy's phone if he agreed to help Tyler with getting backgrounds on people from time to time. He gave Granger his card and told him he had twenty-four hours to get in touch or he would start going after the contacts in Granger's phone.

To Tyler's surprise, Granger called him a few hours later and agreed.

While it was one of the most illegal things Tyler had ever done during his time in narco and vice, it was also, without a doubt, one of the best decisions he had ever made.

It very quickly blossomed into a strange sort of professional relationship. They would never meet up for beers or catch a ballgame, but they came to hold each other in mutual respect.

"I need you to run a profile for me," Tyler said.

"Really? I heard you were out of the vice game."

"Still in the game, just got called up to the big leagues."

"Good for you, I guess."

"Don't worry. I'm sure you're still pulling in more scratch than me."

"Detective Foles, my man, you have no idea. If you ever want to make some cash on the side, I'm sure we could—"

"I'm gonna give you what I got," Tyler said, cutting him off before any offers were made.

"Which is?"

"Name, social security, address, driver's license."

"You sure he's dirty or are you exploring?"

"Exploring. You got a pen?"

"Yeah. Fire away."

Tyler read out Scott Bowers' information.

"How soon do you need it?" Granger asked.

"As soon as you can get it."

"I only ask because I'm working on setting up a fake ID for the daughter of a state representative. You might know him. It's—"

"Granger?"

"Yeah?"

"Stop showing off."

Granger laughed. "It's what I do."

"Call me when you find something."

"*If* I find something," Granger said and hung up.

Chapter 26

Greg Ansley stepped onto the back porch of his house and inhaled the cool night air. The glass in his hand was filled with what? Three fingers? Four fingers? Let's just call it a lot of whiskey.

It may not have been the best thing for his state of mind but who cared?

At the moment, it was the only comfort he had.

There was no comfort in playing with Anthony or holding him in his lap. There was no comfort to be found at his wife's side in the bed upstairs.

He had lied to her. He had lied to everyone.

The lies were going to destroy him—not just the lies about that morning, but the lies about his entire life.

As he thought about his inevitable demise, he happened to glance to his left.

Scott Bowers, that perfect example of suburban masculinity, the kind of guy Greg was certain the women of the neighborhood fantasized about as they made love to their husbands, was fixing the fence that divided their properties. It was a strange time to be working on the fence, but when you didn't have an exhausting wife and son, who knew what you would have the energy for at all hours.

Scott clearly sensed Greg's stare, because he looked up and waved.

Greg toasted his full glass of whiskey but quickly lowered it, worried that Scott might judge him.

Suddenly, Scott dropped the screwdriver in his hand and checked his phone.

He seemed to stare at it for an inordinate amount of time.

"Someone send him a novel or something?" Greg mumbled in a whiskey-laden accent.

*

Scott continued staring at the text on his phone.

His monitoring service had sent him another alert.

He did his best to keep his face placid, knowing that Greg was watching. He wanted to convey that it was a harmless text, but it was so much more.

His monitoring service wasn't some generic company everyone saw commercials for on television. Scott used a "service" that didn't advertise, anywhere. It was able to detect when anyone attempted to examine his carefully constructed life but unfortunately, he couldn't stop whoever was looking. He could only see who was trying to access his credit, social security, criminal records, etc. The service, which was really an automated computer program, was able to instantly trace the email and IP of whoever made the request. The first request, which had been made a mere two days ago, had come from Detective Meredith Somerset of the CCPD.

This time, the one doing the digging had an email address that started with "slideofruin".

Someone thought they were being awfully clever but Scott saw through it in an instant.

"Slide of ruin" was an anagram of "iron sulfide", which was better known as "fool's gold".

173

Scott knew this was coming, but this was faster than he had anticipated.

He picked up the screwdriver from the grass and carried it to the backdoor of the garage, no longer caring if Greg was watching him.

Once inside the garage, Scott hung the screwdriver on the pegboard and surveyed the wall. The tools were spaced apart perfectly, created a pleasing aesthetic.

From there, he went through the door and into the house. He sat at the kitchen table and wondered who was trying to peek behind the curtain.

He had to get ahead of this. He had to take action or everything he'd worked for was over.

He took out his phone and dialed.

Chapter 27

"I love you, too, Mom."

Meredith waited for Allison to end the call and then placed the phone on the table to resume studying the crime scene photos on her laptop, but no sooner had she set the phone down than it began to buzz.

She checked the screen.

"What the—?" she whispered and hit answer. "Heather?"

"Hey, Meredith. You got a minute?"

Heather's voice was low, as if she was worried about being overheard.

"Sure. Is everything all right?" Meredith asked.

"Yeah … well … Hold on a sec. I'm going to step outside."

There's no way things are all right if you have to step outside, Meredith thought.

"Where's Pete?" she asked.

"He's in his office, grading papers."

Meredith heard a door quietly close on Heather's end.

"Okay," Heather said, a little louder. "I'm outside now."

"What's up?"

"I'm really sorry for calling. I know it's kind of late, but I was waiting until you and Allison had said 'goodnight.'"

Oh, good, Meredith thought. *Now, you're eavesdropping on phone calls between me and my daughter.*

"What's going on?" she asked.

"I'm worried that I did something that might have upset Allison. She accidentally called me 'Mom' the other night. I told her it was okay if she wanted to call me that, but I should have spoken to you, first."

"It's all right," Meredith said, not adding that she felt Heather was correct.

"I know Pete's going to propose soon."

Meredith lightly laughed. "Everyone seems to know."

"Yeah. He's terrible at keeping secrets."

"Yes, he is," Meredith said, remembering how Pete had essentially asked her about how she'd like to be proposed to. That's not to say that the proposal was disappointing. Pete just wasn't very spontaneous.

"Meredith, I know that Allison is your daughter and you know I love Allison like she was my own, but there's a little bit more to it."

"Okay …"

"When Allison called me 'Mom', it meant everything to me because … I'm just going to say it: Pete and I won't be able to have kids."

"What?"

"When I was a junior in high school, I had pains in my stomach. We were pretty poor, and my parents really didn't approve of visits to the doctor. They told me I was fine, that I was being dramatic. Then, one afternoon, I passed out. I was taken to the hospital. Turns out, I had ovarian and uterine cysts that had become infected. They were able to remove the cysts, but there was too much scarring in my fallopian tubes and uterus and, well, that was that."

"Heather. I don't know what to say … I'm so sorry."

In addition to her genuine sympathy, Meredith was mortified.

One of the fears that plagued her when she knew Pete and Heather were in it for the long haul, was that they would have a child and favor it over Allison. It was a stupid fear, and one that Meredith now felt like a monster for considering.

"There's really nothing to say. It's rare, but it happens," Heather replied.

Meredith's heart broke.

She had never really thought of her own ability to have children as anything other than a given.

Looking back, Meredith realized that she had even considered it a nuisance. When she'd learned she was pregnant with Allison, she'd worried how it might interfere with her career. Of course, any doubts were obliterated when she held Allison for the first time. Picturing her life without Allison was unimaginable.

"Does Pete know?"

"Yeah. I told him when things started getting serious. I was worried because I knew how much he loves being a dad. We hadn't talked about it in a while, but he brought it up recently. That's when I knew he was thinking about proposing. He's a traditional type of guy, so I knew that getting married would come first."

"What did he say about …?"

"Having kids?"

"Yeah."

"He talked about adopting. I don't know if I'm ready for that, but when Allison called me 'Mom' … I've lived for years knowing I can never have kids of my own. I know we're all close and she's your daughter, but to hear someone you love and are raising call you that when you've told yourself that it will never happen … I can't tell you what that meant to me."

"Heather, you are an amazing mother."

"Thank you but I want you to know; I'm not going to ask Allison to call me 'Mom'. I'm going to leave that up to her, but if she does, I want to know if you're okay with that."

"Absolutely," Meredith replied. There was still an involuntary flash of resentment, but she wouldn't give it air, not after what Heather had just told her.

"And it goes without saying that you're still 'Mom.'"

Meredith laughed.

Heather took another deep breath. "Okay. I should get myself together and head back inside before Pete comes looking for me."

"Yeah. I should get back to work. I really appreciate you talking to me."

"Thank you for understanding. Do you want to set up a time to sit down and talk to Allison?"

Meredith thought it over. "You know what? You talk to her. I think it'll be better. Just let her know that I'll support her decision and that I love her very much."

"I will. Goodnight."

"Goodnight, Heather."

Meredith hung up the phone and flopped back onto the couch, surprised at how tired she suddenly was.

Once again, her phone began to buzz.

Now what? she thought.

The caller ID displayed a number she didn't recognize.

"This is Somerset," she said, bringing the phone to her ear.

"Good evening, detective. It's Scott Bowers."

Meredith sat up. "Mr. Bowers. Hi."

"I'll keep this brief. I know it's late, but I was hoping I could speak with you and Detective Foles tomorrow morning at my house. It's regarding the case."

"Uh, sure. Can you tell me what it's about, specifically?"

"It's a little delicate. I think it would be best to explain it in person. Would that be all right?"

"That would be fine. What time are you available?"

"I'm working from home tomorrow, so I'm available all day, but the earlier, the better."

"How does eight o'clock sound?"

"That would be perfect."

"Great. Detective Foles and I will be there at eight."

"Your coffee will be waiting."

Meredith chuckled. "Sounds like a plan."

"Until then, have a good night, detective."

"You, too."

Scott hung up.

Meredith looked at her phone for a moment, then dialed.

The line rang … and rang … and rang …

"Come on," she grumbled. "Pick up."

She cursed as Tyler's recorded voice sounded in her ear.

"You have reached Tyler Foles. You know how this works."

Beeeeep.

"Tyler, it's Meredith. Need to talk to you. Scott Bowers just called. He wants us to be at his place at eight o'clock tomorrow morning. He wouldn't get into it over the phone. Said it was 'delicate'. Call me as soon as you get this."

Meredith hung up.

Chapter 28

Meredith tapped her finger against the paper coffee cup, the contents of which were long gone. She had already given up her seat on the covered patio and was now standing on the sidewalk in the drizzling rain.

She knew that Scott had said that coffee would be waiting for her, but it was just out of habit that she needed coffee first thing upon waking. She would have no problem enjoying Bowers' brew.

Tyler hadn't returned her call from the previous evening. He did, however, respond to an early morning text and agreed to meet her at the coffeeshop.

Meredith checked her phone. Ten minutes late.

You've got to be kidding me, she thought.

*

A couple of miles away, Tyler was also checking the time on his phone as he quickly exited the brick building from his morning visit.

He cursed and began typing.

*

Meredith's phone buzzed.

Be there in ten, the message from Tyler read.

"Un-freakin'-believable," she quietly said.

They needed to leave ten minutes ago if they were going to be on time for their interview with Scott and the light rain meant that it would take even longer.

Meet me at Bowers, she messaged back and walked to her car.

As she slid into the driver's seat, she received his response.

You got it, boss.

She wanted to erupt. She wanted to call him right then and there and chew his flippant ass out, but it would have made her even more late. Hopefully, he would arrive at Scott Bowers' house a few minutes after her.

"Un-freakin'-believable," she repeated and started the car.

*

"Detective Somerset," Scott said upon opening the door. "Please, come in."

"Thank you."

Meredith stepped into the foyer.

The rain had picked up on the drive over and she had gotten a decent soak hustling from her car, which she had parked in the street.

"Let me help you with that," Scott said, assisting her out of her jacket.

Meredith didn't have much of a chance to decline, which protocol dictated. Scott was a possible murder suspect. There were a lot of suspects, and he seemed fairly harmless, but she shouldn't let him stand behind her. However, it happened so quick, the fastest way to get him back in her line of sight was to go along with the polite gesture.

Of course, he made no sudden moves. He didn't go for her weapon. Meredith didn't expect him to. It had been a flash of police instincts, and then it was gone.

He hung her jacket on the stand next to the door.

"Thanks, again," Meredith said.

"I'm sorry. I should have told you to park in the driveway to save yourself from the rain."

"It's all right."

"Will Detective Foles be joining us?"

"He's running a little late. The rain."

Scott smiled. "Sometimes, I miss going into the office, but not on mornings like this."

"Believe me. You really don't."

As Scott closed the door and reengaged the deadbolt, Meredith noticed the small, abstract painting that was mounted to the wall next to the door that hadn't been there before. It was streaks and splashes of reds, yellows, greens, and blues. There appeared to be no focal point or definitive shapes. It was eye-catching, made even more so by its odd placement on the wall. It was off-center, as though the painting itself wasn't framed by anything.

Meredith pointed. "This is new, isn't it?"

"Yes. I wanted to change things up. It's called 'Meditation' by a man named Gerhard Richter. Ever heard of him?"

"No."

"He's a German visual artist."

"He painted this?"

"Yes. Well, no. He painted the original. This is a high-quality print. The original would set me back a couple million."

"It's stunning," Meredith said, finding the only adjective that seemed to fit.

"It is," Scott concurred. "I love it because it's a different painting every time I look at it."

"It's beautiful, but I'm sure you've got things to get to. Shall we?"

"Of course."

Scott led her down the hall to the kitchen and offered her a seat at the table.

"I'm sorry. I was running a little behind and haven't made the coffee yet," he apologized.

"That's okay. I think I'm good on the coffee."

"Don't tell me you already had coffee when you knew you were coming here. I was looking forward to sharing a brew that was delivered yesterday from Hawaii."

"Maybe next time."

"With all due respect, Detective Somerset, I hope there won't be a next time the police come to my home to talk to me about a murder."

"Fair enough. So, what was it that you wanted to talk to us about?"

Scott walked over and sat in the chair around the corner of the table from Meredith with the door to the basement behind him.

"I'm not sure if you've already checked to see if I logged in to my workout account the morning of the murder."

"No, not yet."

"I know it's not an airtight alibi."

"Is that what you wanted to talk about?" Meredith asked.

He took a moment to look down at the table before meeting her eyes and smiling. His teeth gleamed.

"No. It's not."

*

"Come on!" Tyler groaned over the patter of rain and the incessant *woosh* of the windshield wipers. He was inching along I-85. He only had three more exits to go, but at this rate, it was going to take at least another fifteen minutes to get there.

His phone, which was lying on the passenger seat, began to ring.

"Shit," he muttered, assuming it was Meredith calling to let him have it for being late, again.

He glanced at the caller ID. The number was blocked.

Tyler hit the answer button and put it on speaker phone.

"Hello?"

"Detective. It's Granger."

*

"I know that a standard part of an investigation like this one, is to run background checks on anyone possibly involved," Scott said. "And I assume you ran one on me?"

"Yes ..." Meredith answered.

The hairs on her arms prickled.

Scott studied her.

"Find anything interesting?" he asked.

*

"What's up?" Tyler asked.

"I've been digging into that guy you told me to check out: Scott Bowers."

"Yeah. What have you got?"

Granger went quiet.

"Yo?" Tyler asked.

"Is this guy for real?"

"What are you talking about?"

"Dude's dead."

Tyler's grip on the steering wheel tightened. "Talk fast."

"I started tracking him down based off of the social security number you gave me, and man, did it take me on a trip."

Tyler's pulse began to spike.

"There's a Scott Bowers who had a nearly identical social security number, just one off, but he died ten years ago. *Your* Scott Bowers has been using *that* Scott Bowers' social security number."

"Then, who is this guy?" Tyler asked.

"No idea, but he's someone who doesn't want to be found."

Tyler yanked the wheel, swerving onto the shoulder of the road, and gunned the engine.

*

"There were some discrepancies," Meredith said, her body tensing.

"Discrepancies …" Scott smiled at her. "Detective Somerset, may I show you something?"

"What is it?"

"The truth."

They stared at one another.

"Mr. Bowers, I think it might be best if—"

Scott slowly stood from his chair.

Meredith was instantly on her feet, her hand ready to go for her gun.

Scott calmly turned, keeping his hands out to the sides, and walked toward the basement door.

"Mr. Bowers, I need you to stop right there."

"I'm going to walk very slowly and keep my hands visible the entire time," he said, continuing his slow pace to the door.

"Mr. Bowers," she said forcefully.

He opened the basement door. The light below was on. Scott began gradually descending the stairs.

Meredith raced to the door, keeping him in sight.

Scott slowly laced his fingers behind his head as he continued downward.

"Stop now!" she commanded.

"It's this way," he said quietly.

Meredith hesitated.

He wasn't complying with her orders but his hands were visible and he was going very slowly.

She didn't want to draw her firearm. She knew that it changed the dynamic of every situation. Innocent or guilty, people naturally panicked when a gun was pointed at them. She felt that she still had control over what was happening. She followed him down the stairs, staying a few feet back in case he were to suddenly turn. Her hand hovered close to her gun.

In her pocket, her phone began to ring.

*

"Pick up the fucking phone, Meredith!" Tyler shouted as the ring tone chirped from the passenger seat.

Horns blared all around him as he flew past the line of traffic to his left, the tires spewing gravel in his wake.

The chirping stopped.

"Hi, this is Meredith Somerset. Please leave a mess—"

"FUCK!"

"—age and I'll get back to you."

Beep.

"Somerset! Get out of there! Scott Bowers is not who he says he is! Get the fuck out, now!"

*

Meredith wasn't going to answer her phone.

No way was she going to take her attention off Scott as he led her across the basement to an open door. The room beyond was pitch black.

"Okay. That's enough," she said. "Stop right there."

"It's in here," he replied, inching closer to the door.

"Mr. Bowers, you have to stop." Her hand wrapped around the grip of her Sig Sauer.

Scott slowly stepped inside the door of the darkened room and turned to face her.

"I'm going to show you," he said.

Her thumb flicked open the catch on the holster. "Do not move."

Very slowly, Scott brought one of his hands down from behind his head, keeping it where she could see it.

"Stop!" she commanded.

For a brief second, his hand disappeared behind the doorframe. There was a *click*, and he was bathed in light.

Meredith stared wide-eyed at what was behind him. Her jaw dropped.

In an instant, she pulled the gun from its holster and leveled it directly at his chest.

"ON THE GROUND! GET ON THE GROUND, NOW!"

*

The back end of Tyler's car fishtailed across the wet pavement as he whipped through the turn onto Willow Lane.

He hadn't wasted any more time trying to call Meredith. If she wasn't answering, she was in trouble. The confirmation was there, right in front of him; Meredith's car parked on the street in front of Scott Bowers' house.

The tires of Tyler's car hissed, fighting for traction as he applied the brakes. For a split second, he was sure he was going to skid into the back end of her car, but the tires found purchase and the car stopped with an inch or two to spare.

Seconds later, Tyler was racing across the yard, through the rain, gun in hand. He hurdled onto the porch. Water dripped from his hair into his eyes as he reached for the handle.

It wouldn't budge.

"Somerset!" he yelled.

"Tyler!" Meredith yelled from inside. "Don't—!"

But Tyler was already in motion. His foot was in the air. He kicked just below the handle, throwing all his strength and weight into his leg, morphing it into a battering ram.

The resistance sent a shockwave throughout his entire body, but the door didn't stand a chance. It violently swung inward. A large piece of the doorframe fell to the ground.

Tyler raised his gun, his heart pounding.

He raced inside to see Meredith coming toward him, her arms out, palms up in a pleading gesture.

"Whoa! Whoa! Whoa! Stop!" she yelled.

Tyler quickly turned his gun away and took his finger off the trigger.

They both had their hands up and stared at one another. They leaned against the walls to steady themselves.

"Goddamn, Somerset. What is going on?" he asked.

"I was going to tell you not to break down the door," she replied breathlessly.

"Detective Foles?"

Tyler glanced down the hall to the kitchen to see Scott Bowers sitting in a chair at the kitchen table with his hands cuffed behind his back.

"Won't you come in?"

Chapter 29

"My real name is Scott Rennick. I lived in Chicago for a few years before moving to Atlanta."

The man they had previously known as Scott Bowers was calmly sitting at the table with his hands cuffed behind him as Meredith and Tyler listened from their chairs on the other side.

This new person was a lot like the Scott Bowers they knew: tranquil, polite, articulate.

"I assume you found out that the real Scott Bowers passed away some time ago?"

"Yeah," Tyler said. "You have anything to do with that?"

"No. It was just a name found by the man who set up my false ID."

"Cool," Tyler said wryly.

Meredith let Tyler take the lead since he obviously knew more than she did.

"So, why don't you tell us, Mr … I don't know. Which do you prefer? Rennick or Bowers?" Tyler asked.

"You can call me 'Scott.'"

"Okay, *Scott*," Tyler said, interjecting a little derision. "You want to tell us about the name change, why you lied to us, and what is with the little medieval playroom you got in your basement?"

"First of all," Scott said, "I want to be clear that I wasn't lying about what I did or my whereabouts the morning of that girl's murder. That was all true."

"Why don't you tell us what's going on and then we'll be the judge of that, yeah?" Tyler asked.

Scott nodded.

"As I said, my real name is Scott Rennick, and I used to live in Chicago. I was an architect there, as well. I ... I enjoy physical pleasure and I have very unique tastes."

"Is that what we're calling that?" Tyler asked with a nod toward the basement door.

"You can call it what you'd like, detective."

Meredith felt that he wasn't being a smartass with Tyler. His demeanor was confident, accommodating, as though he wasn't in handcuffs, and there wasn't a sex room in his basement.

"I enjoy different, you could even say 'extreme', physical sensations. I also enjoy inflicting them."

"Yeah? And who do you like inflicting them on?" Tyler asked.

"I'm coming to that, detective."

"Let's speed it up, because I'm getting antsy."

Scott glanced at Meredith but she was letting Tyler have the floor.

"I enjoy a multitude of partners. I rarely like experiencing my tastes with the same woman more than once."

"That's gotta be rough," Tyler said. "Something like that down there? That requires some serious trust. Trust takes time and then to only be interested in one trip to the playground? That doesn't seem too efficient." Tyler leaned forward. "But there's a way around that, though, isn't there Mr. Bowers or Rennick? Oh, sorry, I mean, 'Scott' ... You been hiring girls?"

"Yes," he answered, his demeanor unchanged.

"Is that what got you in trouble back in Chicago?"

"Yes."

"Well, okay then, Scott," Tyler said, sitting back in his chair. "Let's hear it."

"Very well." He shifted his weight and cleared his throat. "I grew up in Chicago and starting in my teens, I knew I had these urges, but I also knew that I needed to keep them under control. I was fascinated by them, but as you said, it takes trust, which takes time. I was able to enjoy my tastes and keep them under wraps. Then, as I got older and a little more successful, I decided to explore. I wasn't interested in waiting for someone to trust me, so I began hiring women."

"I'm sure all of them were willing," Tyler smirked.

"Absolutely. I may be a fetishist, Detective Foles, you could even call me a sadist, but I'm being totally honest when I tell you that every woman I asked to join me—"

"Every woman you *hired*," Tyler corrected.

"Yes, *hired*," Scott admitted, slightly annoyed. "They were fully aware of what we would be doing and agreed. We used safe words and at any point, if they felt that they were in danger, they were free to leave."

"And you just expect us to believe that because you're being so honest with us now, right Mr. Bowers or Rennick, or are you going to tell us a different name in a few minutes?" Tyler asked.

"I know I have nothing to corroborate what I'm telling you, but it is what happened."

"It's not all that happened," Meredith said, finally speaking up. "What made you change your identity?"

Scott hesitated and the annoyance was replaced with a touch of shame. "I do enjoy younger women."

"I'll bet you do," Tyler sneered.

"Let me clarify; I do not mean *underage*," Scott said, as if the word tasted foul in his mouth. "That does not hold any interest for me. Only consenting adults."

"Sure. So, what happened?" Tyler asked.

"I asked every woman their age to specifically avoid something like that."

"You check their IDs?"

"I assume you've worked in this field, Detective Foles?"

"Oh yeah. Got a lot of experience *in this field*."

"Then you know there is a difference between how people are prosecuted for soliciting a prostitute and soliciting a minor."

Tyler shrugged. It was true. The difference was a decade in prison.

"You get caught with a minor?" Tyler asked.

Scott's posture sagged. "There was someone I went to who represented the women."

Tyler sighed. "Come on, man. These women don't have someone *representing* them. They don't have agents. They're called 'Johns' and if they're underage, they're not 'women'. That's a kid, and don't tell me you blame them for you getting busted."

"It is what happened, and no, I'm not blaming them. I want to make it clear that I did my best to avoid something like that. I asked her repres—I mean, her 'John', her age. He told me that she was nineteen. She told me that she was nineteen. I took them at their word."

"And how old was she?"

"Sixteen."

Meredith flinched. Tyler let out a light whistle.

"There was a sting. I was arrested, as were a lot of other people. I spent five years in prison and was released for good behavior. I was placed on probation, but as you know, that wasn't the end of it."

"You had to register as a sex offender?" Tyler asked.

"Yes. For the rest of my life, everywhere I went, I had to go around and tell everyone what I had done. I couldn't explain the finer details. Everyone just thought that I was a pervert. There's no coming back from that. No one was going to hire me. No one was going to rent me an apartment, much less let me buy a house. I knew that if I was ever going to have a life, I had to leave the old one behind. I found a guy who could forge IDs and create false identities. It was very expensive, but it was my only chance.

192

He was able to craft a new life for me. It wasn't ironclad, nothing ever is, but all you need is just enough to cause a little confusion; something you can blame on the system."

"Like using someone else's social security number?" Tyler asked.

"Yes. I was able to start over here in Atlanta, almost entirely free from my past."

"This is all very interesting," Tyler said. "But I know guys like you and they don't change. So, here's the million-dollar question, Scottie: you been hiring girls here in town?"

"Yes."

"Did you hire the girl we found in the street?" Tyler asked. "She freak out in your little sex dungeon down there and make a run for it? Were you choking her so hard, you didn't hear her say the safe word?"

"No. What I told you about that morning was the truth. I had nothing to do with her death."

"Still not particularly sold on that."

"I'm telling you now, without a lawyer present. I showed you the room. I called you here to my home. I'm telling you the truth."

"Only because we were going to find out. Don't play this 'I'm-so-honest-that-I-couldn't-have-done-it' bit. That's not where you want to go, right now."

"I had nothing to do with the girl found in the street," Scott reiterated.

"We're still gonna have to dig around. You said you were hiring girls here in Atlanta. You're gonna have to tell me the name of your John."

"Not a chance."

Tyler cocked his head. "Excuse me?"

"I've told you everything I'm going to tell you. I know that I'm not a perfect person. I've made many mistakes, but I'm trying to help you, and I will continue to do so, but if you want to know anything more about my 'activities', you're going to have to arrest me. Then you'll only deal with me through my lawyer."

Tyler looked at Meredith and back to Scott. "I ain't got a problem with that."

"Detective Foles, can I talk to you for a second?" Meredith asked.

Before he could answer, she stood and walked into the living room.

Tyler blinked in confusion and gave another glance at Scott.

"Excuse us," he said and got up to follow her.

They stopped on the far side of the room with Scott's back to them.

"We can't pop him," she said, keeping her voice low. "At least, we can't pop him right now."

Tyler stared at her as if she was speaking some alien language.

"I'm sorry? What the hell do you mean we can't pop him?" he asked.

"Think about it; if we arrest him now, we're going to have to bring in vice. We'll have two teams working two crimes on one street. Vice is going to have to interview everyone on Willow Lane, and who knows how many more in the neighborhood. It would be a shit show and our case will be all but over."

Tyler fought to keep his voice down. "You've got to be kidding me, Somerset! The dude confessed to hiring girls! He's got a freaking romper room in his basement. You're telling me this *isn't* our guy?"

"No. I don't think he is, and neither do you."

Tyler's hesitation said as much. He looked around, searching for an answer. "Maybe he's having some hanky-panky with her, lets it slip about his past, she runs, he grabs her in the street, and kills her to shut her up."

"You're trying to make it fit. Alexa only arrived in town a few days ago. You think in that time, she got hooked up with a high-class John, and was sent here? If she had, he never would have shown us the basement. He never would have told us about his past. He would have lawyered up and said nothing. You know it and I know it: He's not our guy."

194

"Somerset, we can't let him walk. I've dealt with his type for years. He's gonna keep doing what he does, which is prey on women."

"I'm not saying we let him go forever. I'm saying we can't do this now. It will blow our case to hell and he probably beats this."

"No. No way he beats this. He just confessed to everything. I say we read him his rights and get this show on the road."

"Really? How did you find out about his ID?"

Tyler looked away from her.

"You called your guy, didn't you, even when I told you not to?" Meredith asked. "You want to explain that to his lawyer?"

Tyler had nothing to counter with, other than, "We can't let this guy walk, Somerset."

"He's not walking. We'll put him on a leash."

"And you think he's going to calmly wait for us to wrap up our case and *then* pop him?"

"We'll keep an eye on him."

Tyler snorted in disbelief. "This is a goddamn joke. He slipped the system before. He'll do it again in a heartbeat."

Meredith had had enough. "If you've got a problem with my decision, talk to Sergeant Wheaton."

Tyler froze.

"You telling me to rat you out?" he asked.

"I'm doing what I think is best and I'm telling you to do what you think is best. If that's going to Sergeant Wheaton, then do it and welcome to the big leagues."

He stared at her.

"Your call, Tyler. What's it gonna be?"

Tyler wetted his lips and then reluctantly turned and walked back to the table.

He took out his skeleton cuff key and worked Scott's wrists.

"You're catching one hell of a break today," Tyler growled in his ear.

The cuffs clicked open. Tyler tossed them back to Meredith and walked around to face Scott.

"If you've got any vacations coming up, I'd cancel them. We'll keep in touch. And no more girls. I see or hear of any girls coming through that door, we're taking you up on that offer of talking to your lawyer. Got it?"

Scott nodded.

Tyler turned and walked down the hall and out the broken door.

Scott and Meredith watched him go.

"Don't worry about the door," Scott said, rubbing his wrists. "I'll take care of it."

Meredith nodded. "And everything he just said about leaving town? He's not wrong."

"I understand," Scott replied.

*

Meredith emerged from the front door as Tyler neared his car.

"We're not done, Tyler," she said, striding through the rain.

"Really? What else you got?"

"Where were you this morning?" she asked, stepping into the street and standing in front of him.

"You serious? You're gonna come at me for being a couple minutes late when you just let that guy off the hook?"

"Those couple of minutes could have gotten me killed."

"Then you shouldn't have gone in there."

"You said you were only a few minutes behind. It was more than a few minutes. Are you gonna be a few minutes late next time?"

Tyler snapped. "You really wanna know where I'm at?"

"Yes, and none of this 'it won't happen again' or 'I got the message', because obviously, you haven't."

"Fine," he said. "Follow me."

Chapter 30

Meredith pulled into the spot next to Tyler and killed the engine.

Through the raindrops spattering on the windshield, she stared at the wooden sign that sat next to the concrete walkway leading to the entrance of the squat, brick building: *New Horizons Care & Learning Center*.

Tyler stepped out of his car and began walking toward the door without so much as a glance in her direction.

Meredith got out and followed.

Even though the rain maintained its steady drum, Tyler made no effort to hurry to the door to save them from getting wet. Nor did he hold the door open for Meredith when they reached the front of the building.

They entered the lobby where a young man sat behind the reception desk.

"Mr. Foles. You're back."

"Hey, Nate," Tyler said, running his hand through his hair, shaking out some of the water. "Yeah. I just wanted to introduce her to a friend."

Nate glanced past Tyler to Meredith, even though Tyler had made no physical acknowledgement of her presence. For her part, Meredith was taking in the area behind the reception desk.

It resembled a kindergarten classroom. At different tables, adults were working with children of varying ages with different learning disabilities.

"Is it all right to see her?" Tyler asked.

"Sure," Nate replied. "She's in her room, working with Dr. Holland."

"Cool. Thanks, Nate."

Tyler walked toward one of the hallways that branched off from the lobby.

Meredith was rooted to the spot for a moment longer, still trying to process what she was seeing, until she noticed that Nate was staring at her. Tyler was a few yards away and wasn't slowing down. She went after him, lengthening her stride to catch up.

They entered the hallway, passing open door after open door. Meredith caught a glimpse of the interior of each room as they passed. They appeared to be children's rooms. In some of the rooms, there were more children with advanced learning disabilities being assisted by adults.

Tyler slowed as they approached one of the open doors and came to a stop. He waited, listening.

From inside, Meredith could hear the voice of a woman speaking in a soothing tone.

"Good. Now, which is the fish …? There you go."

Tyler reached out and gently knocked.

"Yes?" the woman's voice softly answered.

Tyler stepped through the door and Meredith followed.

It was another child's room.

There were stuffed animals on the bed, a desk, and construction-paper butterflies on the walls. Sitting on the carpeted floor in the center of the room was a woman in her early fifties with glasses and chestnut hair. She was looking over the shoulder of a teenage girl with advanced Down's Syndrome. In the girl's lap was a large book with pictures.

The girl looked up at Tyler and her face blossomed into a wide smile.

She immediately put the book down, stood, went to Tyler, and embraced him in a hug.

"Hey, Hannah," he said, returning her embrace. He then spoke to Dr. Holland as he continued to hold her, since she showed no signs of letting go. "What are we working on?"

"Reading, and then some spatial exercises later," Dr. Holland replied. "What brings you back?"

"I wanted to introduce someone. Hannah?" he said, gently pulling away, which the girl resisted but Tyler was eventually able to get a little distance between them. "Hannah, I want you to meet a friend of mine."

For the first time since they'd had their standoff on Willow Lane, Tyler turned to Meredith.

"Hannah, this is my friend—Meredith."

With a little trepidation, but still smiling, Hannah stepped over to Meredith.

"Meredith," Tyler said, "this is my sister, Hannah."

Hannah held out her arms.

Tyler nodded to Meredith, who crouched down.

Hannah hugged her.

Meredith closed her arms around her and hugged her back.

"Hi, Hannah," she said.

Hannah gently squeezed. "Hi, Meredith," she said, clearly using a lot of effort to form the words.

Over Hannah's shoulder, Meredith looked at Tyler, whose face remained placid.

Hannah let go, walked back over to Tyler, and held his hand.

"We'll let you get back to your studies," Tyler said to Dr. Holland. "I just wanted them to meet." Tyler got down on one knee to better speak with Hannah at eye-level. "Listen, Hannah,

I'm going to talk to Meredith, but I'll be back to say goodbye in a little bit, okay?"

Hannah's eyes widened and she shook her head. "No!"

Tyler smiled while gently patting her arm. "It's okay, Hannah. It's okay. I'll be right back."

Hannah reached out and tightly embraced him while repeating, "No, no, no, no."

Meredith watched with a stunned expression as Tyler held Hannah and softly whispered, "It's okay … It's okay …"

Chapter 31

"I visit her every morning. It's the only time I can, really. She gets upset when I leave and sometimes, it takes a while to calm her down. It's been especially bad the past few days because there were a couple of weeks where I was getting ready for homicide that I didn't get to see her that much. It was rough on her ... It was rough on me, too."

They were sitting on a covered bench on the playground next to the building, watching the rain.

"Tyler, why didn't you tell me?"

"Can't have people knowing about this."

"What are you talking about? I would have understood."

"It's not about you, Somerset."

She stopped.

Tyler searched for the right words. "What I'm trying to say is that this isn't entirely on the legal side."

Meredith waited as Tyler continued to stare out at the rain.

"I didn't have the best of parents," he began. "Pops was a walking dumpster fire who left when I was five. Mom went to shit shortly after. Drugs. Drinking. One-night stands, sometimes for cash. When I was fourteen, she got pregnant with Hannah. No idea who the father was. We were in a world of hurt. Never had any money and Hannah needed care. I talked to some of Mom's dealers and got a job slinging. I was making enough money to get us by, but unfortunately, by the time I was seventeen, I got a little dust on my nose to deal with the stress."

"You were an addict?" Meredith asked.

"Anyone slinging who says they never took a taste is lying."

"You still use?"

Tyler quicky shook his head. "Those days are long gone."

Meredith felt that there was something wrong with his denial. She knew from her dealings with her father, and the number of times that he told her his drinking days were over, only to relapse a few days later, that a recovering addict never says their addiction is over, but she let Tyler continue despite her suspicions.

"I was keeping us afloat, trying to get Mom's life in order. Then, my guy got popped, along with all of his dealers, including me. The cop in charge of the sweep was a guy named Doc McElwee. Ever heard of him?"

"Not much. Sergeant Wheaton told me a little bit about him."

"They were friends from way back. Anyway, Doc takes notice of me, what I was doing, why I was doing it, and the fact that I was a minor. He also noticed that I was a lot smarter than my compatriots.

"The bust sent Mom over the edge. I was locked up and she didn't have any money coming in. She couldn't handle Hannah. I told Doc about my situation. Told him how I was trying to keep all of our heads above water and I was worried about Hannah and Mom. He went to go check on them. Found my mom in the living room. She had OD'd. Hannah was sitting next to her, waiting for her to wake up. She hadn't eaten in two days. The year before, I'd had Mom sign a life insurance policy, but Doc knew they wouldn't pay out for an overdose …" Tyler hesitated, as if struggling to continue, wondering if he even should continue. Meredith waited until he finally spoke. "So, he found the gun Mom kept in the apartment, and fired a bullet into her dead body to make the whole thing look like a robbery gone wrong. He even altered the autopsy report to say my mom's tox screen was clean and the bullet was the cause of death … The man risked everything for me.

"In exchange for his help, Doc told me that I was going into law enforcement. He didn't have to say anything. I would have done it. He was the father I never had. Being young and what I knew about slinging, I was fire in narco and moved up quick. Things were going great with Hannah. She was getting the care she needed. I would have been more than happy to live out the rest of my days in narco and vice. Then, three years ago, Doc took a bullet. He walked into a 7-11 as it was getting hit. Didn't try to stop the guy. Doc wasn't trying to be a hero. The perp just turned and shot him as he was coming through the door." Tyler bit his lip. "The man who saved my life bled out on the floor of a 7-11 because he happened to wander in at the wrong time. All the perp took was forty-eight dollars and a couple of tallboys of Steel Reserve. They never caught him … That's when I decided I was gonna work homicide … and here you find me, Somerset. That's the story."

They silently watched the rain.

"You could have told me, Tyler. I would have understood."

"I don't doubt that, but we're still getting payments from the insurance company. If they find out that Mom wasn't a botched robbery, it could be a problem for Hannah and me; but more importantly, I don't know if anyone in the department knows what Doc did. That's why I've kept this secret for as long as I have. If someone found out … The man saved my life. He saved Hannah's life. I don't want it getting out and staining his memory, you know?"

She nodded.

"But I promise you this, Somerset. You'll never walk into a suspect's place alone, again. You have my word."

Meredith believed him.

Chapter 32

Armed with the new information they had acquired over the past forty-eight hours, Meredith and Tyler returned to the precinct, determined to establish a definitive timeline of events.

Meredith printed out some of the crime scene photos. She and Tyler then set up shop next to the white markerboard in the corner of the bullpen. She drew a rough outline of Willow Lane, using crude rectangles for the houses, and writing the last name of the occupants on each one. She then taped the photos to the board. Once completed, she and Tyler stepped back to take it in.

"Okay," Meredith began. "For the moment, let's say we take our focus off of Scott Whatever as a suspect—"

"For the moment," Tyler reiterated.

"And what Trevor told us confirms our suspicion that it was someone on Willow Lane. Neither he nor Patricia Crawford heard a car pull up or drive away. So it's unlikely that Alice or her killer—"

"You mean Alexa," Tyler said.

"What?"

"You said Alice."

"I meant Alexa."

"Okay."

Meredith plowed ahead, eager to get past her verbal slip. "It's unlikely that Alexa or her killer ran very far and just happened to wind up on Willow Lane. Even with the fog, that would increase the odds that someone saw them. The most likely scenario is that she and the killer were somewhere nearby, and the killer returned to the same place after the murder."

"So, who's lyin'?"

Meredith studied the board.

"Again, taking a step back from Scott Whatever and working off our theory that the killer is a male, that leaves Dr. Richard Morgan, Greg Ansley, and your favorite, Mr. Thomas Whitaker," she said, writing the names in a column off to the side.

"And I don't like Whitaker's story about going for a jog that morning."

"Me neither," Meredith concurred.

"Maybe we should talk to Natalie Whitaker, again, but alone this time. Find out if his jogs were a regular thing or something that just happened to be a part of his routine that morning."

"Not a bad idea."

"Since I'm starting to agree with you that Scott Whatever is not our guy, I'm leaning toward Whitaker."

"Me too," Meredith said, using the marker to draw a circle around Thomas Whitaker's name.

Sergeant Wheaton's head popped out of his office.

"I've got Mike in the Morgue on the line. He wants to speak to you two."

Meredith and Tyler exchanged a questioning glance and walked across the bullpen to his office.

Sergeant Wheaton was circling back around his desk when they entered.

"Okay, Mike," he said in the direction of the phone on the desk. "I've got the detectives here."

"Detective Somerset?" Mike asked through the speaker phone.

"Yeah. Detective Foles is here, too. What's up?"

"I've got your lab results."

"That was fast," Meredith said.

"Well, we got you the special treatment, but I think we may have broken someone at the lab."

"Okay," Meredith said, confused. "Anything interesting in the results?"

"That's why I'm calling. Can you come down here, please?"

"Uh … sure."

"You should probably come too, Sergeant Wheaton."

*

The three of them rode the elevator down to the basement in silence.

They opened the doors to the morgue to find Mike waiting next to his laptop, which was resting on one of the cookie sheets.

"What's going on, Mike?" Sergeant Wheaton asked.

"First of all, thanks for coming down to speak to me, and before we begin, I'd like you to listen to something."

Mike took out his cellphone, tapped the screen a few times, put it on speakerphone, and then held it up.

A woman's automated voice filled the room. "You have … four … saved messages … First saved message …"

Beep.

"Hey, Mike. It's Jordie," a male voice said, dripping with sarcasm. "I just wanted to let you know that I received the request from you and Sergeant Wheaton to expedite your tests, and since Chickenshit Wheaton isn't answering his damn phone, I thought I'd call you, but it looks like you're also too chickenshit to answer your phone."

Meredith glanced sideways at Sergeant Wheaton, whose placid expression did not change.

"I'm so goddamn sick of everyone's goddamn 'expedite'

requests," Jordie continued. "Don't you assholes realize that if *everyone* is having their superiors app—"

There was a pause.

"Next saved message," the automated woman announced.

"I called back because I'm not done. Don't you assholes realize that if *everyone* is having their superiors approve their requests, the requests become goddamn meaningless?! I'm so goddamn sick of it that I've been running lab work nonstop for twenty-four goddamn hours. Am I getting overtime? Of course not. We can't have budgeting shitting their pants, but as long as it makes you feel special, and I don't have to hear from you people for a few goddamn days, well then I guess it's all worth—"

Pause.

"Next saved message."

"WORTH IT! I ran your samples with the nucleotide markers and did the comparison too, because you're *soooooo* special, and I just emailed you the results. I'm calling because you said that Chickenshit Wheaton was scared that the press was going to get a hold of some story. Well, if you see him, tell him I said 'good-chicken-shit-luck'!"

There was another pause.

Sergeant Wheaton sighed. "Well. That was—"

Mike held up a finger.

"Next saved message," the automated woman said.

"Hey. It's Jordie. Listen, sorry for blowing up your phone. It's, uh, it's been a long day. Anyway, I emailed you the results … and let's keep this between us, okay? … Bye."

"End of messages," the automated woman announced.

They all stared at Mike.

"I felt that if I had to listen to it, so should you," Mike said and returned the phone to his pocket.

"What is he talking about?" Sergeant Wheaton asked. "Why 'good luck'?"

Mike motioned to the laptop. "Check it out."

They stepped closer to the screen, which displayed numbers and graphs that were incomprehensible to Meredith.

"I decided to try to save us some time and batched your Jane Doe DNA samples with the samples we scraped from under her fingernails. I figured since we're asking for favors, let's get two for the price of one. Jordie thought I was asking for a comparison of the two, so he ran it."

"Any hits from the samples under her fingernails?" Tyler asked.

"Yeah," Mike answered.

"Who?" Meredith asked.

"Her."

Sergeant Wheaton blinked. "Wait. You're saying she scratched herself?"

"At first, that's what I thought the tests showed, but it's not," Mike said, indicating the screen, which had terms like "STR", "loci", "markers", and "polymers". He pointed at the bottom of the report, which displayed a number. "The DNA from under her fingernails confirms that her killer was a male, but that's not the interesting part."

"What is the 'interesting' part?" Tyler asked.

"Her killer shared forty-seven percent of her DNA."

"Oh god." Meredith breathed.

"Yeah." Mike nodded.

"Plain English, please," Sergeant Wheaton said.

"What I'm saying, Sergeant Wheaton, is that whoever killed your Jane Doe was her father."

Chapter 33

The late happy hour crowd buzzed around Meredith and Tyler as they sat at the bar in the neighborhood of Little Five Points. The bartender, a good-looking guy with sleeve tattoos and a beard that was trying to hide a scar on his neck, placed two fresh bottles from a local brewery in front of them.

"Thanks," Tyler said.

The bartender nodded and moved off to help other customers.

Tyler picked up his beer and turned to Meredith.

"Her dad offed her. I'd say this changes things."

"It changes what we're looking for, but not how we can look," Meredith replied before taking a sip.

"Come on, Somerset. We've got this guy's DNA. He lives on that street. Hell, we've spoken to him."

"What do you want to do? You want to ask all the grown men on Willow Lane to voluntarily submit to a DNA test?"

"Damn straight."

"You know we can't do that. You think Scott Whatever is going to give us his DNA? He's a registered sex offender. His DNA is already on file. If we ask, he's gonna bolt. Then there's Whitaker.

He would have a field day with that. But you knew that wasn't going to work even before you asked, right?"

He smiled. "Just making sure the bullshit in homicide is the same as narco and vice."

"Don't worry. It is."

They both took a swig of their beers.

Tyler began to pick at the label on his bottle, lost in thought. "Who does that, Somerset? Who strangles their daughter in the middle of the street outside their house?"

"Better question is 'why'. We can assume Alexa ran away from Sisters of Sacred Heart to find her parents, or at least her father, since she clearly found him."

"So, why kill her?"

"I still think it was an accident," Meredith said. "He was trying to keep her quiet."

"Do you think he was being considerate of the neighbors? What was so important that he tried to shut her up so hard, he accidentally killed her? Then, he slinks back home to his family like nothing happened. What was so important that he's pretending not to know who she was?"

"That is an excellent question," Meredith said.

"It's also very fucked up."

"That, too."

They took a few more sips and studied the crowd.

"How do you want to proceed?" Tyler asked.

"We keep this to ourselves. It would definitely catch the eye of any reporter. Also, if the killer doesn't know that we know, maybe we can use it to catch him in a lie."

"Please tell me we can start with my man, Whitaker."

"I agree but I don't think we should talk to him first."

"You want to work on Mrs. Whitaker? Find out some more about their marital bliss?"

"It's our best option."

"I like it, Somerset," Tyler said, tapping his bottle against hers. "I like it a lot."

*

"Dad's finally going to ask Heather to marry him," Allison said through the phone.

"Did he talk to you about it?" Meredith asked from her couch.

"He said he wanted to know if I was okay with it."

"Are you?"

"Yeah."

"Good."

"Heather talked to me, too," Allison said.

"Oh? About what?"

"She knows Dad's gonna ask her and she asked me to be a bridesmaid."

"Baby! That's great. You'll have so much fun." Meredith caught herself. "Wait. What did you tell her?"

"I said 'okay.'"

"That was very nice of Heather."

"Mom?"

"Yeah?"

"What does a bridesmaid do?"

Meredith momentarily wracked her brain and laughed. "Most of the time they wear unflattering dresses and think about how much better their own wedding is going to be."

"What?"

"Nothing, baby. Mommy was making a joke."

Allison grew quiet.

"Baby, it was a joke. I swear. Bridesmaids have a lot of fun. They help plan the wedding and help the bride get ready before the cerem—"

"She also talked to me about calling her 'Mom.'"

Meredith's breath caught in her chest. "And how did that go?"

"She didn't ask me to call her 'Mom.'"

"She didn't?"

"No. She said that if I wanted to, I could, and it would mean a lot to her but that it was up to me. She also said that no matter what, you were always going to be my mom, too."

Meredith felt relief that it was all out in the open and Heather had handled it better than she could have asked.

"So, are you going to call her 'Mom'?" Meredith asked.

"Is that okay?"

Meredith thought she had it under control, but suddenly her eyes burned and her throat closed. There was a whirlwind of emotions. A part of her was sad because she felt as though she was giving something up, but it was only a flash of pride and ego. To her surprise, she found that the stronger emotion she felt was happiness and pride in her daughter.

"Mom?"

"Baby, that's so great."

"You aren't mad?"

"No, baby. Not at all."

"You're sure?"

"I'm so sure. Heather loves you very much and she's raising you, too. Of course, you should call her 'Mom' if you want."

"Okay."

Meredith was finally able to steady her voice, now that it felt like a major hurdle had been cleared.

"Has your father talked about where he wants to have the wedding?"

"No. He only asked—"

Meredith's phone buzzed in her hand, announcing that there was another call. She checked the screen.

At first, it didn't register, but then the phone nearly fell from her hand.

"Allison? Sweetheart?"

"Yeah?"

"I am so sorry, but I have to go. I'm getting another call."

"Oh …"

"Baby, I really want to talk, but I have to take this, okay? It's important."

It has to be, Meredith thought.

"Okay," Allison answered.

"Thank you, baby. I love you and we'll talk more later, okay?"

"Okay."

"Goodnight. I love you."

"Love you too, Mom."

Allison hung up.

Meredith felt terrible for ending the call so abruptly, but she had to grab this one before it went to voicemail.

She took one last look at the screen to confirm that her eyes weren't playing tricks on her.

She took a deep breath and hit the answer button.

"Mom?" she asked.

"Hey, baby," Bethany Somerset replied.

It had been years since she had last heard her mother's voice but it was unmistakable, even if Bethany Somerset sounded tired and perhaps a bit softer.

It was also unnerving to hear her mother address her the same way Meredith addressed Allison, which is where she got it from.

"Is everything okay?" Meredith asked.

"Oh, yes. Everything is fine. I just wanted to speak to you. I know it's been a while."

A floodgate of contradicting thoughts opened in Meredith's mind.

What did her mother mean by *"Oh, yes. Everything is fine"*?

She hadn't spoken to Meredith in years, and the last conversation had ended in a way that precluded the next conversation from starting with "everything's fine".

"How are you?" her mother asked.

"I'm-I'm great, Mom."

"And how is … Allison?"

There it was. That little pause before she said Allison's name.

Meredith had named Allison at a time when she had hoped to repair her relationship with her mother. Instead of viewing it as a loving gesture, Bethany saw it as a constant, hurtful reminder of the daughter she had lost from the daughter she blamed for losing her.

Still, this was the first time they had spoken in years and her mother had made the effort, so Meredith was willing to let it slide.

"She's good. She's really good."

"And Pete?"

"He's good, too. He's getting married pretty soon."

"Oh that's great."

Her mother's uncertainty was understandable. Heather was just stepping into the picture the last time she and Meredith had spoken.

"It is great," Meredith said. "Heather's fantastic for Pete and she loves Allison."

"That's good to hear. And how are you feeling about it?"

Meredith sighed. "Not going to lie. There have been some moments that have been a little tough, but—"

She stopped and shook her head. She wasn't ready to share her insecurities in one or two minutes of conversation after years of silence.

"How are you?" Meredith asked, changing the subject.

"I'm fantastic."

Meredith waited for elaboration, but none came.

"Anything particular that's 'fantastic'?"

"There is," her mother said. "And it's sort of why I'm calling. I mean, I really wanted to talk to you, because I've met someone."

Meredith shut her eyes and hung her head.

After their family fell apart, Bethany Somerset had been

married and divorced twice. Meredith came to believe that her mother was trying to move on by starting a new family. It had been a disaster and was at the center of their final falling out. Meredith worried that the cycle was starting again.

"Mom …"

"No! Nothing like that. This isn't a relationship thing."

Meredith opened her eyes. "Okay. What is it?"

"I really want you to meet him."

"Why?" Meredith asked.

"You'll see."

Chapter 34

"Somerset …? Hey, yo, Somerset?"

Meredith blinked and turned her head from the car window to Tyler, who was watching her from the driver's seat.

"What?"

"Where did you just run off to?" Tyler asked.

"Sorry. My mind was wandering a little bit. What did you say?"

"How long after he leaves until we move?" Tyler asked with a nod toward the Whitaker's house. They were close enough to keep an eye out to see when Thomas Whitaker left for work, but far enough away that he hopefully wouldn't notice them.

"As soon as he's clear," Meredith answered. "I don't want to lose his wife if she tries to go to the store or anything."

"Cool."

Meredith cursed at herself for losing focus. She kept thinking about what was coming after work, when she was going to her mother's house to meet this mysterious stranger. Still, it was no excuse for being distracted, even if this was the tamest of stakeouts, but who would her mom want her to meet when the two of them hadn't spoken in years?

Meredith gritted her teeth.

It took all of fifteen seconds for you to get distracted again, she thought.

The garage door to the Whitakers' house began to roll upwards.

"There's our boy," Tyler said.

The black BMW emerged from the garage and backed down the drive. They watched as it rounded the corner and disappeared at the far end of Willow Lane.

"Let's go," Meredith said.

＊

Upon answering the doorbell and seeing the two detectives on her porch, Natalie Whitaker looked as though she was about to close the door in their faces.

"Mrs. Whitaker?" Meredith asked.

"I'm sorry. You just missed my husband. He'll be back later."

"Actually, ma'am, we'd like to speak to you, if that's okay."

"I—I don't think that's a good idea."

"It's nothing big," Tyler said. "Just a few more questions about that morning."

"I told you everything—"

"Mrs. Whitaker?" Meredith quietly said, and nodded to Natalie's arm, which was resting on the doorframe near her shoulder. The elevated position had caused the loose sleeve of her shirt to fall down to her elbow, exposing the sharp bruises on her forearm.

She quickly lowered her arm and pulled her sleeve down to cover her wrist.

She fidgeted and fumbled for something to say, but couldn't.

"May we come in?" Meredith lightly asked.

＊

"Mrs. Whitaker, we need to know if you're in any danger," Meredith said as they sat at the kitchen table.

217

At their mother's suggestion, Ashton and Kendall had retreated upstairs until the school bus arrived.

Natalie nervously laughed. "It's not what you think. We were in the kitchen and I slipped. Thomas happened to be right there. He grabbed me so I wouldn't fall."

Both Meredith and Tyler had heard similar, flimsy excuses in their separate lines of work and neither bought it for a moment.

Natalie tried to give them a reassuring smile but broke as if it was a physical weight that was too much to bear. She glanced back down the hall toward the stairs, checking to make sure that neither Kendall nor Ashton was eavesdropping before turning back to Meredith and Tyler.

"I'm leaving him," she said, little more than a whisper. "I've spoken to some lawyers. I'm still figuring out what I'm going to do."

"Do you need a place to stay?" Meredith asked, matching Natalie's volume.

"I'll be fine. I need to be here for the kids. It's only for a little while longer. He won't hurt me."

"Mrs. Whitaker," Meredith said. "You're not safe here. We can—"

"I'll be fine."

As Natalie stared at the table, Meredith caught Tyler's eye. This wasn't the conversation they thought they'd be having.

"I can't do it anymore," Natalie said. "I can't put up with the lying. I can't. Not anymore."

"What kind of lying?" Meredith asked.

"Thomas has cheated on me before. I know he's had affairs. It's just who he is but ..." She hesitated but realized that she had already crossed some line from which there was no going back. "He's in trouble, financially, which I guess means we both are. He's doing something to get out of it, but he won't tell me what."

218

"Those jogs in the morning," Meredith said. "Does he do that often?"

"No."

"He just happened to go for a run the morning that girl was found?" Tyler asked.

Natalie shifted uncomfortably in her chair. "I think he was meeting someone."

"Do you know who?"

She shook her head.

Meredith leaned toward her. "Mrs. Whitaker, do you think that your husband killed that girl?"

"… I know this is going to sound strange with all of his lies, but no, I don't think he did it."

"What makes you think that?" Tyler asked.

"Because he was so mad about it. Not upset that someone was killed, but that it was some sort of inconvenience for him. That's what he's like. It's all about him."

"But you can't be sure?"

"No, but he's not acting like he's scared of being caught or anything. He's upset because he says it's 'messing with his life'. He keeps saying, 'Couldn't whoever killed her have done it one block over.'"

*

"Well, that didn't go the way I expected," Tyler mumbled as they walked back to the car.

"Nope," Meredith replied.

They'd left Natalie Whitaker with instructions to call them or the police if she was in danger. Meredith had Natalie's number and told her that she would be checking in. At first, Natalie had resisted, but Meredith had assured her it would be confidential and her husband wouldn't know anything about it.

"You believe her?" Tyler asked as they reached the car. "You think he didn't do it?"

"If what she's saying is true, it doesn't sound like it, but I think we should find out what he's doing for extra cash. It might tie into Alexa's murder."

"Copy that," Tyler said.

Chapter 35

Meredith and Tyler stepped into the bullpen upon their return to the precinct and heard a loud, irate voice coming from the open door to Sergeant Wheaton's office.

"—have no idea what you and your detectives think you're doing, but I guarantee you, if they try anything like that again, I will make your department's life a fucking nightmare!"

Meredith looked at Tyler.

Why did that voice sound familiar?

They maneuvered around the desks so that they could see inside the office, just as Sergeant Wheaton began to speak.

"They're conducting a murder investigation. They have to interview people. I'm still not seeing what—"

Meredith's line of sight cleared the doorframe.

Sergeant Wheaton was seated in the chair behind the desk. A man in a suit was threateningly standing over the desk, resting his hands on the edges, with his back to the door.

Sergeant Wheaton caught the subtle movement out of the corner of his eye and spotted Meredith.

The mystery person saw the flicker of Sergeant Wheaton's eyes, turned, and faced the door. At the sight of Tyler and Meredith, his face contorted with rage.

"Just what the hell do you think you're doing, talking to my wife when I'm not there?!" Thomas Whitaker demanded as he came out of the office and stopped in front of Meredith.

Sergeant Wheaton was out of his chair and right behind Thomas as he stared Meredith down. With a glance, he silently asked Meredith if she wanted help, but she subtly shook her head.

"Did she tell you that we spoke to her?" Meredith asked.

"No. My son texted me that you were at my home, asking questions. I've been trying to call her but she won't answer her phone. My office is only a few blocks away, so I figured I'd come ask you. So, tell me, what did you talk to her about?"

"We had a few more questions about what happened that morning," Meredith calmly replied.

"Bullshit. I know how this works, detective. You were talking to her alone to try to get her to change her answers."

"Mr. Whitaker, if you had been there, we would have gladly asked you—"

Thomas put out his hands. "I'm here, now. Why don't you ask me those same questions? I'll tell you the same thing I told you that morning. Ask away."

Meredith continued to counter his aggressive demeanor with a cool tone. "I think we got what we needed."

Thomas took another small step toward her and leaned in, inches from her face. "Do you, now?"

"Man, you *really* want to take that step back," Tyler said from Meredith's side.

Meredith could sense that Tyler was ready to party, but she wasn't going to take her eyes off Thomas. Over his shoulder, she could see that Sergeant Wheaton was bracing himself.

"You're right, Mr. Whitaker," Meredith said.

Thomas blinked, temporarily thrown, which was Meredith's intention. She seized the opportunity and kept talking.

"As you know, Mr. Whitaker, it's a standard tactic to interview witnesses separately to see if there are any discrepancies in their stories. I'll be honest, Detective Foles and I pressed your wife pretty hard for more details about that morning, but all of her answers were the same."

Thomas searched Meredith's expression for any sign of a lie.

"Detective Foles can back me up on that, right, detective?" Meredith asked, keeping her eyes on Thomas and praying Tyler's improv skills were up to speed.

"Yeah." Tyler nodded. "Which makes me wonder why you're so pissed, Mr. Whitaker."

Thomas broke his stare to scowl at Tyler and back to Meredith.

"Stay out of my business. And both of you need to leave me and my family alone. If you want to talk to them, I want an advanced warning."

"Mr. Whitaker," Sergeant Wheaton said. "They're conducting an inves—"

"Fine," Meredith said.

Everyone, including Thomas, was surprised by her response, which had taken the air out of the room.

"There," Thomas said in Sergeant Wheaton's direction. "You heard her." He then stepped around Meredith and walked out the door.

Once he turned to go down the hall, Meredith quickly reached for her phone.

"Tyler," she said quietly. "Stall him for a minute. Do not let him use his phone. Go."

Tyler immediately understood and raced out the door as Meredith dialed.

"Hello?" Natalie answered.

"Mrs. Whitaker, it's Detective Somerset," Meredith said softly into the phone as she heard Tyler call out to Thomas in the hallway.

*

"Mr. Whitaker! Yo, Mr. Whitaker, hold up!" Tyler called out as he jogged after him.

Sure enough, Thomas had his phone in hand.

"I don't have anything else to say to you," Thomas replied, resuming his stride and going back to his phone.

"Listen, I just want to apologize for my attitude back there," Tyler said, pulling even with him.

Thomas stopped and stared at him in confusion.

"This case, man," Tyler said in an apologetic tone. "It's got us all rattled, but that doesn't excuse what happened back there or showing up unannounced on your family's doorstep."

Thomas continued to stare.

"We good?" Tyler asked, extending his hand.

Thomas regarded Tyler's hand as though it were unclean.

"No, detective," he sneered. "We're not 'good'. If you come near me or my family again, I'll have your badge."

"'You'll have my badge'?" Tyler smiled and looked around. "Where are the cameras? Which version of *Law & Order* are we on?"

Thomas was unamused. "Stay away from me."

He hurriedly walked away, dialing his phone, while leaving Tyler alone in the hall.

*

"Detective, what's going on? Thomas keeps calling me—"

"Ashton texted him. He knows that we were at the house, talking to you this morning," Meredith said. She could hear Tyler speaking to Thomas in the hall.

"Oh no."

"He was here. He wanted to know what we talked about. We told him that we were asking about the morning of the murder, and that none of your answers changed. That's all you need to tell him. Do you think you can do that?"

224

"Yes," Natalie replied. "I can do that."

"Okay, but if he doesn't believe you, if he hurts you again, you have to call us."

"I will."

Meredith wished she believed her.

"He's calling me, right now," Natalie said.

"Just stick with the story."

"I will. Thank you, detective."

Natalie Whitaker hung up the phone just as Tyler re-entered the bullpen.

"You talk to her?" he asked.

Meredith nodded.

"She gonna be okay?"

"I don't know," Meredith said. "We did what we could, for now."

*

"That was great work with our friend Mr. Whitaker," Tyler said as they walked toward their cars at the end of the long day. "Where you off to? Heading home?"

"No, I ... I'm meeting someone," Meredith replied, wishing she hadn't.

"Ooh-la-la. You playing the field, Somerset?"

"No. Nothing like that."

Tyler laughed. "Sure. Right. Gotcha." He mimed locking his lips and throwing away the key.

"See you tomorrow," Meredith said, rolling her eyes. "I want to go over the crime scene photos."

Tyler pretended his lips were still locked and gave her a thumbs-up before climbing into his car and driving off.

Meredith got in her car but paused before starting the engine.

She would have preferred that the meeting she was about to attend was "something like that".

Chapter 36

Meredith pressed the doorbell before she could change her mind. From the time that she heard the chimes inside until the door was opened felt like an eternity filled with apprehension and doubt, but also a sliver of hope.

Had anyone else tried to guess the age of the woman who answered the door, they would have said she was in her early fifties, but Meredith wasn't fooled by the hair dye or makeup.

"Meredith." Bethany smiled.

"Hi, Mom."

She stepped inside and they embraced, but the alarms were already ringing inside Meredith's head.

It had been years since they had seen each other and to say it hadn't ended well would be an understatement. Not only that, Bethany was going to introduce Meredith to "someone". This first meeting between them should have been just that: between them. They should be easing into it. The wounds they had inflicted upon one another had never truly healed, at least not for Meredith, and jumping back into a relationship without establishing some ground rules ran the risk of bringing back the pain of the past; a pain Meredith had worked hard to overcome. So yes, the alarm bells were ringing, but on the other hand, there she was, embracing her mother, something she had written off as an impossibility.

Although it was a different house, it smelled of her childhood home. It brought a wave of memories: of Meredith and Alice racing downstairs to the tree on Christmas morning, of nights staying up late, telling Alice ghost stories.

For a brief moment, Meredith was home.

"How was the drive?" her mother asked.

"It was fine."

Bethany took in her daughter from head to toe. "You look wonderful. Really fit."

"It's the job," Meredith said, glancing around. "Listen, about meeting this guy—"

"He's right this way," Bethany said, turning to walk down the hall to the kitchen.

Meredith reached out and touched her mom's shoulder.

"Mom?"

Bethany stopped and turned to her.

"Don't you think we should talk first? Just you and me?"

"Oh." Bethany looked back toward the kitchen. "But, he's already here."

"I know, but it's been a while—"

Bethany put a reassuring hand on Meredith's arm.

"I know this is all very sudden, and that you and I have a lot to talk about, but this really can't wait."

Meredith gave her a quizzical look.

"You'll see," Bethany said.

She resumed walking down the hall. Meredith followed.

Stepping through the entranceway to the kitchen, Meredith saw the man sitting at the table.

"Meredith," Bethany said. "This is Colin McDowell. Colin, this is my daughter; Meredith."

Colin McDowell looked like he had just stepped off the silver screen. His square jawline was sporting a full, sculpted beard. His dark eyes behind his delicate spectacles gave him a learned look. His shoulders were broad. He wasn't bulky but he definitely took care of himself.

"Hello, Meredith," he said in a clipped English accent. He stood and extended his hand.

"Hi," Meredith replied.

His handshake was firm and went along with his air of confident authority.

He motioned to the chair on the opposite side of the small round table. "Please, have a seat."

The three of them sat down.

Meredith cast her eyes toward her mother, who appeared to be thoroughly enjoying her confusion, like she was relishing the build-up to some big reveal.

"It's very nice to meet you," Colin said to Meredith.

"And I would say the same but I have no idea who you are."

The initial conflicting emotions of embracing her mother for the first time in years were gone, and this stranger was causing her defenses to go back up.

"Meredith, Colin is—"

"No, no, no. It's quite all right," Colin said. "She's right to be skeptical."

There was a long, awkward silence.

"Okay …" Meredith said. "Who are you?"

Colin smiled again and reached down toward a bag on the floor at his feet. He pulled out something that was sealed in clear plastic and placed it on the table.

Meredith's heart slammed into her throat.

It was a piece of light-purple fabric that was riddled with dirt and grime. The color was faded but there was no mistaking it.

Alice's swimsuit.

Meredith looked up at Colin.

"I'm the man who's going to find your sister."

The room began to spin. The contented grins from Colin and

her mother only added speed to the rotation. Finally, her professional instincts exerted themselves and the need to ask questions and understand took control.

Meredith picked up the plastic bag and opened it.

Her mother let out a soft, concerned, "Oh, I don't know if you should—"

A frustrated Meredith looked at Colin. "May I?"

He motioned to the bag. "Please."

Meredith removed the swimsuit and held it in her hand.

The fabric was brittle but more importantly, incomplete. It was only the lower half of the swimsuit. It was the right color and style but the part that would have held the tag with Alice's initial was gone, which meant she couldn't be entirely sure this was Alice's swimsuit, but she couldn't be entirely sure it wasn't.

"Where did you get this?" she asked.

"First off," Colin said, "let me tell you what I do. I worked for many years as a detective in Scotland Yard. Since retiring from the force, I have worked in investigating cold cases. I feel that I have unique skills and the ability to find new angles and construct new theories that the police sometimes miss. My work has led to several cases being reopened and even some arrests."

The alarm bells that had been ringing in Meredith's head were now deafening, but she quietly listened as he continued.

"I found your sister's disappearance among one of the online databases that keeps track of such cases, and thought it was intriguing."

Meredith knew of those "online databases". They were run by armchair detectives who formulated ridiculous theories that ranged from mafia involvement to the supernatural. They tended to be the same type of people who sent in wild suggestions to tip-lines.

"It's such a rarity to have an abduction that leaves absolutely no trace," Colin continued. "There is almost always some shred of evidence, some signal from the kidnapper. All of my years of working in this area led me to believe, after a mere passing glance, that there was something wrong with how your sister's case was conducted."

"I'm sure Meredith knows exactly what you're talking about," Bethany said. "Because I haven't told you the best part, Colin."

"Oh? And what's that?"

"She's a detective, too. She works in homicide."

Colin looked at Meredith. "Really?"

"Yeah." Meredith nodded, noting the tinge of worry in his question.

"See how perfect this is?" Bethany beamed, as though she was setting them up on a date. "The two of you can work together."

"How about it, Meredith?" Colin asked enthusiastically. "Want to help me find your sister?"

"First, tell me where you found this," Meredith said, holding up the fabric.

"Before I decide to offer my services, I always visit the crime scene to establish if there is even any hope of success. I flew to Dalton and retraced everything I could about that day. Now, the police believed that Alice probably got into a car outside of the fence near the diving boards, and I think they're right. A young girl wandering down the road would have been noticed. If she had wandered off into the woods, she wasn't wearing shoes and couldn't have gotten far. If someone did take her into the woods, they would have had to carry her. No. I agree with the police. She got into a car.

"The police tried to get an idea of where the car may have gone by using maps of the area. Here's where I think they got it wrong. Her abductor needed to get her away from the pool to somewhere they could be alone. It would have been too risky on the main roads, especially if Alice began to struggle. My theory is that he would have gotten off any main roads and into a secluded area." Colin paused for dramatic effect. "So, I used aerial photos to look for something that wouldn't show up on the maps the police used:

dirt roads, leading into any wooded area. I found a dirt road, five miles away from the pool, that branches off Route 76, which is one of the main roads that runs past the pool. The police never searched it, because it didn't appear on any maps at the time. The dirt road, which didn't have a name, went two miles into the forest and ended in a pine glen. I canvassed the area for three hours and found that," he said with a nod to the fabric. "It was then I was sure that I could be of help in finding your sister."

"And you just happened to pick the right spot?" Meredith asked.

Colin smiled and shook his head. "I should have been clearer. I explored seven other dirt roads within a five-mile radius of the pool and several likely areas someone would stop. In all honesty, I told myself that the pine glen was the last place I was going to search and if I didn't find anything, I was going to give up."

"And now, you'd like to offer us your 'services'?"

"I want to help you and your mother find Alice and put an end to what I know has been years of suffering. I don't promise a happy ending to our search, but I'm confident that we can get a result."

"And I'm sure your services aren't exactly cheap."

"Meredith," Bethany said. "Colin has been very upfront about all of this."

Colin was undaunted. "The cost of my services is commensurate with my expertise. I can also tailor my fees to the financial situation of my client. My true reward is helping to right the hopeless wrongs of the past."

Meredith stared at him, then at her mom.

"Can I talk to you for a second, please?"

*

"Mom, who is this guy?" Meredith asked as she and her mother stood in the living room. The kitchen was just around the corner through the dining room, but it offered them enough privacy.

"Meredith, I don't know what you mean. He told you everything."

"How did you find him?"

"He found me."

"Yeah. I bet he did."

"Meredith—"

"Have you looked into him at all?"

"Yes."

"And?"

"He's a detective, just like he said he was."

Meredith was still unconvinced. "This is all wrong. Give me some time to check him out."

"He wants to start tomorrow."

"He can't wait a few days?"

"I asked him to come here. I don't want him to wait. I want him to work on your sister's case and I want you to help him."

"Mom—"

"Please, Meredith, think of what finding your sister could do for us. He's not promising to find her alive. He's being honest. What do we have to lose?"

"A couple thousand dollars to start, I'm sure."

Bethany frowned.

"Are you going to help him?" she asked.

There was a pain in Meredith's chest. She needed to check this guy out, but she also didn't want to ruin this small opening between her and her mother.

"Give me until tomorrow morning, okay?" Meredith asked.

Bethany thought it over.

"All right."

*

Later that evening, Meredith was sitting on her couch, staring at her laptop. On the screen was Colin McDowell's website.

Everything looked legit, but she knew that was the point. There were half a dozen cases listed on the site that had been reopened. Meredith studied them, but they made no mention of Colin McDowell, which wasn't much of a surprise. Also, Colin had written little supplemental articles to each one, detailing how he had aided the police. It looked impressive, but there was still no tangible evidence that Colin McDowell had been involved in the cases, at all.

There were phone numbers she could track down and call but not before tomorrow morning. It was well past midnight in the UK.

She needed to find out info about this guy, and fast, but who could—

Meredith suddenly grabbed her phone and dialed.

"Somerset?"

"Tyler, I was wondering if you could do me a favor."

"Uh, sure. Name it."

"Your guy who did the deep dive on Scott Bowers or Rennick or whatever."

"Yeah?"

"Think he'd look up someone for me?"

"I can try. Tell me what you got."

Meredith gave him all the info she had on Colin McDowell, which basically amounted to his website.

"No promises," Tyler said. "But I'll pass it on."

"Thanks, Tyler."

"Welcome to the underworld, Somerset," Tyler said and hung up.

*

Meredith had been expecting a response sometime in the middle of the night, but to her surprise, it only took an hour for her phone to ring with a call from a blocked number.

"This Somerset?" the guy asked.

"Yeah."

"Tyler said that you wanted some info on a guy?"

"Yeah. Did you find him?"

Chapter 37

The next morning, the bag slung over Meredith's shoulder bounced off her hip as she approached the patio of the coffeeshop where Colin and her mother were sitting at a table, deep in conversation.

They noticed her approach and smiled.

Colin stood and, being the perfect gentleman, pulled out a seat for Meredith to join them.

She sat and lowered the bag to the ground.

Bethany's face was flushed with pride and contentment.

"Baby, we're so glad you came."

"Hi, Mom," Meredith said, leaning over and kissing her cheek.

"I'm very happy you decided to join us, Meredith," Colin said, resuming his seat. "I truly believe that we can find your sister. We're going to consider things that would have never occurred to the police in the original investigation. Methods and technology have taken such huge leaps in the past few years. Amateur detectives of the present can be more effective than the professionals of twenty-five years ago, and as I hope you are now aware, I'm no amateur."

"No, you're not," Meredith replied in an icy tone.

Colin's confident shell showed the slightest crack, but instantly mended.

He leaned forward and rested his elbows on the table. "To begin, what I'd like to do is go back to Dalton and start over. I want to requestion everyone. My plan is to reconstruct that day. I can also get access to the FBI's registered sex offender list. I know it's unpleasant but it's something we have to consider." He turned to Bethany. "If your daughter's abduction was sexual in nature, it actually gives us a better chance that she's still alive. Sex offenders have to check in everywhere they go. I want to see if there were any in or around Dalton during the time of your daughter's disappearance."

Bethany was confused. "But they already did that. They told us during the investigation that they checked the registry." She glanced at Meredith for confirmation, but Meredith was still watching Colin.

"True," Colin said. "But here's something they haven't done; I want to check the sex offender registry for people who had to register *after* your daughter's disappearance and see if any of them were in or around Dalton at the time. These perverts don't change. He may have gotten away with it before, but there's a chance he was apprehended years later for some other offense. I want those names, and then I'll run a background check to see if any of them were in the area."

Meredith could see the cruel hope flooding into her mother's eyes. Bethany was on the verge of weeping with happiness and relief, as though Alice was as good as found.

Satisfied with Bethany's awed expression, Colin focused on Meredith.

"What do you say, Meredith? Ready to find Alice?"

"Let me see if I understand this," Meredith said. "What you want is a couple thousand dollars to go to Dalton for a few days, recanvas the case and talk to witnesses, many of whom are long gone. You also want to reconstruct the scene, even though the pool is now a strip mall—"

"But not the terrain, Meredith. You know that being at a crime scene, no matter the changes over time, is the best way to get fresh eyes on a case. There are dozens of cold cases that have been reopened because a visit to an old crime scene has yielded new evidence. I mean, look at the swimsuit fabric I found only five miles from where the pool was."

"Yeah, about that." Meredith reached down and lifted the bag onto her lap. She extracted a sealed plastic bag and placed it on the table. Inside the bag was the bottom half of a girl's one-piece swimsuit. The light-purple fabric was mottled in dirt and grime. It was nearly identical to the fabric Colin had presented to her and Bethany the evening before. Even the bag was similar.

Bethany was mute. Colin was frozen.

"You know what's cheaper than going to Dalton, reinvestigating a cold crime scene, and miraculously discovering some huge clue that every cop and forensic specialist missed?" Meredith asked. "Researching cold cases, finding out what the victim was wearing, going to Kohl's, buying something similar, and running it through the dirt for a while. Then, you try to con someone out of their money by playing off their grief."

Bethany remained speechless but Colin kindly shook his head.

"Meredith, I understand your skepticism. I do, and it's healthy, but the first step to finding your sister is to believe that someone can find her."

"And the second step is giving you money?"

"We've been over this. I've made no secret that it will take investment to track down new leads."

Meredith snorted. "Listen, I'm sure you never would have gone through with this if you knew that I was a detective. That's bad luck for you, but are you really going to try to keep this up?"

"I have decades of experience—"

"Fine," Meredith said. "While you're researching, can you check out a town in Nebraska called 'Revere'?"

This time, Colin couldn't hide his noticeable shock.

"I—I don't know what you mean," he said, his accent momentarily slipping.

"That's where you were born. Isn't it … Larry?"

"I don't know where this is coming f—"

"I have an acquaintance that can track down information, too," Meredith said. "He's very resourceful. I had him look into you and it took all of an hour to find everything. You've never been a detective for Scotland Yard. You've never even left the United States," Meredith said in amused disbelief and turned to Bethany. "Did you do *any* research other than his website?"

Bethany could only sputter, so Meredith continued.

"My friend couldn't find anything about a detective named 'Colin McDowell'. All of the stuff about the cases on your website is public knowledge. You made up the stories tying yourself to the investigation. All my friend had to do was look up the details of your account on the website server. There, he found the credit card you're using to pay for the site. The name on the card is Larry Colin McDowell, who was born in Revere, Nebraska, in 1967. You've never applied for a passport or visa to leave the country. Everything about you is a lie."

Colin had regained a little of his composure. His expression morphed into one of sympathy, as though he pitied Meredith, but the color had drained from his face.

"Meredith?" a confused Bethany asked. "What are you—?"

Meredith ignored her mother and kept her focus on the man across the table. "You were born in Nebraska, Larry. The accent is good. Very convincing, I'll give you that, because if you are going to offer someone the impossible, it helps to sound like Sherlock Holmes, doesn't it?"

Colin exhaled. "Meredith, I don't know what your friend told you, but I have solved dozens of cold cases—"

"Oh, come on. You had nothing to do with those. You found cold cases that were solved, researched them, and then inserted yourself into the story on your website."

"Meredith, please—" Bethany pleaded.

"You're a conman, Larry. Plain and simple."

Larry's face hardened. "I understand that sometimes, it's difficult for professionals such as yourself to acknowledge that an outsider may uncover things that might have been missed."

Meredith laughed.

"Please, Meredith. He could help us," Bethany said.

"No, Mom. No, he can't. Not at all. Even if he was sincere, which he's not."

"You don't think I want to help you find your sister?" Colin asked.

"Absolutely not."

"I have no idea why you would say that when I—"

"Because no one, *no one*, with even the slightest understanding of law enforcement would have *ever* moved that fabric from where they found it. It destroys the chain of evidence to the point where even if we found who took Alice, and that piece of fabric was the key to the whole case, we could never use it. You've taken what would be the most important piece of evidence in twenty-five years and made it worthless. You've guaranteed that the person connected to it would go free, all to make a sales pitch of how you, alone, could catch him. But all of this would only matter if you had actually discovered that fabric in Dalton. You and I both know you didn't. You're Larry Colin McDowell. You were born in Nebraska and you live in Lexington, Kentucky. You're a conman who's trying to make money off my family's tragedy and grief."

There was stunned silence around the table. A few of the people seated nearby had taken notice of the tense conversation.

Colin sadly shook his head.

"I recognize that this is difficult for you, Meredith. I know you blame yourself for Alice's disappearance. Your mother told me that you were supposed to be watching her that day. So, it only makes sense that you would be resistant to opening an old wound."

Meredith turned to her mother.

"You told him?"

"He needed to know for the investigation."

Colin tried to interject. "I needed to know everything about—"

"Shut up!" Meredith spat.

She had hoped that calling his bluff would end the con, that he would leave without Meredith having to make her mother feel foolish, but the only way to lose a mark in a con was to finally admit the truth, which Colin clearly had no intention of doing. He was a pro, willing to push the con all the way to the bitter end.

Meredith reached into her pocket, pulled out a piece of paper she had printed from her laptop, and laid it on the table.

At the top of the page was an image of a driver's license for Larry Colin McDowell. It listed his address in Lexington. Underneath the driver's license was another image: a mugshot of the same man in the driver's license, which was the same man who was sitting across the table.

"You needed a complete understanding of my sister's case?" Meredith asked. "I think it's only fair my mother has a complete understanding of who you are before she hires you. You're Larry Colin McDowell. In 2006, you were arrested for a Ponzi scheme and charged with wire fraud in Wisconsin."

Whatever blood was left in Colin's face promptly fled. The con was over and he turned to the one option he had to save face.

"Bethany, if my services aren't appreciated, then I have plenty of other clients who need my help." He stood up from the table.

"No, please stay," Bethany pleaded.

"I'm sorry, but I can't work with your daughter." He then looked across the table at Meredith. "But I'm most sorry for Alice."

Meredith prided herself on her restraint, but in that moment, she fantasized about pulling her Sig Sauer. Instead, she summoned up every ounce of cold professionalism she had within her. "I know who you are. I know where you live. I know what you do.

You keep pulling shit like this, the FBI will want to have a talk with you."

"Good day, Mrs. Somerset," Colin said to Bethany and walked off.

Meredith watched him go.

Once he was sufficiently down the street, she turned to her mother, who was staring at her with flushed cheeks and burning eyes.

"Why, Meredith?"

"Why what?"

"Why would you do that? He was our best chance in years to find Alice."

"Our best …? Mom, he wasn't going to help us find Alice. He was going to take your money, string you along until he got as much as he could, and then disappear."

Bethany regarded her daughter with a look of disdain.

"I wanted to connect with you. I wanted us to have a life again, and the only way that can happen is for us to find out what happened to Alice."

It was as if she hadn't heard a word Meredith had said.

"Mom, I want nothing more than to have you in my life, in Allison's life, but not like this. We're never going to connect over this. Alice is gone and she's never coming back."

Bethany's rage shifted to smug moral triumph.

"He was right."

"Who was right?"

"Colin. He said that you wouldn't want to find her, because you were supposed to be watching her that day—"

"Stop it."

"—That you wouldn't want to find her, because then you'd have to face what you did."

"Mom—"

"That you wouldn't want to find Alice because that would tear your life apart and you would rather move on."

241

"Mom, please."

"Because you've put it behind you, when I've been stuck there for over twenty years, and it's all your fault."

"STOP IT!"

Every head on the patio turned in their direction.

Meredith didn't care. It was only her and her mother on that patio, just as it had been after her father had died. No. Even before that, since her father had abandoned them to wander the wastelands of the bottle, leaving Bethany to focus all her blame and guilt on her remaining daughter.

Meredith stared at her mother, cursing herself for believing, cursing herself for hoping that there was a future here. There was only the past. She was fifteen all over again, carrying a weight upon her shoulders that had no business being there.

Bethany showed no sign of backing down or apologizing one bit for the horrible wound she had opened in Meredith's chest.

Meredith was right. There was no future here—only pain and guilt.

Meredith stood. "Goodbye, Mom."

In the silence of the patio, she turned and walked away.

The teenager inside Meredith begged and pleaded for Bethany to call her back, but the woman who had built a life for herself in spite of all kept walking, holding the teenager's hand and urging her not to look back.

Bethany never made a sound.

*

Meredith made it to her car intact, got in, and pulled away from the curb, but didn't get far.

She found a dead-end street, parked off to the side, and began screaming and pounding the steering wheel with the palms of her hands.

When she finally calmed down, her hands were red and

throbbing. Her throat was scorched. She had the urge to call Dr. Kaplan, but she wanted to do this on her own.

She steadied herself and took a series of deep breaths.

"I miss you, Meredith," a voice said.

She turned her head.

Alice was sitting in the passenger seat, looking at her with those pleading eyes.

Instead of looking away or trying to shake the vision from her head, Meredith looked directly at her.

"I miss you, too," she said in an unsteady voice. "I miss the life that we should have had and I'm sorry. I'm so sorry I wasn't watching you more closely and I've spent so many years trying to make up for that ..." She closed her eyes. "But it wasn't my fault. What happened wasn't my fault. I have a family. I have a daughter. I'm sorry, but you're never coming back and I have to live my own life now."

Meredith opened her eyes.

Alice was gone.

*

Tyler had already created a collage of crime scene photos on the whiteboard when Meredith entered the bullpen.

He was about to crack a good-natured, retaliatory joke about her tardiness, when he saw her eyes.

Meredith had done her best to pull herself together before walking into the station. She had, mentally, but there was nothing she could do about her bloodshot, puffy eyes.

"Somerset?"

She looked up at him.

"You okay?" he asked.

"Yeah."

Tyler hesitated, in case she wanted to change her answer.

"I'm good," she added.

"Copy that," Tyler said, and turned back to the board.

It wasn't his business and if she didn't need or want to talk about it, there was nothing more to say.

Chapter 38

Hours later, Meredith and Tyler were still studying the wall of photos that Eddie had taken at the crime scene on Willow Lane. Each photo had a timestamp in the bottom right corner.

Tyler's enthusiasm had begun to wane. He was slouched in the chair at the table with his head thrown back. Meredith was standing in front of the photos, peering intently at them.

"We haven't ruled out Whitaker, right?" he asked.

"No. He's still on the board. I'm only taking it into consideration that Natalie Whitaker doesn't think it was him, and based off what she said, that makes sense."

"What does?"

"If he killed her, he wouldn't have taken any time getting out of there and going to work. It was only after he heard Patricia Crawford scream and saw the body in the street that he tried to leave."

"Maybe he wanted it to look that way."

"It's possible," Meredith said, but she didn't think it very likely. She continued examining the photos. Tyler had done his best to arrange them on the wall from the vantage point of where they had been taken. The result was a tight circle of photos of Alexa, lying in the middle of the street, in the center of the diagram.

Was there something they were missing?

These were only some of the photos. Tyler had combed through them, selecting the ones he felt were the clearest and most helpful. Many of them resembled the others so closely, they could have been considered duplicates, but there was the possibility that they needed to examine one of the other dozens of photos.

"You think it's time to start looking outside Willow Lane?" Tyler asked.

"I hope not."

Tyler sat up. "I hope not, too, but it's something we need to start considering."

"He's on that street," Meredith said.

Alexa's lifeless eyes stared back at her from the photos, her mouth slightly open as if trying to tell Meredith the last thing she had seen before life left her body.

"Okay," Tyler said. "Convince me."

"You said it yourself; dumping her from a car is too risky."

"Maybe they were in the car together. She jumps out. He parks the car, chases her, and that was where he happens to catch up with her. He strangles her, runs back to his car, and drives off. No one near the crime scene hears the car drive away."

"No. The clothes? The stains on the socks? She didn't run that far."

"I'm not saying she ran a marathon or anything. I'm saying maybe she was in a car, got out, ran, and he chased her."

"What were they doing?" Meredith asked. "Taking a joyride through Meadowgate? Why wasn't she wearing shoes?"

"There aren't easy answers, Somerset. My point is that it might be time to cast a wider net."

Meredith hated to admit it, but Tyler was right, and if they were going to start looking outside Willow Lane, they needed to start right now, because it was going to be a logistical nightmare that was going to require more time and more manpower, and the odds of catching a break were much, much smaller.

Frustration burned in Meredith's chest. She had done her best to put that morning out of her mind and pour her concentration into Alexa's murder, but the heightened emotions from the coffee shop were adding to her anxiety that the case was getting away from them.

She refocused her gaze, staring closely at each photo, going from one to the other. Nothing about Alexa changed, only the background as Eddie had circled her body, snapping away.

The constant movement from photo to photo was interrupted when she noticed that one of them was in the wrong place. It had been taken from a different perspective than those around it. It showed Alexa lying on the street with the garage of one of the houses in the background. The door of the garage was open. Tyler had placed it with the photos of Alexa with the Whitakers' house in the background, because yes, the Whitakers' garage door was open, but the house in the background of this particular photo was different. It was the Ansleys' house. If you were focusing on the dead body, as Tyler surely had been, it was an easy mistake.

Meredith pulled it, moved it over to the grouping of photos with the Ansley's house in the background, taped it back onto the board, and stopped, her eyes fixed on that photo.

"Somerset?"

"Tell me again, what kind of car does Greg Ansley drive?" she asked.

Tyler quickly shuffled through the papers on the table until he found what he was looking for.

"A black Honda Accord."

Meredith compared the timestamp in the corner of the photo to the ones around it that had the Ansley house in the background.

She spun around and began riffling through the notes.

"Somerset? Talk to me."

"One sec," she said, pushing around sheets of paper.

She found Sheriff Howell's report and set it aside. Then, she found the statement dictated to Officer Hawthorne from Patricia Crawford and compared the two.

It was right there in Sheriff Howell's report and verified by Officer Hawthorne, but she needed to be sure.

Meredith took out her phone.

"Anytime you want to make me a part of this," Tyler said.

She held up her finger as the phone began to ring on the other end.

"Sheriff Howell," the gruff voice answered.

"Sheriff. This is Detective Somerset. How are you?"

"Good. Yourself?"

"Good. I just had a quick follow-up about the Jane Doe we found on Willow Lane."

"You got something?"

"Maybe. I was going over your report and the statement from Patricia Crawford. I want to make absolutely sure that no one left any of the houses on Willow Lane after your team arrived."

"Nope."

"No one drove off?"

"No, ma'am. We sealed it off. From the time I got there, no cars came or went from Willow Lane."

"One hundred percent?"

"One hundred percent."

Meredith inhaled. "Thank you, Sheriff."

"My pleasure. Let me know if you need anything else."

"I will. Thanks again."

Meredith hung up.

Tyler was staring at her. "Do I get to play too?"

Meredith tucked her phone into her pocket, took his arm, pulled him out of the chair, led him to the wall of photos, and pointed. "These two, right here."

Tyler studied the two photos.

The photos appeared to be almost identical. One was close on Alexa's head, taken from street level. The scrape on her forehead was visible. The other was taken a little further back, showing the bruising around her neck.

Tyler kept going back and forth between the photos, as though if he looked fast enough, he might see a difference between them.

"You got me. What's different about her in the two photos?"

"Not her. Back here," Meredith said, pointing to the Ansleys' garage in the background. "Notice the timestamp."

Tyler looked at the corner of the photo. "Okay."

"Now, watch."

Meredith pointed to the timestamp in the next photo. They had been taken roughly ten minutes apart. Once Tyler had nodded, acknowledging the fact, Meredith's finger drifted upwards to the background.

It was instantaneous.

"Holy shit," he breathed.

In the background of the first photo, one of the garage doors to the Ansley house was open, revealing Greg Ansley's Honda Accord parked inside. In the second photo, the garage door was closed, hiding the car from view.

Tyler turned to Meredith.

"No wonder Mrs. Ansley was so rattled."

Meredith nodded. "Greg Ansley was in that house the morning of the murder while we were questioning her."

249

Chapter 39

Meredith turned the car into the entrance to Meadowgate.

"You want me to call and make sure he's not there?" Tyler asked.

"No. He has to be at work and I don't want her to know we're coming. If he's there, we wait him out until we can get her alone. It'll be easier to catch her in a lie than him."

They had checked their notes against the timestamps in the photos. The Ansleys' garage door had been closed while they were talking to Scott Rennick. They also double-checked the notes from their interview with Greg Ansley to make sure that he didn't mention anything about carpooling, which he hadn't.

As they came to a stop outside the house, every instinct in Meredith was telling her that this was the break they were hoping for. They got out and made their way to the front door. Meredith carried a manilla envelope in her hand.

"You taking the lead on questions?" Tyler asked.

"Yeah, but if you've got one, go for it."

"Copy that."

They stepped onto the porch. Meredith pressed the doorbell.

They waited. Meredith was about to reach for the doorbell, again, but they heard the fumbling of the deadbolt.

"Here we go," Tyler whispered.

The door opened and Meghan Ansley stared at them.

"Can I help you?" she asked, a mixture of annoyance and fear.

"We were wondering if we could ask you a few more questions about that morning, Mrs. Ansley," Meredith said.

"I have nothing else to say," she replied. "I mean, I said I would call you if I remembered anything, and I haven't called you, have I?"

"No, you haven't, but there's some more information that has come to our attention and we need some clarification."

*

Meredith sat at the kitchen table, going over her notes. Meghan was sitting next to her with her arms folded across her chest. The manilla envelope rested on the table between them. Tyler was standing off to the side, glancing out the kitchen window to the backyard.

"Just to be clear, your husband left around five-thirty that morning?" Meredith asked.

"Yes." Meghan's answer was accompanied by an eyeroll. "We've been over this."

"As I said, we're just double-checking. And tell me again, what type of car does your husband drive?"

"He drives a black Honda Accord. I don't understand what that has—"

Meredith picked up the envelope, took out the two photos, and placed them on the table in front of her.

"Once the police arrived, we locked down the street. No cars came or went. In this photo, right here," Meredith said, pointing, "there's your husband's car, in the garage. And in this photo, taken ten minutes later, the garage door is closed. The street was locked down, so his car was still in there."

Meghan picked up the photos. There was the beginning of a slight tremor in her hands and a tightening of her jaw.

"Mrs. Ansley, was your husband here when we questioned you?" Meredith asked.

"No … no … He left for work."

"But you can see that his car is still in the garage."

The tremor in Meghan's hands began to grow.

"Mrs. Ans—"

"He took my car," she blurted out.

Meredith and Tyler exchanged an incredulous glance.

"Why would he take your car?" Meredith asked, feigning confusion.

"Sometimes we trade. He'll take my Toyota and I'll take his Honda."

"Oh …"

There was no doubt in Meredith's mind that she was lying, but it presented the detectives with a problem. Since the other garage door was closed in both photos, they couldn't immediately prove that she was lying and the moment they left, Meghan Ansley would be on the phone with her husband to get their story straight.

In the slight hesitation as Meredith turned the possibilities over in her head, Tyler spoke up.

"Your son? What's the little man's name, again?"

"Anthony," she said.

"Yeah. Anthony. You said he was upstairs that morning?"

"Yes."

"We think it might be time to talk to him."

Meghan's face went white.

"I don't want him to get involved," she said.

"Don't worry, Mrs. Ansley. We're not going to ask him about the body in the street. We'll only ask him if Daddy was home that morning." Tyler held up three fingers. "Scout's honor."

Meghan went rigid. She turned to Meredith for help, but found none.

For the love of God, Meredith thought. *Stop digging yourself deeper into a hole.*

252

"Mrs. Ansley?" Tyler asked.

"I think you should leave," Meghan said.

"Mrs. Ansley—?"

Meghan stood. "I just remembered I have to be somewhere."

"We just want to ask him one question," Tyler continued. "It'll take two seconds. You can stand by the little man's side the whole time."

Meghan was a wounded animal backed into a corner.

"You have to go, now," she insisted.

"Mrs. Ansley?" Meredith said, quietly, but forcefully.

She turned to Meredith.

"Your husband was here when we questioned you, wasn't he?"

"Get out. Both of you," she insisted.

Her nervous eyes darted between them and for a brief moment, flashed toward the window, and glanced at the shed.

Meredith and Tyler caught it.

Tyler pointed a thumb in the direction of the window toward the shed. "Mind if we take a look in there before we go?"

"Get out."

*

Meredith and Tyler crossed the lawn, back toward the car.

"Think it's enough for a search warrant, Somerset?" Tyler asked.

"I think we should find out."

*

Amanda Crabtree was sitting behind the reception desk in the lobby of Hopewell & Associates when she suddenly heard the raised voice of Mr. Ansley from his office. The thick, glass walls muffled his speech, but they weren't entirely soundproof. She glanced up to see him seated at his desk, talking into his cellphone. His face was one of barely contained panic.

Suddenly, he slammed his fist onto his desk.

Amanda quickly put her eyes back on her work to pretend like she wasn't watching, but after several seconds, she couldn't help stealing another glimpse.

Mr. Ansley was sitting back in his chair, staring up at the ceiling with a shocked expression. He quickly stood.

Amanda looked down again but strained her eyes so she could see what was happening.

Greg Ansley went to the panel on the wall, hit a button, and the walls went opaque.

A moment later, the intercom buzzed.

"Amanda?"

"Yes, Mr. Ansley?"

"If anyone calls, tell them I've left for the day."

"Yes, Mr. Ansley," she said, trying to mask her confusion.

The intercom clicked off.

Chapter 40

"So, you want a search warrant for the house?" Kelly Yamara asked, sitting across from Meredith and Tyler in the bullpen while Sergeant Wheaton stood off to the side.

"There's a big shed in the backyard where he said he likes to do woodworking," Tyler said. "We'd like to get a peek in there, too."

"And what exactly are you looking for?"

"Sister Mariah from Sisters of Sacred Heart said that Alexa may have been carrying an ID card. We're hoping the killer hasn't gotten rid of it."

"You think it's in the house or the shed? Unless they're incredibly stupid, they would have gotten rid of it by now."

"We've seen stupider," Tyler said.

"It's not only the ID we'd be looking for," Meredith added. "We believe that Alexa was possibly in the Ansleys' home. We'd be looking for anything that would indicate that she was there, such as any personal items or articles of clothing."

"Her shoes," Tyler said.

Kelly grimaced. "It's pretty broad."

Meredith hung her head in frustration.

"Don't get me wrong; it's not impossible," Kelly quickly

continued. "The fact that Mrs. Ansley may have been lying about taking her husband's car—"

"She *was* lying," Tyler sighed.

"She may have been, but her story, however implausible, makes it a little more difficult for a judge to issue a warrant."

"Come on, Kelly," Sergeant Wheaton finally joined in. "Do we really need to bring this to you on a silver platter?"

"You guys have done great and I think you're right. I just need a little more to prove she lied, and the warrant is a slam dunk. Do you want me to try for the warrant now, or do you think you can get a little bit more?"

Tyler looked to Meredith.

"We can get it," Meredith said.

"Okay," Kelly said, rising from her chair. "Keep me posted."

She turned, walked through the bullpen, and out the door.

"What's the plan?" Sergeant Wheaton asked.

"We talk to Greg Ansley," Meredith said. "See if we can trip him up."

"They've probably got their stories worked out by now," Tyler countered.

"She's rattled. They're not going to be able to keep everything straight much longer. I'll call him and see if we can set up an interview tomorrow at his house. If we can get back inside, we can see if there's anything in plain sight that would let us skip the warrant."

"And if not?"

"We'll go to his work. Talk to him there."

Tyler smirked. "Fine by me, but this time, I'm flashing my badge to everyone in that office. I want him uncomfortable."

"Agreed," Meredith said.

Sergeant Wheaton began walking back toward his office.

"I have no idea what the hell you two are talking about, nor do I want to know."

*

256

Greg Ansley inched along I-85, one of the tens of thousands of cars trying to navigate their way through the daily nightmare of Atlanta rush hour.

He would have given anything to change places with any of the other drivers around him. The infuriating crawl of traffic accentuated the sensation of being trapped. He continued replaying the phone call with Meghan in his mind.

She had lied to protect him, to protect their family, but it hadn't been a very good lie. In fact, it had been terribly transparent, but it had bought them time, and what was she supposed to do?

This was his fault. All of it.

But he could still salvage it. He had to believe that because it wasn't only his marriage on the line.

His phone began to ring.

In a panic, he hit the Bluetooth answer button on the steering wheel before checking the caller ID, worried that it was Meghan with more bad news.

"Hello?"

"Mr. Ansley?"

"Yes?"

"It's Detective Meredith Somerset. How are you?"

Greg was motionless.

"Mr. Ansley?"

"I'm fine, detective," he said, wishing he hadn't answered the call. "I'm driving home, though, so I probably shouldn't be on the phone."

"This will be quick."

"Okay …"

"We have some follow-up questions we'd like to ask you."

"What kind of questions?"

"We need to clear up some details. I'm sure your wife told you."

*

Across the desk, Tyler, who was listening in on the call, cracked a smile in Meredith's direction.

"Would that be all right, Mr. Ansley?" Meredith asked.

"Uh, yes. Okay."

"Great. We were wondering if we could stop by your home tomorrow."

"No. I don't think that will work."

"Fine. We can come to your office like last time."

"I—I don't know if that's going to work, either."

"Okay, then you can come into the precinct and talk to us, because there are some things that you need to clarify for us."

"I don't understand why you need to speak to me if you've already spoken to—"

"Mr. Ansley."

"My office, then," he relented. "Is nine o'clock okay?"

"That's great. See you tomorrow."

Greg Ansley hung up without saying another word.

Meredith and Tyler rested their phones back on their respective cradles.

"Great," Tyler said. "He's going to make us fight traffic."

*

Greg stared through the windshield at the endless line of cars stretching out before him; a slow-moving kaleidoscope of brake lights and turn signals. He couldn't move. He couldn't run. He couldn't escape.

The commuters around him, who were likewise being held captive by traffic, noticed movement out of the corners of their eyes, and glanced into the black Honda Accord. Some might tell the brief story to their spouse when they got home. Most would forget what they had seen a few minutes later. They had seen it before. Some of them had done it.

None of them begrudged or questioned the man sitting behind the wheel, screaming his lungs out.

Chapter 41

That night, Scott Rennick sat in one of the kitchen chairs in his silent house, staring at the small suitcase on the table. Inside was everything he needed to start over. When the time came, as he knew it would, he would grab it, walk out the front door and never look back.

But he couldn't leave now.

If he did, all suspicions would fall on him. He would wait until whatever was happening on Willow Lane came to a head. Then, he would use the chaos as a cover to slip away. It would be days before they realized he was gone.

By then, he would have disappeared.

*

Across the street, Thomas Whitaker slid into bed next to his wife, who was lying on her side, facing away from him.

He clicked off the lamp on the nightstand and nestled close while speaking softly into her ear.

"Listen, Natalie, I'm sorry for the way I've been behaving lately. I'm just under a lot of pressure and this whole thing with the police is really piling it on." He tenderly kissed her shoulder. "Do you forgive me?"

His tone was different from the one he had used a few hours earlier, when he was screaming at her, demanding to know what she had told the detectives. She'd insisted that her answers hadn't changed from that morning, infuriating him to the point that he shoved her to the ground. Kendall and Ashton never left their rooms during the altercation. They knew better. Afterwards, Thomas had locked himself in his office, while she went straight for bed, hoping to find sanctuary in sleep. She'd taken one of her pills to hasten the process, but it wasn't working fast enough. She was only just beginning to feel its effects when Thomas had come upstairs. He hadn't said a word as he disappeared into the bathroom to get ready for bed.

Natalie had believed he wouldn't hurt her, but she was wrong.

Now, he was running a classic from the abuser's playbook: acting lovingly and apologizing.

"Do you forgive me?" he asked again.

What could she do? She needed more time.

"Yes," she mumbled, the pill finally exerting itself over her already frayed mind and descending a dark curtain over her thoughts.

He gently squeezed her waist. "I love you."

Before she could answer, Natalie was asleep.

*

At that moment, next door, Richard Morgan emerged from the master bathroom to find Kathy staring out the window.

"What are you up to?" he asked.

She was so lost in thought, the question startled her.

"I was just … nothing."

He walked over, wrapped his arms around her waist, and kissed her cheek.

"Come to bed," he whispered, withdrawing his arms and moving toward the bed.

Kathy did her best not to make her sigh of disappointment audible.

That was Richard's way of initiating sex—a kiss on the cheek, a whisper in her ear.

It had been fine twenty years ago, but it had grown so predictable. The sex would be boring, respectful, the way you figured Ward and Mrs. Cleaver made love. He'd either finish too early or not at all and apologize and she would sooth him and tell him that it was all right and that the sex had been wonderful. Richard would think everything was fine; that he was being romantic. Then, he would doze off with an accomplished, satisfied grin, while she would stare upwards at the darkened ceiling and allow the questions into her head; the questions that she would not dare ask in the light of day, when she was surrounded by her precious and treasured children.

They're what's most important, she thought, and Kathy Morgan would do anything to protect her family.

But it was depressing to know that this routine had happened so many times, that she could automatically play the tape to the end.

Her eyes drifted back to the window. She gazed at the light burning in the upstairs bedroom across the street and, not for the first time, Kathy Morgan wondered …

"Kathy?" Richard quietly said, in a pathetic attempt at seduction.

"Coming," she said, allowing her contemplation to linger a moment longer on the window across the street before joining Richard in bed.

*

Across the street, in the bedroom that Kathy had set her eyes upon, Greg Ansley stepped out of the master bathroom of his own bedroom to find Meghan sitting on the far side of the bed, staring at the wall. She had been quietly crying and her shoulders trembled and hitched intermittently.

He wanted to comfort her, but didn't know how or even if he could.

He sat on his own side of the bed, their backs to one another. The bed had become a mile wide.

He blankly stared toward the window and happened to see a shadow in the window across the street as it turned away. Then, the light in the Morgans' bedroom went dark.

"I can't lie anymore, Greg," Meghan whispered.

Greg's eyes drifted down to his wrists.

"It's almost over," he said.

Chapter 42

Meredith pulled into one of the spots marked "visitor" in the subterranean garage and she and Tyler hopped out.

"Just like we've been doing, I'll take lead on questions," Meredith said as they made their way to the elevators, holding the manilla envelope containing the photos in her hand.

"How are you gonna trip him up?" Tyler asked.

"Not sure. If we keep hammering at how ridiculous their stories are, he might crack. If not, we'll play the 'interrogate their son' card, but I'm hoping we won't have to."

She had continued walking but stopped when she realized that Tyler wasn't behind her. She turned to see him frozen by the parking garage office, which she had just passed.

"Tyler? What's wrong?"

He was grinning from ear to ear. "We might not have to do any of that, Somerset."

"What are you talking about?"

Tyler waved her back. "Come on."

Meredith hurried to him as he stepped over to the open door of the office.

A parking attendant was working on a spreadsheet on a computer.

Tyler knocked on the doorframe.

"Excuse me?"

The parking attendant turned to him.

"Can I help you?" he asked.

Tyler read his nametag.

"Robert, my man, I sure hope so."

*

"Thanks for seeing us again," Meredith said as she and Tyler settled into the chairs on the other side of Greg's desk.

"You didn't give me much of a choice," he said and hit the button on the panel that caused the glass walls to cloud over.

"There are some things we need to clear up."

Greg dropped into his chair.

"My wife told me. She said you startled her by showing up out of nowhere."

"It was important," Tyler said.

"We've already told you everything. I don't see how these constant interviews are supposed to—"

Meredith produced the photos of his car in the garage of his home from the manilla envelope and set them on the desk in front of him.

"Oh," Greg said. "That."

"Yeah. That. Why didn't you tell us that you traded cars with your wife that day?" Meredith asked, her voice bordering on sarcasm.

"There was a lot going on. It slipped my mind."

"When was the last time you did that?" Meredith asked.

"Switched cars? I don't know. A few months ago, maybe."

"When did the two of you start that little tradition?"

"It was when we got the cars, I guess."

"You guess?" Tyler asked.

"I'm saying that I'm not sure, but we've been doing it a while."

"How do you like driving your wife's car?" Meredith asked. She was circling, sparring, looking for an opening.

"I prefer my own."

"Did you do it with the cars you had before this?"

"No, and I see what you're doing."

"And what is that?"

"You're trying to throw me off; drive some sort of wedge between me and my wife and catch us in a lie."

"Are you lying?"

Greg stared at her. "No, and I resent that."

"One last time," Meredith said. "You took your wife's car?"

Greg's irritation grew. "Yes. How many times do I have to—?"

Meredith produced another piece of paper and a photo from the envelope and held them up. The paper had columns of names, numbers, and times on it, while the photo showed a car at the parking gate of the garage downstairs.

"I don't understand," Greg said. "What is that?"

"On our way up, we stopped by the parking garage office," Tyler said. "Had a nice little chat with Robert, the attendant. He did us a solid and let us check the parking logs. You've got one of those parking passes. Whenever you use it to enter the garage, it records the time. We checked the log for that day. You entered the garage at 10:08 that morning. So, we checked the security footage, and there you are," Tyler said, pointing to the photo Meredith was holding up. "Pulling into the garage in your car. Not your wife's."

Greg was motionless.

"Why did you lie to us, Mr. Ansley?" Meredith asked.

"That … That doesn't mean anything. That might not even be me," he said, forcing a nervous laugh while sweat formed on his brow.

"Come on, man," Tyler smirked, as though he was almost impressed that Greg was trying to wriggle out of the question.

"Mr. Ansley," Meredith said. "You're not seriously suggesting that someone else drove your car to work and used your parking pass?"

Greg's mouth was open. His eyes darted back and forth. His breath was shallow.

"I've said all I'm going to say without my lawyer."

Meredith smiled. "That's fine, Mr. Ansley. I believe we've got all we need."

*

"I think that's enough to get our warrant," Meredith said, pulling out her phone as they rode down in the elevator.

"That is a goddamn silver platter," Tyler replied. "You think he's our guy too, right?"

"I don't want to say anything."

"Why not?"

"Because I don't want to jinx it." Meredith placed the phone against her ear. "Kelly, it's Detective Somerset. Meet us at the precinct, ASAP."

Chapter 43

Beep! Beep!

The two sharp hits from the horn of the car that was nearly on top of his rear bumper startled Greg Ansley from his thoughts.

The driver in front of him had progressed a couple of yards while he remained stationary.

Greg allowed his car to slowly roll forward until he was a foot or two from the stopped car ahead and once again applied the brakes.

He had been a world away inside his head, replaying everything in his mind; every mistake he had made that had led him to this moment, and searching for a way out, but it all came back to the same conclusion.

It was over.

As if to emphasize the point, he caught a glimpse of his wrists, which were visible due to the fact that his cuffs had ridden up his forearms with his hands on the wheel. He had tried so hard to hide them from the detectives, but in the end, it didn't matter. And what was worse, he had dragged Meghan into it by telling her to lie.

As he inched along the interstate in silence, creeping closer to home, he made the decision he knew he should have made all along.

*

Kelly Yamara nodded to the paper she was holding in her left hand. "This is the entry log for the parking garage of Greg Ansley's workplace?"

"Yep," Meredith replied.

Kelly nodded to the paper in her right hand. "And this is from the security footage?"

"That is our boy, Mr. Greg Ansley, arriving at 10:08 in his very own car," Tyler said.

"He not only lied about what time he arrived, but he also lied about switching cars with his wife," Meredith added. "Which means she's been lying to us, too. There's only one reason for both of them to be lying about that morning. We're pretty sure this is our guy."

Tyler smiled. "How's that for a silver platter?"

Kelly was impressed. "I'll try to get the warrant tonight, but it probably won't be until tomorrow morning."

"Fine by us," Meredith said.

"We'll be at the Ansleys' bright and early with some fluffy bows on." Tyler nodded.

"Thanks for the imagery," Kelly said and headed for the door. "Great work, detectives."

"Thank you, ma'am!" Tyler called after her and turned to Meredith. "What's it gonna be? You want to wait it out? See if they can get us the warrant before bedtime?"

Meredith shook her head. "It's getting late. Go home. Get some sleep. It's going to be a busy day tomorrow."

"Copy that," Tyler said, getting out of his chair.

"Good work today," Meredith said.

"You too. I could get used to this homicide thing!" he replied and went out the door.

Meredith waited for his footsteps in the hall to fade away, then took out her phone and dialed.

"What happened?" Kelly asked from the other end. "You forget something?"

"No. I need to ask you for a teeny-tiny favor and I couldn't do it with anyone else around."

Chapter 44

Greg stepped inside from the garage to find Meghan at the kitchen table, reading a book to Anthony.

"What happened?" she asked, noticing his tired eyes and defeated posture. "Did you talk to the detectives?"

"Yes."

"And?"

"They know. It's over."

Meghan's face dropped. "What are we going to do?"

"I need you to trust me, okay?"

"Greg—"

"All of this is my fault, but I'm going to try to make it right. I need you to take Anthony and go to your mother's."

"When?"

"Now."

Meghan's eyes widened. "What are you—?"

"It'll be okay," he said, with his best attempt at a smile. "Everything's going to be all right. I promise."

She got up from the table and walked over to him. "Why? Why do you want me and Anthony to go to my mother's?"

"I'm going to tell them, Meghan. It's what I should have done before and I don't want you or Anthony to be here when that happens."

Meghan broke down and leaned into him.

Anthony watched from the kitchen table as his father broke down as well, holding his mother and softly repeating, "I'm sorry ... I'm so sorry ..."

*

Minutes later, Greg kissed Meghan one last time before she got in the car with Anthony.

She had argued and pleaded with Greg to let her stay or at least give her more details. All he would do is ask that she trust him.

Worn down by the last few days and at Greg's insistence that it was what was best for her and Anthony, she'd finally yielded.

He watched the car disappear down Willow Lane. He then turned to look at the house and the open garage door.

The open garage door.

If only he had remembered to close it the night before everything went to hell, he and Meghan might have made it through, but there was so much happening, he simply forgot. It was such a small oversight, completely understandable, but it had sealed his fate.

Greg shook his head. It was too late for that type of thinking.

Instead of feeling anxious or scared, he felt an overwhelming sense of calm. The decision had been made. He was resigned to whatever awaited him.

He turned to the shed across the yard and began walking, like a man walking to the gallows.

The sound of the grass under his shoes was the same as that morning. The air was still, just like that morning, the morning he'd last made that same walk ...

*

271

A piece of toast in one hand, and a glass of juice in the other, he approached the shed, praying that Meghan or Anthony didn't look out the window and wonder what he was doing.

He opened the door and found the daughter he never knew sitting on the floor, wrapped in the sleeping bag he had smuggled out to her last night. Her shoes were off to the side.

Her teeth chattered as she looked up at him.

Twenty-four hours earlier, he'd had no idea of her existence. The night before, he had received a panicked call that she was coming. He'd gotten to her before she reached the house. He'd begged her to listen to him, to give him some time. She had agreed to stay in the shed until he could sort things out, but the look on her face now said she was done waiting.

"I brought you some breakfast," he offered.

"I'm not staying in here."

"It's only for a little while longer until I figure out—"

"No!" she replied. "I've come all this way—"

"Alexa—"

She suddenly got to her feet.

Greg stumbled backwards.

She seized the opportunity and bolted past him into the yard.

Had Greg not been holding the juice and toast, he might have grabbed her. He might have tried to pull her back into the shed and explain again why she had to wait.

Instead, he stupidly hesitated between calmly setting down the juice and toast or dropping them as he saw the calamity that was about to unfold. He finally dropped them and ran after her.

Greg was still spry and agile for his age, but Alexa was fast and, more importantly, determined. As he chased her across the backyard, he didn't call out her name for fear that it would wake the neighbors, but he had to stop her.

He had to.

She was already across the driveway, through the front yard, and onto Willow Lane, but panic fueled Greg's legs and he quickly caught up, extended his arms, and tackled her to the asphalt.

They landed in a heap, her head smacking against the pavement.

"Alexa, you have to listen to me!" he urged her, as quietly as his heaving lungs would allow.

Alexa was dazed.

Greg could see the scrape on her forehead.

As her senses returned, she began to struggle.

"No! No, no, no. Alexa! Shhhhh! Listen to me!" he insisted, trying to press his hand over her mouth.

"Let go of me!" she grunted as she struggled.

He pressed his hand harder over her mouth to keep her quiet, while grabbing her wrists with his other hand.

She flailed at him.

He was able to keep her hands away from his face but her nails raked his wrists.

"Alexa, please stop!"

She inhaled, winding up for a primal scream.

He saw what she was about to do, and without thinking, his hands flew to her throat.

Her cry was cut short by his hands suddenly throttling her windpipe.

She continued to claw at his wrists and face.

Greg held fast, blinded to the fact that her fingernails continued to rip into his skin. He only knew that if he were to let go, everything would be lost.

She would scream so loud that everyone on Willow Lane, everyone who was starting their day, eating breakfast, or watching television, would come outside to see what was happening. His life would be ruined. His marriage would be over and probably his career as well. All because of one mistake, a mistake he had compounded every step of the way since, culminating in moving to Willow Lane, which was supposed to be his one chance at happiness. Instead, it had been *the worst mistake of all. If she screamed, everything he had worked for, everything he had sacrificed, would be for nothing. All of his frustration poured into his forearms as he crushed her throat. She wasn't just some girl. She was the embodiment of everything he had done wrong in his life. Every nightmare that haunted him in his sleep, every voice in his head that ridiculed him and pointed out how miserable his life had become, was right there in his grip and he would silence it.*

Her attempts grew more ineffectual and her eyes went bloodshot.

He only needed her to be quiet. He needed her to understand, that if she carried out what she intended to do, it would lead to not only his own destruction, but so many others.

"Shh! Shhhhhhh!" he insisted, still gripping her throat.

Her flailing slowed to a stop. Her hands slipped from his wrists and dropped to the pavement.

Seconds later, she stopped moving entirely.

Greg looked down at her.

His daughter's lifeless eyes stared back at him.

He held his grip a few moments longer until reality began to creep in. The tsunami of adrenalin subsided and the true horror of what he had just done dawned upon him.

He had killed her. He had killed his daughter.

He slowly withdrew his hands.

"No ..." he whispered. "No, no, no, no ..."

He gently shook her shoulder, but there was no mistaking the fact those unfocused eyes conveyed.

He looked around. The fog-laden air was absolutely still.

Then, a sound reached him through the mist: the steady thwick-thwick *of nylon against nylon and a woman faintly singing.*

Someone was coming.

Greg began lifting Alexa's lifeless body to get her off the road, but it was too late. The woman was too close. He lowered Alexa back to the asphalt, where she rested, face-down. He quickly rifled through her pockets. There, he found an ID card.

274

The singing was getting closer. Any moment, the owner of the voice would emerge from the fog.

Greg sprinted across the lawn to the backyard and to the shed. He stepped inside and shoved the sleeping bag into the corner, out of sight to the casual observer, along with the ID, toast, and empty glass of juice. He then quickly stepped out of the shed, shut the door, and locked it.

Greg raced back to the house. His hand touched the back door just as a woman's screams pierced the air.

He threw open the door and went inside.

Meghan was standing in the kitchen, staring at him.

"Greg ... What did you do?"

*

Meghan's words echoed in his mind now as Greg reached for the door to the shed and opened it.

The sleeping bag was still stuffed in the corner. There was the ID, too.

Just inside the door, a trail of ants traced the path of the spilled juice to the grass at his feet.

Greg stepped inside and closed the door.

Chapter 45

Meredith shuffled the skillet over the burner. The peppers and onions popped and hissed in the sputtering olive oil as she quickly consulted the recipe printed on the cardstock, upon which was printed a photo of what the dish was supposed to look like.

A five-star restaurant couldn't make it look that good, Meredith thought.

The bottle of wine waited on the counter next to the fridge, but she paid it no mind. Dinner was going to be a celebration of the day, but she was still technically on the clock. The warrant could come down at any minute if Kelly pulled some strings, but by the time the meal would be ready, it was a safe bet that she would be done for the night.

She flipped the veggies again and inhaled the aroma. She could never cut it as a chef, but she prided herself on being a little better with a stove and cutting board than most.

Her phone vibrated on the kitchen table with a call from Allison. It was too early for their customary goodnight call.

"Hey, baby," Meredith answered.

Allison was laughing and out of breath. "Guess what?!"

"Give me the phone!" Pete said from somewhere in the background.

"What?"

"Dad asked Heather to marry him!"

"Allison!" Pete good-naturedly cried.

Meredith reached back and turned off the burner. "He did? Wow. That was quick."

"Yeah. He said he was tired of everyone spoiling the surprise," Allison giggled, her voice bouncing as she ran.

"Give it to me!" Pete insisted, his voice growing louder. "Give me that phone, you scamp!"

There was the sound of a playful struggle.

"You're no fun, Dad!" Allison yelled, her voice trailing away.

"Meredith?" Pete asked.

"Yeah. I'm here."

"Believe me, I really wanted to talk to you before our daughter spilled the beans," he said loudly for Allison's benefit.

"It's okay." Meredith smiled.

"Give me a sec," Pete said.

There was the sound of shuffling and then a door closing.

"Meredith. I need to know that you're okay with this."

"Pete, I've already told you; I think it's great."

"Yeah?"

"Heather loves you, you love her, and you both love Allison. That's all I care about."

Pete sighed. "Good ... But, Meredith?"

"Yeah?"

"I'll always love you. You know that, right?"

Meredith suddenly needed to sit in the chair next to her at the kitchen table.

Pete had told her that he still loved her and would always love her. He had said it in the presence of Heather, but it wasn't the love of a husband. It was an acknowledgement of everything that they had been through, and how much they were still a part of each other's lives. Still, Meredith hadn't expected it to hit her so hard. It was that same feeling as before; that the world was moving on without her. Yes, she was happy for Pete, but that pain was there.

"I know and I love you too, Pete."

"Thank you, Meredith," he said, his voice a little unsteady.

"So," Meredith said, wiping her nose. "Um, what kind of wedding are we talking about?"

"I have no idea. I haven't really discussed it with Heather yet, but it goes without saying that we want you there."

"And it also goes without saying that I'll be there."

"Good. Heather might also ask you to help with the planning, if you're okay with that."

Meredith laughed. "Sure. I mean, I've been there before."

Pete chuckled. "It'll be something small. We're not that—"

Meredith's phone vibrated with another call. She checked the screen.

"What the hell?" she breathed.

"What's happening?"

"Listen, Pete, I'm sorry, I've got to go. It's work. I've got a call that I really need to—"

"No, no, no. It's fine."

"It's just that—"

"Meredith," Pete said, cutting her off. "It's fine. Do what you have to do. We'll talk later."

"Thanks. I'll call you back." She ended her call with Pete and tapped the screen to answer the other call.

"Hello?"

Chapter 46

Tyler coughed, pinched his nose shut, and leaned back on the couch as the warm lightning began coursing through his limbs.

He had done a little extra tonight. The past few days had been unbelievably stressful. There was the start of the investigation, running late, the thing at Scott Rennick's place, Hannah, coming clean to Somerset, Thomas Whitaker, but now, they had their guy. If that didn't call for a little extra dessert, Tyler didn't know what did.

But right away, he knew he had pushed it a little too far. The lightning began to crackle and sear his veins. That was fine. He had nowhere to be, other than right there in his living room, savoring the moment.

He was going to close his first homicide case in the morning. He couldn't wait to see the look on Greg Ansley's face when they busted in with the warrant. He wondered if Greg would be shocked. Would he break down? Would he be furious?

Tyler hoped Meredith might let him have a freer hand, it being his first homicide collar and all. He also hoped that Greg would flat-out confess so they could get that shit over with and move on to Scott Rennick's proclivities, and maybe even start digging into Thomas Whitaker.

"Quite the fucked-up street," Tyler said out loud, to his own amusement.

God, he felt good, and not all of it was the blow but a good chunk of it was.

He wanted to get up and do something; go for a run or hit the gym, but he knew better.

"Yeah, Homicide Detective Tyler Foles," he said with a chuckle and a cough. "You may have gone a little heavy on the candy."

He could feel the tips of his fingers sizzling as if they were made of static electricity. It had been a while since he had been this high and the ride was just beginning.

He stood and began pacing around the apartment, but it did little to appease his muscles' desire for movement. He jumped up and down in place and shook out his hands in an attempt to get some of the lightning out of his system, but it only made him glow brighter.

"Okay, okay, okay," he said, sitting back down on the couch. "Overdid it. Overdid it. It's all good. Just take it in and let it out."

While his words were cautious, the feeling of euphoria and invincibility was glorious. His heart was a steady drum of thunder.

This has to be the last ride for a while, he thought.

The drug tests could be coming soon and it would take a few days for this one to clear his system. If he had his wits about him, he might have been worried, but the lightning wouldn't allow that.

He tightly clenched his fists and then attempted to flex every muscle in his body. The lightning had to go somewhere.

His phone, which was on the coffee table, next to the small mirror upon which rested a few stray flecks of powder, began to ring and displayed Meredith's number.

"Shit."

There was no way he couldn't answer. He should have held off on the party, but he was almost in the clear for the evening. Hopefully, Somerset only had some extra info for tomorrow.

"'Sup, Somerset?" he answered, trying to sound casual.

"What are you doing?" she asked, earnestly.

"Just hangin' out."

"You have to get to the Ansleys', right now. I'm on my way there."

"What's going on?"

"Greg Ansley called me. He said he wants to talk to us. Said he was going to 'explain everything.'"

Tyler sat up. "You think he's gonna confess?"

"He might. How soon can you get there?"

"I don't know, Somerset. Not sure it's gonna work for me."

"Seriously?"

Tyler cursed, again, but silently this time.

He knew he should come up with some excuse, some reason why he couldn't go, that he'd had a few whiskies and shouldn't drive, but he'd already promised her that she wouldn't have to walk into a suspect's place alone, and besides, the euphoria and invincibility were quickly overruling any uncertainties. There was no way Tyler was going to miss Greg Ansley confessing to the murder of his daughter. He was going to be there. He was going to see his face. He could play it cool. Somerset wouldn't suspect a thing.

"I can be there in thirty if the traffic ain't bad."

"I'm on 75 and it's died down a little," Meredith said. "I'll meet you there."

She hung up.

Tyler stared at the phone in his hand.

"Fuck it," he said, reaching for his keys.

Chapter 47

Something's up with him, Meredith thought upon hanging up with Tyler.

Why did he seem so reluctant at first to meet her at the Ansleys'? Was he with someone? She had no idea what his social life was like, but he struck her as the kind of guy who would have no problem dropping whatever he was doing for this.

Maybe he was with his sister? That would have made his hesitancy understandable, but why not just say so?

Her speculations were interrupted by a text message from Kelly Yamara.

Caught Judge Tammserson in a good mood. Got your warrant. Covers entire property incld shed. Cleared to search for evidence girl was there. Sent a copy to Wheaton. Happy hunting!

Meredith did her best to keep her eyes on the road as she dialed Sergeant Wheaton and hit the Bluetooth button.

"You calling about the warrant?" he asked through the car's speakers.

"Yeah."

"It's a little late but you want to execute it tonight?"

"I'm actually on my way there, now. Greg Ansley called me and said he wanted to talk."

"Think he wants to get something off his chest?"

"Possibly."

"You're not going alone, are you?" Sergeant Wheaton asked.

"Detective Foles is going to meet me there."

"Good. You want me to send a team to execute the warrant?"

"Yes, please. Detective Foles and I will get there before they do. If he doesn't confess, we'll keep him busy so he doesn't get rid of anything before the team arrives."

"Got it. Be careful and don't go in there without Detective Foles."

"Wouldn't dream of it," Meredith said, knowing Sergeant Wheaton would blow a gasket if he knew what happened with Scott Rennick.

"Go get 'em," Sergeant Wheaton said and hung up.

*

Minutes later, Meredith pulled up outside of the Ansleys' house.

Both garage doors were open but Greg Ansley's Accord was the only car inside.

If Greg saw her parked out front, she wondered how long she would be able to stall until Tyler arrived, but thankfully, Tyler was already pulling up.

He parked behind her and got out.

The moment he stepped out of the car, Meredith knew she had been right; something was up with him.

His breathing was heavier than necessary. His movements were clipped and he avoided eye contact.

"What's going on?" he asked, looking toward the house.

"What I told you earlier; Greg Ansley said he wants to 'explain everything' but we also got the warrant. Sergeant Wheaton is sending some bodies to help us out. If Greg Ansley doesn't confess right away, we keep him talking until they arrive."

"Cool. Let's do this," Tyler said and began walking to the porch.

Meredith didn't move.

"Tyler?"

He stopped and turned back to her.

"You okay?" she asked.

Tyler forced a shrug. "Just want to get this show on the road." He resumed his march to the front door.

Meredith followed.

Tyler pressed the doorbell before Meredith was even on the porch. The chimes had barely died away before he began knocking.

"Give him a chance," Meredith said.

Tyler waited a little longer and knocked again, but there was no answer.

"You said we've got the warrant?" Tyler asked.

"Yeah."

Tyler took a step back and inspected the door.

"Think we need to get this open?"

"No. Come on," Meredith said and walked off the porch.

Tyler followed her down the concrete path and around the side of the house to the driveway. She entered the garage, maneuvered around the Accord, and up to the door where she knocked and waited.

"Mr. Ansley?" she called out.

Nothing.

This time, she pounded on the door. "Mr. Ansley?"

She tried to open it, but it was locked.

"We waiting for the crew or we need to break this down?" Tyler asked.

Meredith turned to him.

His breathing was still off. He couldn't remain still. He was too eager and he continued to avoid eye contact.

"Let's try the backdoor. We'll look in the windows while we're at it," she said as she walked past him and out of the garage.

Tyler fell in line as she led them into the backyard. She was making her way to the backdoor when something caught her eye. She came to a halt so abruptly that Tyler almost walked into her.

The door to the shed was partially open.

The light from the setting sun filtered through the small window in the side of the shed, illuminating the interior just enough for them to see a foot lying on the floor inside.

Meredith instinctively drew her firearm.

Tyler began to do the same.

"Tyler?"

His hand stopped on the grip.

"Don't," she said.

"What are you talking about, Somerset? Why wouldn't I—?"

"Leave it," she insisted and stared at him until he withdrew his hand. "And stay right there."

Tyler shook his head in confusion but held up his hands.

Meredith turned back to the shed and cautiously walked toward the door.

She adjusted the angle of her approach so that she could see more of the interior and watched for any movement inside.

"Mr. Ansley?" she called out.

The person lying on the floor remained motionless.

"CCPD," she announced. "Is anyone in there?"

Silence.

She slowly reached out, grasped the handle of the door, and pulled it open.

She crouched low and aimed her weapon inside.

Greg Ansley was lying on the floor. A good portion of his head was gone, splattered across the wall and ceiling. His half-closed eyes stared upwards. A gun was clutched in his left hand.

Meredith did a quick sweep of the shed to double check that no one was hiding in the shadows. There was a workbench in the middle. The walls were made up of pegboards where tools were hung, except for a small section of framed photos. There were photos of Greg with Meghan and Anthony. A photo of a younger Greg with a man who could only be his father. There was also a photo of Greg Ansley that appeared to have been taken years ago in front of a blue and green glass-paneled building.

Meredith made a closer examination of the shadows.

In the corner of the shed, tucked under a table, was a sleeping bag, pillow, and a pair of girl's sneakers.

Meredith lowered the gun, returned it to the holster, and released the breath that had been trapped in her chest.

She crouched down and inspected the remains of Greg Ansley, paying special attention to the gun in his hand. Her eyes drifted from the gun to his wrists, where she saw the claw marks; claw marks that could have only been from where Alexa scratched him during their struggle.

"Damnit," she whispered.

There was the sound of a car outside.

Meredith turned, as did Tyler, to look back toward the driveway, where a Toyota Tercel was pulling in. Behind the wheel was Meghan Ansley. Her eyes widened as she recognized them. The car lurched as she threw it into park.

"Keep her back!" Meredith shouted at Tyler.

Meghan leaped out of the car. Tyler began moving toward her, putting out his hands for her to stop.

"Where's Greg?" she asked.

She moved to go into the backyard but Tyler stepped in front of her and wrapped her in his arms, holding her back.

Meghan struggled at first, but looked toward the shed. Through the open door, she could see the body lying on the floor and immediately understood.

"No … no … Greg?! GREG?!!!"

She continued to cry, thrash, and scream, but Tyler held her fast.

After a few moments, she went limp in his arms as she continued to weep and call out Greg's name. Tyler gently lowered her to the ground where she sat and sobbed.

Over Meghan Ansley's agonized grief, Meredith heard another sound.

Police sirens.

She quickly went to Tyler and grabbed his arm. "Come here."

She led him away from Meghan, but made sure they stayed between her and the shed in case she tried to get inside.

Meredith stopped and turned him so that they were face to face.

"What are you doing, Somerset?" Tyler asked, the setting sunlight streaming into his face.

"Look at me," she said.

Tyler looked anywhere but as he attempted to wriggle out of her hold and avoid the sunlight.

"Get off me," he said.

Meredith tightened her grip. "Look at me!"

Tyler once again tried to wrest himself away from her. "Get off!"

"Tyler, look at me!"

"GET THE FUCK OFF OF ME!" he raged and violently threw Meredith's hands from his arms.

Even Meghan stopped crying, startled by the sudden anger in his voice.

The action had stunned them all, but Meredith quickly recovered, and grabbed his arms again and studied his face.

The breathing. The movements. The dilated pupils that weren't reacting to the changing light from the setting sun.

She looked into his face and knew.

They both knew.

Tyler's rage was gone, replaced by apprehension and guilt.

In the distance, the sound of the police sirens was growing.

"Somerset. Listen, it's nothing. I got this under contr—"

"Go home," she said.

"No. I'm fine. This isn't a big deal."

"Tyler," she said urgently. "You have to get out of here."

He opened his mouth to argue but stopped in the knowledge that she was right.

He turned and began walking back toward the front yard.

Meredith went over and stood next to Meghan, who was still sitting on the grass and had resumed crying.

Moments later, Tyler pulled around the corner. He cast a quick glance in Meredith's direction as he drove off.

All the while, the sound of police sirens continued to grow.

Chapter 48

Tyler sat on the couch in his darkened apartment, staring into the void.

Attempts at sleep had been pointless. The lightning was still faintly crackling beneath his skin when he returned home. However, the euphoria and invincibility had faded, giving way to heightened dread. At first, he simply waited for Meredith to call him. She had to call, right? They could work it out. Maybe he could convince her that what she suspected was wrong. He had just been amped for the confession they were sure Greg Ansley was about to make, but killed himself instead. Tyler was sure there was some way he could talk himself out of trouble.

He even considered coming clean with her.

'Yes, Meredith. You were right. I had a little before I got your call, and believe me, this is not a normal thing. It was incredibly stupid, but I'm good now, and I promise it won't happen again. Now, let's get back to work.'

He talked himself in circles for hours.

Then came the crash.

He had conditioned himself for crashes with his normal "party nights". Knowing the crash was coming went a long way toward mitigating its effects. There would be irritability and the feeling that you had run a marathon with stones around your shoulders and then went straight to a boxing match, in which you got pummeled. Then, Tyler would smoke a cigarette to ease himself down and that was that. He had become such a pro, he could get through it believing that the crash had been worth the high.

This was not one of those crashes.

He hadn't hit the ground this hard in years. The endorphins flat-lined, while the worry and dread continued to grow. By the time he was reasonably clear-headed, it was far too late to call Meredith. He no longer believed he could, nor did he want to try to talk his way out of anything. All he wanted to know was what she was going to do.

There would be no early morning visit with Hannah. He had other things on his mind.

He got dressed obscenely early and joined the onslaught of morning traffic, believing that he could salvage the situation and his career.

*

The elevator doors opened.

Tyler stepped out and glanced around, unsurprised that the hallway was empty at such an early hour. He made his way down the hall and slipped in the door to the office, which, like the hallway, appeared empty. He was still in the process of crashing, and desperately needed coffee.

He slung his bag into Somerset's chair and nearly jumped out of his skin when he heard a voice from Sergeant Wheaton's office.

"Detective Foles? That you?" Sergeant Wheaton asked.

"Y-Yeah, boss. It's me."

"Why don't you come in here?"

Stepping through the door, he found Sergeant Wheaton sitting at his desk and Meredith in a chair on the other side. Sergeant Wheaton was smiling while Meredith wouldn't look at him.

"Have a seat," Sergeant Wheaton said, nodding to the empty chair next to Meredith.

Tyler hesitated but took up him up on his offer.

Sergeant Wheaton sized him up. "Busy day, yesterday?"

"Yeah," Tyler responded.

"Well, it looks like this Jane Doe case is pretty wrapped up. Detective Somerset here, has spent almost all night filling out the paperwork and has submitted a preliminary report."

Tyler blinked. "She has? Already?"

"Yes. She has. There will be an autopsy later this afternoon, but her report says that Mr. Ansley was this girl's father and that he killed her for reasons we have yet to ascertain. We're going to run Mr. Ansley's DNA against Alexa's, but Detective Somerset is fairly certain it will be a match."

"I agree," Tyler said, "but we still need to know why he did it."

"Yes, and Detective Somerset will handle that. Detective Somerset has also made a recommendation."

Tyler's expression darkened. "What kind of recommendation?"

"I'm perfectly aware that she gave you a vote of confidence not that long ago—"

"Yeah, like three days ago."

Sergeant Wheaton silenced Tyler with a glare. "But in her preliminary report, she recommends that you be moved back down to narco and vice and be given a re-evaluation after one year if you want to come back to homicide. I'm putting her recommendation into effect immediately."

Tyler turned his head to stare at Somerset, who kept her gaze straight ahead.

"And did Detective Somerset give a reason for her recommendation?" he asked.

"She mentioned that you had been tardy on multiple occasions in the few days you've been in homicide."

Tyler scoffed, derisively.

"I trust Detective Somerset completely," Sergeant Wheaton

said, "but I'm glad you came in early, because I wanted to give you the chance to respond. In fact, Detective Somerset insisted that you have that opportunity."

Tyler shook his head and chuckled to himself. He was still coming down and the irritability was flaring. He didn't care that she was presenting tardiness as the reason for his demotion and not the other thing. This was going to ruin his career.

"So, this is the one chance I have to stand up for myself against someone who's dinging me for being late?"

Sergeant Wheaton shrugged. "That's all she would say, but yes."

"Okay," Tyler said. "What I have to say is this …"

He once again turned to Meredith.

She tried to avoid his stare but couldn't and met his eye.

"Fuck you, Somerset."

Meredith returned to staring ahead.

Sergeant Wheaton smiled in a way that was both uneasy and ominous.

"I get your frustration, Detective Foles, and you're right; a few days ago, she was in here backing you up, and the fact that her recommendation was because of 'tardiness' leads me to believe that she's full of shit. She's not telling me something and it's pissing me off. She's covering for you, son. She wanted to wait until the case was officially wrapped, but I'm enacting her recommendation immediately. I also want to make myself perfectly clear." Sergeant Wheaton leaned forward and glared at Tyler. "One more word like that, and you'll never wear a fucking badge again. Got it?"

Meredith had known Sergeant Wheaton to curse only when he was joking. Not this time.

"Yeah," Tyler said. "I got it."

"Good," Sergeant Wheaton said. "Now, it's been a crazy forty-eight hours. The case is over. Why don't you take the rest of the day off to decompress and we'll figure out where to go from there, okay?"

Tyler was immediately out of his chair.

"Thanks, boss," he barely got out as he walked through the door.

Meredith hesitated, and then stood.

"Let him go," Sergeant Wheaton said.

"I got it," she said.

＊

By the time Meredith shoved open the door to the parking lot, Tyler was halfway to his car.

"Tyler!"

He kept walking.

"Tyler!" she shouted, going after him.

"Listen, Somerset," he replied without stopping, "I'm really not interested in waiting around to see if another bus comes along that you can throw me under."

"Are you kidding me?!" she snapped as she fell in behind him. "You're really gonna pull this shit?!"

They reached his car. Tyler opened the door but Meredith pushed it shut.

"Look, Somerset, you got me demoted and put a cap on my career. If you're looking for a 'thank you', it ain't happening."

"What I did in there was save any chance you have at a career."

"That really how you see things?"

"That's exactly how they are. As it stands, you get to stay on the force in narco and vice, where you'll have an easier time getting your shit together."

"And how do you think that's gonna look? That I couldn't hack it in the big leagues? And do you think they'll ever give me another shot at homicide? They'll sit me at a desk, rubberstamping shit until I retire or trade it in for a job as a mall cop."

"It's a hell of a lot better than if I had told Sergeant Wheaton that you showed up last night high as a kite."

"I had it under control."

"Oh, you had it under control? Is that supposed to be enough for me to trust you? What if Greg Ansley had been alive in that shed and instead of using the gun on himself, it went to a standoff? You really think you had it 'under control' then?"

Tyler sneered.

Meredith was right, but he was running too hot to admit it.

"You didn't have to do it like this," he said. "You could have talked to me first. Given me a chance."

"A chance is what I just gave you."

"You and I both know that's not how this is gonna play out."

"Fine. Then I was looking out for myself because I would never risk you showing up to a scene like that, again."

They stared at one another.

Tyler finally blinked but his scowl lost none of its hatred for Meredith.

"See you around, Somerset," he said, once more opening the door and stepping into his car.

Meredith moved back and watched as he started the engine, pulled out of the spot, and drove away.

*

Meredith went back upstairs to her desk to finish typing up her notes for the autopsy that afternoon. They were pretty straight-forward: an obvious suicide brought on by the guilt of strangling his daughter. That final point had yet to be proven definitively, but it was a foregone conclusion. Greg Ansley realized that he was minutes away from confessing to the murder and spending the rest of his life in prison. Instead, he decided to take an alternative route.

As she slumped into her chair, Sergeant Wheaton emerged from his office.

"Everything all right?"

"It's taken care of," she replied.

"Meredith, you know that's not true." It was a rare occasion when he addressed her by her first name. "You're covering something for him, something serious, and you've got to tell me. What happens if he's paired with someone in narco and vice, and whatever you're lying about costs that partner their life?"

Meredith stared at the screen of her computer.

"What are you covering up for him?"

"I'm sorry, Sergeant Wheaton, I didn't catch that."

She didn't need to look at him to register his condemnation.

"Wrap this shit up," he said. "And when you're done, we're going to have a talk."

Sergeant Wheaton went back into his office.

Meredith waited until she heard the creaking of his office chair before rubbing her weary eyes. She had grabbed a thirty-minute nap at her desk a few hours ago, but that was all the sleep she could manage.

Why was she was covering for Tyler? Why was she putting her relationship with Sergeant Wheaton on the line for a partner she had worked with for only a few days and who had colossally screwed up?

It was because she saw that spark. Tyler was good at what he did. His "rough-around-the-edges" exterior concealed a sharp mind. She knew about addiction and wanted to give him the benefit of the doubt, but Sergeant Wheaton was right.

If Tyler didn't get clean, he was a danger to any partner he was paired with. Meredith had already taken that into account. With Greg Ansley's suicide, she thought she would have some more time for the dust to settle and she and Tyler would have a chance to talk, but Sergeant Wheaton had pulled the trigger immediately by removing him from the case rather than after it was closed. Now, Tyler's outburst had poured gasoline on his own fire, but his reasoning hadn't been entirely wrong, even if his actions were. Getting knocked back down before his first case was finished would effectively put a lid on his career. He would lose his status as a senior detective in narco and vice. He would have to claw his way back up, if that was even possible, because the demotion on his record would be a stone around his neck. Sergeant Wheaton sure as hell wouldn't want him in his department and, of course, everything was dependent on Tyler getting clean, which was a big question mark.

You're getting ahead of yourself, Meredith thought.

She needed more time for everyone to cool off, and Sergeant Wheaton was right: before any of this could happen, she needed to wrap this shit up.

Chapter 49

The chimes of the doorbell were answered by a frail, elderly woman, but her delicate frame belied the fierce stare with which she greeted Meredith.

"What do you want?" she asked.

"I'm Detective Meredith Somerset. I'm here to speak to Meghan, your daughter. We set up an appointment."

"I don't care what you say, she doesn't want to talk to you."

"It's okay, Mom," Meghan answered from somewhere behind her.

The elderly woman continued to glower.

"Mom, let her in."

*

"You'll have to excuse her," Meghan said, cradling a cup of coffee as she and Meredith sat alone on the back porch.

"It's okay," Meredith said.

There was still a morning chill in the air, but Meghan wanted to speak away from Anthony, who they could see through the window, sitting with his grandmother at the kitchen table, playing with action figures.

"How is Anthony taking it?" Meredith asked.

"He doesn't understand what happened. He doesn't realize his father's dead. I'm not sure I do, either ... I'm sorry I wasn't more helpful last night."

The night before, Meredith had gently tried to get Meghan to explain the previous couple of days, but all she could manage was that Greg had told her to take Anthony and go to her mother's. After a few hours, Meghan had grown worried because Greg wasn't answering his phone and came back to the house. That's when she found Meredith and Tyler in the backyard. Eventually, Meredith had one of the officers drive her back to her mother's while another officer followed in Meghan's car. In the chaos, they had forgotten to ask Meghan to unlock the house so that they could execute the search warrant. Meghan told them about the spare key in the shed. They found no evidence that Alexa had been inside the house, but they didn't need any more than what they found in the shed.

"I do need to ask you why you lied to us the morning we found the girl," Meredith said.

"Greg told me I had to. That morning, I watched him run through the backyard to the shed. He threw something inside, locked it, and ran back to the house. I asked him, 'What did you do?' and he said there was a dead girl in the street. He said he didn't have anything to do with it but worried that someone had seen him looking at the body and he would be blamed." She shook her head. "It was so stupid. I knew he was lying, but I couldn't believe it was happening. I didn't understand how in the space of thirty seconds, the man who I loved and had a child with, might be capable of killing someone. Then, I started thinking about Anthony and what would happen to him if I said something. I was still in shock when I spoke to you. I'm sorry."

Meredith did understand. She in no way condoned it, but she had seen good people make a situation worse by denying that someone they loved could do the unthinkable; that everything had changed in the blink of an eye and the life they knew was over.

"Am I in trouble?" Meghan asked.

"I can't really speak to that," Meredith calmly replied.

She couldn't rule it out. Meghan had lied to the police and obstructed a murder investigation, even if Greg hadn't outright told her that he killed Alexa. She would have to talk to Kelly, but Meredith felt reasonably sure that she wouldn't pursue it. If anything, maybe probation. The case was over and enough damage had been done.

"I know you and Anthony have been through a lot. The best thing to do would be to tell me everything and I'll speak to the district attorney's office."

Meghan nodded in resignation.

"Did Greg ever explicitly tell you that he killed her?" Meredith asked.

"Not until the night before last. He told me that it was his daughter from an affair that he had a long time ago. He said he didn't even know she existed until she showed up. I asked him 'why?', why did he do it, and he said he didn't mean to, but that she would ruin everything. I begged him to tell me what that meant, but he told me to go, and that I would understand after he spoke to you."

"This may sound like an odd question, but did Greg seem nervous or out of sorts when he told you this last night?"

Meghan let out a sad, quiet laugh. "Did he seem like he was about to kill himself? I don't know. He seemed calm. Maybe he was going to do it all along and told me all that just to get me to take Anthony and leave."

It was something Meredith had considered, but there were still questions.

"Mrs. Ansley, did you and your husband own a gun?"

Meghan shook her head. "My father committed suicide with one when I was four. I would never allow a gun in the house with Anthony."

"Did you know your husband had one?"

"No, but I guess there was a lot Greg was hiding from me."

"It looks like he was hiding it from everyone," Meredith replied, as if it might lessen the blow. "He never registered for one and the serial number on the gun was filed down. It appears to have been done recently. It's likely he bought it in the last few days, off market, when he decided to … to do what he was going to do."

"How would Greg even know where to get a gun?"

"It's not that difficult. A couple of clicks on Craigslist or he could have gone to one of the weekly gun shows they have around here and purchased it illegally out of the trunk of a car. It's a pretty easy thing to do."

Meghan looked back toward the kitchen window and watched Anthony playing with his toys at the kitchen table.

"So, that's it?" she asked. "My husband had a secret daughter that he strangled to keep it from getting out and then killed himself? That's what my husband and the father of my child did?"

"It looks that way, but there's still a lot we don't know."

"Like if I'm going to prison?"

"As I said, I'll talk to the district attorney's office."

"Please do," Meghan said, her eyes never leaving Anthony.

Chapter 50

Mike in the Morgue took his foot off the recording pedal under the cookie sheet at the sight of Meredith walking through the door.

"You can stop bringing me dead people, Detective Somerset. You've met your quota." His jocular tone faded as she drew near. "Wow. You look like shit. You okay?"

"It's been a long couple of days."

"So I've heard."

"Yeah? What have you heard?"

Mike shrugged. "Not much. Just that your partner may have been put out to not-so-greener pastures."

"Something like that."

"Want to fill me in on the gossip?"

"Not really." Meredith sighed and looked at Greg Ansley's nude, dead body on the cookie sheet.

His skin was pasty-white, his eyes were still half-open. The blood around what was left of his scalp had been cleaned and the contents of his skull laid bare. The corpse had the appearance of a prop you might see in a cheap haunted house attraction.

"What can you tell me?" Meredith asked.

"Like your notes say, it looks like a straightforward suicide."

Mike pressed his foot on the pedal and spoke toward the microphone hanging over the cookie sheet. "Time is 1:27 p.m. I have been joined by Detective Somerset to go over my preliminary findings in the death of Gregory Jacob Ansley. The cause of death is—" Mike took his foot off the recording pedal, "—really obvious—" he said in an attempt at a joke and put his foot back down "—a gunshot wound to the left-hand side of the head. The bullet entered below the temple, traveled upwards at a fifty-degree angle, causing extensive damage to the brain, and exited at the top of the skull. Death was instantaneous." Mike moved down to Greg's left hand. "Gunshot was likely self-inflicted, as evidenced by the powder burns on the left hand. The only other markings or injuries of note are numerous scratches on the wrists. I note them because of the ongoing investigation into a body that was found on the street outside the deceased's home. The victim in that case scratched their assailant and we were able to collect DNA from under the victim's fingernails. The scratches on Greg Ansley's wrists are consistent with such a struggle. An analysis of Greg Ansley's DNA will be conducted to definitively conclude if he was involved in the previous case." Once again, Mike took his foot off the pedal and turned to Meredith. "Off the record, I'm willing to bet my obscenely underfunded retirement account that this is the guy who strangled your Jane Doe and that he's her dad."

He expected at least a chuckle or some sign of relief from Meredith, but instead, she creased her brow.

"What's wrong?"

Meredith shook her head. "I'm just seeing things."

"Like what?"

"He was right-handed."

Mike glanced back at the body. "Yeah?"

"But he shot himself with his left hand?"

"I was going to talk to you about that."

"Is it bothering you too?" Meredith asked.

"It did at first, and I'll admit, it's strange, but I've seen a lot of suicides. Too many, in fact, and sometimes, they don't make any sense at all. People get weird when they're about to end their own life. I had a woman, who for seemingly no apparent reason, used her toes to pull the trigger, when there was nothing wrong with her hands."

Meredith was still focused on the corpse, unconvinced.

Mike noted her expression.

"I don't think we should overcomplicate this one, detective. He strangled his daughter, was overcome with grief and guilt, knew you were closing in, and decided to do us all a favor and punch out early." He stopped and held up his hands. "Sorry. I don't mean to tell you how to do your job. I only wanted to point out that the fact that he used his left hand when he was right-handed is weird but not unheard of, and the powder burns on his left-hand seal the deal."

"What about the angle?" Meredith asked, unable to let it go. "Why would he have been aiming upwards?"

"It's possible he was having second thoughts when he pulled the trigger. I had one guy who did almost the exact same thing. It looked like he was aiming up at the ceiling. The bullet did just enough damage to turn out his lights. Made no sense at first, but then we found out that his legs gave out just as he pulled the trigger. He was fainting as he shot, which made it look weird, but it was definitely a suicide."

"How could you possibly know that?"

"Because he filmed it. He decided to record some last words for his kids. Me and the detectives watched the tape and every-thing matched up. When he was done talking, he stood there for a couple of seconds with the gun to his head, working himself up. He started breathing really heavy and shaking. He hyperven-tilated just as he started to pull the trigger. Legs gave out. His hand was starting to fall away from his head, causing the gun to point upwards, and *bang*! Game over. I'm relatively certain that's exactly what happened to Mr. Ansley, here."

Meredith reluctantly nodded.

Mike was right. She was seeing things that weren't there because it was all so unsatisfying. They should have gotten to Greg Ansley sooner. She hated that he had killed his daughter, and for that, only had to endure a brief second of punishment, and avoided paying a larger price for what he had done. His actions had caused harm to others on Willow Lane, and in a sense, he had gotten away.

"Detective?" Mike asked, snapping her out of it. "You good?"

"Yeah, I'm good. Thanks, Mike. I appreciate it. I'm gonna go upstairs and put the finishing touches on this mess."

"Trust me; this is a suicide, but if I find a poison dart or anything, I'll let you know."

She looked at the body. "I don't think there's anywhere left to hide one."

"Oh, there is," Mike responded, deadpan.

Meredith smiled, turned, and headed toward the door. "Thanks, Mike."

"I mean it about the quota!" Mike called after her. "Stop bringing me bodies!"

"I'll try!" she called back as the door swung shut behind her.

Chapter 51

Meredith was back at her desk, slogging through the paperwork.

She had filled out the forms for the DNA analysis, leaving out the request to expedite the results, which she was sure the lab guys would appreciate. She had put in a request to see if they could get the serial number off the gun, but she wasn't hopeful. As she had told Meghan, the number had been filed down. It looked to have been done recently and not very well, but well enough.

She was dotting the i's and crossing the t's. It was a tedious but necessary part of. the job. She had done it more times than she could count, but that nagging feeling was starting to grow; the feeling that this wasn't done. It had started with the trip to see Mike in the Morgue.

Meredith dropped her pen onto the desk and leaned back in her chair.

Mike was right; a slight oddity in a suicide didn't point to something bigger. They were just that: oddities, an errant brush stroke in a macabre painting where the artist was under duress, not trying to convey some secret message.

If she needed any more confirmation, all she had to do was walk into Sergeant Wheaton's office, explain everything that had happened, and he would tell her the same thing Mike had. It was open and shut. Was it satisfying? Nope, but she should take the win, or at least what could be called a draw, and move on.

But in her mind, she kept going back to the shed. It wasn't the image of Greg Ansley, a quarter of his head splattered on the ceiling that was bothering her.

She had seen something; something that didn't fit.

Yes, Meredith, she told herself. *You saw the proof Alexa was there. You saw a suicide. If you need more convincing, go talk to Sergeant Wheaton.*

She didn't want to talk to Sergeant Wheaton because she knew the conversation would turn to Tyler, and she needed more time.

Meredith was suddenly struck by an idea.

If it was closure she was after, she might find a little in someone who would be happy that the case was over and Alexa's killer was dead.

*

"Sister Mariah?"

"Yes?"

"Hi. This is Detective Meredith Somerset. How are you?"

"I'm fine," she answered tentatively. "And you?"

"I'm okay." Meredith lazily twirled a pen in her hand as she spoke. "I was calling because we closed the case on Alexa's killing. I thought you would want to know."

"Oh. Does that mean you found whoever did it?"

"Yes and no. We were about to apprehend him, but he, uh … Before we could arrest him, he decided to take matters into his own hands."

"I'm afraid I don't understand. What do you mean he 'took matters into his own hands'?"

"He killed himself."

Meredith had hoped to be a little more delicate, but she was going on almost no sleep.

"He killed himself?" Sister Mariah asked.

"Yes. Turned out it was her father who strangled her. Greg Ansley? I assume that was the name Alexa found on your computer."

There was a pause.

"Detective, I'm sorry but I can't—"

"Yeah, I know," Meredith said, exasperated. "You can't go into it, even though I just told you that we know his name."

The call was supposed to put Meredith at ease, but the realization that Greg Ansley would still be alive if Sister Mariah had simply given her his name in that first phone call caused Meredith's blood to boil.

"Sister Mariah?" Meredith asked.

"I'm sorry, detective. It's not that I ..."

The pen in Meredith's hand stopped twirling.

"Go on."

"I didn't ... We didn't ..."

"Sister Mariah?"

Meredith waited, listening for any whisper that Sister Mariah might make.

"No. I'm sorry. I can't," Sister Mariah replied.

Meredith was filled with the sudden urge to hurl the pen across the room.

"All right, then," she said in disgust. "Just wanted you to know, since you cared so much about Alexa. If there's anything else, I'll be sure to give you a call."

"Th-Thank you, detec—"

For the first, and what Meredith could only assume would be the last time in her life, she hung up on a nun.

Chapter 52

Meredith kept at it for another two hours and was nearing the end, but she finally had to surrender. She had to get out of there, away from Alexa, and Willow Lane, and thoughts of Tyler, and Sergeant Wheaton, and unfounded suspicions that would not go away.

She crossed the bullpen and knocked on Sergeant Wheaton's open door.

He looked up from his computer and took in her heavy eyes. "I'd ask how you're holding up, but Jesus, I don't have to."

"That obvious?" she said with a failed attempt at a smile.

"Yeah."

There was an awkward silence fueled by the fact that they hadn't spoken since that morning.

"I've finished most of the paperwork," Meredith finally said, "but as you can tell, it's been a long day. Well, two days, actually ... It's been a long week, and I—"

"Go home, Meredith."

"Is that okay? I know it's still a little early."

"I should have told you to go home hours ago."

"I'll have everything done by tomorrow. I'll try to—"

"Meredith. Go home. In fact, take a day or two off. Greg Ansley's not going anywhere and you need some rest."

Meredith would normally flat-out refuse, or at least bristle at such a suggestion, but under the circumstances, she wanted nothing more.

"Okay. I'll still work on it some more tonight and send you what I've got."

She turned to leave.

"Meredith?"

"Yeah?"

"We're not done with this Foles thing. Before he's reassigned, you and I are having a talk, and we're not doing the whole 'I didn't catch that' routine. Got it?"

"Got it," Meredith said, unable to argue.

All she wanted to do was go home.

*

But that wasn't enough.

Having walked through the door and locked her firearm in the safe, she stood in the silence of the living room and looked around. That feeling, gnawing at the base of her brain, would not go away.

She thought about working some more on her laptop, but that was the last thing she needed. Instead, she changed into comfy clothes, put on a movie she had seen a hundred times before, and tried to take a nap on the couch. It was late in the day, but given her fatigue, she was confident a nap wouldn't keep her up later.

But a nap was not in the cards.

As the opening credits started, her thoughts continued to spiral.

Frustrated, she changed into her running clothes, popped in her earbuds, cranked up the music, and went for an extended run.

She once again pushed herself to the extreme, hoping to exhaust the nameless suspicion that continued festering in her skull.

By the time she finally slowed down outside of her apartment, she was gasping for air. Instead of exhausting her worries, she had exhausted her defenses against them, and they grew louder than before.

A stinging hot shower and a glass of wine did nothing to silence them, and it was still early in the evening.

She needed to interact with someone.

She could have called Tyler to see if he had cooled off, but if he hadn't, it would only make things worse.

She wanted to talk to someone who had no connection to the case, whatsoever.

Meredith grabbed her phone and tapped Allison's number on her contact list.

"Meredith?" the voice on the other end asked.

"Heather?"

"Yeah."

"Where's Allison?"

"She's upstairs, doing homework. Sorry, I know I shouldn't be answering Allison's phone, but I've been wanting to talk to you and I saw your name pop up on the caller ID. I know Pete and Allison told you the news."

"They did and congratulations. I couldn't be happier for you guys."

"Thanks."

"You have to tell me; what are the plans for the wedding?"

"It's going to be a low-key affair. We don't want anything crazy, but I'm going to need help and if you say 'no', I'll completely understand, but … Meredith, can you please help me plan this thing?"

Meredith laughed. "Of course, but I have one condition."

"Name it."

"You have to uphold the bridesmaid tradition and put Allison in the gaudiest dress imaginable."

"Okay, but are you going to be comfortable in it? Because I'd love for you to be one of my bridesmaids, too. You've been an amazing part of my life. I really want you and Allison up there with me."

Meredith was deeply touched. "Heather, I'd be honored. Thank you."

Heather breathed a sigh of relief. "Good. I still might go with the gaudy dresses, though."

"Then I'll help you plan the reception at Waffle House."

They broke down laughing and proceeded to talk for another hour about everything, spit-balling ideas for the ceremony and reception, about colors and menus, bands versus a DJ (the vote for a DJ was unanimous). What Meredith worried might drive a wedge between them was actually bringing them closer. They talked about venue-shopping and cake-tasting and bringing Allison along.

As if on cue, there was Allison's voice in the background.

"I'm done with my homew— why are you on my phone?"

"I was just talking to your mom. Are you ready for your daughter?"

"Sure," Meredith replied. "Throw her on."

"Okay. Thank you, Meredith. I love you."

Meredith smiled. "I love you, too, Heather."

"Here you go," Heather said, handing the phone to Allison.

"Umm, what was that?" Allison asked.

"We had a long talk and Heather asked me to help plan the wedding. I'm also going to be one of her bridesmaids, so I'll be standing right up there with you during the ceremony. And you, me, and Heather are going to go venue-shopping and cake-tasting."

"What does that mean?"

"It means we're going to go to neat places and people are going to give us lots of free cake."

They spoke a little while longer about the wedding before Meredith finally checked the time on her phone.

"Okay. It's getting late. Time for you to go to bed."

"Mom … Do you really love Heather? Even though she's marrying Dad?"

"Baby, I love her *because* she's marrying Dad and because she loves you. You love her too, right?"

"Yeah," Allison answered confidently.

"Good. And I love you, too, baby."

"Love you, Mom."

"Goodnight."

"Goodnight," Allison said and hung up.

Meredith put down the phone and leaned back on the couch.

Her heart was full. She couldn't remember the last time she had been this content. Not once during the conversation with Allison and Heather had Alexa, or Greg Ansley, or Tyler, entered her thoughts.

Mike was right. Greg Ansley committed suicide. The case was over.

If the events of the last few days, from the murder of Alexa by her father, to Meredith's own dealings with her mother had taught her anything, it was that she needed to seize this and not dwell on the past for one moment longer.

She had been so concerned about the world leaving her behind again, and here was the world, welcoming her aboard.

Last time, after the disappearance of Alice, she had not been offered a choice to move on.

This time, she was, and Meredith was taking it.

*

The warm glow of contentment continued throughout the evening and was still with Meredith as she slid under the sheets.

She had cooked a wonderful late dinner of salmon and rice

that she ate while watching a television show she had been meaning to catch up on. She read a couple chapters of a book she had purchased ages ago that had been gathering dust on the nightstand. She had started making plans for tomorrow but said, "forget it". She was going to do whatever her whims dictated. If she wanted to be productive, she would be. If she wanted to be selfish and catch a movie or go to the High Museum of Art, she would. If she didn't want to change out of her pajamas all day, so be it.

She clicked off the lights and nestled her head into the pillow.

After a few minutes, the dreams began, something about a Ferris Wheel suspended over the ocean, but it was cut short by the ringing of her phone.

Meredith sluggishly blinked her eyes open.

Her phone continued to glow and chime on the nightstand.

She checked the screen. It was 11:33 and the call was coming from a New York area code.

"This is Somerset," she answered groggily.

"Detective Somerset? It's Sister Mariah. I'm sorry to be calling so late."

"No. It's fine," Meredith said, clicking on the light.

"I wanted to speak to you, detective. I wanted to apologize."

"For what?"

"For not helping you catch Alexa's killer."

Meredith appreciated the gesture, but it was late and she had had her fill of Sisters of Sacred Heart.

"Okay. Thank you … Is that all?"

"No. I want you to know that I loved Alexa and that I cared for her and I wanted to help."

We're not going over this again, Meredith thought.

"Sister Mariah, the case is closed. I understand you wanted to help but the opportunity for that has passed."

"I also want you to know that she didn't find the man who killed her because of me."

"What?"

"This afternoon when we spoke, there was something I wanted to tell you, but I wasn't sure if I could. I wanted you to know that Alexa didn't find the name and address of the man who killed her from me."

Meredith shook her head, trying to clear the cobwebs. "What are you saying?"

"I'm not allowed to give you any names, so I'm not going to, but I can tell you—"

"Wait. Before you go any further, and I hate to say this, but it might be best if we have this conversation tomorrow with Sister Anna on the phone."

"I don't care," Sister Mariah insisted with an intensity that Meredith assumed was as close as she got to pissed off. "From my understanding, I've found a way to say what I want without jeopardizing anyone here at Sisters of Sacred Heart, and if I'm wrong, I'll suffer the consequences."

"Okay …"

"I wanted you to know that Alexa didn't find her father through me. I had never heard the name 'Greg Ansley' until our conversation this afternoon. We only had the name of Alexa's mother in our system."

Meredith stared at the ceiling overhead.

It all came roaring back, louder than before; the gnawing at the base of her brain, the sensation that something was off, that this was all far from over.

"Detective Somerset?"

Meredith snapped out of her daze. "Wait. Hold on. Then, how did she find her father?"

"I don't know, Detective Somerset. I just needed you to know that I didn't send Alexa to her killer."

"Sister Mariah, I have to know. If you really cared for Alexa—"

"I told you; I love all my children here at Sisters of Sacred Heart and you said that Greg Ansley killed her."

"He did, but—"

"Then, I guess it's over."

"Sister Mariah, you've got to give me her mother's name—"

"I can't."

"Sister Mariah, please—"

"I'm sorry," Sister Mariah said, the confidence she possessed moments ago quickly fleeing. "Good night."

"No, don't hang up!"

The line went dead.

Meredith stared at the phone in her hand before setting it back on the nightstand.

She clicked off the light and lowered her head back to the pillow, but she was wide awake, her brain a firestorm of questions.

If Alexa didn't know Greg Ansley was her father, what was she doing on Willow Lane? Who told her? Did Alexa contact her mother first? Would her mother know where Greg Ansley was? Was there any other way that Alexa could have found her father? No. Alexa had to have gotten the information from her mother. So, where was she? Did she know that Greg was dead?

"I miss you, Meredith."

Meredith bolted upright.

Alice was standing in the shadows at the foot of her bed.

Meredith frantically reached over and turned on the light, banishing the shadows.

Alice was gone.

Chapter 53

The smell of chlorine filled Meredith's nostrils. She could feel the sun warming her hair.

The pool was packed. Children ran past her, but their faces were blurry as they jumped in the pool or strolled to the concession stand, unaware of Meredith's presence.

Meredith stared across the pool toward the diving boards, her eyes locked onto the one figure who did have a face: Alice.

She was standing at the back of the line for the high dive. A few feet behind her, watching her from the other side of the fence, was a figure. Its face was also blurry.

The figure tilted its head and Alice turned as if it had addressed her.

Meredith helplessly watched as Alice spoke to the faceless figure, unable to hear what was said over the sounds of splashing and the playful screams of children.

Alice turned and began making her way toward the main entrance.

"Alice!" Meredith screamed, but it had no effect.

Alice couldn't hear her. No one could, except for the figure behind the fence.

Even though he didn't have eyes, Meredith could feel him looking at her.

They stared at one another.

Gradually, the figure's face became clear.

Hot tears stung Meredith's eyes as she looked upon the smiling face of her father.

Then, as quickly as her father's face had appeared, the figure's face blurred again, only to be replaced by that of Wallace Hogan, the mentally unstable loner who lived in the woods near the pool. The face changed again to Meredith's childhood neighbor, Mr. Rawlins. Another blur, and the face was suddenly her history teacher, Mr. Snyder. Then, she saw the face of Detective Reed. More faces appeared, all of them she knew. Some of them people she cared for, trusted. More faces appeared; Mike in the Morgue, Tyler, Greg Ansley, Sergeant Wheaton, Scott Rennick, people who it was impossible to have been involved in her sister's disappearance.

Alice reached the figure's side and took his hand.

The face blurred again, but this time, remained blurred.

The figure looked at Meredith one last time before he and Alice turned and began walking away.

"Alice!" Meredith screamed. "Alice!!!"

Alice began to turn toward her, but then she and the figure disappeared.

Meredith's eyes flew open. In a breathless panic, she took in her darkened room and pressed the palms of her hands against her eyes.

The nightmares were back.

317

Chapter 54

The warmth from the Styrofoam cup filled with coffee radiated through Meredith's hands as she sat on the leather couch. Dr. Kaplan was sitting in the chair across from her, holding her own mug. The clock above the wall of photos and certificates read 7:19.

"Thank you for seeing me so early," Meredith said.

"Of course. You called my personal line at one in the morning."

"Sorry about that."

"No. I'm saying you did the right thing."

"It was an emergency."

"I should think so. Tell me what happened."

Meredith did the best she could to recount everything that had happened over the last few days in the shortest time possible. She described the case, the developments with her mother, with Tyler, Greg Ansley's suicide, Pete and Heather's engagement, and wrapped it up with the phone call from Sister Mariah and the appearance of Alice at the foot of her bed only a few hours earlier.

"And the nightmares have started again," Meredith finished.

She looked up to see Dr. Kaplan staring at her.

"Okay," Dr. Kaplan said. "I'd say it's been a pretty eventful couple of days."

"Yeah," Meredith concurred. She had spent the rest of the night unsuccessfully chasing sleep.

"There's a lot to talk about, but was there something in particular that you wanted to focus on?"

"I know this is going to sound crazy, but out of all of this, it's the case that's bugging me the most," Meredith said, rising to her feet. She began pacing back and forth. "I mean, why can't I let this go? He killed his daughter and committed suicide. It's obvious. So, why do I feel like I'm missing something? Why did the call from Sister Mariah set off another, I don't know what to call it, 'thing' with Alice and the nightmares? I really thought I was done with that after shutting out any future with Mom."

"We've talked about that, Meredith. It's never going to be completely over. You can only continue to deal with it, to process it."

"I know, but I really believed that I had put that part of the 'processing' behind me. I thought I had a handle on it ... I can't do that all over again."

"Meredith, this isn't a relapse. You're not backsliding. This is perfectly understandable after the events of this week. You had a murder investigation where the victim resembled Alice. You started working with a new partner who put you in an incredibly difficult situation. Pete and Heather got engaged. Your mother re-entered your life in a terribly destructive way. Then, the prime suspect in your case committed suicide. Am I leaving anything out?"

Meredith stopped pacing by the wall of pictures. "No. I think you covered all of it."

"My god, Meredith. Of course, you're shaken. How could you not be? And when was the last time you slept?"

"I've caught a nap here and there."

"I'm talking about real sleep."

"Two days ago."

Hearing the words caused the fatigue to renew its assault on Meredith's senses.

"Then it's good James gave you a couple days off," Dr. Kaplan said. "You need to do everything you can to process all of this, and no one can tell you how to do that but you. We can find some time to talk if you think that would help or you can stay far away from here."

"Is that what you think I should do?"

"I can't make that decision for you, Meredith. My advice is to take this afternoon and come up with a plan. I also think you should request a few more days off ... and you're going to have to tell James about what's happening."

Those had been the words Meredith was dreading.

To have to admit to Sergeant Wheaton that Alice was back would make Meredith feel weak, like she was letting him down, and that years of work had been wiped away, but Dr. Kaplan was right.

Tears of frustration rushed to Meredith's eyes. She turned and pretended to be observing the degrees and photos mounted to the wall to hide them from Dr. Kaplan.

"You can't look at this as some sort of failure, Meredith. That's not what it is."

Meredith listened as her eyes drifted from picture to picture. Here was Dr. Kaplan receiving the diploma that was in the adjacent frame. There was a photo of Dr. Kaplan at a lecture. Below that was a photo of Dr. Kaplan with a group of people at what appeared to be a symposium of some kind. There was another photo with a different group of people, but the building in the background was the same. She guessed it was the same symposium but a different year.

"This is a natural result of everything that's going on," Dr. Kaplan continued. "But there are also a lot of positives. Look at Heather asking you and Allison to be a part of the wedding."

Meredith still had her back to her, gazing at the photos, while trying to hide her reaction. There were more photos of Dr. Kaplan with other groups of people.

"And I can't tell you how proud I am of how you handled the situation with your mother. You did the right thing."

Meredith's eyes snapped back to the photos of the same symposium from different years. A different group of people, standing in front of the same building in two different photos.

"You were right to cut her out of your life until she puts in the work to move on," Dr. Kaplan was saying. "You can't completely cut out your past. You of all people know that, but it's up to you how you move forward, and the people tangled up in the past will have to deal with that."

Her words probably would have helped, but Meredith didn't hear them. She wasn't thinking about her mother, or Sergeant Wheaton, or Pete, or Heather, or Allison, or Tyler, or even Dr. Kaplan.

It was right there in front of her, the thing she had seen in the shed. Seeing the photos on Dr. Kaplan's wall of the same building in the background of two different photos had triggered it. She knew what she had seen in that shed. It was the photo of a younger Greg Ansley with a group of people standing in front of the blue and green glass-paneled building. She had seen that building in the background of another photo on Willow Lane.

"Meredith …? Meredith?"

She turned back to Dr. Kaplan.

"Are you okay?" Dr. Kaplan asked.

"Yeah. Yeah, I'm fine, but I should probably be going. I've taken up too much of your time this morning." Meredith went back to the couch and began collecting her things.

"What just happened?" Dr. Kaplan asked.

"Nothing. This has been great. Thank you."

Dr. Kaplan stood.

"Meredith—?"

"I really have to go," Meredith said, heading for the door.

Dr. Kaplan stepped into her path, blocking the door.

"Meredith, what's going on?"

Meredith remembered that first rule that Dr. Kaplan had established when they began their sessions: don't lie. It was a waste of both their time and she would never get better, but in this one instance, Meredith felt she had no choice.

"Everything's fine, Dr. Kaplan. I promise."

*

Meredith wasn't sure if the morning traffic was as bad as it always was or if it was her heightened state, but after what felt like an agonizingly long drive, she turned into the entrance to Meadowgate. A few more twists and turns and she stopped in front of the Ansley house.

She wished there was some way to hide her presence—some trees to obscure the view of her car or hedgerows to hide behind as she got out and walked across the lawn—but there were none. She moved quickly, hoping to get out of there before she was spotted.

The morning dew began to dampen her shoes as she approached the shed. The police tape still hung across the door. She gently pulled it down and let it hang to the side as she opened the door and stepped inside.

She was met with the smell of cut wood, metal, and grease. The bloodstains were still there on the floor and opposite wall, but they held no interest for her.

She closed the door behind her and went to the wall with the small collection of photos. There were the ones of Greg with Meghan and Anthony. There was one that Meredith assumed was Greg's father, taken years ago.

Meredith zeroed in on the photo of Greg standing with a group of people in front of the entrance to the blue and green, glass-paneled building. Everyone in the photo was wearing matching hunter-green polos and khakis, with lanyards hanging from their necks. Compared to the other photos, this one stuck out like a sore thumb. There didn't seem to be anything in this particular photo that would hold any emotional resonance for Greg Ansley, but it clearly meant something to him. Why else would it be included with the photos of people he cherished most in a place where only he would see it? Meredith peered closer. The Greg Ansley in the photo was younger with a much slimmer figure, more hair, and fewer wrinkles. He looked handsome and vibrant, but that only occupied Meredith's attention for a second.

She focused on the building behind them.

The wall of blue and green panes of glass.

No. Her tired mind wasn't playing tricks on her.

She knew that building. She had seen it before.

It might have been a coincidence, but Meredith had stopped believing in coincidences long ago.

She carefully removed the photo from the wall. She flipped up the clasps on the back and removed the picture from the frame. The resolution was grainy, due to the fact that it was an enlargement of the original photo and had been printed on a computer. Meredith turned the photo over, hoping to see a date or location written on the back, but there was none.

She quickly folded the photo, tucked it into her pocket, and replaced the frame on the wall.

She had to get out of there.

Meredith stepped out of the shed and replaced the police tape across the door.

She kept her eyes down as she hurriedly crossed the lawn, worried that if someone were watching, she would give herself away by looking in a certain direction.

She reached her car, got inside, started the engine, and drove off, hitting the gas just enough for a hasty getaway, but not enough to squeal the tires and draw attention.

As she drove away, Meredith said a silent prayer. *Please, please say that no one saw me.*

Chapter 55

Meredith hustled into the office and slid into her chair. She took out the photo, unfolded it, laid it on the desk next to the keyboard, and fired up the computer.

There was the creaking of Sergeant Wheaton's chair from his office and a moment later he emerged.

"Our definitions of 'take the day off' must vary, widely," he said upon seeing her.

"I need to check something," Meredith replied.

Sergeant Wheaton spotted the photo on the desk. He walked over, picked it up, and inspected it.

"Meredith," he sighed. "What are you doing?"

"Something doesn't feel right."

"I know that feeling. It's caused me plenty of pain and has gotten me in a lot of trouble, especially when I was wrong."

"This will be quick. Then, I'll get out of here and sleep a lot better."

"Will you?" he asked doubtfully.

Meredith stopped typing, wondering if Dr. Kaplan had called Sergeant Wheaton. It would be a terrible breach of trust, but she had to have known Meredith was lying when she said everything was okay. Meredith couldn't call Sergeant Wheaton on it, because if Dr. Kaplan hadn't, she would have to explain.

"It'll be quick. I promise," Meredith said.

Sergeant Wheaton held the picture a moment longer before setting it back down on the desk.

"Be careful," he said and went back into his office.

Again, Meredith didn't know if he was referring to the case, or Dr. Kaplan, or both of them, or maybe neither of them, but there was nothing she could do about it.

Instead, she finished bringing up her notes from the casefile in one window and Google in a web browser.

She glanced at the photo and the question haunted her: Why this photo? What was it doing among those other treasured memories in that shed? And there was no way that it was just a coincidence that Meredith had seen that building before.

She had a creeping suspicion, but she had to be sure it wasn't some imaginary connection that her frazzled, sleep-deprived mind had concocted.

She pulled up Greg Ansley's background check and employment history from the casefile.

There it was: Cloverfield Construction in Charleston. He had been a consultant, just like his most current job at Hopewell & Associates.

I had to travel around a lot. It put a strain on our marriage, he had told them at their first interview.

Meredith clicked back onto Google and found the company website. Thankfully, they were still around.

Now, it was about to get tricky.

She dialed the company's general info line, which was answered by a chipper female voice with a southern accent.

"Cloverfield Construction. How may I direct your call?"

"Hi. My name is Detective Meredith Somerset. I'm with the Cobb County Police Department outside of Atlanta. How are you this morning?"

"Very well, thank you," the woman answered, slightly on edge at the knowledge she was talking to a detective.

"I was wondering if I could speak to someone about a previous employee."

"I suppose," the woman said. "But it depends on the information you're looking for."

"I'm trying to trace his business travels from 2001 to 2005. I was wondering if you still had the records of the trips he took for the company over that time."

Meredith had taken a guess on the timeframe, based on Alexa's age.

"Certainly. Let me connect you. One moment, please," the woman said, sounding relieved that this was going to be someone else's problem.

Tinny, poor-quality elevator music filled Meredith's ear.

Moments later, the music clicked off just as suddenly as it had begun.

"Hello?" an uncertain voice asked.

"Hello?" Meredith asked back.

"This is Kevin Amero. I'm one of Cloverfield Construction's accountants and bookkeepers."

"Hi, Kevin. My name is Detective Meredith Somerset."

"I was told you had a question about the business travels of a former employee?"

"That's correct."

"I'm not sure what I can tell you. I may have to contact our attorneys."

"I totally understand, but I don't think that'll be necessary," Meredith said.

"Okay. Tell me what you need and I'll see what I can do. Who's the employee?"

"A guy named Greg Ansley."

There was a pause.

"Greg?" Kevin asked.

"You know him?"

"Yeah. Not well. I was just starting out as an assistant with the company when he was here. We weren't, like, friendly, but we knew each other. It's not a big company. Is, uh, is he in some kind of trouble?"

"No. Not really."

"What does that mean?"

"I'm sorry, but he's dead."

Meredith probably shouldn't have told him, but she hoped some sympathy might grease the wheels to get what she needed.

"Oh my god. Are you serious?"

"Yes, but I'd appreciate it if you didn't spread that around."

"No, no, no. Of course not," he said, but Meredith was relatively certain he would. "Is what you're looking for connected to his death? I mean, it has to be, right?"

"I can't go into any further details."

"I understand. I only just … wow."

"Would it be possible to get the records of his travels?"

"Yeah. I don't see a problem with it if it'll help the investigation. We keep records of everything. Let me grab a pen. What is it you were looking for again?"

"His business travels from 2001 through 2005. Any expos and conventions he attended, those sorts of things."

Meredith could hear Kevin mumbling to himself as he wrote.

"There's going to be a lot of them," Kevin said. "Greg was one of our head consultants during that time. He was kind of a 'golden boy'. He attended a lot of junkets and conventions and generated a ton of contacts that brought the company a lot of business. I know the higher-ups were sorry when he quit."

There was the tapping of keys.

"Okay," Kevin said. "I can start combing through our accounting and expense reports and flag all of his business travels. I'll put them in a spreadsheet and email it to you in a couple of hours. Does that work?"

"That would be great."

"I could also find copies of receipts for any other expenses, like meals and stuff, but it may take longer."

"Thanks, but I think the general travel is perfect."

She gave him her email address, thanked him for his time, and hung up.

"One down," she said, looking at the photo. "One to go."

She went back to the casefile and pulled up the background check and the employment history of Kathy Morgan.

That's where she had seen that building behind Greg Ansley in the photo.

She had seen Kathy Morgan standing in almost the exact same spot in a photo hanging on the wall of her office the morning of the murder as she was telling Meredith and Tyler about the job she gave up when she and her husband decided to start their family.

A job that she said required her to travel, a job that meant she and her husband had been apart for more than a year.

Chapter 56

"Atlantic Engineering. How can I help you?" a man sighed.

His tired and annoyed tone rendered Meredith speechless.

"Is someone there?" he asked.

"Yes. Hi. I'm Detective Meredith Somerset with the Cobb County Police Department outside of Atlanta. How are you?"

"Great," was his unenthusiastic reply. "What can I do for you?"

Meredith was still confused by his demeanor but avoided lapsing into silence. "I wanted to know if you kept records of the conventions and expos that your employees attended—"

The line clicked and went silent.

Did this guy just hang up on me? she thought.

"Hello?" Meredith asked. The silence continued. She waited another couple of seconds. "Is someone th—"

There was a click and a woman answered.

"Accounting. This is Sarah."

Her tone was the same as the previous guy: bored, annoyed, and distracted.

"Hi. I'm Detective Meredith Somerset with the Cobb County Police Department. How are you doing?"

"I'm fine. How are you?"

"I'm good, thanks. I was wondering if you could do me a favor."

"What kind of favor?"

"I'm trying to piece together the movements of someone who was once employed there, specifically the conferences and expositions that they may have attended. Can you tell me if you keep those records?"

"How far back you looking?"

"2001 through 2005."

"Yeah. I got those. Who's the employee?"

"A woman named Kathy Morgan. Do you know her?"

"I've only been with the company for five years. She would have been before my time."

"But you still have access to that information?"

"You're a detective?"

"Yes, and if there's any problem with your boss, I'd be more than happy—"

Sarah laughed. "No. There won't be."

"You sure?"

"We're shutting down in two weeks. There's only a handful of us here to man the phones and offices. Boss told us we were closing down, then suddenly decided to take a three-week trip to the Bahamas. I kind of hoped you were calling about him. It's a good thing you called. Two more weeks and there wouldn't have been anyone here to answer the phone and the records would probably have been scrapped."

As with Kevin over at Cloverfield Construction, Meredith gave Sarah a few more specifics on what she needed, her email address, and thanked her.

Once Meredith hung up, she sat back in her chair.

There was nothing to do now but wait.

*

One hour became two. Two rolled into three …

Meredith picked up Alice's ball from her desk and began tossing it in the air above her with one hand, catching it with the other, transferring it back, and starting the process over again. Sometimes, she would hold on to the ball and stare at her computer screen, willing one or both of the emails to arrive. After a few minutes of waiting that reinforced her lack of psychic powers, she would go back to tossing the ball to herself.

Other people came and went.

Sergeant Wheaton left for lunch and returned to find her in the same spot. He may have hesitated slightly at the sight of her upon his return, but she didn't notice as she was too busy staring at the unchanging computer screen.

She got up from her desk a total of three times. Once to get coffee, and the other two times were to go to the bathroom, a consequence of the first time.

Four o'clock rolled around and her arms had grown tired from tossing the ball to herself, but she continued.

Finally, just as the ball reached its apex above her, there was a ping from her computer. Meredith sat up and reached for the keyboard. The ball fell, hitting her on the shoulder. It bounced down her arm, where it lightly ricocheted off the coffee mug full of pens, which was perched on the edge of the desk.

Meredith quickly shifted and grabbed the mug before it plummeted to certain annihilation.

The typing in Sergeant Wheaton's office paused for a moment, then continued.

Meredith hastily put her desk back together and went back to her computer.

The first email was from Kevin at Cloverfield Construction.

Hope this helps. Let me know if there is anything else I can do.

He had attached an Excel spreadsheet that plainly laid out the dates and locations of the conferences that Greg Ansley attended while working at Cloverfield Construction. There were a lot of them, scattered around the country. There were even a few in Canada and France. Meredith printed out a copy of the spreadsheet and began researching the cities where they were held and the specific venues that hosted them.

Minutes later, her computer pinged again.

This time, it was an email from Sarah at Atlantic Engineering.

Sorry it took so long. Kathy Morgan was an assistant to one of our execs, so it was a little harder to track down if she went with him to a conference or not. There are some occasions where she's noted as definitely going, and others where she probably went, but I can't be sure. Sorry I couldn't be more specific. It's all I've got. On a side note, in addition to the stuff you asked for, I'm also attaching my resumé in case you're hiring.

Meredith ignored the resumé, opened the file named *kmorgantravel*, and hit print.

It was a Word document that had been haphazardly thrown together, but after a few minutes of studying it, Meredith was able to piece it together and sort out the dates, which were out of order, and when Sarah was certain that Kathy Morgan had attended a conference and when she only might have attended.

There were probably half as many entries as Greg Ansley's travelogue, and only a quarter of those were conventions that Sarah was sure that Kathy Morgan had attended.

Meredith laid the papers side by side and compared them. Sometimes there was a match, most of the time, there wasn't, but steadily, the number of matches began to grow.

When she reached the end of Kathy's entries, she had eight possible matches and four definite matches.

Greg Ansley and Kathy Morgan had been at the same convention at least four times, and maybe more.

It didn't prove that they had met, but each possible match increased the odds that they had.

She then researched the venues where Greg and Kathy were at the same convention.

The Collection at McCormick Square in Chicago? Meredith did an image search. No. That wasn't it.

The Orange County Convention Center in Orlando? Nope.

The Colorado Convention Center in Denver?

Meredith clicked on the "images" tab, but from the thumbnail, she already knew that was it.

She stared at the blue and green glass-paneled structure on the screen. It was the same one that was in the photo she had taken from the shed, and the same one that was in the photo in Kathy Morgan's office. Meredith checked the date of the convention.

September of 2003.

She checked the dates in the travelogues. Chronologically, it was the first match between the two, meaning it may have been the first time Greg Ansley and Kathy Morgan had ever met. If Meredith's hunch was right, that would explain why this seemingly random photo was hanging in Greg Ansley's shed. It was a way of remembering the significance of that trip, without the reason actually being in it. It would also explain why it was hanging in Kathy Morgan's office, as well.

Meredith was struck by another idea.

She went back to the entries for Greg Ansley and this time started checking for conventions he attended in the northeast. That gave her five more entries that were within driving distance of Providence, Rhode Island, where the Morgans were living at the time. Another quick check of the timeline and a consultation of the case files put three of those during the time that Richard Morgan was doing his traveling residency.

There was even the convention in Boston where Greg Ansley got the …

Meredith flew back to her notes and feverishly searched through Greg Ansley's background until she found it; the DUI he had gotten outside of Boston.

Meredith pulled up the info on the convention.

There it was. Greg Ansley, along with everyone else from Cloverfield Construction, stayed at the Hilton, which was right next to the Boston Convention & Exhibition Center.

So, why did Greg Ansley rent a car?

Meredith checked the citation and found the location where Greg Ansley had been pulled over and pinned it on Google Maps. Then, she entered in two addresses; the Hilton where Greg Ansley was staying for the convention, and the Morgans' address in Providence.

Meredith clicked "get directions".

The map filled the screen.

The route from the Hilton in Boston to the Morgans' house in Providence ran right through the pin where Greg Ansley had been pulled over.

Chapter 57

Tyler opened the door to his apartment to find Meredith standing on his doorstep.

He poked his head out and looked around.

"What is this? A one-woman intervention?" he asked.

"I need to talk to you."

"Not sure I have anything to say to you."

Meredith cocked her head and stared at him until he finally rolled his eyes and held open the door.

"Yeah. Whatever."

*

He led her into the living room, which was dark due to the blinds being drawn. Empty beer cans littered the coffee table.

"You'll have to excuse the mess. I didn't know I'd be having company."

"How you holding up?" Meredith asked.

Tyler picked up a pack of cigarettes and a lighter from among the beer cans. "Oh, you know, I haven't OD'd and hit rock bottom yet, but it's only been twenty-four hours. There's still time." He stuck a cigarette between his lips, flicked the lighter, touched the flame to the end, and took a deep drag.

"You smoke?" Meredith asked.

"You care?" Tyler replied, exhaling a plume that caught the setting sunlight that snuck past the edge of the blinds.

"You don't strike me as the self-pitying type," Meredith said.

"Yeah? Well, you didn't strike me as the 'throw-your-partner-under-the-bus' type, but here we are. World's full of disappointment."

"You still think that's what happened? You threw yourself under the bus, Tyler."

"Yeah, I know!" he snapped. "I fucked up. I get it. I'm just saying you should have talked to me first. I could have handled it. I could have been the one to ask Sergeant Wheaton to send me back down. It would have let me save some face. Instead, I'm yanked before my first case is even over and kicked out of homicide. No way I stick that landing."

"I didn't recommend your immediate dismissal from the case. That was Sergeant Wheaton's call."

"How hard did you fight?"

"He knew the tardiness thing was bullshit. If I had fought any harder, he would have demanded to know the real reason I was lying for you."

"My point exactly! All of this could have been avoided if you had spoken to me first."

"Really?"

"Yeah."

"Were you going to let me know when you were sober enough to have that conversation?"

"Man," Tyler chuckled sarcastically. "To think I didn't want to talk to you."

Meredith took a breath of the stale, stagnant air and glanced around.

"What?" Tyler asked. "What is it?"

She stared at him, uncertain of what to say.

"Oh, now you're gonna be shy, Somerset? Here. Let me help you." Tyler went over and opened the door. "Fly, Somerset. Be free and may we never cross paths again."

"I'm not sure Greg Ansley killed himself," Meredith said.

Tyler stared at her in confusion. "What are you talking about?"

Meredith went over to the couch and sat down.

"I found something."

Tyler looked outside and squinted into the setting sun.

"Shit. I guess it's good to know that this wasn't entirely about your concern for my well-being," he said and closed the door.

*

Over the course of the next hour, Meredith laid out everything she had discovered. She had brought the emails, travelogues, photo, and the route from the Boston Convention Center to the Morgans' house in Providence, with a pin in the location of Greg Ansley's DUI.

At the outset, Tyler was bewildered and attempted multiple times to interrupt Meredith, but she continued with her theory. Finally, Tyler sat back and listened to the end, dutifully examining the images and entries when she asked him to.

"Let me get this straight," Tyler said, once she had concluded. "You think that Kathy Morgan and Greg Ansley met on the road some sixteen years ago, and started an affair that they carried on all over the country—"

"And sometimes at her place when he was at a convention that was close enough."

"What about Kathy's doctor husband?"

"It was during the eighteen months he was in residency, which, remember, was on the road. Kathy Morgan was by herself."

"Okay," Tyler said, still trying to take it in. "You think they had an affair and that, what, Alexa was their love child?"

"Yes." Meredith nodded. "And do you know what else was only an hour and a half drive from where the Morgans lived at the time?"

"Nope," Tyler said. "Wow me."

"Sisters of Sacred Heart."

Tyler studied the papers on the coffee table, which had been cleared of the beer cans, and ran his fingers through his hair.

"Okay, but you're also saying that, and this is where you lose me, you're saying Greg Ansley was so busted up over Kathy Morgan, that he quit his job at Cloverfield Construction in Charleston and moved his family so that he could live across the street from her?"

"Yes. I mean, it has to be, right?"

Tyler was less convinced.

"You don't believe me?" Meredith asked, feeling some of the wind go out of her sails.

Tyler took a drag on his cigarette. "I'm not saying you're wrong, Somerset. I'm saying you don't have it locked in yet."

"Are you kidding? The conventions they both *happened* to be at and the location of the DUI on the route from the hotel to her place? You're telling me—"

"You ever see one of those conventions? If it's like anything I've seen, then there are hundreds, if not thousands of people. That's like saying everyone who goes to Comic Con knows every other nerd there. I'm not saying you're wrong, Somerset. I'm saying you need more for that silver platter."

"And the location of the DUI?"

"That spot is on a million different routes to a million different places. Look, the directions say that it's over an hour's drive between Boston and the Morgans' house. The DUI happened about twenty miles from the hotel. If it was even halfway, I'd say you were definitely on to something, but I can't do that with this. Should you look some more? Yeah, but don't start connecting dots that aren't there. From what I learned in our very short partnership, that ain't like you, Somerset."

Meredith wiped her hand across her tired eyes.

"What kicked all this off?" Tyler asked. "You saw a photo in the shed and just happened to remember the photo in Kathy Morgan's office?"

Meredith sighed. "There was a photo on my therapist's wall this morning that made me think—"

"Whoa," Tyler said, his eyes suddenly wide. "I'm sorry. Did you just say you were at your *therapist's* office this morning?"

Meredith silently cursed. It was a mental stumble, brought on by fatigue.

"It's not important," she replied, trying to push it aside.

"Bullshit, it ain't important," Tyler said, no longer caring about Meredith's theories on Greg Ansley and Kathy Morgan. "Why are you talkin' to a shrink?"

"It's none of your business."

"That depends. What's got you so fucked in the head that you gotta talk about your feelings to a professional while I get kicked out of homicide?"

"You're really going to compare talking with a therapist to showing up at a scene while you're high?"

"Yes. Yes, I am, because tell me, what are you seeing a therapist for? Depression? Don't you think that could affect your judgment while you're waving a gun around at a scene? As your partner, don't you think that's something I should know?"

"We're not having this conversation."

Meredith didn't want to have the conversation, partly because it was none of his business.

"Does Sergeant Wheaton know?" Tyler asked.

Her silence was his answer.

"Holy shit," Tyler breathed. "And *you* threw *me* under the bus? Maybe I should repay the favor. Maybe I should tell him about the head shrink sessions that you so conveniently forgot to mention."

Meredith met his accusatory stare.

"You know what, Tyler? Do it. Go ahead. It might get me in trouble, but you'll still be out of homicide, you'll lose the only person on your side right now, and you'll still be a junkie."

"Yeah. I could definitely do that, but I'm not gonna and do you know why?"

"Why?"

"Because I don't throw partners under the bus."

Meredith bit her lip so hard, she almost drew blood.

"You're right," she said and began collecting her things.

"About the bus thing?"

"No. About not having the connection between Greg Ansley and Kathy Morgan yet."

She finished getting everything together and made her way toward the door.

"Where are you going?" Tyler asked.

"The Ansleys' house. I want to see if there is anything else that might connect them." She stopped by the door. "You know more about the case than anyone else. Want to help?"

Tyler put his hands in his pocket. "You know, I'd love to, but I'm worried about my safety around you, and besides, thanks to you, I'm not a detective. So, you know, sorry."

Meredith opened the door. "I gave you the chance to finish what you started and help find who killed that girl, but your ego won't let you, which proves you right: you're not a detective, Tyler."

She stepped outside and forcefully closed the door behind her.

Chapter 58

Night had fallen by the time Meredith pulled into the driveway of the darkened Ansley house.

The motion sensor light above the garage door startled her as it flared to life but her vision quickly adjusted.

She stepped out of her car and scanned the street. Scattered lights glowed in windows, except the Ansley house, which sat like some sort of beast, trying to hide in the shadows of Willow Lane.

Meredith walked into the backyard, toward the shed. At the halfway mark, the light over the garage shut off, throwing her into darkness. The shed became a vague shape in front of her. She took out her phone and pulled up the flashlight app to light her way, giving up on the secretive pretext of that morning. Either her theory was right, or it was wrong, and it might not even be decided that night.

She once again removed the police tape, opened the door, and stepped inside.

The air in the shed was a few degrees warmer than outside, but that wouldn't last long. Meredith realized what a miserable night Alexa must have spent there.

She swung the beam of light from her phone over the wall containing the collection of photos. There was the empty frame where she had removed the photo of Greg and his coworkers outside the Denver Convention Center.

She went over to the workbench, opened the third drawer down, and found the key at the bottom of the drawer, where they had replaced it after searching the house.

*

Meredith exited the shed and closed the door behind her, not bothering with the tape. She walked across the lawn toward the backdoor of the Ansley house. The key slipped easily into the lock and with a simple twist and push, Meredith was inside.

The interior of the house was silent, save for the breath of warm air coming through the vent overhead. The light above the stove was on, casting an eerie glow through the kitchen that struggled to reach across the family room.

Meredith flicked the switch next to the door and the lights mounted to the ceiling fan illuminated the room.

She stood absolutely still, taking in her surroundings.

Everything appeared to be in order, even after the team had executed the search warrant. They hadn't found anything in the house that indicated that Alexa had been inside, but they had all they needed from the shed. That, combined with Greg Ansley's apparent suicide, might have caused the team to lessen their intensity while searching the house.

The search warrant stated that they could only look for evidence of Alexa being in the house, so Meredith didn't necessarily have the authority to search for evidence of a connection between Kathy Morgan and Greg Ansley, but she knew she'd have no problem crossing that bridge if she found some.

She started over at the shelves mounted to the wall above the television, upon which rested some framed photos of the Ansley family. The frames had sayings like *Bless This Family*, *Memories*, and *LOVE*. They were frames you'd find at any store. Charming, but not unique, and Meredith saw no hidden messages connecting Greg to Kathy.

She moved to the kitchen, but there was really nothing there to search. There were some dishes in the sink and two towels on the counter.

She entered the dining room and turned on the light. Like the kitchen, there wasn't much there to investigate. There was a table and chairs that gave the appearance of rarely being used. Meredith understood. Growing up, her family's meals were eaten at the kitchen table. The dining room was for when family and friends came over for Thanksgiving or Christmas. Meredith moved to the living room, leaving the light on in the dining room. She'd work her way back, turning off all the lights when she was finished.

The living room, like the dining room, felt impersonal. There was a couch and love seat situated around a low table and a large print of the courtyard of an Italian villa hanging on the wall. There was also a plant clinging to life in the corner of the room. Just like the dining room, Meredith assumed that this room was reserved for company and rarely used. At least, there was nothing there that told her otherwise.

Meredith once again left the light on as she crossed the room, which brought her to the front door. She could have taken a left down the short, darkened hallway to go back to the kitchen, but instead, went for the stairs, and began to climb.

At the top of the stairs, Meredith turned on the lights and took an immediate right into the master bedroom.

If there was going to be any evidence of a connection between Kathy Morgan and Greg Ansley, she believed this would be her best bet, but also wondered if Greg would dare to hide something in the room he shared with his wife.

After turning on the lights, Meredith wandered about the space.

The bedsheets were piled onto the mattress. The drawers in the dresser were slightly askew. Meredith rifled through the night-stand, hoping for any small clue, something like the convention photo, that felt out of place. All she could find were signs of Greg Ansley's affection for his wife and son.

Striking out in the master bedroom, Meredith felt her doubts double upon themselves as she walked out into the hall. She had to again remind herself that it was likely she wouldn't find anything in the house. Greg Ansley had been careful. He had hidden his affair for the better part of two decades, and even concealed his daughter for a day. So, it was possible—

Meredith stopped at the top of the stairs. She thought she had heard something, possibly a footstep or maybe just the house settling. She waited and was rewarded by the faint sound of the compressor in the refrigerator kicking on from the kitchen.

Meredith continued on.

Anthony's room was like any other child's room. The illusion of it being somewhat tidy was maintained by the toys that littered the floor being pushed up against the walls.

She had almost passed by Anthony's room altogether. There was no way Greg Ansley would have used his son's room to hide some coded token of his feelings for the woman across the street, but Meredith had come all this way and decided to be thorough.

She stepped into the room and worked her way around.

No. There was no secret payoff in the *Paw Patrol* poster or a hidden Kathy Morgan action figure among the toys on his dresser.

Meredith went back into the hall, her hopes fading.

If there was ever a room devoid of personal affections, it was the guestroom. There was the bed with nightstands on either side and a wicker chair in the corner by the window. The inspection took even less time than Anthony's room, but Meredith did her due diligence, checking the nearly empty closet and under the bed.

Upon standing with a grunt, Meredith surrendered. Whatever she had hoped to find wasn't in the house.

She turned off the lights in the guest room and went back into the hall. As she passed Anthony's room, she reached inside and hit the switch to turn off the lights. She did the same for the master bedroom and retraced her steps down the stairs, already thinking about the warm bed back in her apartment.

As she reached the bottom of the stairs, Meredith crossed the darkened hall and went back into the living room.

She was halfway across the floor, her hand already reaching for the light switch, when she heard the front door being thrown open behind her.

"Somerset!" Tyler's voice cried.

Meredith spun around to see Tyler standing just inside the front door, reaching for his sidearm.

The view of Tyler was partially obscured by Kathy Morgan, who had been behind Meredith. She was in the process of turning to Tyler as well, and Meredith only caught a glimpse of the gun in her hand.

Meredith reached for her Sig Sauer as a gunshot ripped through the air.

She watched over Kathy Morgan's shoulder as Tyler fell.

Kathy charged toward the door and the sound of a second gunshot split Meredith's ears. Kathy let out a short scream of pain as she ran out the door and into the night.

Meredith raised her weapon to fire, but Kathy was gone.

"Tyler?!" she cried.

He was slumped against the bottom step. His face was contorted in agony. He hissed through clenched teeth as he writhed. A red bloom was spreading across the left side of his shirt.

Meredith raced over and crouched next to him.

"I think I tagged her in the leg," he said between grunts.

Meredith took the gun from his hand and set it aside.

"What happened?" she asked.

"I told you I wasn't letting you go into a place by yourself," Tyler said. His attempt at bravado ended as his whole body started to shake.

"Hold still," Meredith said. She gripped the sides of his shirt next to the bullet hole.

"I saw her behind you through the window as I was walking up," Tyler groaned. "The front door was unlocked, so I—"

"Hold still," Meredith commanded again.

She ripped open Tyler's shirt. The motion jerked him forward, causing him to cry out.

Meredith inspected the wound. The bullet had definitely punctured his lung. She leaned over his shoulder to check his back. There was no exit wound.

"How bad?" Tyler asked, his breathing shallow and his face pale.

"The bullet's still in you, which is good, but we've got to get you some help."

"I'll be fine," he coughed, his hands continuing to shake. "Go after her."

"Tyler, listen to me—"

"Go after her, Somer—!" Tyler's demand was cut short by a grunt of pain.

Meredith looked from his face to the wound, and back again.

"Get out your phone," she said, and ran for the kitchen.

"What?"

"Get out your phone!"

In the kitchen, Meredith grabbed the two dish towels near the sink and sprinted back down the hall to the stairs.

Tyler's hands fumbled, but he was finally able to get his phone out of his pocket as Meredith returned to his side. He unlocked the home screen and sat the phone on the step.

"Tyler, I need you to lie down," Meredith said, gently coaxing him onto his back. "We're going to use gravity to slow the bleeding, okay?"

Tyler allowed her to ease him down.

"Please," he whispered, fearfully. "Please, I really don't want to go out like Doc."

"Here," she said, placing one of the towels over the wound.

She then took Tyler's wrist and placed his own hand over the towel. "You need to hold this here as tight as you can."

Tyler nodded.

Meredith picked up his phone, dialed, and hit speakerphone.

"Nine-one-one. What is the nature of your—"

"This is Detective Meredith Somerset. I need dispatch to 147 Willow Lane. Officer down. Gunshot left-hand side of the chest. He's losing blood. Get an ambulance here, now."

"Yes, ma'am," the operator replied.

Meredith put the phone on the floor next to Tyler's head.

"I'm going to pursue an armed suspect. I'm putting Detective Foles on the line."

"Yes, ma'am," the operator said.

"Tyler, listen to me," Meredith said.

He looked at her with tears rolling down the sides of his face.

"You do not stop talking to her. Do you understand?"

Tyler nodded.

Meredith pulled her gun, ran out the door into the yard, and scanned the street.

There was no sign of Kathy Morgan, but the Whitakers were on their porch, watching, as was Richard Morgan across the street. Only Scott Rennick's porch remained dark.

Meredith hustled across the road and stood in the Morgans' front yard.

"Is your wife inside?" she asked.

"What?" He blinked.

"Is your wife inside?" Meredith repeated, louder.

"N—No," he sputtered.

Her grip on the Sig Sauer tightened. "Now would be a terrible time to lie to me."

Richard Morgan vigorously shook his head. "No. I swear! I thought she was in her office, but then I heard gunshots and I called out to her. I can't find her."

Meredith believed him and changed gears.

"My partner's been shot. Left-hand side of the chest. He's just inside," she said, motioning over her shoulder toward the Ansley house. "I need you to help him."

Richard nodded. "I'll get my kit."

He quickly turned and opened the door to his house.

"Hurry!" Meredith said as he went back inside.

Meredith hustled back to the Ansley home.

Tyler was still lying on the floor, holding the blood-soaked towel in place and talking to the operator. His voice was weak and his breathing remained shallow, but his eyes focused on her as she re-entered.

Meredith kneeled beside him and gently took his hand off the towel.

"Operator, how we doing on that ambulance?" Meredith asked, gently replacing the blood-soaked towel with the dry one.

"I've dispatched two ambulances along with backup. They're a few minutes out."

"I have a doctor who lives across the street who's coming to help until they arrive. His name is Richard Morgan. He'll be here when the EMT's arrive, but I won't."

"Understood," the operator said.

Tyler's eyes widened.

"It's okay," Meredith said and looked back through the open door to see Richard Morgan jogging across the street with a bag in his hand. Meredith turned back to Tyler. "Don't tell him who shot you," she whispered.

Tyler nodded.

Meredith stood just as Richard stepped through the door.

"Ambulance is on the way," Meredith said.

"Got it," Richard replied and set the bag down next to Tyler. The confusion he had exhibited a few moments ago on his porch was gone and he snapped into "doctor mode".

"Detective, I'm Doctor Richard Morgan. We spoke a few days ago. Let me take a look at this, okay?"

Meredith locked eyes with Tyler over Richard Morgan's shoulder. Tyler blinked, his eyes still full of fear, but nodded.

Meredith nodded back and went back outside.

She didn't know if Tyler was going to make it, but she had done everything she could for him. The only thing Meredith could do was go after Kathy Morgan.

Stepping onto the porch, Meredith looked down and saw a spot of streaked blood on the step, leading into the yard. She pulled up her flashlight app once more and aimed it into the grass. It took some searching, but she found another spot. The wet blood gleamed in the harsh light.

Tyler's shot had hit her.

Kathy Morgan hadn't run back to her house, probably because she knew that she would be found, but where could she have gone?

Meredith kept the beam of light from the phone pointed down the barrel of her weapon toward the grass. There was another streak of blood, glinting in the light, and then another. She followed the spots of blood into the street, and it became obvious where it was leading: the unfinished house next to the Morgans.

Meredith looked at the spot on Willow Lane where Greg had murdered his daughter. She turned to see the outline of the shed in the Ansleys' backyard, where she was now certain Kathy had killed Greg. Meredith glanced back toward the Ansley house, wondering if Dr. Morgan could save Tyler or if Kathy had taken another life.

Meredith then turned back to the dark, half-finished house and was suddenly filled with wrath.

Inside was the woman who killed Greg Ansley and who might have just killed her partner.

She clenched her jaw as she made her way up the drive and mounted the steps to the front entrance.

"Meredith?" a small voice next to her said.

Meredith stopped and looked down.

Alice was standing next to her on the porch, looking up at her.

"What are you going to do?" she asked.

Meredith went through the door without answering.

Chapter 59

Meredith cautiously stepped inside, sweeping the light through the shadows.

The blood trail led up the stairs.

She remained still and listened.

There was the faint sound of someone crying coming from the second floor.

Meredith began slowly creeping up the stairs. The light scuffing of her feet as she climbed was masked by the sound of Kathy Morgan's stifled sobs.

At the top of the stairs, the blood trail led down the hall, where a loose plastic tarp was serving as a door to an unfinished bedroom.

Meredith kept her gun at the ready as she moved down the hall. She arrived at the tarp, slowly pushed it aside, and stepped into the room.

It was the master suite, but only two of the walls were finished. The others were open to a view of Willow Lane.

Kathy Morgan was standing next to the edge, trying to keep her weight off her injured leg. Blood was running down her jeans but Meredith was more concerned with the gun Kathy Morgan was pointing at her own head.

Meredith stopped.

"Kathy?"

"I saw you," Kathy said in between sobs. "I saw you this morning go into the shed. I wondered what you were doing, so I went in and saw that the picture was gone and I knew. I had to make sure there was nothing else in the house that tied me to him."

Meredith slowly put down her phone so that she had use of both hands. She rested the phone so that the light pointed out to the street. She hoped it would serve two purposes: to illuminate the room and also as a signal to the backup when they arrived.

"Kathy, I need you to put the gun down."

"Greg was going to tell. He was going to ruin my family. He was going to take them away from me," she said earnestly, still holding the gun to her head.

"What happened to Greg?" Meredith asked as calmly as possible. She wanted to know, but she also needed Kathy to keep talking. She needed to distract her as she inched almost imperceptibly closer. Meredith had to get to her before she pulled the trigger or took a step backwards and fell to what would most likely be her death, but Meredith also kept her Sig Sauer at the ready. If Kathy pointed the gun at her, Meredith would be forced to fire. She already had the sight trained on Kathy, and she wouldn't miss.

"He was going to tell everyone," Kathy repeated, pitifully.

"That Alexa was your daughter?" Meredith asked, inching closer.

Kathy nodded. "It would have ruined my life, my marriage. It would have ruined his life. He should have just stayed quiet."

"Tell me what happened."

Another inch closer.

"It was so long ago," Kathy muttered. "It was a mistake. Richard was gone ... and Greg and I started seeing each other, but ... It wasn't supposed to happen ..."

"'It'? You mean Alexa?"

Kathy closed her eyes and nodded.

Meredith took the opportunity to edge closer.

"When I couldn't hide it anymore, I stayed away from Greg. From everyone. Richard was gone, but Greg knew. We hadn't seen each other in months. I had the baby at home, in my house, and I took her to the children's home. I told Greg that I lost it. That I had miscarried."

"What happened that night when Greg came to see you from Boston?" Meredith asked.

Kathy shifted and continued to grimace in pain. "That's when I told him that I miscarried. He was so upset. He told me that he thought that we might be a family. That he had never been happier than when we were together ... I felt the same but I told him it was over. I couldn't have a family like that, from an affair. That we were a mistake. He stopped at a bar on his way back to Boston ..."

That explains the DUI, Meredith thought but she didn't have the luxury of contemplation at the moment. She needed to keep her talking. She had already closed half of the gap between them without Kathy noticing. She was too wrapped up in her own pain.

"What happened after that?" Meredith asked.

Some of the tension seemed to flow from Kathy and her shoulders sagged, but the gun still remained at her head, finger on the trigger.

"We stopped for a while. Neither of us were happy in our marriages. Richard decided to set up practice here and we moved to Willow Lane ... Greg and I still talked. Finally, he said he couldn't take it anymore. He quit his job and got the job here and moved across the street. He said we could still be together and no one would know. I told him I didn't want him to, but I did ... He gave me a key to his place and we tried to start over, but it was different ... I ended it. I told him it was over."

Meredith wanted to explode at her selfishness and self-pity, but she couldn't because in the distance, there was the sound of sirens. Instead, she continued inching closer.

"What happened with Alexa?"

The mention of Alexa brought a new wave of physical grief and Kathy appeared as though she was about to scream.

"Alexa called me a few days ago and said she was coming. She had learned about me from one of the nuns at the children's home and had hitchhiked from New York. I told her not to. I told her that she wasn't my daughter, but she refused. I panicked. I told Greg. I told him about our daughter and that she was coming and that it would ruin our lives and I didn't know what to do. He said he would try to take care of it. When she arrived, he convinced her to stay in the shed for the night, but the next morning, she tried to run to my house. She wouldn't listen. She didn't care what it did to our lives. Greg stopped her and tried to keep her quiet but … You have to understand that he didn't mean to do it. It wasn't his fault. He was only trying to protect me."

Meredith stopped her incremental advance, unable to control herself any longer.

"Not his fault? He killed your daughter."

"She wasn't my daughter!" Kathy shrieked, causing Meredith to raise her gun. "She wasn't a part of my life! She wasn't supposed to be here! She was a mistake! She wasn't my family."

Meredith began to seethe.

Yes, Alexa coming into her life would have made things difficult and awkward, but she was her daughter. You dealt with it. If you didn't, it led to destruction, just as her family's unresolved grief over Alice's disappearance had torn them apart and destroyed her father and nearly destroyed her.

And Tyler.

Tyler had done whatever it took to take care of his sister because that was what families who loved each other did. They were unselfish and would do whatever it takes for the ones they loved, no matter how much it hurt, like when she signed over custody of Allison to Pete, because she knew it was the right thing for Allison.

And Kathy Morgan's selfishness, her misguided, destructive desire to keep Alexa a secret had led to the deaths of two people, and possibly a third, who had taken the bullet that would have killed Meredith.

Suddenly, it wasn't just Kathy Morgan standing in front of her.

It was the person who had taken Alice for their own selfish reasons, regardless of what it meant for Meredith or her family. It was her mother's hurtful attempts to lay the blame at Meredith's feet. It was the guy who shot Doc McElwee for no other reason than he walked in the wrong door at the wrong time. It was the selfishness of people like Scott Rennick and Thomas Whitaker who preyed upon and ruined the lives of those around them for their own ends. It was the selfishness of someone who would kill Greg Ansley to keep him quiet, not caring about what it did to his wife or his young son.

"And Greg? Was that not your fault?" Meredith asked, resuming her slow advance. She was about ten feet away, praying that Kathy didn't move.

"He was going to admit everything. I told him that it wouldn't solve anything. Alexa was dead, but he couldn't take it. He called me and said that you had figured it out. He was going to confess and that he wanted me to be there. He said that I was the only woman he ever loved and that I was the last thing he wanted to see before he was taken away." Kathy's hand began to shake. "He told me what he was going to do and to meet him in the shed so he could show you her things, but I couldn't let that happen. I had to protect my family. So, I grabbed one of Richard's guns and I went to the garage and scratched off the numbers as quickly as I could. I met Greg in the shed. He told me how sorry he was and we kissed. I had the gun behind me and put it against his head. He saw it at the last second and tried to grab it but ... I did it."

Meredith could see it in her mind's eye. It explained everything. That's why it looked like he used his left hand. That was the hand he had grabbed the gun with. It explained the powder burns and the odd angle.

Behind Kathy, the first cop car swerved onto Willow Lane, then another, and another, as well as two ambulances.

Kathy furtively glanced over her shoulder. Her breathing quickened. She turned back to Meredith and seemed to finally realize that she was only a few feet away.

"Please, Kathy. I need you to put the gun down, okay?"

"What happens to me? What happens to my children?"

"We can talk about that, but you have to put the gun down," Meredith said, trying to push her own feelings out of her mind.

"But, my family—?"

"She was part of your family," Meredith said, unable to stop herself. "You at least owed her that."

Kathy stared at her.

There were voices on the street below.

The tears that were pouring over Kathy's cheeks slowly gave way to a steely resolve.

"You're going to do it, aren't you?" she asked.

"Do what?"

"You're going to take me away from my family."

"Kathy …"

"I can't let you do that."

Meredith steadied the grip on her gun.

"Kathy, listen to me—"

"You can't take away my family. I won't let you!"

Suddenly, Kathy pulled the gun away from her temple and began to aim it at Meredith.

At that moment, a search light mounted to the hood of one of the police cars down below sparked on, flooding the room with light just as Meredith inched within striking distance.

Meredith moved to the side and stepped forward, putting Kathy's gun past her. With her free hand, she grabbed at Kathy's wrist, but only succeeded in grabbing the barrel of the gun as

Kathy pulled the trigger. The gun roared. The hot metal singed Meredith's hand, but she was not letting go, and she pulled Kathy away from the ledge.

No, Meredith wasn't going to kill her, no matter how enraged Kathy's actions made her feel, because that would have given into the very selfishness that was fueling Meredith's rage. It would have been a destructive act for her own selfish reasons, and Meredith had fought her whole life to be better than that—to not give in to that selfishness that ultimately destroyed everyone who expressed it.

As Kathy stumbled forward to the ground, Meredith threw her weight behind her elbow, and slammed it into Kathy's face as she fell. The gun slipped from Kathy's hand. Meredith still held fast to the smoking barrel. A dazed Kathy stumbled to the floor. Meredith was on top of her in an instant, pinning her with her knee. She returned her gun to its holster, ejected the clip from Kathy's gun, and racked the slide, ejecting the bullet in the chamber. She slid the gun away across the floor, got out her cuffs, pulled Kathy's arms back, and snapped the cuffs over her wrists as voices began calling out from downstairs.

Meredith climbed off Kathy and crawled away until her back hit the wall.

"Up here!" Meredith shouted. "We're up here!"

Police officers burst through the tarp to find Kathy Morgan lying face-down on the floor, weeping inconsolably.

Meredith watched as the police swarmed her.

For a few brief moments, it was chaos.

"Detective Somerset?" a voice asked.

Meredith looked up to see Sheriff Howell standing over her. "Are you all right?"

"Yeah," Meredith said quietly. "It's over."

*

Once back on Willow Lane, Meredith hurried down the street back to the Ansleys' house.

Tyler was being brought out on a gurney by two EMTs. His torso was wrapped and there was an oxygen mask over his nose and mouth. His skin was still ashen, but his eyes were open and alert.

Sergeant Wheaton walked behind the gurney as they made their way down the drive to the waiting ambulance.

"How's he doing?" Meredith asked as she approached.

"He's stable," said one of the EMTs.

"Actually, we keep having to tell him to shut up," the other EMT added.

Tyler gave Meredith a weak, sly smile.

He reached up and lowered the oxygen mask off from his nose and mouth. "All I'm saying, Sergeant Wheaton, is that it was kind of dark, and it may have been Detective Somerset who put a slug in me."

"Please stop talking," the EMT said, replacing the oxygen mask over Tyler's face.

Tyler winked at Somerset. He started to lightly laugh but coughed and groaned in pain.

"Yeah, he's all right," Sergeant Wheaton said.

The EMTs brought the gurney to a stop next to the back of the waiting ambulance. They collapsed the legs, lifted it up, and rolled it through the open doors. One of the EMTs then went and got into the driver's seat.

"You said he's stable?" Meredith asked the remaining EMT.

"Yeah."

"Then I'm riding with you," Meredith said and climbed into the back of the ambulance.

"Wait," the EMT protested. "That's not really—"

"Son?" Sergeant Wheaton interjected. "She's going to ride with you."

Knowing better than to argue, the EMT shrugged and followed Meredith into the ambulance.

Sergeant Wheaton closed the doors and gave them two sharp slaps with the palm of his hand.

The driver blasted the siren twice, turned on the strobing lights, and threw it into gear.

Inside the ambulance, the EMT went to work and began hooking Tyler up to different monitors and an IV.

Tyler's searching eyes found Meredith.

Meredith reached over, took his hand, and held it.

Tyler returned her grip.

As the ambulance rolled away down Willow Lane, neither one let go.

Chapter 60

Like nearly every night since the discovery of the dead girl on Willow Lane, Scott Rennick was sitting at his kitchen table, staring at the small suitcase that contained everything he needed to start over.

Bang! … Bang!

Scott nearly jumped out of his seat at the faint sound.

Those were gunshots. It sounded like they came from the Ansleys' house.

Whatever Scott had been waiting for, he knew this was it.

He grabbed the suitcase, ran out the front door, and was gone.

*

Memphis was the perfect place to lie low for a few days. It had a tourist industry with people coming and going. He could cool off, have some fun, and put into motion his plan to start over. He had plenty of cash to float him for a few weeks.

He wasn't a fan of the scarce amenities of The McClarren Hotel on Beale Street, nor did he like the noise of the drunken tourists below his window, but he could live with it.

After a quick dinner, he drifted a few blocks from Beale Street, away from the touristy sheen.

He settled into a side street and watched a corner where three women were gathered. Their attention was drawn by any man who happened to walk by.

He selected one and waited before making his approach.

His target was more attractive from a distance than close up. Her face and body still had a youthful quality, but the strain of her profession was beginning to show. Her eyes were dark and her skin was blotchy, but he wasn't looking for one of those all-night sessions he had enjoyed on Willow Lane. He was an addict looking for a fix.

He walked directly to her.

"Hi."

"Hi," the woman said, sizing him up.

"Are you working?" he asked with a warm smile.

The other two girls quickly turned and walked away, smelling a bust.

"You a cop?" she asked.

Such a stupid question, Scott thought. There was this urban myth that undercover cops had to out themselves if asked if they were a cop, which was total bullshit.

"No," he laughed. "I'm only looking for a good time."

"I can do that," she said after a moment's consideration. "Two-hundred. I'm not getting in a car and I'm not going back to your house. You need to have a hotel room."

"I'm staying at The McClarren on Beale Street. You know it?"

"Yeah."

"Room 110. Thirty minutes. And here's a little bit down," he said, extending his hand in a gesture that would appear to be a handshake to anyone watching.

She took his hand and felt him press a bill into it.

"My name is Brian," he lied.

"I'm Rose."

"It's nice to meet you, Rose," Scott said, assuming she was also lying about her name. "We'll talk more when you arrive."

He released her hand and walked away.

Rose looked down at the $100 bill in her palm.

*

Scott slipped back into his room at The McClarren, already anticipating what was to come.

He was taking a chance but it was a small one. She wasn't a cop and the hotel wasn't going to say a thing. There was too much business for them to worry about.

He placed a couple hundred-dollar bills on the nightstand, then took some of the toys from the suitcase and laid them on the bed.

He then dragged one of the chairs to the window, sat down facing the door, and waited.

Minutes later, he was rewarded with a knock.

"Come in," he said.

The door opened and Rose poked her head inside.

"Thank you for coming," he said.

Rose stepped into the room and looked around. She spotted the cash on the nightstand, which was obviously more than she had quoted him, but she also saw the toys.

"Please, have a seat," Scott offered, noting her concern.

She cautiously made her way to the chair and sat.

"I'm not really used to stuff like that," she said with a nod toward the bed.

"I understand, and that's what I wanted to discuss. We'll use safe words and at any time you wish to stop, we stop. However, if you make it without using the safe word, I'm willing to pay you five times your normal rate."

"Okay," she said. "But I'm not making any promises."

"Perfect. Now, let me begin by telling you what I want and what I—"

The door flew open and bodies flooded into the room, accompanied by cries of "POLICE!".

Scott's eyes bulged. He turned to Rose and before he could stop himself, he asked the stupid question.

"Are you a cop?!"

She didn't answer. She was too busy screaming. An officer quickly restrained her.

Scott exhaled and shook his head in defeat.

Of course, she wasn't a cop.

"On the ground!" one of the officers demanded.

Scott lowered himself to the floor.

In the blink of an eye, a policeman was on his back, driving a knee into his spine.

As his arms were pulled behind him and he felt the cuffs encircle his wrists, he knew exactly who had outplayed him.

Chapter 61

"Natalie, please, please, call me," Thomas begged. "I know I screwed up. I know that I've been an ass, but I promise that things will be different. I love you and I miss you. Please, call me. I love you. I love you so m—"

Beep.

The line went dead.

"FUCK!" he screamed.

He put the phone down and rested his head on the table in the darkened kitchen.

Thomas Whitaker was freaking out.

It had all begun to fall apart that night four weeks ago—the night of the gunshots on Willow Lane. He still didn't know exactly what had happened. All he knew was that Kathy Morgan had been arrested.

He had bigger problems.

In the midst of the chaos, he had seen Scott Bowers get in his car and drive away.

That was the last he had seen or heard from him.

Scott Bowers' departure and absence was a blow to Thomas' side-hustle, but not a fatal one. He could still work toward paying off his debts.

That was until two weeks ago when everything stopped.

He couldn't get in contact with his "business associates". He had no "requests" to fill.

Thomas had worked in the world of law enforcement long enough to know that it could only mean one thing: something had gone horribly wrong.

His frustration and paranoia exploded, and Thomas focused those explosions at his wife. He did it regularly and with confidence, because it was what he had always done, and what was she going to do?

Five days later, he returned home to find an empty house.

At first, he thought she was hiding. He marched through the rooms, calling her name, and demanding she come out. Ashton and Kendall were probably at a friend's house. Natalie must have sent them away, fearful of what he would do, with good reason.

His righteous anger grew until he found the note on the kitchen counter, written in Natalie's hand.

She had taken the kids and gone. Her attorney would be in touch. If he tried to find her or make contact, she would call the police.

His first instinct was to laugh. This was a joke, or at most a bluff.

He waited, secure that before midnight, she and the kids would walk through the door, and man oh man, would he let her have it. Until then, he was going to work himself into a lather, gaming out what he would say for maximum pain.

She didn't return that night.

Okay, he thought. *She wants me to come after her. She's got a little more of a backbone than I thought, but I'll take care of that.*

He was about to start making calls, starting with Natalie's sister in Florida, but stopped when he remembered her threat to call the police if he tried to contact her.

That was a bluff. It had to be, but then he started putting two and two together.

Was the sudden disruption in his side-hustle her doing? No. It couldn't be. She didn't know anything about it … did she?

He became paralyzed, and each day that passed with no word from his "business associates" only caused his paranoia to grow.

He started showing up late for his clients' hearings, and even when he was there, his brain wasn't.

Before long, he was no longer attending the court hearings, at all. He was removed from his cases. He was dodging calls from his lenders. He would sit in the house with the lights off in case they showed up.

He needed to talk to Natalie and it was for the most pathetic of reasons. It wasn't out of love or concern for the woman he married who was the mother of his children.

He needed to talk to her because he could feel himself losing control and it terrified him.

The world he had convinced himself that he commanded was falling apart, and she was always the easiest target to feed his need for power and control.

That was why he broke down and made that call and left that pleading, pitiful message, but it had been for nothing. By sounding so weak and confessing how much he needed her, he had given up more control.

And there he sat, in the darkness of the kitchen, hiding from lenders, his life in tatters, and his head down on the table because he felt weak for needing his wife which is why he didn't see the red and blue strobing lights growing brighter through the windows by the door.

There was a crash and he looked up.

The front door was open and police officers were pouring through.

Thomas sat with his mouth open as an officer approached and read him his rights while another officer cuffed his hands behind his back.

It was at this point that Thomas Whitaker would always advise his clients to keep their mouths shut, and he took his own advice.

He did, however, begin sobbing like a child, because for the first time since he could remember, he felt utterly powerless.

Chapter 62

Meredith sat on the hood of her car and looked out over Willow Lane as the sun began to rise over the rooftops.

A little over a month and a half had passed since that night. The press storm around the story had begun to fade.

An approaching car caught her attention but only for a second before she resumed her gaze of Willow Lane.

The car parked next to her. Tyler got out, walked over, leaned against the hood of her car by her side, and joined her quiet vigil.

She had spent a lot of afternoons and evenings at the hospital with Tyler as he recovered. She explained everything that happened and would give him sporadic updates about the case but nothing too in-depth. She wanted him to focus on getting better.

"Stopped by the station," Tyler said. "Sergeant Wheaton told me I'd probably find you here."

"How are you feeling?" she asked.

"Good. Still hurts to laugh, so don't go using that world-class stand-up routine on me."

Meredith smiled.

"Heard Kathy Morgan might be cutting a deal," Tyler said. "Is that true?"

"She won't spend the rest of her life in prison, but most of it."

"I'm the one she shot," Tyler said. "No one asked me about it."

"Yeah. They usually don't, but I do have some news you might like."

"What's that?"

"They picked up Scott Rennick at a hotel in Memphis."

"What are you talking about?"

"He was trying to make a run for it. We were watching him."

Tyler was confused, but Meredith's knowing smile gave it away.

"You put a tail on him?" he asked.

Meredith nodded. "I asked Kelly Yamara for a teeny-tiny favor."

"Why didn't you say something?"

"I figured the less people who knew about it, the better. I've spoken with the DA in Memphis. They have no problem sending him back to us, but do you want to hear the best part?"

"That's not the best part?"

"The first thing Rennick did when he knew he was busted was roll over on his contact for hiring girls."

"Anyone we know?"

"Thomas Whitaker."

Tyler's eyebrows shot up. "No shit?"

"Yep. Whitaker was trying to pay off his debts. He decided to make a little money on the side. He'd recruit women he represented who were down on their luck for a high-end pimp downtown to get a kick-back. The case is going to take years but I thought you should know we got them both."

Tyler chuckled in disbelief. "I do like your style, Somerset."

"Thank you."

They stared out at the street in silence for a few moments.

"Somerset, I need to apologize, again."

"Tyler, you don't have to—"

"Yeah, I do. You were trying to look out for me, and I was a little shit. Recommending my demotion back to narco and vice was the right call. Hell, it's more than I deserve. So, thank you, and I'm sorry."

Meredith nodded.

"And you said we'd talk about what comes next after I was off the ice chip dinners and sponge baths. So … what happens now?"

"That's up to you, Tyler. Do you want to work homicide?"

"Yes," he answered without hesitation.

"Okay. Then this is how it's going to be: you're going to go back down to narco and vice. You are going to bust your ass and do everything by the book."

"I can do that."

"You're also going to NarcAnon. At least one meeting a week or whenever you feel you need to. I'll go with you if you want."

Tyler nodded.

"And," Meredith continued, "we're going to find a private lab. You are going to submit to random drug tests at my choosing. You'll have no idea when they're coming. When I say it's time, if you're not peeing in a cup in twelve hours, we're through. You understand?"

Tyler nodded again. "Copy that."

"You do all of that for eighteen months, I'll recommend your promotion to Sergeant Wheaton and you can put in the transfer request. I can't make any promises, but I still have some pull with him. Think you can do all that?"

"I'll have a NarcAnon schedule and a list of private labs by the end of the day."

"Good."

There was a long silence. Meredith was going to stick to her rules, but she also had no trouble believing Tyler when he said he would do it.

"Why you doing this, Somerset?"

"Doing what?"

"Giving me a second chance. Doesn't seem entirely like you."

"You're a good detective, Tyler. You'll be a great one if you put the junk away … and you took a bullet for me. That's not something you overlook when considering a partner."

Tyler smiled. "I'm still on the fence on whether that was the right thing to do."

"Too late now."

"What's next for you?"

Meredith shrugged. "There's always going to be more cases, but I'm going to take a little time off for some personal stuff, which reminds me, my ex is getting married in a few months. You want to be my plus one? I'm helping plan it, so I'll make sure it's fun."

Tyler cocked his head. "Why, Detective Somerset, are you taking a shine to me?"

She looked at him dead in the eye and answered with complete honesty. "God, no."

"Good," he chuckled. "I'm still gonna tell everyone at the wedding that I'm the hot, younger piece of ass you traded up for."

Meredith laughed. "Whatever."

They both turned to Willow Lane. The sun continued to peek over the houses.

"Why does it feel like this, Somerset?" Tyler asked.

"What do you mean?"

"I thought it would be different. I got into homicide because of what happened to Doc. It made me open my eyes, you know? There were plenty of scumbags in narco and vice, but there were also a lot of people who needed help, not a jail cell. I wanted to work homicide because I wanted to catch the *real* bad guys, the people who deserve it, and we did that. Things got a little crazy, but we got Kathy Morgan and we would have gotten Greg Ansley, and we did it quick … So, why does it feel like this?"

"Like what?"

"Empty. Alexa ain't coming back. The Morgan family is ripped apart. So are the Whitakers, and Anthony Ansley is gonna grow up without a father. I just feel like we left a lot of busted stuff in our wake."

"You expected a happy ending?"

"Nah. I ain't naive. I'm just sayin' that I thought this would feel better."

"I know," Meredith said. "And you're right; Alexa isn't coming back, but we got the people responsible, which is always the best outcome when you consider the alternative. We also got Scott Rennick. We got Thomas Whitaker. It was their actions, the actions of Kathy Morgan and Greg Ansley. Their actions were the cause of all the pain, here. Not us. And thanks to you, Scott Rennick won't be hiring any more girls and Thomas Whitaker will never be able to hit his wife again."

Tyler took in Meredith's words while watching as the sunlight crept over the rooftops.

"Is everything perfect?" Meredith asked. "No. It's a mess but we did our jobs, and hopefully, the next time someone thinks of killing someone else, they'll think again. But if you're looking for a totally happy ending, this is about as happy as it gets. If you don't like that, then you should stay in narco and vice."

"Nah," Tyler said. "I'll get used to it."

"Good. Because I'm looking forward to working with you again, Detective Foles."

They enjoyed one more shared silence before Tyler stood.

"All right. Like I said, I'll have the NarcAnon schedule and list of labs for you later in the day," he said, walking to his car. "Catch you later, Somerset."

"See you around, Tyler."

He gave a salute, got in his car, and drove away.

Meredith watched until he rounded the corner, out of sight, and then drank in Willow Lane one last time.

It was time to go.

She hopped off the hood of her car and got in.

As she drove off, the sunlight finally crept down to the lawns of the houses on Willow Lane.

There was a "FOR SALE" sign in every yard.

*

Upon returning home from her final visit to Willow Lane, Meredith walked up the path to the door of her apartment. She was looking forward to a hot shower and a change of clothes before picking up Allison for their monthly trip to the Marietta Farmers' Market.

As she approached her door, she spotted the manilla envelope resting on the ground.

She picked it up and turned it over in her hand.

There was no postage or address, only her name written in marker across the front. It felt like the envelope contained some type of padding.

Meredith opened the door and stepped inside.

She tossed her keys onto the table and inspected the envelope again. Maybe Pete had dropped something off.

She opened the flap and reached inside.

Her fingers closed around fabric and pulled it from the envelope.

It didn't register at first, then Meredith went numb.

In her hand, she held a girl's light-purple bathing suit. It was dirty and aged. The label was visible, as was the "A" written upon it in Alice's hand.

Pinned to the bathing suit was a note.

Still clutching the bathing suit, Meredith raced back to the door, threw it open, and sprinted down the path to the road.

She looked around, taking in every corner and shadow, searching for anyone who might be waiting to observe her reaction.

There was no movement, no sign that whoever had left the envelope was still there.

Meredith once again read the note pinned to Alice's bathing suit:

She still misses you, Meredith.

Acknowledgements

A huge thank you to everyone who made this book possible.

As always, thanks Mom, Dad, Amanda, and Stephanie. You were the first people to be introduced to Meredith and Tyler. Thank you, Olivia, for the sanity and for being a sounding board. Thank you, Dushiyanthi Horti, and all of my HQ family for shepherding Meredith and Tyler into existence. Thank you to everyone who has read and enjoyed my previous books, which gave me the confidence to try my hand at a detective novel.

I would also like to apologize to any authorities who are now monitoring my search history; I have no plans to produce high-quality fake IDs, cheat on any sort of drug test, shoot anyone in the chest, etc. Researching for a crime novel can take you to some pretty strange places … We're cool, right?

Keep reading for an excerpt from
Deadly Games …

Chapter 1

My phone pings with a text.

I'm not going to answer it. Not even going to look.

When you're being led by a detective down a hall at a police station to be interviewed, it's not the time to respond to what is probably a message from your boss, asking you to come in twenty minutes early for your shift tomorrow.

At the end of the hall, Detective Mendez motions to an open door and I step inside.

The walls are painted cinderblock. The floor is concrete.

In the middle of the room is a metal table with metal chairs on either side. There's a file resting on the corner of the table.

"Again, I'd like to thank you for coming in and talking to me," Detective Mendez says, following me into the room. "Please, have a seat."

He indicates the chair on the other side of the table, away from the file.

"Of course." The confusion in my voice is genuine as I ease myself into the chair.

He comfortably lowers himself into the chair on the other side of the table.

"I'll try to make this as quick as I can. We're just asking some questions, trying to get an overall picture of things."

"Okay." I nod. "Um, what things?"

He leans forward, resting his elbows on the table and lacing his fingers together.

"How well do you know Emily Parker?"

How well do I know Emily Parker?

I know everything about her, the same way I know everything about a lot of people. I know their name, their birthday, their kids' names, where they live, where they work. I know when they get that big promotion. I know how they feel about that cute coworker they haven't told their spouse about. I know when things are bad at home. Hell, I know when people are on antibiotics. I know all this stuff because they tell it to me; freely, willingly, because everyone wants to be my friend, even though they don't know a thing about me.

They tell me all these things because I'm their bartender.

Of course, with Emily Parker, it's a little more complicated but I sort of knew this was coming.

Katie, my coworker, was interviewed earlier this morning by Detective Mendez and as I pulled into the parking lot of the police station, she texted me the heads-up that they had asked her about Emily. She said she didn't know why they were asking, but that she had kept me out of it; a fact I very much appreciated.

"Mr. Davis?" Detective Mendez asks from the other side of the table.

There are some things about Emily and I that I'd rather not discuss and I know she feels the same way. I need to buy a little more time so I can figure out what's going on and talk to Emily.

Luckily, I have the training to bullshit all day, if need be.

"You can call me Clay."

"Your ID says that your name is Franklin Davis."

"Yeah, but everyone calls me Clay. In my business, you make a lot more in tips with a cool name. I found that out when I worked at one of those corporate chains where you have to wear a nametag and like, buttons with witty sayings, you know? Well, one day, I forgot my nametag, so I had to wear a spare one we had in the office. For one shift, my name was 'Clay', and you wouldn't believe how much more in tips I made that day. So, I decided to stick with it."

"That's really interesting," Detective Mendez says, dryly, while making a note on his pad.

"Thanks."

I can't tell if he's being sarcastic or not. He's got this perfectly neutral, bulldog expression and while bulldogs look kind of dumb, you're pretty sure they could rip your arm off if they felt so inclined.

"Do you often do that?" he asks.

"Do what?"

"Lie to people."

Is he being serious? What is happening, right now?

"It's just a work thing." I shrug.

He makes another note and looks up from his pad.

"So, Mr. Davis … I'm sorry, Clay," Detective Mendez says, maybe sincerely. "You still haven't answered my question."

"I'm sorry. What was the question?"

"How did you know Emily Parker?"

"Well, she's a regular at my bar. She comes in from time to time. She's one of my best regulars, actually— Wait … Wait. What do you mean 'how *did* I know Emily Parker'?"

Detective Mendez gets a slight, pained expression and his eyes inadvertently glance at the file resting on the table.

"Mr. Davis, we're just asking some questions and we know that she was at the bar two nights ago," he says, trying to be reassuring.

"No. What did you mean by that?" I can't help the worry that finds its way into my tone. "Has something happened to her?"

"Mr. Davis, I'm not sure it's the right time—"

"Please. Tell me, did something happen to her?"

Detective Mendez sighs, reaches over, flips open the file, takes out a photo, and slides it in front of me. And then another. And another.

At first, I can't process what I'm seeing. Then, it becomes clear. The horror sets in and bile climbs up my throat.

This can't be real. It can't be, but it is.

Oh my god.

Cold beads of sweat pop from my forehead. My heart is slamming into my chest.

Detective Mendez leans forward further.

"Mr. Davis … Clay … How did you know Emily Parker?"

Let me back this up to that night.

"Goose martini. Filthy. One olive!" Mr. Collins calls over the din of the crowd.

"You got it."

Good. He's in a chipper mood. Things must be going better at home.

Mr. Collins, a retired fifty-something aerospace engineering consultant, has been coming to The Gryphon for years. A filthy Goose martini was his standard drink and I used to start making it the second I saw him walk through the door, but for the past few weeks, he's been drinking cheap scotch, neat. He and his wife have been having problems. He's never told me this, directly, but it's obvious to me. He's been down, quiet, and the times he's come into The Gryphon recently, he goes outside whenever he gets a phone call. He doesn't want anyone to hear him, which is what you do when it's personal. On slow nights, I've watched him through the window while he was on the phone. The body language, the pleading posture, all point to problems at home. This is the kind of stuff you notice when you work behind the bar; the stuff that you as a patron don't realize you're doing, but your bartender sees all of it. And if Mr. Collins is back to his favorite drink, that means he's happy, which means I'm happy, because he'll be tipping big.

I head to the well and start working on his martini.

My partner in crime, Katie Watson, one of the main attractions at The Gryphon, is holding court at the end of the bar. She brings in tons of business and I'm the one to grind out the drinks. Don't get me wrong, I'm a good-looking guy. I've got a thick, sculpted beard, sleeves of tattoos, keep a regular schedule at the gym, and I've got a sharp wit that has earned me my own little knot of admirers, but Katie is straight out of a 1950's pinup calendar, and she's wearing a black leather corset that is fighting a losing battle with her breasts.

I can't keep up with that, not even going to try and that's what makes us a perfect team.

"Coming right up!" Katie shouts to someone and goes for the beer taps behind me. "Clay!" she calls out as she approaches. "Can you make me a Bullet Rye Old Fashioned while you're at the well?"

"Yep."

"Thank you," she says, and slaps my ass as she passes.

I do not recommend doing this at your place of employment, but this is not sexual harassment. I'm not going to call HR. This is bartending. When you bartend with someone, you're going to experience a lot of physical contact with them; a *lot* of physical contact. Your bodies are going to press together and you're gonna bump uglies as you try to get around each other. You have to get physically comfortable with your coworkers very quickly. Katie and I passed that obstacle a long time ago. We've been working together for years and we do it so well, people have nicknamed us "The Dream Team". We've developed such a rhythm that we know when to help each other without asking, we silently agree on who should handle which customers, we know when the other is having a bad night, and out of that working relationship, we've grown into best friends.

The group of guys standing near the well are staring at me

with what I can only describe as the equivalent of high-fives.

"You have the best job in the world," one of them says.

"Damn right," I reply.

It is pretty great.

The Gryphon is a block from the ocean in the town of Avalon, which is about halfway between San Francisco and Monterey. I literally found this place by throwing a dart at a map. Not kidding. I had gotten fed up with living and working in Los Angeles. All the bartenders who were waiting to be discovered by a casting agent had done my head in. I pinned a map of the US to my wall, took a couple steps back, and fired. I knew I wanted to stay in California, so I took a general aim in that direction. The nearest town to the point of the dart was Avalon. That was that. I didn't worry about finding a job. I had the experience where I could walk in and get a job at any bar that was hiring, and people drink everywhere. They drink when times are good and when times are bad. Bartending is the only job that is bulletproof.

So, I packed up my stuff, moved to Avalon, and found my current employment: The Gryphon.

This town is a mix of everything, and from the first time I stepped through the door of The Gryphon, I knew I had found something special. Nowhere on the building does it say "The Gryphon". It's too hip for that. Instead, there's this cool neon sign in the shape of a gryphon above the door as you enter. I've been working here for five years and it's by far the best gig I've ever had. It has this cool, library vibe with some subtle hints of steam-punk thrown in. It brings in everyone from locals, to surfers, to hipsters, to yuppies, to businessmen, to you name it.

Such is life on the central California coast.

The Gryphon isn't a dive, so I don't have to deal with the bums or the seedy crowd, and it isn't corporate, so I don't have to worry about ridiculous oversight, company mantras, or secret shoppers coming in to make sure I was pushing the specials. The money is really good for how easy the work is. Of course, I don't want to bartend forever, but for now, I'm perfectly happy where I'm at.

I pop the shaker tin onto the cup containing Mr. Collins' martini, raise it above my head, and start to shake it. The rattling ice makes a sound like maracas.

Before I get started on the Old Fashioned, I glance to the slender guy with the shock of wiry red hair, long, spindly nose, and tortoise-shell glasses sitting at the bar, writing in his little notebook.

"You doing okay, Mr. Loomis?" I ask.

He nods without looking up.

Sydney Loomis is a weird dude.

He's been coming to The Gryphon since before I showed up. He walks in, sits in the same chair, orders three gins on the rocks with lemon over the span of a few hours, simply watches everyone and everything, but never says a word, only writes in his notebook, and then leaves. He's incredibly out of place, but he's an institution at The Gryphon. The one night a week that we're closed, he drinks at a bar down the street. He's not a big tipper, but he always tips, and any bartender will tell you those are the people who pay the rent. You always make sure they are happy, and since Mr. Loomis is happy, it's time to start the show.

With my free hand, I begin to build the Old Fashioned. I glance down the bar to my left to make sure a certain someone is watching.

She is.

Emily Parker.

She's in her forties and impossibly sexy. She's got blond, wavy hair, and a body born of yoga and morning jogs on the beach. She's watching me with an appreciative eye as she takes a sip from her almost spent vodka tonic.

I bring the martini down, hit the shaker against the side of the bar, which causes the tin to jump off, and strain the martini into the chilled glass. Then, I grab a cherry and toss it high in the air above the Old Fashioned. I quickly dump the shaker into the sink next to me, snatch an olive, and drop it into the martini, just as the cherry falls into the Old Fashioned with a light *plop*.

The crowd around me applauds and I take a bow.

Katie finishes pouring the beer and joins in the applause by adding a loud "whoop". With her free hand, she slaps my ass, again, and reaches around my waist to grab the Old Fashioned.

"Thank you, Clay!" she says.

"Can you take this martini over to Mr. Collins?" I ask.

"Sure," she says, carefully adding the martini to the drinks she's carrying. "By the way, can we switch 'out-times' tonight?"

"Tonight?"

"Yeah. I want to go home early."

"You want to leave early, but you're not going home," I say with mock disapproval.

"Not really your business, but you owe me for all the times I've traded with you so you could 'leave early but not go home'."

Damn.

I do owe her for multiple occasions in the past where she's traded with me so that I could leave early.

I roll my eyes. "Yeah. Okay. Fine."

"Thanks," she says, kissing my cheek and carrying the drinks away.

Time to deliver some bad news.

Avoiding all the outstretched hands and requests for drinks, I slink down the bar to Emily.

The one person I make certain to avoid is the customer that I've labelled 'The Blonde'. She's been coming in from time to time over the past couple of months, always on her own. Unlike almost everyone else in here, I don't know who she is or what she does. She's never hung out at the bar or tried to strike up a conversation with me. She keeps to herself, which I would totally respect, except for the fact that she's insistent to the point of being rude if she's not served right away, even if the bar is busy. Also, she doesn't tip, and carries herself with a "holier-than-thou" air. One time, she felt that I took too long getting her a Cape Cod and complained to our manager, Alex, about my service. She treats Katie the same way. So, we've had a not-so-pleasant relationship. I still haven't caught her name. Kind of don't care, but unfortunately, I've accidentally locked eyes with her as she uses her elbows to knife her way to the bar.

"Can I get a Stella?" she asks.

"You got it!" I reply and keep moving.

I have no intention of pouring her beer.

Katie can take care of her, but that's only if Katie wants to, which I doubt. If she tries to get Katie's attention, there's enough people for Katie to pretend like she didn't hear her. We bartenders do it all the time to customers we don't care for.

"Doing okay over here?" I ask, pulling up across the bar from Emily.

"Just fine, Mr. Showoff."

"Gotta give them what they want."

"I wasn't complaining," she says, giving me a seductive glance and taking the last sip of her drink.

"Another one?"

She ponders the wet ice in her glass. "Nah. I'll settle up."

She reaches into her sleek, expensive handbag, extracts a couple of twenties, and hands them to me.

I reach for the cash. "Listen, I'm gonna be a little late, tonight. I have to close."

She pulls the cash back. "I thought you were going to be cut first."

"I was, but I kind of owe Katie for our last time … and the time before that."

Emily gets a dreamy, far-away look. "I remember those times."

"Sorry. You know that I would do anything—"

"It's okay," she sighs. "I may just get started without you."

"I promise I won't keep you waiting."

"You'd better not." She hands me the cash.

"I'll be right back," I say with a sly smile.

After closing out her tab at the register, I put the change and receipt into a faux-leather check presenter embossed with The Gryphon logo. Even though there's nothing for her to sign, I slip a pen into the presenter and lay it on the bar in front of her.

"Have a good night."

"I'd better," she replies.

We hold each other's gaze before the surrounding requests for drinks become too much.

I turn to the thirsty crowd and start knocking them down, taking three orders at a time, mentally triaging them to be the most effective with my time. I bury myself "in the weeds" and do what I do best, which is crank out drinks.

Occasionally, I'll steal a glance back towards Emily to catch her watching me, but finally, after a blitz of pouring beers and shaking cocktails, I turn to look and she's gone.

The countdown to last call begins …

The evening settles into a steady hum.

Katie takes advantage of the lull and begins clearing the bar top of empty pints and highballs. She reaches for the check presenter left by Emily on the bar.

"No, no, no! I got that one. That's for me!" I call out, quickly moving towards her.

She picks up the check presenter and turns to me.

"You two are ridiculous. You know that, right?"

"I have no idea what you mean," I reply as though I'm offended.

"Cut the crap, Clay. Yes, you do."

Of course, I do. Others may have their suspicions, but Katie is the only one who knows for sure about Emily and I.

"Okay. Fine. You think we're ridiculous?" I ask.

She nods, emphatically.

"Two words, Katie: Nick McDermitt."

Her cheeks flush with anger.

Nick McDermitt is an ex-ballplayer for the Giants. He and his wife used to occasionally stop by The Gryphon until the night Mrs. McDermitt found Katie and her husband in the parking lot being a little too flirty. In fact, they were being waaaaaay too flirty. After that, we never saw the McDermitts again.

Our manager, Alex, who's in the office right now, had a talk with Katie. He wasn't going to fire her. She brings in too much business for that, but it was a bad look for the bar. Since then, there has been an informal "Please Don't Bang the Spouses of Our Customers" policy.

Katie presses the check presenter into my chest.

"Just be careful, okay?"

"If by 'careful', you mean 'no nookie in the parking lot', I think I can do that."

She groans and walks away, remembering to toss up a middle finger at me over her shoulder.

I laugh and open the check presenter.

Emily has left all the change, which comes out to about a fifty-dollar tip on a thirty-five-dollar tab. I toss the cash into the tip jar to split with Katie. The receipt is what I'm after, and I'm not disappointed.

Written on the receipt with the pen I provided is a message: "Seaside Motel. Room 37. Don't keep me waiting. You promised."

Tucking the slip of paper into my wallet, I glance up to see Katie shaking her head at me in disgust.

I make the sign of the cross and press my hands together, as if begging for forgiveness.

She gives me one last shake of her head and goes back to cleaning bottles.

It's five past midnight. I'm wiping down the bar while Katie enters her credit card tips into the register. We've stopped serving and the few remaining customers are finishing up their drinks. The music has been turned off and the lights are turned up, which is the universal sign for everyone to get out.

Alex emerges from the office.

"Okay, who is leaving first?"

Katie raises her hand. "That would be me."

Alex pops open Katie's register and runs her sales report.

They disappear into the office to do her checkout. A few minutes later, she reappears, holding her check presenter and counting her credit card tips. She tips out Tommy, our barback, who is mopping the floor, and comes to sit at the bar.

"You want to hand me the tip bucket?" she asks, settling onto a barstool.

Instead of handing it to her, I extract the cash from the bucket and lay the bills on the bar in front of her.

"Keep it. It's yours."

"Seriously?"

"Yeah. I still owe you." I tip the bucket over in my hand. A mass of coins slides into my palm and I deposit it into my pocket. "I'll keep the change."

I really do owe her and I'll still get my credit card tips for tonight. Besides, I love taking the change. I keep it in a jar on my dresser. Every month or so, I'll cash it in. It's usually a couple hundred bucks and I treat it like that ten-dollar bill you find in your jacket pocket at the beginning of autumn. I'll go out for a steak dinner or take a day trip to Napa.

"Thanks," she says, placing the bills in her personal check presenter, which is already stuffed with slips of paper.

"How many numbers you stack?" I ask.

We each have our own check presenter where we keep our change, credit card receipts, cash, order pad. A bartender never wants to leave their check presenter behind. It's also where we keep the phone numbers customers give us. Katie and I have our own little rivalry. We call it "Stacking Numbers". At the end of the night, we'll see who got more phone numbers. It's always Katie, to the point that I have a "ten-phone-number" handicap.

"You don't want to know," she replies, confidently.

"I would like to know who you're having dirty sex time with tonight."

She tuts her tongue at me and takes my hand. "Oh, Clay. Are you jealous?"

"Hey, don't worry about me. I'm having my fun."

"Yeah," she says, sadly. "But it's not with me, is it?"

I snatch my hand away. "I hate you."

"No, you don't." She laughs and gives me a knowing wink.

"Then get out of here before I do."

She hops off the stool and heads for the door. "Good night, Tommy!"

"Good night, Katie!" he replies, bent over the mop.

"Good night, Clay!"

"Good night, Worst Person in the World!"

She stops in the door, turns, and blows me a kiss. I grudgingly return the gesture. She "catches" it, slaps it on her backside, and heads out into the street.

"You two are a walking lawsuit."

I spin around to see Alex standing at the end of the bar.

"You ready?" he asks.

"Yeah."

"Let's go," he says, popping my drawer and running the sales report.

I grab the drawer and follow him into the office.

Alex sits at his computer, working on the inventory while I count my drawer.

I quickly make sure that the amount in the drawer is the same as when I started, minus my sales and credit card tips.

"I'm dropping four-hundred-twelve dollars and sixty-two cents and my credit card tips are two-seventy-four-eighty," I announce and hold the drawer out to Alex.

"Give me a sec," he says, slowly pecking away on the keyboard.

I keep the drawer right where it is, hovering near his face, and don't say a word.

Unable to ignore it any longer, he looks at me. "You got somewhere to be?"

"Maybe. And she doesn't like to be kept waiting."

He snatches the drawer. "I don't want to know."

He double checks my figures and counts the money.

"Perfect, as always," he says, signing my drop slip. "Get out of here and do whatever it is you need to do."

I pop out of my chair and head for the door. I know I shouldn't, but I can't resist getting one last dig before I go.

"I'll tell her you said 'hi.'"

He jams his fingers into his ears. "La-la-la-la-can't-hear-you-la-la-la-don't-want-to-know-la-la-la."

"Have a good night!" I shout as I exit the office.

A couple minutes later, I'm driving past the gazebo in the town square, which is festooned with lights, as I head towards to the ocean. I'm already anticipating the sex that is mere minutes away.

Emily and I have been seeing each other for months and it hasn't lost any of its shine. It's fun, thrilling, and a challenge in its own way. It's almost entirely physical. That's not to say that I don't care about her. I do, but we've laid our cards on the table and "love" was not one of them. We are fine with it.

I didn't even know that she was married the first time it happened. She conveniently forgot to mention it. She came into the bar by herself, we flirted all night, and ended up in bed together. It was fun and I thought it was a casual, one-night stand.

Then, a few nights later, she came into The Gryphon with her husband. They were a total physical mismatch. She was stunning, sensual. He was a short, thin, balding man. He was also arrogant, demanding, and eager to show her off. To put it another way, he was that stereotypical short, incredibly insecure guy with a massive chip on his shoulder, but as a hedge fund manager, he possessed the one asset that leveled the playing field: money. For Emily's part, she was bored.

I was speechless.

She and I kept exchanging glances while he would speak too loudly about his business deals in an attempt to impress those around him, many of whom were also millionaires and didn't care for his grandstanding.

At one point, he theatrically announced that he was stepping outside to take a phone call about a "billion-dollar project". After our shared glances, I took the opportunity to approach her.

"So, who exactly is that?" I asked.

"My husband," she casually remarked.

"You didn't tell me you were married."

"You didn't ask." She smiled. "Don't worry. You're not in danger of breaking up a happy family or anything. There's no kids. We're only married in a legal sense."

"Isn't that kind of the only sense that matters?"

"Do you regret the other night?"

My hesitation was all the answer she needed.

"Good," she said with a look that intimated we were just getting started.

I liked her little game. I liked her confidence. I liked her.

Just then, her husband re-entered the bar with a swagger and a sense of self-congratulation that was almost comical. He ordered a round of shots for the bar in celebration of the deal he had just closed. I was pretty sure he was lying but he paid the exorbitant tab and insisted that Katie and I join in by taking a shot. We were more than happy to oblige. Emily and I locked eyes as we took our shot.

In that moment, I knew that what I had thought was a one-night stand was far from over.

When they closed out their tab, I thanked them, saying I hoped they would be back soon, all the while keeping my eyes on her.

* * *

A week later, she did come back, sans husband.

"No date, tonight?" I asked as she settled into the bar, surprised at how happy I was to see her.

"Nope."

"That's too bad."

"Isn't it? I'm so distraught. I'm going to be so lonely."

"Tragic." I nodded. "Well, I suppose I can keep you company if you don't mind me working for a bit."

She gave me a hungry look from head to toe. "Not at all."

She and I continued our parries and jabs of innuendo all night.

When I got off work, we went back to her place. Her husband was in San Francisco at some conference, so we had sex on his prized pool table. I was in a little bit of a dry spell, but from our two encounters, it was obvious that she had been starved for a long time.

Ever since then, we had seized every opportunity offered to us.

I turn right onto Kensington, which runs along the beach, and will take me right to the Seaside Motel. If I had kept going straight instead of turning, I would have eventually reached the Parker house.

When we first started sleeping together, that's exactly what I would have done, but not anymore. We've stopped meeting there. We had been on a mission to break in every room in the house while her husband was away. It was fantastic. We'd have sex, and afterwards I'd walk naked out of their bedroom onto the massive balcony, which was cantilevered out over the sea, and marvel at the view. Then, I'd go back inside and we'd have sex in another room. I would spend the night. We'd fall asleep around eight in the morning. I'd wake up and leave from her place to go to work in the afternoon with a flushed glow and receive looks of scorn from Katie and Alex. Alex knew I was seeing someone but he didn't know who. Katie figured it out because she had seen us flirting at the bar multiple times.

Emily isn't a fan of being a trophy wife. In fact, she hates it and she's most definitely not a fan of her husband. She's talked about leaving him, but she loves the perks and she's not in a hurry to part with them. Eventually, she began swinging from paranoid about being caught to "devil-may-care". Sometimes, she would be overly worried about someone finding out and cancel plans at the last minute. Other times, she would rail about how much she didn't care and we'd take ridiculous risks, like the time during one of my shift breaks when we had sex on the hood of a car on a side street next to The Gryphon. Then there were the times when we'd just go back to her place.

But we were sloppy and almost got caught at her house.

After that, she decided that we would only meet up at motels, and not good ones, either. In my opinion, I think it's lame but after a world of fine Egyptian cotton sheets, marble floors, and a private wine cellar, she finds it a turn-on to meet at these "seedy" establishments. Whatever. I'm not going to say no to getting the chance to see her.

Which is why I'm already fantasizing about what I'll find in room 37 as I pull into the Seaside Motel parking lot. It's an L-shaped, single-story structure forever stuck in the 1960s, but it's not without its charm. They've embraced the retro look and there's a stunning view of the ocean across the road. Avalon is full of places like this.

I park in one of the numerous open spots. The air is heavy with the taste of salt, churned up by the low tide. I notice that there's another gray Honda Civic just like mine occupying one of the spaces near the office. I don't see her car, which is not a surprise. Like I said, since we were almost caught, she's become much more paranoid. She always pays cash at the bar. She also bought a burner phone for us to text each other. She finds Uber and Lyft drivers that will accept cash to drive her to our hookups. There's always a handful of them outside The Gryphon. They don't want to split the fare with the rideshare company. They also don't want to pay the taxes and their riders don't want anything showing up on their credit card statements for their spouses to find. Emily also discovered that motels like the Seaside often don't need to see your ID or make a record of your stay if you offer to pay double their nightly rate in cash. She's become very good at making sure that her husband's assistant won't find something that will raise any red flags on her credit cards, which her husband pays, and that he won't see anything in her bank accounts, which he controls.

I stroll down the row of numbered doors. Next to each is a large window. Some have the curtains drawn and are illuminated by the soft, flickering glow of a television but at this hour, most of them are dark.

I arrive at number 37.

The lights are on inside.

On the other side of this door, I'm going to find her on the bed, naked, lying on her side, head propped up in her hand. She'll ask something like "What took you so long?". That'll be the extent of our conversation. I'm already anticipating her hungry touch, her skill, and reveling in the abandon that comes from two people who are comfortable with the fact that they are using each other for physical pleasure.

I push on the door, but it doesn't budge. She normally leaves it open a fraction of an inch so that she doesn't have to get up to let me in, but there's a problem; the deadbolt is engaged.

What the hell?

I check the number on the door.

Yeah, this is room 37.

I lightly knock.

"Emily?"

There's no answer.

Maybe she fell asleep.

I knock again. No response.

I take out my phone, dial her burner phone, and press my ear to the door. There's the sound of a cellphone ringing inside. If she fell asleep, I'm hoping the call will wake her up, even though the knocking should have.

The call goes to the generic, automated voicemail.

I glance around. The Seaside Motel is quiet. There's only the soft buzz of the lamps in the parking lot and the crashing of waves from across the road.

I'm about to knock again when my phone pings with a text message.

I don't want to do this tonight.

Damnit.

Sorry I'm late, I text back. *But it doesn't have to ruin our evening.* I hit send.

I'm too tired, is her reply.

My thumbs fly across the screen. *Okay, but can you please open the door?*

There's a long pause and then my phone pings again.

No. Leave me alone.

Great. She's having one of *those* nights, but even on nights that she's suddenly canceled plans in the past, we'd at least talk for a little bit.

It's no good trying to get her to reconsider. She's made up her mind.

So, that's tonight down the drain. It's a little weird but I'm not gonna waste any more time with this. If it's not happening, it's not happening.

Good night, I text.

She doesn't answer.

Once inside my apartment, I head straight for the bathroom. I hop in the shower, scrub down, towel off, and climb into bed, not a little frustrated.

She'll be back at the bar in a week or two, and we'll pick up where we left off.

Still, that was odd.

She's run hot and cold but that felt different.

Oh, well.

As I drift off to sleep, I think about what was behind that door, waiting for me …

Sitting across from Detective Mendez, staring at these photos, now, I know.

Even though there is a Post-it Note covering a section of the image, I can see Emily's face.

Mechanically and in utter shock, I reach towards the photo.

"Mr. Davis, I'm sorry but you can't—"

I remove the Post-it.

There's Emily, just as I had envisioned her, lying naked on the bed, but her throat has been cut by an angry slash across her windpipe. Her lifeless eyes stare up at the ceiling. The mattress is soaked in blood.

"Mr. Davis!"

The photo is snatched away but the image is seared into my brain.

"I'm— I'm sorry. I didn't mean to—" I stammer. "I wasn't thinking."

"It's my fault," Detective Mendez says, replacing the photo into the folder. "I shouldn't have shown you that."

While he collects himself, I stare at the other photos which show the rest of the room; there's her clothes placed neatly on a chair, her purse, keys, and cellphone on the table.

I'm able to choke down the bile in my throat, but my hands continue to shake. The beads of sweat that popped on my forehead have run down into my eyes. In all of this, there's this strange thought in my head amidst the chaos that something was wrong about the photos; something other than the woman I was sleeping with lying naked on the bed with her throat cut. Something was missing.

"Mr. Davis? … Clay?" Detective Mendez asks.

Of course, I'm going to tell him. I'm going to tell him everything; the affair, the sneaking around, the motels, all of it but with everything that's happened in the past thirty seconds, I've forgotten how to speak.

Wait. I know what was missing in the photo: Emily's burner phone.

I check the photos again, to be sure. There's no sign of it.

Which means whoever killed her took it and …

I suddenly remember the text I received as I was walking down the hall into this room.

My brain on autopilot, I reach into my pocket for my phone. "Clay?"

"I'm sorry, Detective. I just need to check something …"

Detective Mendez may as well be on the other side of the world, and it's a good thing that my expression is already at "maximum bewildered" because this text message, sent from Emily's burner phone, has taken what was a surreal situation and turned it into a nightmare.

Keep your mouth shut or I'll tell them about the blood in your car, MY SWEET LITTLE CUPCAKE.

This can't be happening.

Another realization causes my stomach to plummet into my shoes: last night, as I stood outside the door of number 37 at the Seaside Motel, it wasn't Emily that I was texting. It was this guy. He knows who I am. He knows my number … and he knows about "my sweet little cupcake".

That's impossible! It was a joke!

"Clay? Are you all right?"

My mind snaps into horrible focus.

Whoever this is can easily make the cops think I killed Emily. I didn't, but how can I explain that to Detective Mendez? Yes, we were having an affair. Yes, I was at the Seaside Motel and yes, my fingerprints are on the door, but I didn't kill her. And if I show him this text, and there is blood in my car, how do I explain that? Even if there's not, he's going to ask what "my sweet little cupcake" means, and if I tell him, that's it. I'll be locked up in a cell and whoever did this to Emily goes free.

"Mr. Davis?"

Some sort of survival instinct is triggered. The chaos happening in my head is swept away and I see my situation, clearly. If I try to tell him everything and show him the text, they'll think I did it. I'll be locked up. No one will ever believe me and this guy, whoever he is, walks away.

I can't believe I'm about to do this, but I see no other option. I have to lie.

I blink my eyes and shake my head in an attempt to concentrate.

"I'm sorry, Detective Mendez. I just—I can't believe it."

"It's all right," Detective Mendez says, picking up the rest of the photos and putting them back in the file folder. "I know it's a shock but I need you to tell me: how did you know Emily Parker?"

"She, um, she was a regular at the bar."

"That's how you met?"

"Yeah ..."

All I can do is keep the panic at bay. This guy, whoever he is, knows who I am. He knows things about me and Emily that no one could possibly know.

"When was the last time you saw her?"

"Um ... two nights ago when she came in."

"Did you talk to her?"

"Yes. I served her some drinks."

"How many drinks?"

"A couple of vodka tonics."

"How many?"

"Like, maybe four."

"Did she seem strange to you?"

"No."

"Did she say if she was meeting anyone?"

"No."

He nods and makes a note on his pad of paper. "Who texted you?"

"It was a work thing."

He nods again, not looking up at me.

I'm keeping my trembling hands under the table so he can't see them. I don't know if he believes me. Is he like this all the time, or is this an act to get me to break?

"So, you two were … friendly?"

"I'm a bartender. I'm friendly with everyone. It's my job."

Something about his question causes my mind to click.

What can I get you?

It's the old bartender question. I know it sounds like I'm being subservient to you when I ask, but your answer, what you ask for, your body language, your tone, tells me everything I need to know. Are you happy? Sad? Do you have money? Do you want someone to talk to or do you want to be left alone? You tell me everything about yourself and I'm going to use that to get what I want, which is the biggest tip. But now, looking at Detective Mendez, I think, "What can I get you?" What is it that you want that I can give you that will get me what I want, which is out of this room?

His demeanor is infuriating. He's not intense. He's not digging too deep. He just wants some answers. He seems like kind of a loner, someone without many social skills; a Sydney Loomis-type. I need to be casual with him. Make him forget about his social awkwardness.

"Did she ever come into your bar with anyone?" he asks.

There. Right there is my "out".

I try to relax or at least appear to relax because relaxation is not possible under the circumstances, and treat the table between us like it's the bar. I slip into my bartending persona, which makes me feel gross, but I have to get out of this room.

"Yeah," I say with a slight roll of the eyes. "Her husband. Have you seen that guy?"

The change in him is instant. He loosens up.

"Yes," he says, mirroring my eyeroll. His lips tighten into something almost like a smile.

My tactic worked. Now, we're just two guys talking.

"He's a piece of work."

"Mmm-hmm," he says, making another note. "How did they seem to you?"

I shift uncomfortably in my seat.

"It's okay," he says. "I'm only asking for your opinion."

"They were … not great."

"Really?"

"Well, yeah, but nothing like that," I quickly add, pointing to the file. I may have overplayed this. I wanted to get on Detective Mendez's good side to loosen him up so I can get out of here, but I don't want to insinuate some other innocent person is guilty of Emily's murder.

"I see," he says, taking more notes. He's much more at ease. "But she came in by herself two nights ago?"

"Yes."

"And where did you go after you got off work?"

"Home."

"Can anyone vouch for you?"

"Bachelor for life," I reply with a shrug and a sheepish grin.

He makes a note. "Okay. That's all I've got for now." He takes something from his pocket and slides it across the table. "Here's my card. If you think of anything else, please tell me."

There are a million things I could tell him, right now, a million things I want to tell him because I want him to catch whoever did this to Emily, but if her blood is in my car, he will never believe me. No one will.

"Okay." I deposit the card in my pocket and try not to rise too quickly from my chair. I have to get to Katie. I need to know what they asked her. Why did Detective Mendez show me those photos? There's no way he showed them to Katie because she would have said something. So, why me?

Detective Mendez stands. "And let me know if you plan to go out of town any time soon, okay?"

"Sure."

"Thank you, Mr. Davis," he says, extending his hand. "Oh, I'm sorry. I mean 'Clay'."

"No problem," I reply, shaking his hand. He's got a grip.

I being walking towards the door.

"I'm sorry, Clay. One last question."

Well, there it is.

He's done it. He's spotted a crack in my story. He's been playing me. I don't know what this question is, but I'm sure it's going to pin me to the wall and slap handcuffs on my wrists.

"Yeah?"

"Your bar; The Gryphon. Is it any good?"

Seriously?

"… yeah."

"What makes it good?"

"Me."

He laughs, proving it was the perfect response.

"What's your favorite drink to make?" he asks.

Bartenders hate this question. It's like someone asking you what's your favorite sales report to compile. There are drinks that we know we make well, but that's different than what's our favorite drink to make. I always give the smartass answer of "bottles of Bud Lite", but this is the one time that I'm relieved someone is asking me this question. This guy wants a friend.

"I make a mean margarita."

"Really? Well, I may just have to come by and see if you're telling the truth."

The way he says that last part about telling the truth, I'm back to not knowing if he's messing with me, but I've already committed.

"The first one's on me."

He smiles. "Well, all right. Thanks for coming in and, remember; if you think of anything, don't hesitate to call me. I mean that."

"Will do, and I mean it about the margarita, too."

He nods and I head out the door.

I'm staring at my Civic like it's radioactive. My initial urge was to search the inside of the car right then and there, but it would look really suspicious right in the middle of the police station parking lot. I do a quick scan through the windows. I don't see anything, but it could only be a drop or two somewhere. Or there might not be any blood at all.

I didn't see anything when I drove over here but I wasn't really looking for—

My phone pings again.

It's another text from Emily's burner phone. Up until a few minutes ago, I would have expected it to have been a flirtatious message about how she couldn't wait until she saw me again and I would try to convince her to meet up with me as soon as possible.

I'll never receive another message from her like that again.

Instead, this one reads:

447 Sweetgrass Road. Evergreen Terrace Apartments. #208. Inside the apartment you'll find something that will help you. It's blue. You'll know it when you see it. The key to the apartment is under the doormat.

Once more, I glance to the packed park across the street and the countless cafés and restaurant patios that stretch into the distance.

He's here. He has to be, right? He had to have been watching me as I walked into the station. That's how he knew when to send that first message. How else—

Another text message arrives and answers my question.

You look nervous. Don't be nervous. It's time to play.

404

Dear Reader,

We hope you enjoyed reading this book. If you did, we'd be so appreciative if you left a review. It really helps us and the author to bring more books like this to you.

Here at HQ Digital we are dedicated to publishing fiction that will keep you turning the pages into the early hours. Don't want to miss a thing? To find out more about our books, promotions, discover exclusive content and enter competitions you can keep in touch in the following ways:

JOIN OUR COMMUNITY:
Sign up to our new email newsletter:
http://smarturl.it/SignUpHQ
Read our new blog www.hqstories.co.uk
🐦 https://twitter.com/HQStories
📘 www.facebook.com/HQStories

BUDDING WRITER?
We're also looking for authors to join the HQ Digital family!
Find out more here:
https://www.hqstories.co.uk/want-to-write-for-us/
Thanks for reading, from the HQ Digital team.

ONE PLACE. MANY STORIES

**If you enjoyed *Secrets to the Grave*,
then why not try another gripping thriller
from HQ Digital?**